THE HEART'S HARD TURNING

JOHN FARR ROTHROCK

 FriesenPress

Suite 300 - 990 Fort St
Victoria, BC, V8V 3K2
Canada

www.friesenpress.com

ISBN
978-1-5255-0839-4 (Hardcover)
978-1-5255-0840-0 (Paperback)
978-1-5255-0841-7 (eBook)

1. FICTION, ACTION & ADVENTURE

Distributed to the trade by The Ingram Book Company

FOR DIANE

There are no events but thoughts and the heart's hard turning, the heart's slow learning where to love and whom. The rest is merely gossip, and tales for other times.

Annie Dillard
Holy the Firm

Part I

DESGRACIADO

Do you think your fathers are watching? That they weigh you in their ledgerbook? ...There is no book and your fathers are dead in the ground.

Cormac McCarthy
The Road

PRODROME

In those days the interstate highway south of the city unwound straight and true through a land largely free of man, a sixty-mile arrow launched to puncture the crusty hide of Mexico. Around the halfway mark were the incongruously green pecan groves that drank the waters of the Rio Rico, but aside from those few verdant acres the landscape was typical of the Sonoran zone: ocotillo, cacti, creosote bush; stunted mesquite and *palo verde,* trees barely taller than an adult man. And everywhere, providing a monotonous beige canvas for the rest was the *caliche, the* "desert pavement", crisscrossed by an infinity of sandy washes.

It was not visually inspiring, and particularly in the unshadowed glare of a mid-summer's day the land's uninviting aspect suggested no respite to humans weary of the road. Most were content to put the region quickly behind them, stopping only if in need of gas and a cool drink at one of the highway's infrequent exits. Hurtling along the road in their air-conditioned cocoons, they left behind no trace of their passing save a brief swaying of the desert broom that encroached upon the highway's narrow shoulders.

From the window of a speeding car the desert appears drab and inanimate, but closer inspection would reveal a vital community more fecund than that of any alpine forest or grassy meadow. Everywhere in the Sonoran desert there is life, scratching, clawing and poisoning for its place; bugs bite, snakes rattle and venomous scorpions lurk beneath the rocks. Few humans are inclined to pause and take notice.

Even now, forty-odd miles south of the city you still can see to the west an enormous pair of longhorns protruding from a small rectangular steakhouse, now abandoned, whose façade unfortunately was more compelling than the meat it served; the restaurant has been closed for years. Ten miles further on the previously flat highway begins to undulate as the road carves through the low hills that mark the southwestern boundary of Arizona. Drive up the last rise and then, suddenly, there is Old Mexico.

The American side of Nogales is bland, nondescript and notable only for the availability of clean, well-functioning public restrooms, a luxury all too rare once the border is traversed. The Mexican side is distinct. Different. A mélange of chaotic traffic; street vendors peddling every product from shaved ices and *churros* to *las virgenes autenticas*; bright pink, turquoise and yellow shacks clinging to the hillsides; *taquerias* with their complimentary bowls of breathtakingly hot carrots and jalapeños; cheesy discothèques; "ladies bars"; and, everywhere…people. Swarms of people. Especially children. Hordes of them. Crowding the sidewalks and filling the alleys. Dusty, vivid Mexico. Only a few steps from *yanquiland*, and yet all one sees, smells and hears is redolent with its differentness.

Navigate through the sprawling city, and the confusing array of streets coalescences into a single two lane road which serves as the sole direct route to Hermosillo, the capital of Sonora some 250 kilometers to the south. On the southern outskirts of Hermosillo an unmarked asphalt road, easily overlooked, abruptly exits the main highway. Take that road, and then drive

100 kilometers westward through a land that appears so dry as to have never tasted rain.

Comes at last a low-lying range of volcanic mounds and, just beyond…a sea. A *sea*. After the long, hot journey through a bleak and silent desert, a sudden cacophony of life and sound. *Que milagro!* A sea. Pelicans circle above in a cloudless blue sky. Waves break against rock and sand. And beneath the water's surface, a living banquet that extends from the smallest marine organism to the largest whale.

A desert sea. *El Mar de Cortez.*

Chapter 1

ARIZONA

The shrill ring of the telephone cut rudely through the darkness. Awake now but continuing to lie motionless in his bed, Will imagined he was in a submarine. While the room he occupied was on the seventh floor of a building whose foundation rested within dry desert soil far from any ocean, the illusion had some basis. The room was – or, at least, felt - hermetically sealed. When he closed the door upon entering, he could feel his ear drums recoil from the increased pressure. At night, with the lights out and shade closed, the cubicle was utterly dark, chilled by the building's powerful air conditioning and, absent the telephone's intrusions, typically as silent as a long-forgotten tomb.

He'd undertaken several liaisons in that cold, lightless chamber, and the results had been inconsistent. While one woman might find its nihilistic aspect arousing, the next was just as likely to recoil from the prevailing sensory deprivation.

Himself, he found the room more conducive to sleep than any social intercourse, and up until the last thirty seconds he'd been slumbering peacefully. Ironically, these nights of hospital duty provided his only respite from the insomnia that dogged him, and while he hardly looked forward to taking call in-house,

1

he appreciated the opportunity to sleep and resented its premature termination. He consequently continued to lie in his bed, patiently waiting for the insistent ringing to subside and allow him once again to drift back into unconsciousness.

He dozed lightly when the phone was silent at last, hoping the call would not be repeated. Over their long association, now approaching a decade in its length, the night shift charge nurse for the ER had learned his habits well. If she, Nicki, was working, the calls would continue until he answered. If he was in luck and it was her night off, a more inexperienced nurse would conclude that he was busy with another emergency or otherwise unreachable and so leave him to his bed.

Once again the phone began to ring. He sighed and answered.

Greeting his ear was Nicki's soft, laconic drawl, an enduring artifact of her Alabama heritage. How this fifty-something nurse had come to forsake the steamy bayous of Mobile for the Arizona desert was a story she'd not shared with Will. Nicki kept her work and personal lives distinctly separate.

"Dr. Rawlins," she said. "We need you down here." Although they'd worked together for over ten years, and while they'd learned to respect and count on one another's clinical competence, not once had she ever called him by his first name.

With effortful politeness he acknowledged her request. Replacing the receiver, he fought the impulse to snatch a few more minutes of sleep; the poor scrap of additional rest was not worth the reproachful look such delay would bring. He flicked on the bedside lamp, glanced at his watch and comforted himself with the knowledge that this task was likely to be his last.

He arose from the narrow bed, threw on his scrubs and did what he could at the sink to make himself presentable. Although the night had been uncharacteristically quiet for a Friday and he'd slept uninterrupted for almost four hours, the face he saw reflected in the mirror appeared drawn and haggard. He shrugged, drew tighter his drawstring and exited the dark cube into a brightly lit hallway that led to the elevators.

Riding down to ground level, he checked his baggy pockets to ensure they held his stethoscope and a pen, the only tools he now bothered to carry. The elevator descended without any stops, and its doors opened upon another bright, empty hallway. He turned left twice and punched the metal disc that automatically opened the saloon-like doors of the ER.

Hospitals late at night are curious places, seas of hushed tranquility punctuated by islands of action. On the quieter wards patients seduced into slumber by sunny yellow capsules of temazepam lie quietly while the nurses gossip at their communal station. The intensive care units are more lively, their ventilators beeping like discordant calliopes; around this bed or that one may observe a bored senior resident instructing his junior in the insertion of a tube, a line, a catheter or a needle. In the OR, a room or two is occupied by teams intent upon an emergency surgery, repairing a perforated bowel or a foot gone blue from blockage of its sustaining artery.

But no other compartment within a hospital can match the ER for its capacity to generate a full spectrum of clinical activity and variety. If one had only hours available within which to sample at first hand the full spectrum of human behavior, the ER would serve as an unsurpassable vantage point. It is a place where pie-in-the-face comedy exists cheek-to-cheek with unspeakable tragedy. An infinity of vivid images are crammed within five thousand square feet and a twelve hour shift: the plaintive whine of a demented patient; a coked-out prostitute's manic laughter; sudden death; resuscitation; unbearable pain; the blessed release from pain; the lonely, old and forgotten; the loved and cherished; blood on the floor and urine in the sheets; the scattered debris of a code gone badly; a baby's scream; a grateful smile; gallantry, sympathy, kindness; fatigue, anger, impatience. Splinters, colds, constipation; sepsis, fractures, infarcting hearts; the child miserable with croup who tonight will return to her own bed and live to see her parents buried; the child in blast crisis whose parent's prayers will not prevent her death by sunrise. Boredom. Anxiety. Terror. Relief.

Yes, Will thought, *a remarkable place is the emergency room.* Were it not for his instinctive dislike of the ER's physical confinement, he once might have taken that path himself. But the time for such choices was now long past, and tonight he simply wished to be done with it all.

He glanced around the wide expanse. Most of the examining rooms were empty, and the few patients being evaluated by sleepy, disinterested interns did not appear to be acutely ill. As he walked towards the centrally situated nurses' station, Nicki looked up from her paperwork, gravely met his gaze and then without speaking inclined her chin towards the closed door of the trauma room. As he walked towards that door, she called after him quietly, "Remember, you're on probation."

Some weeks prior he'd left off suturing a routine scalp laceration to attend to a prisoner from the county jail who, according to the burly guard accompanying him, "slipped, fell and hit his dumb-ass Mexican head on the goddamned floor". Will glanced dubiously at the guard and then suggested that, being as the prisoner was comatose and thus in no condition to flee, he remove the man's shackles. When the guard refused to do so, Will pointed out that the shackles were inhibiting his access to his patient, that the man would be more likely to die should this situation persist and that his death would result in an extensive investigation.

The guard cursed but had complied, and in examining the patient - a thin, heavily tatted Hispanic male of about thirty - Will noted the multiple skull fractures and the cerebrospinal fluid leaking from his left ear. "Must have been one hell of a fall," he remarked to the scowling guard.

When he returned at last to complete suturing the superficial scalp wound, the patient, an inebriated but well-groomed man in his early 60's, complained bitterly of the delay in his treatment.

"If you're in such a fucking hurry, flash, then you can finish the fucking job yourself," Will told him at last. And then walked away.

As it turned out, the offended party was a prominent attorney and alumnus who played golf regularly with the university's president, and his strongly worded complaint had produced rapid repercussions.

He opened the door to the trauma room and entered a charged atmosphere that contrasted sharply with the slow-paced activity outside. Both beds were occupied, but all upright bodies present were huddled around the larger of the two patients. Unattended in the far bed was a young girl who lay unmoving with her eyes closed, a single IV` line running into her left forearm. Will could see her chest wall moving, but from where he stood the rhythm of her breathing appeared uneven.

Stepping closer, he checked the monitor and noted that her last recorded blood pressure was 90 systolic. About right for a girl her age; she looked to be nine or ten. Given the late hour, the abrasions and contusions on her forehead and her presence with the older female patient in the room typically devoted to trauma cases, Will assumed the two had been involved in an MVA.

He glanced over at the other bed. A chunky male physician dressed in rumpled blue scrubs was bending over the supine woman and gesticulating frantically with his left hand as he kept his right index finger firmly pressed against the woman's temple. Three nurses and a female surgical intern clustered about him while two medical students held the flanks, standing on tiptoe and peering over the shoulders of the team at work. As Will watched, one of the nurses shaved off a patch of the woman's hair directly over the left temporal bone, and another opened a sterile surgical tray bundled in towels and lying on a stand by the bed, its tidy array of instruments now exposed and gleaming wickedly under the harsh light of the surgical lamp overhead. She selected a scalpel and briskly slapped its handle onto the outstretched hand of the impatient doctor garbed in blue. As he grasped the scalpel, he turned his head briefly towards the nurse to bark a command unintelligible from where Will stood.

Recognizing him, Will groaned inwardly. Abner Cupp was a neurosurgery resident in his mid-thirties, a Mormon from St. David's who would have done well to forego a career in medicine and instead remain at home amongst people whom he understood and who understood him in return; he could have been modestly successful running a small hardware store or selling life insurance to his Mormon brethren.

Unfortunately, Abner had eked through medical school by working twice as hard as any of his classmates, and after six years of post-graduate training he had become adept at cloaking his horrific clinical judgment by adopting an attitude of unshakable self-confidence as repulsive as it was ill-founded. By sheer dint of perseverance, like a limpet clinging to its rock through the surge of countless tides, he had remained solidly in place until the year had come when, absolutely lacking in other potential candidates, the faculty reluctantly had appointed him chief resident. This unfortunate promotion only reinforced his native arrogance and, worse, freed him from the restraints previously imposed by more senior and capable house staff.

Abner's medical missteps were innumerable, and over the years many had achieved the stuff of legend. Although Will avoided him when he could, he did respect Abner for his consistency of performance: whatever the diagnosis proclaimed or clinical management undertaken, he invariably was wrong. Such consistency could be useful, and whenever Will found himself in agreement with Abner in regard to anything - an MRI abnormality, choice of antibiotic, movie review, restaurant recommendation - he knew to give his position careful reconsideration.

Now Abner was carving a two-inch incision within the unresisting scalp of the latest victim of his ineptitude. Will remained silent through this, but when the hapless surgeon commanded he be given the twist drill, he finally spoke up.

"What are you doing, Abner?" he asked calmly.

Without shifting his eyes from his target, the pride of St. David visibly bristled. "Get lost, Rawlins," he snapped in response. "You're not a neurosurgeon any more, and there's no place for you here." He began to assemble the drill.

Ignoring him, Will walked to the head of the bed and briefly opened the unconscious woman's eyes. Her pupils were widely dilated and failed to constrict when exposed to the bright surgical light. Removing an ophthalmoscope from its cradle on the adjacent wall, he examined her right optic nerve and retina. In the instant before Abner elbowed him sharply aside he was able to make out several unmistakable blotches of hemorrhage over the retinal background, like swaths of acrylic red paint smeared at random.

When he turned back to the table after replacing the ophthalmoscope, Abner was staring at him popeyed, red-faced and furious.

"What's the matter with you, Rawlins?" he shouted. "Are you deaf? I told you to get out of here. This is *my* patient!"

Abner picked up the drill and depressed its trigger. An ominous metallic whine rose and fell repeatedly. Standing his ground resolutely, he resembled a dumpy version of Gary Cooper in an *ersatz* neurosurgical remake of *High Noon*.

Will ignored the neurosurgeon's theatrics and spoke to the nurse closest to him. "What happened?" he asked.

Her summary was concise and confirmed his suspicions. According to observers, the woman had been driving with her young daughter in the passenger seat when she suddenly and inexplicably veered from an overpass and plunged fifteen feet into the concrete culvert below. Her car was a total loss. So was she.

By the time the nurse finished, Abner had positioned the distal point of the drill bit firmly against the patient's shaved scalp, adjusted the safety flange and begun to drill. The acrid smell of burning bone filled the air.

Short on options and time, Will punched Abner squarely in the right temple and watched the surgeon tumble to the tile floor. His large square head rebounded impressively off the hard surface.

Will turned to the horrified nurses, all now staring at him with alarm after first tracking Abner's trajectory. Addressing them, he fired off a string of commands. "Get me a number 12 ET tube and an Ambu bag. Call RT *stat*. Put in a Foley, and give her a hundred grams of mannitol now. And get Nicki in here." When they failed immediately to obey, he spoke to them more curtly. "*Now!*"

They scattered to carry out his orders, and a moment later Nicki entered the room. She glanced briefly at Abner's prostrate form and as she hung the mannitol remarked mildly to Will, "I thought I told you to stay out of trouble."

"Couldn't help it," he replied, distractedly. "It was just one of those Abner things." He was busy sliding the ET tube between the woman's vocal cords and was relieved to find it an easy intubation. Silently he gave thanks that Abner had not seen fit to complicate matters by attempting this job himself and producing laryngeal edema from his aggressive but ineffectual thrusts. "Besides," he added, "it's my last day. What are they going to do? Fire me?"

He connected the Ambu bag to the tube, began to squeeze it rhythmically and elevated the head of the bed from horizontal to 30 degrees. "Here, Nicki," he said, "take the bag for a second while I check the little girl." Silently she complied.

The girl was densely stuporous but arousable. She had a livid bruise that spread across the skin over her mastoid bone at the base of the skull, a sign of basilar skull fracture. She moved her right arm and leg less than their counterparts when he pinched her nail bed, and by squirting a bit of ice water into both ears he found her to have a distinctive pattern of disconjugate eye movement.

By now the pulmonary tech had arrived and attached the woman to a ventilator. Glancing down, Will could see that the intravenous mannitol already was causing her Foley bag to bulge with straw-colored urine. Lifting her lids, Will also saw that the woman's pupils remained fixed and dilated. *Hopeless*, he thought. He noticed Abner was off the floor and nowhere to be seen. Apparently he'd left the room while Will was preoccupied with his examination of the girl.

He looked up from his contemplation of Abner's absence to find Nicki fixing him with her calm, unwavering gaze. "What gives?" she asked.

"The mother ruptured an aneurysm while she was driving," he answered. "That's why she ran off the road. When you look at her retinas, she's got subhyaloid hemorrhages, and it takes the force of an aneurysmal bleed to create them. Trauma alone won't do it. When you see eyes like that, it means a high volume bleed, and that means a lot of brain swelling. She's herniated from her increased ICP. Ballgame's over."

If Abner had had his way with the drill, he thought, *the woman's brain would have squirted out from the burr hole like toothpaste from a tightly squeezed tube. Not that it would have made any real difference.*

"It's bad enough she has to die," he concluded, unaware he now was speaking aloud. "Why make things any uglier by drilling a bunch of holes in her head?"

The mannitol bag had emptied, and Nicki thumbed down the clamp on the IV line to allow a rate of saline flow just sufficient to prevent it from clotting off. "What about the child?" she asked.

"She's got a brain stem contusion," Will answered. "She needs a non-contrasted CT to rule out an epidural, but everything she showed me on exam could be explained by a lesion in the left stem. She may have some swelling tonight and tomorrow, and she'll need close observation and maybe intubation, but I think she'll come out of this okay." He directed the pulmonary tech to check blood gases on the girl and to bring another ventilator.

The tall, slender woman looked at him more closely now and with clear concern. "What about Abner?" she asked.

"What about him?" Will shrugged. Dismissing Abner from his thoughts long ago had become reflexive.

"You apparently hit him pretty hard, Dr. Rawlins," she reminded him. "He'll be back here any minute with Security, and knowing him, he's likely to make a real fuss about this."

"Well, Nicki," he sighed. "It really doesn't matter much at this point, does it?" He sank into a handy chair. Suddenly he was exhausted.

"Maybe not, but I wouldn't be surprised if he calls the police and tries to have you arrested," she replied.

They both glanced up at the clock. Seven a.m. "Your shift's about over, anyway," she observed. "Why don't you skedaddle out of here, and I'll call you if anything comes up in the next hour."

Will rose from the chair where he'd sat sprawling. He grinned. "You're a good woman, Nicki," he told her. "Probably best we just go ahead and get married."

Solemnly she walked over to where he stood and kissed him lightly on the forehead. "Over my dead body," she assured him. Turning her attention back to her work, she began to phone radiology to arrange the girl's CT. "Take care of yourself, Will," she said.

Unsure how to interpret this unprecedented use of his first name, he stepped through the ER doors a final time and walked out into the morning, the sunlight glaring and the heat already rising.

———

His house was located midway between the hospital and the university's main campus. Built in the '20s, the house was a *faux* adobe *casita* characteristic of that period, with heavy wooden lentils over the doorways and windows, a thickly stuccoed exterior, high ceilings lined with *vigas*, tile floors, deeply recessed windows, and a brick courtyard shaded by mature *palo verde* and mesquite. It was a beautiful little house in one of the few old central neighborhoods that had resisted decay, and only the fact that it was slated for destruction as part of the university's long-range expansion plan had enabled Will to afford his home.

It was a short walk from hospital to house, but even at that early hour it was uncomfortably hot. Entering through the arched front door, Will sank into a soft chair and absorbed the welcome breeze produced by the swamp cooler. To his surprise, Brian was reclining on the couch across from him.

Since his fall from grace Brian had been living in Will's home, and as the arrangement had persisted since Will had moved from Michael's house to this one almost a year prior, they were well versed in one another's eccentricities. For his part, although Brian contributed no rent and served as a potential magnet for the narcotics division of the Tucson Metropolitan Police, he was in all other aspects an ideal roommate. Rarely home, meticulously neat, invariably pleasant, and an engaging conversationalist, Will found him now to be the only person whose extended presence he could endure.

Brian had been the most gifted of their intern group, as well as the most personally appealing of the entire house staff. During tense situations in the units, ED or OR, his calm good humor was infectious. If he felt fatigue, annoyance, anxiety or impatience, his unruffled demeanor never betrayed him. He was well-liked by his patients and invariably competent in his clinical management.

As if this weren't sufficient to mark him, Brian was perhaps the most attractive man Will had ever known. He was Black Irish to the core, with raven hair, startlingly blue eyes, pale skin and a tall, slender body that he manipulated with the grace of a cat. Every young nurse in the hospital bemoaned his apparently seamless marriage to Becky, a trim, clever and clear-eyed young woman from Nebraska who lived with Brian and their three small children in a little *hacienda* on the Rillito that he'd inherited from his father.

Brian was a rarity in that city of transplants and transients, a fourth generation Tucsonan. His paternal great-grandfather, Alvin McCoy, had stepped off the boat from Dublin onto the crowded streets of New York and, apparently repelled by what he' observed of immigrant life in the teeming city, somehow made his way to what was then a tiny, unprepossessing outpost located at the very southwestern edge of civilization. Tucson. The Old Pueblo. He'd prospered as a merchant, and once he felt himself sufficiently established, he married a beautiful, dark-eyed *senorita* who bore him seven children. With his own hands he'd built for his family the *hacienda* where until recently had resided his erstwhile great-grandson.

Brian had chosen anesthesiology as his field. To all evidence he'd seemed to thrive in his residency and subsequent fellowship until the past February, when he was discovered on a bench in the OR's dressing room slumped over and deep into a drug overdose, the incriminating syringe still dangling from his arm. In the investigation that followed, a careful check of the OR's narcotics record revealed that a surprisingly high quantity of fentanyl had been expended during the cases Brian attended. When questioned, he freely admitted to theft and chronic intravenous drug use but denied any diversion of the narcotic for sale.

His medical license was suspended. He spent several months in an outpatient rehab program and eventually returned to work on probationary status. Within weeks he relapsed, and despite the administration's threats and Becky's imprecations, he steadfastly refused admission to an inpatient facility. The university consequently fired him, and the state board revoked his medical license. Becky drew the line; he could remain at home only if he stayed clean and either sought reinstatement of his license or pursued another line of work. When he showed no inclination to comply, she threw him out. No enabler, she.

So now Brian occupied Will's spare bedroom, slipping in through the back door in the early morning hours and sleeping into the afternoon. Will rarely saw him at home, and their few face-to-face interactions generally occurred when they ran into one another at a bar. At such times Alex seemed precisely his old self: physically attractive, charming and cheerful. To Will he belied every cliché attributed to junkies. For one thing, although he had no discernible source of income to fund his habit, he never asked Will for money, and no cash or personal possessions went missing at their home. Even his complexion remained perfect.

Brian lay on his back, staring at the ceiling. "You're up early," Will observed. "Have an early night?'

His friend yawned, arose to a seated position and stretched. "The early bird gets the worm," he proclaimed. "But then, what sane man would covet a worm?"

Will turned his head toward the large front window and the courtyard visible beyond. Despite the heat of early summer, the *palo verde's* branches were thick with long, needlelike leaves, and their pale green hue contrasted appealingly with the tiny yellow blossoms that blanketed the tree. He could never tell when Brian was high; to Will he seemed always indistinguishable from the Brian of old. He turned back from the window to address his friend. "Now would be a good time to sign those papers," he suggested.

Brian frowned and looked away. "I know we've covered this ground already, *amigo*," he said, "but this is *not* a good idea. There's nothing to be gained by just walking away. If you feel like you've gotta go, then ask for a formal leave of absence. Take a vacation. Take me with you."

Will shifted his long frame lower in the chair, extending his legs to use the coffee table as a footstool and clasping his hands behind his head. The room was blessedly cool, and the tension provoked by the morning's fracas was dissipating.

"It's too late," he replied. "I've resigned, and I doubt they'll be sad to see me go. Especially after this morning." Briefly he described his dust-up with Abner.

Brian sighed when Will had finished. "Abner's not worth the effort," he said with conviction. "And it sounds like the woman was dead anyway. You're just trying to burn your bridges."

You're a great one to criticize another man for burning bridges, Will thought, but he didn't bother to voice his opinion. He knew from many previous conversations that Brian was impervious to any suggestion that his behavior might contradict his counsel. Instead` he addressed Brian's earlier suggestion. "Yeah," he said, nodding with mock seriousness. "I really should take you with me. You'd be like one of the *milagros* those kids were hawking in Mexicali."

Some years before they'd driven to San Felipe, an endless expanse of Mexican beach at the apex of *el golfo de California*, to camp and windsurf. Driving south through Mexicali swarms of scrawny brown children had descended upon their truck at every stop light, imploring them to buy cheaply printed leaflets that were purported to serve more or less the same purpose as the "Get our of Jail" card from a Monopoly game. If stopped by the Mexican police for a driving infraction, supposedly all one had to do was hand this leaflet to the officer, and even the most flagrant transgression immediately would be forgiven.

Amused by what seemed an obvious scam, they declined and drove on their way. Before they reached the city's southern limits, however, they were stopped three separate times to pay "fines" so as to avoid being detoured to the central station for potential incarceration; their last infraction had something to do with their failure to have a flag- specifically, a *yellow* flag- tied to the protruding ends of the windsurfer masts resting in the truck's bed. They immediately bought several leaflets at the next opportunity and successfully used each of them throughout the remainder of their journey. It clearly had been a major fund-raising weekend for the cities and towns of the northern Gulf region.

Will shook his head with mock sadness. "But if it's an extended trip I guess you might start to miss your recreational activities here in Tucson," he suggested.

Brian ignored the oblique reference to his addiction. From the outset he'd maintained a steadfast loyalty to the use of intravenous narcotics, but the where, how and when of this personal sacrament he kept entirely to himself.

"Aren't you getting a little tired of wearing your hair shirt?" he asked Will. "Why not give the self-flagellation a rest and just take a damned vacation?"

Will brought his feet to the floor and leaned forward on the chair's edge, his hands braced on his thighs. "Why don't we just go sign those papers?" he suggested

Brian gave out an exasperated sigh. "Will," he said, speaking intently. "This is all so *pointless*! There is no one who cares. *No one*. Michael doesn't, obviously." He paused a long moment to examine Will's face closely and then continued, his tone suddenly harsh.

"It's all about that *girl*, isn't it?" he demanded, spitting out the noun like a bad taste. "That goddamned girl." He shook his head dismissively. "She's not worth it, *amigo*," he said with conviction. "She never was."

How would you know? What *do you know?* Will thought. But aloud he said only, "It's not 'about that girl', Brian. It's not 'about' anything."

Many times Brian before had been tempted to tell his friend all he knew concerning the provocative young Maria, but it had long been his habit to avoid such personal intrusions. He'd consequently kept his silence, but circumstances now had progressed to the point that he decided all at once to violate his customary reticence. As if anticipating his revelations, however, Will interupted him before he could speak.

"Brian," he said, "you've always been good about leaving other people to their business. And I've always admired that about you. I'd really appreciate your not making me the exception."

Before Brian could respond, Will rose and walked into his bedroom, collected a short stack of documents and then returned to the living room. Within the pile was an agreement that would designate Brian as tenant, co-owner and legal guardian *de la casa* for the next twenty-four months. Surely, he thought, Brian would exit his self-imposed purgatory within the next two years, one way or another.

Also included were documents related to the mortgage. On the chance that any money he provided Brian might be diverted towards the purchase of narcotics, he'd sent the mortgage holder two year's worth of payments. Even as he'd done so, however, he'd felt reasonably certain that Brian's peculiar set of ethics was such that this precaution was unnecessary. Given that Brian had no identifiable source of income or support, he'd had some difficulty convincing the bank's representative to accept Brian as co-holder of the mortgage, but what won the man over was the inevitability that the university would soon be exercising its right of eminent domain and purchase the property. If that occurred in his absence, Will hoped the university would ante up enough money to provide Brian sufficient financial support should he decide to abandon his current lifestyle and opt for something more conventional.

He'd paid the equivalent of a year's worth of property taxes and utilities in advance. Counting on Becky to maintain some link to Brian and a corresponding concern for his circumstances, he'd set aside another $5,000 in an account that only she could access should Brian's unaccountable ability to keep himself clean, fed and well-clothed desert him.

Without bothering to read the documents, Brian signed on each line that Will indicated. Finished, he gave Will a taut look and asked, "What now?"

"Well," Will answered, "If you're not otherwise engaged, what do you say we meet at the El Corral tonight for a few beers?"

"How about the Monte V?" Brian countered, naming a smaller and more obscure bar on Grant Road.

The Monte V sat conveniently between two of the hospitals they'd had to cover as residents, and Will had spent many call nights there, shooting pool and restricting his beer intake so as to remain functional should he be summoned to serve. The juke box was loud and unfortunately tended to obscure the alert emitted by his beeper when he was paged. When he did manage to retrieve a message, he would wait for a brief remission from the blaring of the juke to return the call. If questioned as to his whereabouts, he honestly could reply, "Between hospitals".

Will shook his head. "No," he said, "The Dusty Chaps are playing. Let's make it an El Corral night."

Brian shrugged. "It's your party," he said, his lack of enthusiasm palpable. He left the room, and in a moment Will heard the back door open and close.

By the time Will reached El Corral the place was rocking. Pretty girls in tank tops, long denim skirts and cowboy boots twirled and pranced with their partners to music fit for the western swing, their long hair whipping across their faces as they danced, their bare thighs suddenly exposed to the hips as they spun. Every table was full, and patrons stood three deep at the bar. Hard-faced waitresses determinedly picked their way through the crowd, two brim-full pitchers clenched in each hand.

Here and there Will saw a familiar face, but all were attached to individuals best avoided. Abner sat resplendent in an enormous black Stetson, dominating the conversation at a tableful of duckling-like students and interns in a far corner. On the dance floor was Penelope, a cute surgery resident whom he'd rashly invited along on a skiing weekend just two winters past, only to regret every interminable minute of the time they'd consequently spent together.

Also dancing enthusiastically but with less grace was Kristi, once a lissome medical student whose slender good looks had given way to stunning obesity almost overnight, testimony to her demanding OB/GYN residency. As if to remind Will of their brief fling years ago, she was prone to greeting him with highly public embraces that transcended the boundaries of mere friendship.

At another table sat a group of medical students whom he knew from working in the ED. Pleasant enough they were, but so young and earnest. Several had shadowed him as he evaluated and treated his patients, impervious to his long silences and disinclination to acknowledge their insightful questions. Just seeing them, fresh-faced, laughing and clearly at ease, he felt himself a virtual Methuselah. *Why am I here?* he wondered.

He'd just decided to exit the bar when he felt a hand come to rest on his shoulder. He turned around, and there was Becky standing before him.

"You take yourself far too seriously, Will Rawlins," she said. She rose on her tiptoes to peer more closely into his eyes, swaying a bit as she did. Will could tell she was drunk. He knew her well, and at this level of intoxication she tended towards belligerence and an uncharacteristic compulsion to lace her speech with profanity. If she continued to drink, she soon would become morose and sentimental, with irresistible sleep quickly following.

"Well, I don't know about that, Becky," he said, "but you surely look beautiful tonight." He paused and then added, "*Como siempre.*"

She settled back on her booted feet and regarded him sternly. "Don't think you can distract me with your stupid sweet talk," she said. "Will, my friend so serious, how come you to be here?"

As if on cue, Brian moved gracefully through the mass of bodies clustered around the bar's entrance and spotted them immediately. Smiling, he greeted Will cheerfully and directed a friendly nod Becky's way.

The young woman bristled visibly in response. "And what are *you* doing here?" she demanded.

Brian's smile never faltered. "It's good to see you, too, Becky," he said. "And it's always nice to be back in the old Corral." He raised his hand, and a harried, heretofore oblivious waitress responded at once, her circular plastic tray balanced gracefully on her fingertips. "What'll it be, sugar?" she asked coyly.

Becky gave a brief shake of her head and returned to her table. Brian focused his full attention on the waitress, favoring her with a beguiling smile. "My repressed friend here needs a shot of tequila and a cold Coors draft," he answered.

"And how 'bout you, cowboy?" she asked, beaming and ignoring Will entirely. "Are you just buyin'? or will you be drinkin', too?"

Brian continued to smile down at her. "No drink," he assured her. "I'm okay." He paused. "On second thought," he said, "I could sure use a big glass of ice water." From the waitress' reaction you'd have thought that with this request he'd bestowed upon her a gift of inestimable value. His effect on women was both profound and consistent.

As the waitress rushed off to comply, Brian turned back to Will and shook his head. "Curious creatures, women," he mused. "Hostile one minute and sweet as candy the next. They've got moods as labile as a desert wash during a *chubasco*: dry as a bone at noon, flooding its banks by 1, and then"- he snapped his fingers - "dry as dust again. Their feelings run deep, but they never seem to run any one way but for so long."

Will watched Becky across the room as he absorbed this insight. There were women, and there were women, he decided. While his Maria was clearly of the type Brian described, Becky was anything but fickle. Whatever feelings she might profess to the contrary, he knew it was Brian she loved. Her emotional commitment was irrevocable. Irrevocable, but not unconditional.

He turned his attention back to Brian, now sipping at the glass of water he'd graciously accepted from the adoring waitress, and inspected him in profile. They were approximately the same height and weight - too lean, most would say. Brian wore his clothes with the same casual grace that attended his movements and speech: tonight a long sleeved black shirt of some light, rough-textured cotton fabric with thin veins of white threaded longitudinally through the dark background, his sleeves rolled up neatly above the elbow. His boots and jeans were black as well, and the effect - pale face and deep blue eyes framed by his inky black hair, eyebrows and attire - was only heightened by his uncultivated insouciance. It was easy enough to see why women found him so irresistable.

Will glanced again over at Becky's table and saw she was watching them. Catching his look, she abruptly turned away and began to talk to the woman sitting beside her. He felt a sudden sadness. Brian had betrayed this good woman - betrayed her trust, generosity and love. And for what? Just as well the waitress appeared to have forgotten his drinks. It had been a bad idea to come here. Why awaken ghosts?

Brian broke the silence. "Deep *ennui*, is it?" he asked, inspecting his friend. "Stare not too long into the abyss, my friend. The past is a door forever closed, no matter how long and loudly one may knock."

Will made no reply. He disagreed with Brian — that door hung wide open. As another had said: the past isn't dead…it's not even past. So it was for him.

They stood together for a few minutes and watched the dancers. Then Brian drained his glass of ice water and excused himself. He had business on the south side, he said. In the *barrio*. Will waited a moment to give Brian time to clear the parking lot and then slipped out quickly himself without bidding Becky goodbye. The racous din from inside diminished at once as the door swung shut.

Chapter 2

MEXICO

The road curves treacherously through the hills that border the narrow canyon, and to travel the road after dark is to court disaster. Unfenced cattle wander casually into the lanes, presenting their huge dumb shapes to startled motorists who happen suddenly upon them and so lack sufficient time to swerve or brake. Massive buses and tractor trailers hurtle down the center of what the maps generously designate a "highway", their cabs decorated as gaily as store windows at Christmas with strands of multicolored lights and signs emblazoned with religious entreaties: *Madre, Oyenos!* (Hear us, Mother!). In their great bulk, speed and apparent heedlessness, it seems impossible that any human intelligence could be lending these brutes guidance. Like chariots from hell they roar through the night, and woe to him who dares to impede their tumultuous passage.

Illusory was any perception that nocturnal travel through the canyon was daunting but ultimately innocuous. With regularity, the coming of daylight revealed roadside monuments of carnage both recent and remote: crumpled buses lying on their sides like ships beached far from sea; human bodies strewn about the wreckage of an overturned flatbed truck; a cluster of white crosses commemorating the sudden, violent deaths of loved ones, the sad memorial adorned by garlands of plastic flowers that substituted for the live petals which rapidly would turn to dust in this hot, arid land.

The man knew all of this and so had left early from his city of origin. It was now just midday, and already he had cleared the canyon and was driving southward towards Hermosillo on a flat sweep of desert that stretched endlessly in all directions. In another hour he would reach the *tienda* maintained by *el Senor* Jesus Caballero, an oasis most humble but assuredly welcome amidst the surrounding miles of empty lunar landscape. Until then, however, there was precious little beyond the windshield that a traveler could look to for succor.

The hour passed slowly, but at last he could see the store just ahead. It was a small, shabby building that measured no more than twenty feet on the longest of its mismatched sides. Its walls were plywood fortified externally by sheets of scrap metal and an assortment of highway signs. The commands the signs once presented to motorists were largely indecipherable, their letters and figures now faded from years of exposure to the scorching Sonoran sun. A flimsy ramada constructed from saguaro ribs projected from the building's rear, and there the aged proprietor customarily could be found in its shade, resting on a rusty beach lounger of similarly ancient vintage.

Inside, the *tienda's* floor was dirt. Until the death of *la senora* Caballero some years past it had been kept tidy, well-swept and hardpacked, but now any movement disturbing its surface would raise small clouds of dust to reveal what lay beneath: old cigarette butts, dried remnants of tortillas, bottle caps, an occasional coin, the desiccated husk of a centipede. The precariously tilting shelves held a few cans, beans mostly, that only the most desperately voracious would dare sample, and on the plywood counter sat huge jars of brine within which floated jalapeños, pig's feet and pickled eggs, all pre-Revolutionary in aspect. The store itself seemed never to be open, and yet it was always so. As for the proprieter, where Jesus lived, slept and prepared his meals was a mystery.

To balance its unabashed squalor, the *tienda* could boast a saving grace or two. For one, it was the only source of diesel and gasoline on the 120 kilometers of highway that extended southward to Hermosillo from Benjamin Hill, the latter a tiny speck of a village unaccountably named for a Confederate senator from Georgia notable primarily for his baseless optimism ("*We shall conquer all enemies yet*," he'd assured President Jefferson Davis in the spring of 1865, just ten days before Lee surrendered his decimated, starving and thoroughly defeated army).

No less important, and the sparsity of his other merchandise notwithstanding, Jesus invariably maintained a supply of iced-down beer abundant in quantity but limited in variety to one brand: Carta Blanca. The old Mexican saw no need to stock any competing *cerveza*. Carta Blanca was tasty and cheap - virtually free, in fact. His brother-in-law, who worked for a beer distributor, stopped by each week while en route to Mexicali and was given to off-loading from his truck four or five cases unlikely to be missed amongst the hundreds it carried.

To make matters yet more convenient, in those days the base of the Carta Blanca bottle contained an indentation cleverly designed to serve as a bottle opener, and in the hot months, April through November, it was a great satisfaction for *el viejo* to sit in the ramada's shade and sequentially open a cool replacement with the empty remains of its predecessor.

As he drew closer to the *tienda*, the American could distinguish the familiar form of Jesus reclining on his lounger. No other vehicles were about. Pulling up to the single gasoline pump in the dirt parking lot, he opened his door and slowly emerged from the cab, his legs stiff from the long drive and his shirt sticking wetly to his back. In the sudden glare he almost failed to notice the four young people sitting in a patch of shade cast by the Pemex sign. Two males and two females, all young, white and draped limply over an assortment of brightly colored backpacks.

They appeared a motley group. The boys stood up as he walked by, as if intending to speak, but they remained silent. One was tall, thin and adorned with stringy long blonde locks. From his chin sprouted a patch of scraggly, rust-colored hair, and the overall effect suggested a peroxided billy goat. The other boy was much shorter, with a mane of thick, black curls that obscured his forehead and fell helmet-like to his shoulders. From a distance his face appeared hairless, but as the two approached he could detect on this boy's upper lip a modest sprinkling of black that approximated a mustache.

Behind them the two girls continued to sit. Her body concealed within a grossly oversized flannel shirt, one was notable only for her shockingly white hair. The other presented a more promising aspect, with long brown hair pinned up to reveal a shapely neck and angular cheek bones.

When he failed to acknowledge them, the two boys halted in unison and continued to gape silently after him as he walked around the *tienda* to *el senor's* refuge. Jesus was sprawled upon his chaise, facing away from his store and towards the west, a half-full bottle of Carta Blanca in his hand and four empties lined up neatly on the ground beside him. Although the two men had known each other for years, their greeting was circumspect and restrained in the *campesino* manner.

"*Buenas a usted. Es un dia muy caliente,*" he greeted the older man, making a brief reference to the oppressive heat.

"*Buenas. Si. Muy caliente, como todos los dias,*" Jesus answered, shading his eyes with his wrinkled brown hand as he peered up at the other man. It was a hot day, he agreed, but then so it was with most days.

"*Espero que en la noche haya menos calor, pero eso es muy raro en este mes.*" The American expressed his hope that the night would bring with it some coolness but conceded that during this season such relief was not to be expected.

"*Verdad,*" the old man replied. He continued to hold his bottle but would not drink from it. This was not the border. In rural Mexico the old customs still held. In his home, a man would never show disrespect to a guest – even one uninvited – by eating or drinking in that guest's presence.

Verbal formalities concluded, the bony old Mexican unfolded himself slowly and arose from his rusty lounger to face the younger man. He proffered his hand, and the other gripped it limply, taking care to avoid the firm American handshake offensive to *los campesinos*.

Having nearly completed the quietly elaborate choreography required to re-establish their social bond, the two men turned away to face westward, both gazing towards the distant mountains as if they held some portent. He was standing slightly behind the Mexican and from his vantage point could look him over unobserved. He judged Jesus to be of Yaqui lineage, a scion of *los indios* indigenous to northwestern Mexico and long persecuted by a succession of despotic regimes both central and provincial. Many Yaqui had died violently in the horrific mines of the region, slaves of Spanish masters whose inclination towards such brutality gradually waned as, generation by generation, their pure Iberian blood progressively was diluted to a *mestizo* composition.

The Yaqui themselves had been no angels. In their time they'd remorselessly preyed upon the docile Seri of the coast, repeatedly raiding the latter's humble camps to kill, rape and carry off whom and what they could. Their history mirrored that of Mexico itself, a pungent stew redolent of paroxysmal violence, intense religiosity, paganism, revolution, reactionism, democracy, fascism, *machismo*, fidelity, betrayal, and so on...and on.

While he'd read much regarding the country, was fluent in its language and had traveled there extensively, he suffered no illusion that he understood Mexico. He knew that a foreigner did best to watch much, speak little and interfere never. This was a country that revealed itself slowly to outsiders, if at all, and to the uninitiated who sought to embrace her too enthusiastically, Mexico could prove lethal.

Even so, he'd often been surprised by the reflexive generosity of these people of the *campos* who were, with the exception of the urban squatters inhabiting the dumps of Tijuana, the most impoverished of Sonora's citizenry.

———

Once, years ago, his radiator had blown during a hot, labored ascent of the mountains north of San Quintín, and at the road's summit he shut off his engine and coasted down the far side. Once on level ground again his momentum carried him to a small *ranchero*. The family who lived there and farmed its scrubby fields consented to watch his truck until he could hitchhike to San Diego, buy a replacement radiator and return.

He was gone almost a week. He drove south with a friend, and when they arrived, the *campesino's* large family spilled out of their tiny home to welcome his return. The pope himself could not have received a more radiantly enthusiastic greeting. During his absence the farmer had removed the ruined radiator, and now he took charge of installing its replacement.

Once the new radiator was seated and bolted to his satisfaction, he and his family formed a bucket brigade to transport water from a small creek that meandered through their property. In the interim, *la esposa de la casa* had prepared a meal, and sitting outside at a large, hand-hewn wooden table they celebrated the truck's restoration with a feast of homemade tortillas, beans, *salsa fresca* and freshly killed chicken prepared *asado*.

When at last he and his friend took their leave, the *campensino* politely but firmly refused the payment he'd pressed upon him.

"Vayan con Dios. Su visita trajo bendiciones a nuestra casa." Go with God, he'd said. Their company had honored his home.

———

A strange country is Mexico, he thought. A maze in which a man might lose himself and forever wander anonymous. In all aspects, it was a country well-suited to his present needs. If one adjective could serve as a man's defining characteristic, his own was *solitary*. Only two people had managed to penetrate his preference for solitude. One now was dead, and the other… well, the other had left for parts unknown and was better left forgotten. Ideal for him was the vast anonymity of Mexico.

31

For his own part, and although he'd given no external indication of his feelings, Jesus was shocked by the *gringo's* physical appearance. Despite an acquaintanceship spanning years, he'd at first failed to recognize the man. While always lean, the tall American had grown alarmingly thin. More than that, however, he somehow seemed no longer young. Once smiling and gay, he'd grown solemn. His gaze was flat and dull, and his face was taut in the manner of one whose stomach was sour from a night spent in the bottle, swimming in *mezcal*. Was it possible he had the wasting disease of which his brother-in-law had told him, the illness that afflicted *las mariposas*, those men who inexplicably lay with other men? He stole another look at the *gringo* and shook his head imperceptibly. *No lo creo.* He thought this unlikely.

After the long silence Jesus was prepared for more substantial conversation. *"Esos muchachos no hablan espanol,"* he began, referring to the group presently encamped by his store. *"Alguien queria que se vayan, pero no hablaba ingles."* The young ones spoke no Spanish. One desired they leave, but that person spoke no English and so could not make them understand.

He paused to spit, vehemently, upon the unyielding *caliche*. *"Para dos dias han estado holgozaneando al frente de mi tienda,"* he exclaimed. *"No vendemos nada, y creo que no tienen dinero. Hippies! Tengo miedo que asusten a mis clientes."* For two days they had lounged in front of his store. They'd bought nothing, and Jesus was certain they had no money. They were hippies! They would frighten away his regular customers.

The tall American suppressed a smile at this. The ruggedly independent clientele Jesus served was unlikely to be intimidated by four slovenly young *gringos* and their backpacks.

"*Como llegaron aqui?*" he asked the old man. How had they come to be here?

Jesus spat again. "*En un camión muy grande,*" he answered disgustedly. "*Con un camionero que le vio los tetas a las chicas y queria que se sentaran cerca de el. Hacen autostop, como lo hacen los hippies.*" They'd arrived in a big truck with a driver who'd ogled the girls' breasts and desired to have *los tetas* pressed against him in his cramped cab. They were hitchhiking, he'd added, as hippies were wont to do.

"*Quizas los jovenes hacen autostop como nene,*" the American suggested. Then surely they would resume their hitchhiking, leaving as they'd come.

Jesus shook his head regretfully. "*No,*" he answered. "*Es un milagro que llegaron tan lejos. Por todo un dia intentaron que alguien los recogiera. Nadie, menos ese bufon de camionero, recogena los hippies como de esos. El se haido para el este y no regresara pronto*" It was a miracle they'd managed to make their way even this far, he declared. He'd watched for an entire day as they stood by the highway and tried without success to induce someone to stop and pick them up; now they seemed to have abandoned the effort. He was sure that except for that fool of a truck driver there was no one sufficiently ignorant to invite these *hippies* into his vehicle. And that *bufon* had turned east and would not soon return.

El viejo paused a moment and then, without looking directly at the younger man, spoke with some firmness. "*Es necesario que se estos vayan ahora,*" he proclaimed. It was necessary that they leave…and the sooner the better.

This was the Mexican's means of inquiring obliquely whether the American would accept responsibility for removing his unwanted guests.

He considered the implied request. While he owed Jesus no favors, there was also no compelling reason to deny him. The *jovenes* presumably were heading south, as he was, and Hermosillo was not far distant. *Quien sabe,* he thought. Acceding to the old man's plea might come to assist him in some manner presently inconceivable.

So without further hesitation, he replied, *"Conmigo, como no? Primero necesito algo de gasolina y mas cervazas. Despues todos los gringos nos iremos a Hermosillo."* Why not leave them to me? he suggested, as if the idea were his own. He required only some gasoline and more beer, and then all the *gringos* could depart for Hermosillo.

The old man frowned in consternation. *"Cerveza yo tengo, como no? Pero, necesitas la gasolina ahora? No puedes llegar a Hermosillo con la que tienes?"* Beer he had, of course. But did one truly require gasoline now? Could one not reach Hermosillo with that fuel already residing in his tank?

When the American confirmed that he could not, Jesus stared in mournful silence at the distant mountains for a full minute before speaking once again. *"Yo no tengo gasolina ahora, y el camión de* Pemex *esta atrasado,"* he explained. *"Sin telefono, yo no se cuando viene."* He had no gasoline. The Pemex truck was late. Without a telephone, he had no idea when it would arrive. The Mexican continued to gaze sorrowfully at some distant point.

He glanced sideways at the old man. Although his placid *mestizo* visage typically concealed all emotion, Jesus was clearly miserable with frustration. *"Oye, amigo, "*he reassured the old man.

"Yo los llerare al desierto. Alli esperaremos a que el camion de Pemex venga de nuevo. Entonces iremos a Hermosillo.". He would take the young ones into the desert and remain there until the Pemex truck's arrival. Then he would drive them to Hermosillo.

"Por que querrian ir al desierto?" the old man asked doubtfully. Why would they willingly go into the desert?

"Porque pensaron que seria una gran aventura. A los hippies les gusta dormir en la tierra," he replied. He told Jesus that they would consider it a very great adventure, that hippies enjoyed sleeping on the ground.

The Mexican looked at him disbelievingly. Among the *campesinos* of rural Sonora the concept of recreational camping was unknown or incomprehensible. To forsake one's bed voluntarily to sleep on the hard ground and so expose the body to the nocturnal *aires malos*, the"bad airs", were the actions of a lunatic.

"Es esto posible?" he asked. This was possible?

"Claro," the American assured him. Believe it.

———

As it happened, however, it had not been so easy to convince the group to relocate. The boys were game, but the pretty brunette seemed less enthusiastic at the prospect of camping amidst the splendors of the Sonoran desert, and the girl with the Andy Warhol hair expressed a more specific and practical concern.

"How will we know when the gas truck gets here?" she asked.

"I'll drive in tomorrow at midday," he replied. "If the truck hasn't come, I'll check again in the evening. Once the truck has come, I'll gas up and stop to get you."

She looked at him dubiously. "How do we know you won't just drive off by yourself and leave us?" she asked.

He glanced back at her briefly. "You don't," he conceded. "Stay here if it suits you." He turned and walked away, leaving them to confer amongst themselves.

In the end it was their collective boredom that swayed them. They'd been languishing at the store for over two days, and the heat and inactivity had worn them down. Even the open desert seemed inviting after their extended layover at *la tienda de Jesus.*

Before they left he bought some ice and *cerveza* and told the relieved old man he'd be back in the morning. The truck's bed was packed with provisions, but for the short trip his passengers could manage within the cramped space. As if preordained, however, the white-haired girl broke off from the others and joined him in the cab, tossing her cheap purple backpack to the floorboards as she settled herself in the passenger's seat. He was more bemused than annoyed by her presumptuousness. They weren't traveling far.

Jesus had told him of a spur that departed from the main highway two kilometers south of the store, a narrow dirt path that led through the ubiquitous creosote bush to the ruins of a small corral once used for the gathering and loading of cattle. It sounded as if it would suffice as a campsite, and he drove slowly, squinting through the sun's glare as he searched for the turn-off.

The girl sat on the seat beside him, staring out the window at the featureless desert. Glancing over at him quickly and then looking away, she asked, "Where were you going when you stopped at that store? Do you live here?"

He paused before answering. "I have business in Hermosillo," he answered, finally.

"Is it this bad all the way?" she asked. He assumed she was referring to the desert all about them, a discouraging land seared to a state of near-lifelessness. Ceaselessly arid. Hopelessly empty.

"Yeah," he answered. "Believe it or not, it gets even drier if you keep heading south."

"We're on our way to Guaymas," she advised him. "It's beautiful there. We're going to camp on the beach."

Guaymas was a largish city about fifteen kilometers south of San Carlos, his own destination. While it might be many things, he reflected, the city could not in any sense be described as "beautiful". It served primarily as the home port for western Mexico's seafood industry, and if one knew where to look there were a small number of no-frills restaurants that offered excellent *camarones, calamar, cabrilla* and *ceviche* - literally fresh off the boat. Those restaurants catered primarily to locals and to Mexican families from Hermosillo fleeing the inland summer heat for the relative cool of the coast.

Under no circumstances, however, could one envision Guaymas itself as a vacation destination, and the city consequently took no pains to offer the amenities typically associated with tourism. It was a working-class, industrial city, and its sole public beach was a sad narrow ribbon of oily sand, heavily littered and located on the town's uninspiring inner harbor. He doubted that within the city's entire history anyone previously had undertaken such a long journey for the express purpose of spending an extended amount of time on that particular beach. With the exception of young couples intent on romance and desperate for privacy, even the locals shunned it.

But this information he kept to himself. If these kids were hell-bent on Guaymas and its purported charms, why disillusion them prematurely? Let them figure it out. Once they recovered from the initial shock, perhaps they'd be sufficiently resourceful to migrate a few miles to the north and discover the pristine bays and beaches of San Carlos.

"Good for you," he replied. And they drove on in silence.

———

Their campsite's appeal increased considerably with nightfall, and the group's spirits rose correspondingly. In the heat and glare of the afternoon it had appeared to be nothing more than a small clearing in the barren desert, empty save for the weathered wooden rails of the abandoned corral and an abundance of desiccated cow pies. Darkness transformed the site into something almost magical. The desert air cooled rapidly once the sun set beyond the mountains, and they'd used the old rails to make a fire. Above them were arraigned the constellations, complete and distinct due to the remarkable clarity produced by the absence of moisture or city lights.

He'd remained apart from the group throughout the evening. He prepared a cold dinner - tortillas, some carrots and a wedge of *queso fresco*, the ubiquitous white cheese produced on farms throughout northern Sonora - but wound up tossing most of his meal to the antelope squirrels watching silently from their outposts in the underbrush. Using old blankets, he made himself a pallet in the bed of the truck and settled back with a plastic cup of red wine to observe the night sky.

The moon was near full. Earlier it had risen orange from its position behind the hills to the northwest and then faded to white as it gradually ascended. Lying in his truck fifty yards from the bonfire, he could detect the heavy sweet scent of dope, and for a moment he worried that the smell might drift abroad and attract unwanted attention. No, he decided. They were two miles in from the main road, and aside from the *tienda* the desert was uninhabited for ten miles or more in all directions.

Unable to sleep, he was rooting through his medicine kit for 2mg of clonazepam to add to his wine when he heard footsteps approaching the truck. By their light tread he guessed the intruder to be barefoot and female, and on both counts he was correct. Above where he lay appeared suddenly the head and torso of the white-haired girl. She looked down at him thoughtfully.

"Why are you staying over here by yourself?" she asked. Despite the smell of dope that had wafted over intermittently throughout the evening, her speech was clear.

Not bothering to answer, he took another sip of his wine and shifted his gaze back to the moon. It was now at its zenith and would soon begin its slow descent.

"Okay if I join you?" she asked, and although he still made no response she climbed into the truck bed and sat beside him.

"What are you drinking?" she asked, and when he told her asked, "May I have some?" The moonshine cast odd shadows on her face. Her white hair glistened, and her cheeks shone palely, but her eyes were dark. Obscured.

He motioned towards the open bottle, and she poured her cup full. It was a cheap but respectable red. Dry. Would have complimented a steak nicely. Few decent wines were produced in Sonora, and as it was likely to be a long time before he found himself in a place where wine would be abundant or even available, before leaving home he bought several cases of an inexpensive *rioja*, along with a few pricier bottles to be saved for a time worthy of celebration. This was not such a time.

He watched her as she knocked back half the cup's contents in one long swallow. "You seem to be more of a drinker than a smoker," he observed.

"I don't care for weed," she replied. She paused for another substantial swallow of the wine. "It makes me feel wired," she added, "and then I can't sleep."

He made no comment and resumed his stargazing as she finished off the cup and poured herself another.

"There's another bottle in that box over there," he told her. "Why don't you take it back to the bonfire and drink it with your friends?"

"Nah," she replied gloomily. "The guys are into Anna. They think she's hot." She shifted her gaze to contemplate her bare toes and continued in a disconsolate tone. "They could care less whether I'm around."

He turned on his side to address her more directly. "That's too bad," he said, "but if you don't want to party with your friends, there's plenty of desert out there where you can be alone." He shifted to a supine position and closed his eyes, suddenly exhausted and ready for sleep.

"I don't want to be alone," she replied softly. "Please."

When he failed to answer, she carefully lowered herself to lie beside him on the blankets. For what seemed a long time he lay beneath the stars and listened as the pattern of her breathing shifted to the rhythmic undulations of sleep. The moonlight was bright, but eventually he slept as well.

When he awoke in the early morning, he was alone in the truck bed.

Chapter 3

WILL

To the telling it seemed a hard tale. His parents divorced when he was ten, and both were dead by his early teens. His stepmother died shortly thereafter, and at seventeen the boy was living on his own. His only sibling, a half-brother thirteen years his junior, was taken in by an uncle.

And yet, although divorce and death had led early in life to the disintegration of his family, Will was in many ways favored. His genes had blessed him with height, athletic ability, good looks and intelligence, and the circumstances of his childhood and teenage years had combined to render him self-sufficient, emotionally and physically durable and, despite the absence of much early nurturing, light-hearted and kind. His manner and wit drew others to him.

This was, ironically, his greatest liability in interacting with his peers. Although his personal warmth seemed to indicate otherwise, his capacity for participation in any truly close relationship was limited. The solitude he'd experienced involuntarily as a youth evolved into an irrevocable necessity as he grew into adulthood. Those who succumbed to his charm and sought greater closeness were quickly disappointed when the easy intimacy he'd initially appeared to offer receded into an impenetrable aloofness. Correspondingly, whenever he was called upon to direct others (to be a class president, team captain, chief resident, etc), he declined the opportunity. Jokingly, he referred to what he claimed was the Rawlins family motto: "Too lazy to lead. Too proud to follow".

He was good at most of what he determined to undertake but excelled at nothing in particular. He performed well - often very well - but rarely was he superb. Blended with a solid but unspectacular performance on the football and basketball teams, his academic record in high school was sufficient to earn him a scholarship to the University of Chicago, but the allure of California and the vaguely conceived notion of a career in marine biology led him to Stanford instead.

There his grades were mediocre. An inheritance left to him by his grandfather sufficed to cover the cost of tuition, not an inconsiderable sum at that institution, but to support himself otherwise he worked at a variety of jobs both during and after classes. Coupled with the multitude of other distractions offered by life on and off campus, his grade point average hovered well below what would be required to gain acceptance to any of the more elite graduate programs.

By that time he didn't much care. He'd seen and heard enough to discern that marine biology as a career involved window-less laboratories and libraries more than diving expeditions to exotic locales, *a la* Jacques Cousteau. As his graduation date approached he applied for various positions as a high school teacher and coach, but his lack of a teaching degree restricted him to private schools, where the pay was miserable. He'd earned more tending bar.

While discussing his prospects with one of his biology professors, he casually mentioned to the older man the possibility
of his applying to medical school. Although up until then he'd
never actually given any serious thought to a medical career, his
professor's adamantly stated conviction that he would never be
able to gain acceptance was sufficiently annoying to trigger in
him a stubborn determination to pursue that option.

And so he stayed on at the university after graduation, taking
the required pre-med classes over the summer and the academic
year that followed. He did well in those classes, scored highly on
the standardized tests required of applicants, and in the spring
was accepted to Stanford's medical school.

Unlike most of his classmates, Will found medical school far
more appealing than college. For once he had no real financial worries. He'd received a Public Health Service grant that
covered all his educational expenses and provided him with a
stipend of almost $20,000 annually for living expenses. After
the lean undergraduate years spent sharing a succession of
overcrowded apartments, toiling at menial jobs for low pay and
enduring used cars that refused to perform faithfully, this was
luxury. At the completion of his internship he would have the
choice of either paying off his financial debt as one would any
low-interest loan or serving an equivalent number of years in
the PHS, but that decision lay well downstream.

Will managed to survive the drudgery of his first two years
of medical school, time spent largely in lecture halls or laboratories. Once freed of the classroom in his third and fourth
years, he found the clinical work engaging and began to earn
recognition for his skill in managing patients. The strong letters
of recommendation he consequently received from the clinical

faculty enabled him to secure a competitive internship in general surgery at a private hospital in San Diego, and he spent that year improving his clinical skills and learning how to surf. Eventually he'd decided to choose the PHS over an infinity of monthly loan payments, and so at the conclusion of his internship in June he journeyed to the White Mountain Apache reservation in central Arizona to repay his debt to the government.

His four years in the White Mountains passed quickly. While initially he chafed at the social isolation, in time he grew to appreciate the area's remoteness and to revel in the wild ruggedness of the land. When the snows came, he sometimes would ski with friends from work at a nearby resort owned and operated by the tribe. More often he simply snapped into his cross-country skis and set out alone on one of the many trails that meandered through the woods behind his cabin to the Mogollon Rim several miles to the south. The view from the Rim was spectacular, especially in winter, when the trees had shed their obscuring leaves. Far below him spread the vastness of the Sonoran high desert, a tableland bare naked save for scattered stands of stunted juniper and criss-crossed by a multitude of canyons, their rock walls sporting hues of yellow, rosy pink and red according to the sun's changing angle.

Throughout high school, college, medical school and his internship Will had a series of girlfriends, and with time those liaisons had taken on a discernible pattern. At the outset the relationship would blossom rapidly, and for a time - months, even a year or two - all was well. Then, abruptly, he would have had enough, and the young woman would be left dazed by the rapidity of his departure in the absence of any antecedent indication that his affection was waning. For a period he would keep to himself before emerging from his self-imposed isolation to spread himself thin amongst those women who were willing and immediately available. Once he tired of this, he would revert to monogamy, and the cycle would repeat itself.

Those young women with whom he chose serially to partner were a varied lot, but in general they were attractive, athletic, bright, capable and engaged in a job, sport or profession that consumed much of their time and attention. In short, they were women who tended to demand little of him and were both easy to be with and easy to leave. He'd no experience with relationships, romantic or otherwise, that involved any true commitment. He'd learned early in life to expect loss and so to look to himself for constancy.

If in those first months in the mountains he yearned for a companion with whom to share the viscerally stirring scenery, he had but little time to wait. Early in the winter he met Karin, a tall, leggy blonde with the sunny good looks of a classic southern California beach girl but in fact a product of Nebraska. Two years prior she'd accompanied her then-husband, fresh from his residency at Creighton, to his new job in Phoenix. Disappointed by her marriage and repelled by the sprawling monotomy of that hot desert city, she divorced her fellow Nebraskan and migrated to Show Low, a town in the White Mountains, to work as a lab tech at its small hospital.

Will first became aware of Karin when he read in the local weekly that a woman had won the annual Payson cross-country ski race, beating not only the other females but also the male competitors. The margin of her victory apparently was not small. Intrigued by this startling accomplishment and the flattering photograph that accompanied the article, Will located

Karin's number in the thin directory that served the region and called to invite her to accompany him on one of his Sunday afternoon treks to the Rim.

At first meeting he'd marveled at her legs. Although she was at least two inches shy of six feet in height, the inseam of her jeans was longer than his own. She put those long legs to good use, both on the trail, where easily she outpaced his best efforts, and some few nights later in bed, as they encircled his waist.

Their romance developed quickly. Although Karin continued to maintain her apartment in Show Low, not much time passed before she was spending most nights at Will's cabin.

With their shared passion for outdoor adventure and their contrasting good looks – hers fair and his dark; both lean, tall and graceful – they seemed to friends and acquaintances the mythical perfect couple. Were Will not so perpetually restless or, in the end, so attuned to solitude, it's possible they'd have wed and shared a happy life ever after in the mountainous West. As it was, however, Will resisted such domestication, and when his commitment to the Service ended, he left Karin behind and moved south to Tucson. There he entered a rigorous program in neurosurgery that combined both laboratory research and the care of critically ill patients.

As had been his experience at Stanford and in the mountains, Will adapted quickly to life in this new city. His days alternated between the demands of the OR, ER and ICU and the less dramatic but more intellectually draining efforts related to his graduate seminars and laboratory work. As to the last, he was attempting to decipher how one might manipulate the immune system to treat glioblastoma, the most malignant of the primary brain tumors.

His nights he often spent making the rounds of the city's saloons and dance halls with friends he met through his work at the hospital, and amongst them was a group of anesthesiology residents. Although he was uncomfortable with their alarmingly conspicuous drug use, one of them, Brian, was notable for his moderation in that regard as well as his open, friendly manner. And it was through Brian that Will met Michael, the Minnesota internist who became his closest friend.

———

In the tradition of his large family, Michael had attended the University of Minnesota to pursue a graduate degree in physics. Shortly after obtaining his master's and within his first few days in the doctoral program, however, he looked about him and observed that while the ranks of his classmates had thinned notably, this attrition had been accompanied by dramatic increases in both the proportion of Asian students and the level of academic competition. Weighing his lukewarm enthusiasm for physics against the effort it would take to achieve his PhD, Michael opted out and –to the dismay of his father and siblings, physicists all – applied to the state university's medical school. After graduation he left behind the long, cold winters of Minnesota for an internship and residency at the University of Arizona.

Although both were residents when they met, each previously had experienced a diversion from his ultimate career path – Will through his years in the White Mountains and Michael by way of his aborted quest for a PhD – and they consequently were older than most of their peers. Beyond this they appeared superficially quite dissimilar, both physically and behaviorally.

Will was extroverted and athletic in appearance, while Michael was reserved and quite thin, almost frail.

In reality, however, Will's gregarious charm masked a taste for solitude, while Michael's solemn Midwestern affect concealed a dry wit and talent for story-telling. At gatherings of friends, he would entertain those assembled with expressive renditions of the poetry of Robert Service, quoted from memory. As for athleticism, Michael's skill at downhill skiing was pitched at the professional level, and Will eventually gave up making any attempt to follow his friend down the more challenging runs.

Will found Michael's impromptu monologues enormously entertaining, and camping together under the stars or driving for hours on their way to or from another expedition into the Arizona back country, he learned much from the ex-physicist of how and why the natural world functioned as it did. In turn, Michael was amused by his friend's enthusiasm and energy, yet sympathetic to his need for privacy.

Although both had enrolled in residency training programs, each had diverged from the usual path such training offered. For his part, Will became increasingly absorbed in the basic science of brain tumor research and thus reluctant to spend precious lab time dealing with the unending demands of clinical neurosurgery. Michael, unwilling to be tethered to the central lines and respirators of the ICU, was carving out his own unique niche by investigating the management of acute myocardial ischemia and stroke in the ER. To him fell the task of arranging the university hospital's complex ER call schedule, populated by a mélange of senior residents, fellows, and other moonlighters who, like Will, found themselves in need of extra revenue.

They were sufficiently compatible that when Will's lease expired at the completion of his residency, he moved into the small guest suite of the old house Michael had bought upon moving to Tucson, a year in advance of Will's own arrival. The arrangement suited them both. Will was busy with a post-residency fellowship and Michael with his duties as a hospital-ist, and they consequently spent little time together at home. Compounding this, Michael frequently signed up to moonlight at the university hospital's ED or, for entire weekends, at one of the small hospitals that dotted the region: in San Manuel, Globe, Nogales. On Friday afternoons after his VA clinic he would climb aboard his ancient Vespa scooter, wrapped up against the cold in the winter months, and motor off to a 36 hour shift at a tiny ER two hours distant.

This last puzzled Will. His room-mate didn't seem to need the additional income generated by his moonlighting, and consequent to his extended hours at work Michael's social life was largely restricted to an occasional evening - usually spent at home - drinking beer and playing board games with their mutual friends. He apparently had no girlfriend; there was no time for one while he was working, and his vacations he typically spent travelling with Will or visiting his family back in Minnesota. Somewhere along the way Will had heard Michael was married, but in their many conversations his friend had made no refer-ence to a wife. Brian, who somehow seemed to know, warned him off the topic, and eventually Will forgot about it altogether.

Chapter 4

MEXICO

Despite his initial inclination to deposit his passengers in Hermosillo, he wound up driving them to Guaymas, all the way to the dreary city beach. Parking his truck by its crumbling *malecon* and leaving the engine on, he turned to the girl sitting beside him. "Here you are," he told her.

She looked out for a moment at the discouraging bay, the oily gray sand, and the broad assortment of trash that marked the tide line. Then, without a word or backward glance, she clambered out of the cab and with her three companions began to unload their gear from the truck bed. Save for the small waves rippling on the beach, all was silence as they hoisted their backpacks and piled them on the filthy concrete. That task completed, he left them huddled together by the sea wall, and in his rearview mirror he could see that all but the white-haired girl stared after him as he drove away.

Cursing softly, he circled the block and returned to where he'd unloaded his hapless human cargo. There they stood as before, forlorn and motionless. He drew up beside them and rolled down his window. "Get in", he told them. "You can do better than this".

The girl with the white hair climbed in to sit beside him as before while the others resumed their accustomed positions in back. He began to drive eastward, to the main highway that led to San Carlos.

———

While he'd become increasingly possessive of the Midriff region and resented the addition of each new tourist who "discovered" its particular charms, San Carlos hardly qualified as a well-kept secret. In that time the small town boasted the only decent marina and boat ramp to be found along the entire eastern coast, and for years many Arizonians had used it to access the Sea of Cortez. A few dozen kept boats there year-round, either on shore or in slips with rental fees a tenth of what they'd cost in San Diego.

For the less nautically inclined there was one decent hotel. *La Posada* made at least a passing attempt at simulating what an inexperienced American tourist would expect of a Mexican coastal resort after hours spent leafing through the glossy pages of a travel magazine. The rooms were spare but reasonably clean, and those on the higher floors of the ten-story tower offered impressive views of Topolobampo Bay. There were a restaurant, bar and disco on site, and the resort's buildings framed a small but appealing section of beach where the swimming immediately off-shore was safe.

Even so, from its very inception the resort had projected an inescapable atmosphere of seediness and slow decay. The brilliantly colored bougainvillea that grew luxuriantly on the hotel's façade did not quite obscure the mangy patches of exposed cinder-block where huge slabs of cheap stucco had yielded to gravity and the coastal elements. Fallen fragments lay in huge piles at the towers's base, each year rising a few more feet in height and taking on something of the aspect of an unexcavated Mayan ruin as the trumpet vine and sea grape gained purchase and covered the mounting debris.

The services provided by the hotel were decidedly uneven. The staff, all Mexican, was mystified by the American clientele's preference for dining efficiently, with a haste they considered pointless and even unseemly. In Sonora, and especially when friends and family were gathered together, the evening meal involved more than simply eating. It was instead a social event, an entertainment that might last hours, and in even the most modest *restaurantes* a waiter would take great pains to avoid being perceived as rudely intrusive. All of this clashed badly with the hit and run dining tactics of the typical American tourist.

The attempt to obtain any breakfast whatsoever in Mexico can prove especially vexing. The concept of "a hearty breakfast" is foreign and peculiar, and *La Posada*'s best efforts to accommodate this *yanqui* affectation tended to produce meals notable primarily for the prodigious time required to obtain service and the anemic portions of the mediocre product eventually delivered.

Then there was the faint but unmistakably rank aroma of raw sewage that arose each time the wind shifted to off-shore. There was the hair-raising cost of a brief phone call back to the States. And there was the sad little disco, a cramped concrete cube bare of furnishings save for a ball of multi-faceted mirrors revolving gamely above the dance floor, the room sporadically populated by a surly group of local teenagers hungry for entertainment, posturing and gyrating to outdated American rock blaring from the large speakers that loomed in each corner. It was a grim scene, and the few guests who dared enter either beat a hasty retreat or were too inebriated to care.

In the guest rooms were damp, threadbare sheets, limp pillows, and air conditioning units that generated more clatter than cooling. At the front desk the staff's responses to inquiries ran the gamut from embarrassed bewilderment to unfeigned indifference. There were bugs in the air, bugs in the bed, and bugs in the sink. Exotic bugs. Big and seemingly fearless.. It was small wonder that the exclamations of pleasure emitted by uninitiated tourists at their first glance of the resort deteriorated so rapidly into disappointed grumblings.

All other lodging in the town possessed a distinctly Mexican flair and catered almost exclusively to citizens of Hermosillo unable to afford *La Posada's* alarmingly high rates, too inexperienced to know that the hotel industry might offer a more sophisticated alternative, or so desperate to escape the heat and aridity of the interior that the specific amenities offered by the lodging engaged were of little importance. These were the families who gathered together each day on the beach in large multi-generational groups. The women remained fully clad and preoccupied with the preparation of food. The men blithely stripped to their BVDs and busily engaged themselves in rudimentary food gathering: fishing with hand lines, scooping up tiny clams and snapping mussels to fill their plastic buckets. The small children ran about naked, their sand-splattered brown bodies glistening in the sunlight, shrieking as they played their simple games and scurried excitedly from one group of elders to the other. At sunset they all returned to their shabby motels, sleeping eight or ten to a room, windows shut against *los aires malos*, the "bad airs" of the night, seemingly impervious to the heat and lack of air conditioning.

In any event, the tatterdemalions he now transported were likely to lack even the modest sum required to stay at one of these humbler motels, and *La Posada* (*muy rico!*) was out of the question. Besides, as it might increase the odds of their drifting back into his path, he was loath to deposit them anywhere in town or close to the marina. He was wary of any ongoing association with these four vagabonds.

Although the beach he now sought lay only minutes by boat from *La Posada* and the center of town, the coastline's contour was such that it would take a solid hour of steady walking to bring the traveler from one to the other. They would be far enough distant to do no harm and yet close enough to town that they could exit under their own power when they became bored or hungry. In a way he was doing them a favor. That they would find this beach on their own initiative was highly unlikely, and the immediate area held no other alternative for a campsite even remotely as appealing.

At the far end of the town he turned left onto an unmarked and unpaved single lane road that wound up and around a short volcanic peak and then down its seaward slope. As they descended, he could see spread out below, incongruously, the pockmarked asphalt airstrip of the old movie set and, beyond it, the pretty, crescent-shaped beach. Catch-22 Beach.

The girl remained mute beside him, making no comment even as they skidded and slid alarmingly over the crumbly rock and sand during the steeper portions of the descent. In fact, except for asking him to stop once by the roadside so she could urinate, they'd not exchanged more than a few brief sentences all the way from Jesus's store to Guaymas, a journey of hours. While he had no particular desire to speak with her, he nonetheless found her extended silence a little unnerving.

———

To punctuate the tedium of that drive he'd drunk one cold Carta Blanca after another, retrieving the bottles from the small ice chest he kept on the floorboard beneath his legs. By the time they reached Hermosillo he'd finished off a sixpack, and he could feel the beer working on him. It provoked a certain giddiness, a softening of mood.

He glanced at the girl beside him. Her albino hair hung lankly in the heat, and her face was drawn into a frown against the glare of the sun beyond the windshield. She turned and caught him looking. "What?" she asked.

He paused before responding, keeping one hand on the wheel while he groped in the icy water for yet another *cerveza*. With an ease born of familiarity he used his empty to open the fresh bottle and poured back a long swallow of its fine, bitter contents. "I was thinking about a girl I knew once," he answered. "Back in the States. You remind me of her." He regretted his words immediately; clearly he'd drunk too much.

"You mean I look like her?" the girl asked.

"Not really," he said, hoping to end it. He recalled the other woman's long, boot-clad legs and her lean body. She had a thick mane of black hair that swished and swayed when she sauntered about on her long limbs. With her boots on she easily topped six feet, and she towered over her ferret-faced boyfriend, whose putrescent behavior was legendary. Even with her unpleasantly aggressive temperament it had seemed to him the young woman deserved better.

"Then how do I remind you of her?" the girl persisted.

He considered how to answer this, and as he did he wondered what had compelled him to make such an unlikely connection in the first place. They were about as physically distinct from one another as two females could be, and that similarity carried over into the lives they led. A successful professional woman ruthlessly slicing her way to the top, the woman he'd known back in the city was a relentlessly ambitious vixen distrusted by those with whom she worked, but she'd also been sufficiently attractive to arouse his lust. The pale quiet girl who was curled up now in his passenger's seat had none of the other's aggressive sexuality, and from what little he'd observed it seemed unlikely she was bound for great professional success.

"I first met her years ago, when we were students in the same class," he said.

"What does she do now?" the girl asked.

He looked out his window at a large, rotund shape lying inert within the opposite lane. Another dead cow, another reminder why it was unwise to drive at night in these parts. "She's in her next to the last year of a cardiothoracic surgery residency at the university hospital in Tucson," he replied.

It seemed like a good time to change topics. "What's your name, anyway?" he asked her.

"Olivia," she said, staring straight ahead. "My name's Olivia."

Following this revelation she'd lapsed into an impenetrable silence that lasted for the rest of the drive.

———

They drove the length of the airstrip, and at its far end he parked beside the unspoiled beach and its cobalt-colored bay. The girl, Olivia, exclaimed with delight at its beauty, pushed open her door and ran out onto the sand towards the water. As he watched, the attractive brunette jumped from the truck bed, performed a hasty striptease and then ran across the sand to plunge into the water. As the two young women frolicked in the small waves, one naked and the other still fully clothed, he beckoned to their male companions to unload their meager belongings. The young men moved listlessly, stupefied by their long ride under the hot sun, and they spoke neitherf to each other nor to him.

The unloading completed, he climbed back into his truck and unceremoniously drove off without any parting words or gesture. Glancing back in his rearview mirror, he saw the two young men standing together and staring at the departing truck. His spirits lifted at the prospect of once again traveling alone, and he celebrated by drinking another cold Carta Blanca during the short drive to the marina.

———

By the time he'd parked, checked in with the dockmaster and transferred his gear and provisions from truck to boat, the sun had begun to set. All seemed aright with his sailboat, *Celerity,* a twenty-four foot sloop whose shoal keel drew less than two feet of water, a decided advantage when one wished to anchor just off an inviting beach.

Content that all was in order aboard, he made himself a comfortable nest of cushions in a corner of the cockpit and watched the turquoise sky turn orange beyond the rocky hills that enclosed and protected the marina. With the onset of night the air had cooled enough to become comfortable, and so tranquil was this place after the complicated journey south that he considered forsaking the seafood dinner in Guaymas he'd been anticipating for the past two days.

He lay sprawled on the cushions, sipping from a glass of wine, and felt the tenseness gradually fall from him. He thought of Jesus faithfully keeping his vigil far to the northeast, perhaps, like him, enjoying this same sunset. He thought of Olivia and her sad relationship to her traveling companions, and he wondered if her night would again be lonely. He thought of his sailing friend and wished he were present to share this voyage. And, inevitably, he thought of the woman.

It was the last that brought him to his feet and set him to action. He slipped on his sandals and grabbed his truck keys.

Such is the rhythm of living that the most inconsequential decision can set into motion an irreversible cascade of events that leads to destinations unforeseen. The trivial gives way to the tragic, and the ambiguous collides with the absolute.

He hopped from the rail to the dock and walked towards his truck, Guaymas and the fate awaiting him

Chapter 5

MARIA

It was a warm Thursday evening in mid October. Although the day had been hot, the long Tucson summer at last was releasing its grip, and with nightfall the air had cooled sufficiently to allow them to turn off the swamp cooler and open the doors and dusty windows. Will was in the kitchen and Michael in his bedroom, presumably reading or already asleep. They'd been sharing Michael's home for almost a year now and had settled into a comfortable routine. Days might pass wherein they'd see little of one another and rarely speak, and then an evening would come when they'd sit by the ancient swimming pool out back, drink beer and talk for hours.

Tonight had been one of those nights. There had been disturbing rumors recently regarding to Brian, rumors of drug use, specifically, and each shared with the other what fragments he'd heard. It was all quite vague, and none of it squared with what they knew of their friend. When he'd gone hiking with them last Saturday, he seemed entirely himself, and when that evening he'd brought Becky with him to their house, there was no discernible evidence of strain between them.

As he cleaned up the kitchen, Will abruptly was startled out of his reverie by a loud knocking at the front door that persisted for ten seconds and then was firmly repeated. It was almost ten o'clock. In anticipation of going to bed himself, he was wearing only a t-shirt and boxers, and he decided anyone intruding at this hour would have to take him as he was.

He opened the door to find standing before him an unfamiliar female of average height who looked to be in her late twenties. The doorstep was poorly illuminated, but even in the dim light cast outward by the lamps in their great room he could see that the young woman was strikingly attractive. "Can I help you?" he asked her.

She had a certain boldness about her. Taking her time to respond, she first gave him a long, cool stare, breaking off briefly to look him up and down as if to inspect his immodest apparel before returning her gaze to his face. "Is Michael here?" she asked, finally. Her voice was pitched as low and even as her gaze.

"Yeah," Will replied. "He's here, but he may be asleep." The beautiful young woman continued to stare directly at him, and he found it unsettling. "It's pretty late," he continued. "Is he expecting you?"

Again she paused before responding. Her eyes shone in the reflected light, and she seemed faintly amused by his query. "In a manner of speaking," she answered at last. And as she did so, she stepped past Will into the great room and began walking directly down the hall that led to Michael's room.

"Hey, wait a minute," Will called after her. "Where are you going?"

She answered without any break in stride or backward look. "To my husband's bedroom," she called out to him. Her long brown hair swished back and forth behind her like the tail of a thoroughbred.

———

Will had long since gone to bed, and they were alone on the sofa. Michael was sitting warily at one end and Maria sprawled face-first towards him from the other. Her long, copper-streaked hair framed a face that was perfectly oval, with full lips and large, moist brown eyes that– ever so slightly slanted at their margins – belied her heritage. Her skin was perfect: soft, smooth and toffee-colored. As she lay on her stomach, elbows to couch, hands cupping her face and her torso raised slightly, her blouse hung down loosely.

No one can deny her beauty, he thought Adding to her allure, her speech, manner and movements projected a compelling sensuality, her attractiveness rendered all the more powerful by her apparent indifference to its effect. So had Michael first perceived her five years ago at at otherwise unremarkable cocktail reception hosted by a pharmaceutical company: an exotic blossom, her sultry darkness contrasting sharply with the pale generic faces surrounding her. For the first time in his life he'd been mesmerized by a woman.

Yes, without question she was a lovely and provocative woman, but time and bitter experience had taught him all too well how calculated was her manner and how dire the consequences for those who succumbed to her manifest charms. Her course through life had cut a wide swath; sorrow and betrayal and littered her wake. He could see her shining eyes and the toffee breasts, and he knew no panties lay beneath the jeans stretched snugly over her rounded rump, but the view and that knowledge sparked no answering response within him.

Seeming to sense his indifference, Maria dropped her pose and gathered herself up into a seated position at the opposite end of the sofa. She glanced at him appraisingly and after a few moments spoke. "You look tired, Michael," she observed.

He ignored this. "Why are you here, Maria?"

She stretched her arms and yawned luxuriously before she answered. "I like Tucson," she declared. "It's dry." Her blouse had lifted as she stretched, yielding a flash of taut brown belly.

"There's nothing for you here," he said with conviction. "And no reason to be here. I know you've been getting my checks." A pause. "And cashing them," he added.

"Oh, I'm not here for your money, Michael," she said dismissively. "Don't you worry yourself about that." She lifted her eyes to the saguaro-ribbed ceiling. "I *like* it here," she repeated. "British Columbia is so damp. It gets depressing after a while."

He'd told himself beforehand not to probe, to resist rising to her conversational bait. He knew that she thrived on provoking extreme emotional reactions, and whether the reaction was positive or negative appeared to make little difference to her. He fought down the impulse to question her. Some cataclysm undoubtedly had torn asunder Maria's most recent relationship, job, her life generally. Whatever the inciting event, it was likely Vancouver was now home to at least one more embittered soul than had existed there prior to her arrival.

"You can't stay here," he said, indicating the house.

She briefly flashed a hostile glance his way. "Oh, Michael," she responded sarcastically. "Would you deny your wife the small comfort of a roof over her head? There was a time when I knew you to be more hospitable." She arose slowly, languorously, walking towards the kitchen to retrieve another beer from the refrigerator. She called back over her shoulder as she slinked away. "Don't flatter yourself, *chico*. I've got better options than this old dust bin."

He wondered at this but maintained his silence. *No personal questions!* he commanded himself. Maria's explanations tended to be as insubstantial as cobwebs and just as likely to entrap. Or simply lies.

She sat back down on the couch and drank her beer quickly. He knew she could out-drink most men, himself included, and the prodigious amounts of weed and coke she could consume seemed to have no effect other than to stimulate her already unrestrained libido. She stretched one last time, arching her back to allow him a final opportunity to admire her lithe brown body. Shrugging at his indifference, she arose swiftly from the couch in one smooth motion and sashayed wordlessly into his bedroom, leaving the door open behind her.

Michael gathered up his keys, a sleeping bag, his pipe and a small bag of dope. Exiting the house, he drove the old Saab twenty minutes to a secluded overlook near Gates Pass and there spent some hours sitting, smoking and watching the lights of the city before finally he fell asleep.

When he awoke in the morning, stiff from sleeping on the rocky ledge, he returned home and found that Maria had departed. All that was left to mark her passage were the empty beer bottles scattered about and her almond scent on his unmade sheets.

———

Will had arisen early that morning. Lifting the shade of his bedroom's only window, he saw Michael's car was absent from its accustomed position within their ramshackle carport. Perhaps he'd left early to take the young woman - Maria, his *wife,* Will recalled, incredulously - back to wherever it was she'd come from.

Will had spent little time with them the night before. Michael remained almost entirely silent, his obvious unease unprecedented during the time Will had known him. Maria appeared content simply to lounge on the couch and drink her beer. He'd been relieved to excuse himself and escape to his suite at the south end of the house.

To call his motley nook a "suite" was admittedly hyperbolic: the closet was absurdly oversized (particularly given his sparse wardrobe), the bedroom just large enough to contain his bed and the chest he used as a bedside table, and the bathroom tiny and dark. On the other hand, through the window he could see the entirety of the Catalina Mountains, their highest peaks dense with pine forests and laced with perennial streams, a landscape as different from the desert floor as is Mars from Mercury. And when he closed the heavy oak door that separated his humble warren from the house proper, his privacy was absolute, a feature he'd especially appreciated the night before.

He was standing within the deep closet and considering which of his shirts might be sufficiently presentable for work when he suddenly heard a voice behind him. "Coffee?"

Startled, he spun around to find Maria standing there, gazing at him solemnly and holding a mug of coffee in each hand. She was wearing a man's dress shirt, Michael's presumably, with its oversized sleeves rolled up and a single button drawing the two halves together. Whatever modesty the voluminous shirt could offer was undone by the bright sun shining through the

66

window immediately behind her and penetrating the thin fabric to outline precisely her form within. Nonplussed, he quickly took from her hand the mug she extended and turned around to contemplate once again the shirts hanging before him.

"Thanks, he replied, taking a sip from the mug. "Good coffee."

But Maria had stepped out of the closet and missed his words. "What did you say?" she called from his bedroom.

He turned to find her now on his bed. She'd arranged his pillows to form a backrest and was gazing out the window, intermittently sipping at her coffee. The position she'd assumed caused the hem of the shirt to rise high upon her smooth brown thighs and its largely unfettered front to gape open widely at the neck. Once again he turned his attention to his closet.

"How about we do something?" he heard her say.

He turned around to face her once again. "Excuse me?" he said.

"How about we do something?" she repeated. "Together." Her tone and expression were neutral. "Maybe have breakfast. Then go for a hike."

"I don't have time for breakfast or anything like that," he replied, flustered. "I have to get to work." He turned away and hurriedly pulled a on a shirt.

"That's too bad," she told him. "Maybe another time." Noiselessly she quit his bed and left the room.

———

While she invariably was described as "exotic" in appearance, Maria's ethnicity was not easily discerned. Although she stood only a shade over five and a half feet, her long legs and erect, slightly hyperextended posture gave the impression she was taller and emphasized her firm, round breasts. Her long, thick mahogany-hued hair, smooth, tawny skin, full lips and the slight upward slant of her eyes hinted at an Asian heritage that belied her long legs and height. Many who knew her speculated that she was "Polynesian", a misperception she neither confirmed nor corrected.

In fact, she was the unintended progeny of a Filipino deckhand on shore leave and a young Mexican prostitute who met in an Ensenada bar and coupled briefly while standing in a dark narrow alley that smelled strongly of urine. Her mother had wrapped her legs around the man's slim waist and braced her shoulders against a rough block wall.

Shortly after giving birth, her mother deposited her infant at an *orfanatorio* in Manandero, a small, dusty and uninspiring city. Although located only 21 kilometers to the south, Manandero contrasted poorly to her site of conception, Ensenada, with its sparkling bay and *malecón* bustling with taco stands, street vendors and happy tourists from the cruise ships lined up at the congested port like piglets suckling at the sow.

The orphanage was managed by a young American couple and supported with funds from a prosperous Unitarian church in San Diego. Although the living arrangements were spartan and the food monotonous, it was a pleasant enough environment within which to grow up. Despite this, shortly after turning seventeen Maria – as she'd been named by the *orfanatorio's* caretakers – left at the earliest opportunity, moving to San Diego to live with Bruce, a San Diego State graduate student. They'd met at Hussong's, a notorious bar that catered to *gringos*, after she'd abandoned her bed at the orphanage one evening to hitchhike north to Ensenada. Like a salmon returning to its birthplace to spawn.

If she was searching for a human catalyst to propel her from the limited prospects of the *orfanatorio*, Manandero and northern Baja generally upward into the beckoning affluence of southern California, Maria could have done worse. Bruce was a streetwise but decent young man who harbored no illusions in regards to Maria and her motivations. He was older than most of his classmates, and although he seldom spoke of his experiences prior to beginning his graduate program, his background was far more eclectic than that of the typical PhD candidate. For him, Maria was merely an amusement, an ornament to be admired and savored but kept emotionally at arm's length.

———

They'd lived together for a year in his modest apartment, Bruce advancing steadily towards his doctoral degree while Maria gradually shed all vestiges of Manandero and became a Californian. He was fluent in Spanish, and she proved herself to be a talented student. Within a few months she spoke and understood idiomatic English well enough to navigate her way around San Diego and to work – as an unregistered alien, always for cash – at a series of menial jobs.

Her brief stint as maid and nanny for a vacuously arrogant young La Jolla matron was sufficient to convince her that she should aspire to something more rewarding, and with Bruce's help she managed to obtain her GED and begin classes at Mesa College. After an academically successful semester she transferred to San Diego State. She started working towards a degree in fine arts and in short order seduced her faculty advisor, a professor in his late 40s whose previously satisfactory marriage would not survive this detour.

One evening Maria casually informed Bruce that she was leaving him to move in with her professor, and their consequent parting was amicable enough. Examined with a calculating eye, their relationship had served each of them well. With Bruce's assistance and support, Maria had evolved from a socially inexperienced teenager with no real prospects into an attractive, self-assured and determined young woman with her own agenda, while Bruce experienced the pleasure of a companion who had grown to be as passionate in bed as she was intelligent and humorous in conversation. He'd taught her to swim, to surf, how and what to order off a menu and how to dress provocatively without resembling a prostitute from *la zona roja* of Tijuana.

Although from the age of twelve on Maria had experimented with the boys of the *orfanatorio*, she came to Bruce an inexperienced and awkward lover. Within weeks she had repaired this deficiency, but he could sense that the pleasure she so obviously derived from their lovemaking was largely impersonal and unrelated to him, her partner, in anything but the most technical sense. Almonds, he recalled. When aroused, she gave off the scent of almonds.

Bruce knew that Maria was amoral, possessing no conscience to speak of, and he pitied any poor soul who had the misfortune to mistake her lust for affection, her self-serving acts of apparent generosity for love. They parted as they had met: two attractive strangers, each inherently self-sufficient but not without certain transitory needs that the other could fulfill. He doubted they'd ever meet again, and he suspected that neither would miss the other. He was correct on both counts.

He watched from his apartment window as Maria's new *hombre* pulled into the parking lot in a borrowed Ford pickup, embraced Maria briefly and began to load her belongings into the truck bed. *Buena suerte*, he thought to himself. Good luck. Unless you were born without a heart, you'll need it.

———

Maria's liaison with her professor was short-lived, and her course over the two years following was peripatetic but ever-ascending. During her brief time spent in the fine arts program she became adept at fashioning what she called her *regalos de milagros* ("gifts of miracles") from scraps she found in the university's workshop and odds and ends purchased in the *tiendas* of nearby Tecate and Tijuana. The small sculptures were oddly compelling - exotic fusions of skulls, stars, skeletons, angels and the like - all cheap bits of metal of the type affixed to altars and the effigies of saints by *los campesinos* seeking *un milagro*...or, at least, a turn of good luck. There rapidly developed a demand for her work throughout greater San Diego, and eventually she received solicitations from the owners of galleries as far afield as Santa Barbara, Tucson, Scottsdale, and Santa Fe.

Forsaking her professor, southern California and her studies at the university, she moved to New Mexico and soon found herself involved, professionally and sexually, with the female owner of Santa Fe's most exclusive (and expensive) gallery. Encouraged and financially supported by Melinda, her middle-aged patron-ess, she expanded her artistic repertoire to include painting – primitive in style, with oils – her subject the landscapes familiar to her from her early years in Baja, later along the Rio Tijuana and now in the foothills of the Sangre de Cristo Mountains.

Previously a professional ballerina who long had performed for a leading New York-based company, Melinda encouraged her young protégé to begin taking lessons in dance. While she was starting far too late to develop professional aptitude, Maria's body type and inherent sense of rhythm lent well to her efforts. She liked how dancing enhanced her muscle tone and flexibility, and she found the dance crowd appealingly eccentric.

Given her physical attractions and multiple talents, it was hardly surprising that she developed a wide circle of admirers, male and female, in Santa Fe's eclectic community, and whatever influence Melinda had exerted upon her correspondingly waned. Maria was stubborn and independent; the more Melinda threatened, wheedled and (finally) begged, the more the younger woman devalued their alliance. Their sexual relationship had been dormant for months, and Maria began to take her pleasure where, when and with whom she pleased. Melinda's consequent distress was to her a matter of no concern.

Desperate, the older woman threatened suicide, a ploy culminating finally in a clumsily-executed overdose involving modest quantities of Xanax and Ambien chased down by a bottle of expensive vodka. Indifferent to the act and her ex-lover's despair, Maria instructed the housekeeper to call 911 and packed up her belongings while the paramedics bundled Melinda into their ambulance for the short ride to the hospital.

By the time Melinda was released and home once again, Maria was living on Paseo de Peralta with two gay male dancers whom she'd met while their company was summering in Santa Fe. Searching the house they'd shared, the only trace of Maria's presence Melinda could find were a few long strands of mahogany colored hair scattered about their bathroom and the faint scent of almonds arising from the tousled sheets of the guest bedroom where her ex-lover had slept the last few months.

For the first time in her life Melinda felt herself old. The young woman from Manandero left few physical marks of her passage, but the emotional wounds she inflicted cut deep.

———

After two years spent in Santa Fe, Maria was ready for a change. The revenue stream from the sale of her *regalos* was erratic, and at times she was unable to pay the rent for her tiny studio apartment located in a charmless area south of the city. On one memorably cold Friday in February the electric company made good on its repeated threats to cut off her power, and she'd had to endure the weekend wrapped in blankets with candles as her only source of illumination. Her inability to influence her environment was unpleasantly reminiscent of her years in the *orfanatorio*.

Besides, Santa Fe had become too small, too claustrophobic. While people were always flowing in and out, the indigenous population was socially inbred and rather small, especially so in that portion of the citizenry Maria considered relevant to her needs. Her abandonment of Melinda, a venerable resident popular within the local community, was common knowledge, and many of those who initially had embraced Maria now had grown wary. Her immediate prospects did not appear promising.

It was against this background that she happened to attend a random social affair held at La Posada. The hotel was hosting a small medical conference, and for the attendees there was to be a cocktail reception on Saturday evening. The hotel's concierge was a casual friend, and knowing that the presence of attractive young women was likely to be appreciated by the largely male gathering, he'd invited Maria. She'd receive no financial compensation, he advised her, but the food and drink would be abundant and free.

She'd been ambivalent, but as the sun set on that cold March afternoon she found herself unable to tolerate the prospect of another long evening spent alone in her cramped apartment. She washed her hair, retrieved from her closet a skimpy black cocktail dress and at the bottom of a drawer found her silver and onyx earrings. Carefully descending the icy steps outside, she slid into her battered Volvo, drove to La Posada and parked in its covered deck.

As she entered the large dining room given over that night to the reception, her stiletto heels clicking on the clay tile floor, Maria could feel the men's eyes upon her. She stood by the fireplace, enjoying a particularly fine Malbec, and at some point between her third and fourth glass one young man summoned the courage to approach her. He tried awkwardly at first to make conversation, but encouraged by her responsiveness he gradually relaxed.

His name was Michael, and although he currently was attending medical school in Minnesota, he told her that in June he was moving to Tucson to begin his internship. Always quick to apprise others, Maria decided that she found him sufficiently attractive, and the smile she gave Michael positively shown with unspoken promise.

Maria's seduction of Michael was rapidly accomplished. As they talked by the fire, she confessed her preference for marijuana over alcohol and confided that she had with her a small amount in her purse. Michael seemed to find this intriguing, and after a moment she suggested they retire to his room and share her stash.

On the elevator ride up they shared a long and passionate kiss that was broken only by the untimely entrance of additional passengers. Once in his room, the joint they shared was followed by more kissing that rapidly escalated to a prolonged interlude of enthusiastic sex. By its conclusion the young man was hopelessly ensnared. Although not completely naïve in the ways of women, the force that was Maria lay far beyond the limits of Michael's experience. Her sexual magnetism was overpowering, her body as irresistible as a sweet but potent tropical drink that he quaffed to delicious excess.

———

Immediately prior to their departure for Arizona Michael and Maria married. It was a simple ceremony held at a fine old church in downtown St. Paul. Michael was the last of ten children, and his elderly parents, the immediate descendants of Norwegian immigrant farmers who'd worked hard, saved much and traveled little, clearly didn't know what to make of Maria.

As had been the case with his male classmates, Michael's older brothers were bedazzled by her looks and correspondingly attentive, but his sisters kept their physical and emotional distance, conversing little with this flashy young woman who'd so rapidly attached herself to their baby brother. When they did speak to her, it was in that flat Norwegian tone that evokes images of a bleak, limitless Dakota prairie under a grey winter sky.

Maria ignored the parents' confusion and the sisters' icy reserve as effortlessly as she charmed all the males at the reception, young and old alike. What did she care? She had no intention of ever returning to Minnesota, and whatever modest commitment she'd made to Michael certainly did not extend to her in-laws. She'd suffered the vertiginous descent that could befall the single woman who finds herself suddenly bereft of another's support and lacking her own financial resources, and she'd thoroughly disliked the inconvenience involved. This marriage, then, was for her an insurance policy. A revocable contract.

Inspired by sudden generosity fueled by three tequila shots, she strolled across the room to where Michael stood talking with his friends, slid her slim bare arm around his waist and looked up at him with an adoring smile. *Lucky bastard,* his friends thought.

———

At first Michael was tireless in his efforts to please her. Although its price was far beyond the means of a modestly paid intern, they bought a house that Maria craved. It was a two story contemporary nestled in the foothills of the Catalinas, and they immediately took out a second mortgage to construct a patio and pool complex where Maria could sunbathe and swim naked in privacy. To finance these expenditures Michael was compelled to spend most of his free weekends moonlighting.

Given this, his 1 in 4 call schedule as an intern and the long workdays at the hospital, he rarely was at home except to sleep. On those few days or nights when he was home and conscious, he deferred to Maria in regards to whatever diversion she happened to require, and he deeply regretted his long separations from her.

To her his absences were of little consequence. She spent many hours painting in the sunlit studio they'd constructed for her in a large open space on the second story. Still left with time on her hands, she'd fallen in with a group of young male anesthesiology residents who were more than happy to provide her with recreation and entertainment on those nights and weekends when Michael was working. Often one or another of their group would have early cases and so be free by midafternoon. Maria fell in the habit of receiving the lucky man of the day at home, enjoying a swim, allowing the hot sun to dry her body and then moving on to emotionally unfettered coupling under the blue desert sky.

That this was Maria's first plunge into the treacherous waters of adulterous intercourse neither restrained her passion nor caused her any pangs of guilt. If anything, she found her adultery more erotic than any previous sexual indulgence she'd felt inclined to pursue, and whether this heightened enjoyment derived from the taboo inherent in the transgression or the drugs she shared with her lovers she cared not one whit.

But it was the drugs, not the adultery, that precipitated the ultimate disintegration of her marriage, such as it was.

———

While he was attempting to cope with a busy clinic at the county hospital one Thursday afternoon, Michael received a call from a local pharmacist. As he stood listening to the man's words, he felt his body grow numb and his heart turn cold.

" . . . an exceptionally large quantity of Ritalin over the past few months," the disembodied voice was saying. "It's unclear to me why you would prescribe such high quantities to Ms. Gonzales, and I wanted to check and see if there was some mistake." Gonzales was Maria's seldom-used maiden name, an artifact of her early years in the *orfanatorio*.

Michael recovered quickly. "There's been no mistake", he replied evenly. "Ms. Gonzales, my patient, has severe narcolepsy, and the high quantity of dextroamphetamine reflects her having recently developed a partial resistance to the Ritalin. We're in the process of searching for a more suitable treatment."

There was a long pause on the other end of the line, and finally the pharmacist spoke. "I'll accept that for the record, doc," he said, "but this prescription is the last I'll fill. I'm not comfortable dispensing such high quantities of Ritalin or any amphetamine."

"That's fine," Michael responded automatically. And he hung up the phone.

———

Maria had learned of Ritalin's appeal from one of her anesthesiology companions. While coke provided a rush, she'd learned that with continued use it became difficult to remain high for long, and to respond by stepping up her inhalatory frequency was both expensive and hard on the nasal passages. She found that Ritalin preserved the speedy euphoria that the cocaine so rapidly induced but failed to maintain.

Time passed, and her tolerance to Ritalin increased, and so she'd added an amphetamine chaser. Her initial apprehension at forging Michael's name on prescriptions long before had dissipated, but she continued some modest attempt at subterfuge by filling the prescriptions at multiple pharmacies. At last, however, even this ploy had failed to conceal the truly astounding extent of her dependence, and now she was caught.

When Michael arrived home primed for a confrontation, she'd been absent, a consequence of her having dallied at a downtown bar with a friend from her dance class. She was feeling the margaritas when she finally walked through the front door, but despite her intoxication she initially made a half-hearted attempt to deflect his angry accusations by promising to desist and to seek "counseling". Finally, however, she tired of his fretting and badgering.

"Look," she suggested wearily from her position sprawled on the couch with Michael, clearly distressed, looming above her. "Why don't you just get over it?"

"Get over it," he repeated wonderingly. "You want me to 'get over it'? Get over the fact that you committed forgery to abuse schedule II drugs? That I've lied to protect you and have risked losing my license?" His voice was rising again.

"Well," she said, rising up from the couch, spreading her arms and yawning expansively. "Either get over it or don't. I don't care. I'm going to bed."

He watched as she walked away, and even then, at the nadir of their relationship, he could feel himself desiring her still. And despised himself for it.

———

Although Michael and Maria continued to live together in the foothills house for the remainder of that year, theirs was a marriage in name only. By the time Maria left Tucson altogether, to Michael's immense relief, they shared little more than a mailing address. As those last months had passed and she made ever less effort to disguise her infidelities, Michael disassociated himself from her to such an extent that only those who'd known the couple when they'd arrived in Tucson were aware he even had a wife.

Michael was powerfully embarrassed by the situation. Although popular, he was a private person and far more meticulous in his choices and behavior than his relaxed manner would have suggested. He hated to make mistakes, and to make one so extreme and so public struck at his core. Only Brian, his closest friend in the city and a man of particular sensitivity, could sense his torment, and, thankfully, he never spoke of it.

When finally she left for good, Maria had given him no indication of her destination or plans. He hoped that she would go far away, never to return. But now she had.

Chapter 6

MEXICO

His evening excursion to Guaymas proved a disappointment. Although for days he'd anticipated the ceviche at El Paraiso, he found that once he stood before the restaurant he couldn't bring himself to face the friendly inquiries of Arturo, its owner, and his family who served as staff. So he turned his back on the brightly lit façade – its sign proclaiming *"Mariscos Frescos! Camarones y Pescados,"* with "English Speaks!" at the bottom in smaller letters – and unable to think of any more palatable destination continued to walk through downtown, circling back along the seedy waterfront to his truck.

The streets were filthy and unwelcoming. No adult met his eye or offered any greeting, and as he passed the children would pause in their play to stare at him silently. He decided to forsake a seafood dinner in favor of canned chili and a cold beer on the boat.

As he drove along the highway back to San Carlos, he glanced down at the floorboard on the passenger's side and saw Olivia's purple backpack. He groaned softly and briefly considered dropping it on the roadside for the enrichment of a passing *campesino*. Tired, hungry and intending to depart early in the morning, he was anxious to return to the marina. *Leave it be*, he told himself. *You owe this girl nothing.*

For no particular reason he later could remember, he finally decided to return the backpack after all. He drove past the entrance to the marina, turning off instead onto the dirt road that traversed the base of the headland and then wove down through the hills to Catch-22 Beach. Dirt turned to sand, and the sand grew increasingly soft. He shifted to low gear and slowed his speed. Finding it difficult to make out the narrow road —no more than a path, really — in the darkness, he extinguished his headlights. It was easier to proceed by moonlight alone.

As he reached the summit of the last small hill before the descent to the runway and the beach beyond, he thought he could make out the shape of a vehicle parked at the far end of the airstrip, where the pockmarked asphalt gave way to sand. He stopped and pulled out the binoculars he kept in his glove compartment. A head-high berm separated the airstrip from the crescent-shaped beach, and a truck was parked on the near side of the berm. He glassed the area, and while in the thick darkness it was impossible to be certain, the truck's box-like aspect was distinctly military in appearance. There was a faint yellowish glow just beyond the berm, and from time to time sparks from a bonfire popped brightly above its crest.

He edged his truck quietly down the hillside, taking care not to activate his brake lights, and drove slowly down the length of the airstrip, and stopped 50 yards short of the other vehicle. He reached behind his seat and grasped a heavy iron toolbar. His pistol and knives were back on the boat. He thought briefly of returning for the gun, but if his suspicions were correct the delay involved might render that effort irrelevant.

He left his truck, ran quickly to the airstrip's dark periphery, and then scuttled like a land crab along the base of the berm towards the bonfire. Peering over the crest, he saw there were six people in various positions around the fire, the four young hitchhikers and two uniformed Mexicans. They were *federales*, not local police. One *federal* had his carbine unslung and pointed at the two young men and the girl who'd slept beside him in the truck the night before. Her shirt open and bra exposed, the pretty brunette was in the process of being fondled by the second *federal*. Gone was all vestige of the provocative young woman who'd plunged naked and heedless into the sea just hours before. In her place was a helpless teenager, clearly terrified.

Both Mexicans were small men, most likely *indios* infused with small boluses of Spanish blood and culture, thus destined to hover uncomfortably between the ancient, hot-blooded passions of pagan times and the forbidding taboos of more recently imposed Catholicism. At the moment they clearly were yielding to the influence of the former.

The *federal* ceased his groping and settled back on his haunches a few feet from the girl. Weeping, she stood and began to disrobe, her head obscured in darkness but her pale trunk and legs illuminated by the bonfire.

He took advantage of the Mexicans' distraction to crawl over the berm and come up on the group quietly from behind. The captives were facing his line of approach, and he prayed that none would startle and betray his presence. Fortunately the young *touristas* were too preoccupied with their predicament to take any notice, and the *federales* were heedlessly intent upon the girl before them.

Now naked from the waist up, she managed despite her sobbing to tug her tight cutoff jeans below her knees, raising first one slim leg and then the other to shed them entirely. She wore no panties. The Mexican still crouching before her motioned with his hand that she should lie down, and when she failed to obey, he arose and pushed her chest roughly with both hands, causing her to stumble and fall backwards to the sand.

He briefly considered the situation from his position just beyond the periphery of light cast by the bonfire. The Sonoran *federales* were for the most part poorly paid, ill-trained and unschooled men who unfortunately were all too aware of the power and authority that was theirs in this isolated, sparsely settled corner of northwestern Mexico. They could be brutish and were not above intimidating foreign tourists, especially if those travelers were young hippies of meager financial resources who took no pains to remain inconspicuous. But rape was an altogether different matter, a serious crime in a country where the roots of Catholicism ran deep. Even the *machismo* ethic fell far short of supporting the forcible taking of a female who, after all, might be another man's daughter, sister or, most unforgivable, *madre*.

On the other hand, if drugs were involved, all bets were off. Possession of any illegal drug in any amount, however minute, afforded the officials of law enforcement *carte blanche* in their dealings with foreigners. Mexico was no Jamaica. Drugs or no, there also existed the possibility that these two were simply *hombres malos*, thugs who would use their uniforms and carbines to extort, rape and potentially murder, the last to insure the silence of their victims.

A fateful decision, he thought as he moved rapidly forward. He swung the toolbar hard, catching the *federal* with the carbine solidly behind the right ear. The man collapsed in a heap, obviously unconscious, the rifle pinned beneath his supine body. Using his bare foot, he quickly shoved the man over onto his back, gathered up the weapon and wheeled around to level its barrel at the other Mexican. That man was scrambling backwards, comically sliding his bare butt through the sand, wide-eyed with fear. The naked girl was kneeling with her hands clutched together at her chin as if praying. Her keening penetrated loudly into the quiet night.

"*Alto!*" he commanded the Mexican. "*Si tu mueves, yo disparo su cabeza.*" He told the *federal* he'd blow off his head if he moved.

Keeping the rifle trained on the man, he spoke to the weeping girl. "You're all right now," he told her as soothingly as he could. "Put your clothes on, and try to be quiet."

He addressed the other three. "Get her to calm down," he told them. Noise sufficiently loud would travel across the bay to town, and even the indolent San Carlos police might choose to investigate a commotion arising from this particular beach. He knew from experience that the otherwise phlegmatic *policia* of San Carlos enjoyed any excuse to cruise the informal camping area, especially during the vacation times that brought hordes of scantily clad *rubias* from the colleges and universities of Arizona.

The girl with the odd white hair immediately moved to help her weeping companion gather her clothes strewn about on the sand. The two young men, however, made no move to assist her, remaining where they'd stood throughout, silent and staring. He spoke to the taller of the two, the skinny boy with the mop of stringy blond hair. "Are you carrying any drugs?" he asked.

The boy shifted his feet and looked away, aiming his response in the general direction of the twin-peaked hill known locally as Goat's Tits. "No, man," he stammered. "All we have is a few ounces of dope we picked up from some kid on the beach." He sounded thoroughly stoned.

The older man reflexively shook his head in disgust. "It's a real bad idea to carry dope in Mexico," he said. He didn't add that to buy drugs here was even more foolish, as odds were good that the seller would promptly turn in his client. He got paid coming and going, first by the purchaser and then by the *policia*. The *policia* then would extort what they could from the fingered buyer. Everybody profited save for the hapless tourist with a taste for weed.

The blond boy made no answer to this, simply continuing to stare back at him with a vacant expression. *Useless*, he thought. He turned to the other boy, the one with the aboriginal hair whom the others called Pico, and saw that he seemed only marginally more attuned to the situation unfolding around him. Lacking any better alternative, he handed the carbine to the second boy and briefly instructed him to keep his finger off its trigger but its barrel trained upon the unharmed Mexican while he attended to the man he'd struck.

Kneeling by the *federal*, he was relieved to see the man's chest wall moving rhythmically with regular respirations. His pupils were briskly reactive, and when he knuckled his sternum, the man emitted a low groan. He was palpating the man's skull to check for evidence of fracture when three loud explosions erupted in quick succession.

He spun around to find that Pico had shot the other *federal* in the chest at point-blank range. The would-be rapist was a mess, and he died quickly as his lacerated aorta disgorged a pulsating fountain of bright red arterial blood. Watching the man's blood congeal on the sand, it occurred to him that in this moment his own life was forever changed.

The boy then pivoted towards the two girls, the brunette now fully dressed and each clinging terrified to the other. He seemed bemused by what he'd accomplished. The gun was pointed directly at the girls, and his finger remained on the trigger. He leapt at the boy and in one motion snatched the carbine from his grip and knocked him to the ground with its stock. "Why, you dumb little fuck," he said wonderingly. "Look what you've gone and done."

He fought against his rising apprehension and tried to think clearly. The surviving *federal* was moaning softly now, and his eyes were open. Left alive, he'd soon recover enough to stagger back to town to report his version of these lurid events. He could kill the man, load the body in the truck's cab, and at least temporarily preserve his anonymity by heaving the corpse off some nearby cliff and into the sea. Quickly he dismissed that option. The circumstances were dire, beyond question, but even so he chose to believe that premeditated murder lay outside his behavioral repertoire.

Grabbing the *federal's* carbine, he turned and began to sprint towards his truck. Behind him he could hear a female voice calling out. "Stop! Wait! Where are you going?"

Without pausing to look back or reply, he continued on his way. As he reached the truck, he could hear someone running towards him on the airstrip, and in a moment the white-haired girl was at his side, panting heavily. She was barefoot and wore a white t-shirt. The t-shirt was smattered with blood and bits of gore from the slain *federal*. Shot repeatedly at close range with a high velocity weapon, his chest literally had exploded, and she'd been standing sufficiently close to be showered by his displaced parts.

Finally she caught her breath enough to speak. "Please take me with you," she gasped.

"What about your friends?" he asked her. "You're better off with them," he added, thoroughly doubting this to be true.

"I want to come with *you*," the girl pleaded. "I'm afraid."

He shook his head and climbed behind the wheel of his truck. Shutting his door, he leaned out the window and faced her. *I need to travel fast,* he thought, *and she'd only slow me down.* "No," he said aloud. "You don't know me, and you don't know where I'm going. You might as well stick with your friends."

Not bothering to wait for any reply, he started the engine and backed up a few feet before accelerating forward to exit the area. He drove slowly over the hilly portion of the washboard dirt road that linked the beach with town, but once he hit the flats he pushed the accelerator to the floor and covered the last two miles quickly. Reaching the asphalt road that eventually led to the harbor, he slowed to avoid attention and after five minutes of painstakingly sedate driving pulled into the marina's gravel parking lot.

Climbing out of the truck, he stepped back to its bed to retrieve the few provisions he'd bought that night in Guaymas. There sat the girl, Olivia, her back against the external wall of the cab, her hair tousled and her face dusty from the ride. "Get out," he told her.

Eyes downcast and averting his gaze, she hopped to the ground and stood before him. Pondering this new development, he decided there was no choice but to bring her along. He could drive her back to the beach, but he needed all the time he could get to gain a head start on the pursuit that was sure to follow. If he left her where she was, her conspicuousness in this small town would insure she'd be picked up rapidly. Once in custody, she'd soon tell all she knew.

"Let's go," he said. "Grab a couple of those bags out of the back of the truck, and follow me."

He briefly considered trying to conceal his truck by submerging it within the marina's waters but concluded the potential gain wasn't worth the time required to accomplish the task. He settled for moving it behind an old shed where it might not be so easily discovered.

He led Olivia to the boat and helped her aboard. After stashing his provisions and the *federal's* carbine in a storage locker below, he freed the dock lines and started the outboard. It engaged immediately, and he was grateful that he'd taken the time to check the engine prior to his evening excursion to Guaymas. *Jesus*, he thought, *what a disaster*.

They backed out of the slip quietly and glided between the rows of boats into the channel that led to the open gulf. It was late, and he could see no one about. The lights in the dockmaster's office and apartment above were extinguished, and the marina was silent save for the sound of rigging as it tinkled against the spars in what was a surprisingly fresh breeze for a summer's night.

The moon was near-full, and he had no difficulty in finding the channel. Gradually accelerating as they left the marina astern, he guided the boat between the headlands that led into Topolabampo Bay. *Topolabampo* is Spanish for "sea serpent", and the bay derived its name from the arches of volcanic rock that dotted its waters. Most of the houses scattered on the hillsides of the headlands were the vacation homes of Americans or wealthy Mexicans, and few windows were lit. With their running lights off, he was reasonably sure the late hour and darkness would combine to produce an unobserved passage.

Once beyond the protection of the northern headlands the boat immediately reacted to the force of a strong northwesterly wind and its accompanying swells. Because the summer winds typically were light, he wondered at this but was pleased to have the added propulsion. Even on a flat sea, the fuel they carried would permit a range of less than a hundred miles with the boat strictly under power.

The girl was sitting motionless on the port lazarrette as he stood at the tiller. He instructed her to take the helm and point the boat directly into the wind to facilitate his raising the sails, but she was inadequate to the task. With each large swell that slapped their hull, she'd veer off course and struggle unsuccessfully to bring the bow around to the required point.

Giving up, he flipped the clutch to neutral and resigned himself to raising the sails on a pitching deck. With considerable effort, struggling to maintain his balance, he managed to raise and set the main and the 150 jibsail. The wind was brisk, a steady twenty knots gusting to thirty, and to take advantage of this he'd decided to leave the main unreefed and to use this larger of his two foresails.

The boat heeled over sharply to port. Preferring distance to direction and so seeing no reason to strive for a higher point, he gave the sails more sheet, accepted the southwesterly course and immediately felt the boat's hull speed increase. With *Celerity* on a broad reach and the swells providing some added push, she was cruising along at well over eight knots. Under these conditions there was no real need for the outboard, and so he cut the engine to conserve fuel. The night suddenly was quiet save for the swish of the bow as it cut through the water, the occasional *thunk* of a swell colliding with the hull and the rushing of the wind itself. They sailed on into a dark night and uncertain future.

Chapter 7

ARIZONA

Leaving the hospital after Saturday morning rounds, Brian and Will made plans to meet at Will's house that evening and depart from there for the *El Bandito*. Brian would be bringing Becky, and he told Will he planned to ask some others to join them. The *Bandito* had a rough edge, and there was some safety to be had in numbers.

For three weeks following her sudden and unheralded nocturnal appearance, Will saw and heard nothing more of Maria. That next evening Michael had been uncharacteristically terse. In clipped sentences he briefly informed Will that he and Maria were married but had been living apart for some time. He offered no details, and his manner was such that Will asked no questions. They spoke no more of the matter, and his memory of the alluring young woman gradually began to fade. Then that afternoon, while Will was relaxing at home alone, the telephone rang. He answered, and suddenly her melodious, self-assured voice was caressing his ear.

"Is Michael there?" she asked, adding, unnecessarily, "It's Maria."

"No," Will answered. "He's on call today and won't be home until tomorrow morning."

There followed a long pause on the other end, and just as he was about to break the silence she spoke again. "Mind if I come over?" she asked.

Taken aback, he responded reflexively. "Why?"

After another long pause she transformed her question into a declaration. "I'd like to come over," she said calmly.

Despite the neutral tone in which her words were spoken, to Will they fairly screamed of erotic promise. *Am I imagining this?* he wondered.

He tried to make his response non-committal. "Sure. Why not?" he replied. "I mean, you're welcome to come over." As he spoke, it occurred to him that as Michael's wife, her rights to the house – legally speaking – exceeded his own.

"But I've got plans for the evening," he continued, "and I might be gone. You may have the place to yourself. It's pretty hot, and you can hang out by the pool. If you don't get here before I leave, the back door will be unlocked."

"I'll be there in 30 minutes," she said. And promptly hung up.

———

True to her word, Maria was rapping on the front door within a half an hour of their phone conversation's abrupt conclusion. She was dressed simply in a plain white t-shirt, denim cut-offs and sandals, and her mane of thick hair was tied back in a long ponytail. As far as he could tell, she wore no makeup, but to his dismay he found her lack of adornment did not prevent him from feeling immediately that same powerful sexual attraction he'd experienced at their first meeting.

He offered her something to drink, and she accepted a cold bottle of Tecate. While he felt awkward in her presence, Maria seemed relaxed and perfectly at home, chatting with him easily as if they were old friends. Beers finished, they moved outside to the pool, and without any trace of self-consciousness she kicked off her sandals, stripped off the t-shirt and stepped out of her shorts, revealing a minimalistic bikini she wore beneath her clothes.

Will tried not to stare too obviously at Maria as she sat at the pool's edge in the skimpy suit, dangling her slender brown legs in the water. On display was an abundance of long, sun-streaked hair nearly identical in tone to the smooth, tawny skin left uncovered by her suit. Whenever she leaned forward, exposing the tops of her breasts, Will could see no evidence of a tan line. He wondered whether this continuity of skin tone was natural, a consequence of her ethnicity, or a result of naked sun bathing, and the visions conjured up by the latter caused him to avert his gaze.

Despite the erotic gravitational pull she continued to exert, Will found it easier to relax outdoors, where he could put some physical distance between them. Periodically he left her to retrieve another round of beers from the kitchen, and their conversation was punctuated by periods of silence when each would submerge beneath the water to cool off or lie on the poolside concrete to bask in the sunshine and the dry desert air.

It was just then that Brian emerged suddenly from the back door and onto the ramada-shaded patio. He required only a brief glance to assess the prevailing social axis before he turned to his friend and asked nonchalantly, "Got any beer?"

By the time Will returned from the kitchen with three bottles of Tecate, Maria had donned her white t-shirt and sat demurely upon the chaise. Brian stood some distance away, his arms braced against the ancient rock wall that encircled the pool area and gazing southeastward back towards the city. Their pool reputedly was the first to have been constructed in greater Tucson. As with the rugged wall, its many cracks, fissures and leaks bore convincing testimony to its venerability.

Brian and Maria silently maintained their respective positions as Will distributed the beers, but any impending awkwardness was averted by an infusion of new blood. In rapid sequence over the next ten minutes Damien, Gene, Becky and a familiar-appearing young woman whose name was unknown to Will made their respective entrances.

Damien ("Action") Jackson was a doughy, squat émigré from New Jersey who was notable primarily for having been one of the few blacks with superior academic credentials to have failed to gain admission to an American medical school, an anomaly that presumably was a direct consequence of the impressive police record he'd compiled as a teenager in Newark. No matter the color of one's skin and the prevailing cultural winds, grand theft auto, possession of illegal drugs with intent to sell and, an odd appendage to his record, mail fraud made for a hurdle not readily overcome.

Yet Damien was a determined young man. Having survived medical school in Guadalajara he came to Arizona via the so-called "fifth pathway", performed well enough to earn a position in the emergency medicine residency program and now was in his final year of training. His criminal years well behind him, he nonetheless still affected a menacing style of dress that was thoroughly negated by his unprepossessing physique. Standing five foot four and weighing 260 pounds, he closely resembled a large, dark brown beach ball. Undeterred as always by this discrepancy, tonight he wore a sleeveless denim jacket, its back emblazoned with a single word (*"Burn"*) spelled out in metal rivets; matching denim jeans cinched far below his patulous abdomen with a wide black leather belt also studded with rivets; expensive high-topped sneakers whose purchase had further enriched the coffers of an NBA star; and, despite the heat, a black woolen stocking cap. Will observed that the jacket possessed only just enough clearance for Damien's thick, flabby arms to protrude through the openings where its sleeves had been dissected, and he wondered how much searching had been required for the young man to find a store that carried his size in jeans. He estimated their circumference at the waist to be roughly twice the length of their inseam.

Becky was dressed more appropriately for a night to be spent at a raucous western bar: tee-shirt, jeans and boots. Although she was no great fan of *El Bandito* (*"Grow up, you two"*, she'd advise Brian and Will, exasperated. *"Playing cowboy's for kids."*), she was delighted to be freed from her maternal responsibilities for the evening thanks to the good graces of her mother-in-law.

As for the others, Gene was a young orthopedics attending from Texas who was single and often roamed the city with Damien in an eternally futile search for willing young females. Despite his diminutive size and skinny frame (which contrasted sharply with the flabby bulk of his black *amigo*), Gene affected a deep Texas drawl and swaggering attitude that after a few beers deteriorated into a belligerent obnoxiousness that not infrequently earned him a barroom thrashing. Will could do without the man's bluster, but he had to admire his enduring spunk in the face of a long series of public humiliations.

The second girl - Becky introduced her as "Deb" - was younger than the rest, an anesthesiology intern recently arrived from Chicago and still a bit bewildered by the foreign climate, topography and cultural environment of her new hometown. Like many Easterners, within six months she'd either be busy applying for transfer to greener and otherwise more familiar pastures or passionately in love with the desert and its eccentricities, human included. Although she still projected a certain deer-in-the-headlights look, her inherent cheerfulness predicted the latter outcome would prevail. That Brian and Becky unobtrusively had taken her under their collective wing would help, as would her dark good looks that already were attracting attention from fellow housestaff and the younger male faculty.

They all settled around the pool, knocked back a few beers and enjoyed the slow evolution of another glorious desert sunset. When the sun had dropped well below the mountains, Brian arose from his chair and addressed those assembled. "Well, boys and girls" he said. "*Vamanos.* It's time for the Bandit."

Will turned to Maria, sitting behind him and slightly to his right. She'd barely spoken since the others arrived. "We're all heading out to a bar and dance hall that's about twenty minutes away," he explained. "You're welcome to join us, but I'll warn you: it's a real dive."

He fully expected her to decline, but she surprised him. "I like dives," she declared, arising from her chaise. "Count me in."

Brian dropped his head to hide a scowl, and uncharacteristic for her in such scenarios, Becky kept her silence. Unsettled by this unexpected response, Will backtracked. "What I meant was, this place can get pretty rowdy," he said. "We're just taking one car, and if you didn't like it there, you'd be stuck."

She lifted her head to smile up at him, her thick brown hair sliding back to expose her long, angular cheekbones. "I'll manage," she assured him.

Ignoring Brian's sidelong glance, Will replied, "Great, then. Let's get going."

Within ten minutes the seven of them were headed north on Silverbell Road, *Bandito*-bound.

———

El Bandito was an eclectic establishment – bar, dancehall, package store and strip joint – located on the northern outskirts of the city, just off I-10 and about ten miles from the house Will shared with Michael. Immediately inside the main entrance was a small but well-equipped package store where clerks cheerfully dispensed beer, tequila and Wild Turkey to truckers and cowboys already too inebriated to navigate their mounts safely.

Continuing on and bearing left, one entered a large saloon. The room was flanked by a long bar that occupied the entire eastern wall and looked out upon a jumble of tables and a raised plywood platform where the house band of the moment performed. On a busy night it could take ten minutes to traverse the saloon, to push one's way through the high tide of bodies that jammed up against the bar and merged with the hordes seated around the tables or packed tightly together on the tiny dance floor. The room's acoustics were terrible, and the blasting of the band's speakers joined with the incomprehensible roar of voices to produce a mind-numbing din that blended with the overcrowding to heighten an atmosphere of alcohol-fueled frenzy.

Beyond lay a smaller and quieter bar where one could wager money on darts or pool and observe the trading of insults and brief but spirited fist fights that often followed. Outside the gaming parlor was a large deck that served equally well as an alternative to the crowded, filthy restrooms for the emptying of a beer-laden bladder or a romantic tryst with a drunken stranger.

Upstairs was a lounge that catered to bikers and long-haul truckers. While a mere five dollars would gain you access to the festivities downstairs, it required another twenty to sample the pleasures of the upstairs lounge. And although that twenty bought you no drinks or snacks, it did afford you a nice view of the raised stage, where "exotic" dancing was performed. The dancing ostensibly was topless and advertised as such in accordance with county ordinance, but on a busy weekend night that ordinance was often ignored.

The indisputable star of *El Bandito's* lounge was the locally renowned *La Amazonia*, a true professional who (*que milagro!*) had endured in her trade for over two decades. *La senorita Amazonia,* whose baptismal name was Belinda Gomez, initially had performed in Juarez at the tender age of fourteen. She was a long-legged beauty of mixed extraction (Mexican, French and Pueblo Indian) who stood well over six feet tall in the stiletto heels she wore on stage. Her raven hair fell thickly to her waist, and her surgically enhanced breasts beamed out at the audience like the headlights of a speeding Peterbilt. Although the gravitational pull inherent to 38 years of life had taken its toll, her excellent genes, the nightly dancing and her healthy habits had served to prolong her career well beyond the norm.

Will first met Belinda in the emergency room. While performing at a private party thrown by one of Tucson's Mexican *mafiosos*, she'd slipped off the wooden deck upon which she gyrated and fallen into a patch of *cholla* below. They'd had plenty of time to talk as he sutured her scalp laceration and plucked out with forceps the largest of the *cholla* spines painfully embedded in her back, arms, buttocks and legs. He'd admired her stoicism and been surprised by her erudition. Belinda was no floozy. At one time she'd aspired to become a psychologist, she confessed to him, but the immediate financial rewards her dancing provided had led her to stray off the academic path.

From this late night encounter had developed a friendship of sorts. He sometimes met Belinda for dinner at a restaurant near her apartment in the *barrio* district, and when he came to the *Bandito,* she would sit with him during her break and nurse a glass of wine. Their relationship remained entirely platonic. Perhaps it was the perspective derived from twenty-four years of dancing near-naked in lounges crammed with drunken louts, but Belinda regarded as fantastical the concepts of "love" and "romance". With the exception of her brothers, nephews and Will, she appeared to have no particular interest in men. And while she enjoyed his friendship, friendship was clearly all she sought.

Most important to her Belinda was the fulfillment of her dream: to stop dancing and live alone, financially independent, in a fine house of her own choosing. She was single-minded in her determination that this dream would become reality. She worked at the Bandit six nights a week, took moonlighting jobs when she could and saved most of what she made. Ironically, it was other's (men's) extreme interest in *her* that would deliver her the quiet, solitary life she craved.

Because Brian's old Comet Caliente was the only vehicle large enough to contain them all, it had fallen to him to serve as designated driver. With its candy apple red paint job, white convertible top, an over-powered 8 cylinder under the hood and a manual transmission controlled from the steering column ("3 on the tree"), the Comet was a fitting ride for a night at the Bandit.

Brian had been quiet as he drove, his silence masked by the raucous conversation catalyzed by Damien and Gene. He deeply resented Maria's presence, was alarmed by Will's obvious infatuation and could not shake his sense that the developing situation pointed towards some as yet unidentifiable catastrophe.

He'd first met this young woman shortly after he'd come to know Michael and just prior to the *de facto* dissolution of their marriage. He'd been invited to a dinner sponsored by his anesthesiology department at a swanky restaurant whose prices ranged far beyond the means of a modestly paid resident, and due to her grandmother having fractured a hip Becky was in Prescott and unable to accompany him. On a last minute impulse he'd asked Michael if he'd like to stand in for his wife. His new friend had agreed, on the condition that he could bring *his* wife, whose dinner he'd pay for himself. Brian assured him that would be fine.

When he was introduced to Maria, standing beside Michael at the restaurant's entrance, he was stunned to find that his friend had wed a woman so discordant with the Brian's expectations. She was wearing an obviously expensive black cocktail dress that was cut just a bit too low and too short to be appropriate for the occasion, and to him her affect seemed as unsuitable as her dress. They'd instinctively disliked each other from the start, he and Maria, and he took pains at dinner to ensure Michael sat between the two of them.

To Maria's left had sat a senior anesthesiology resident whom she seemed to know well, and throughout the endless dinner the two of them chattered incessantly. At one point Maria excused herself from the table, and Brian noticed that the resident soon followed her lead. Just before they finally returned to their seats, he caught a glimpse of them from the periphery of his vision, walking slowly together, Maria laughing and clinging to the young physician as if unsteady from intoxication.

Seating herself at the table, Maria's eyes shone with excitement, and where before she had contributed little to the general conversation, now she spoke frequently to those around her at a rapid pace. She drank heavily, and at the dinner's end, as she stood propped in a corner by the entrance and enthusiastically engaging in a prolonged farewell embrace with her anesthesiologist, he'd assisted Michael in extricating her from the restaurant and depositing her in their car. Far from resisting them, he recalled that Maria had merely laughed at their efforts.

Will had known nothing of that evening two years prior, but he was nevertheless feeling apprehensive. Before they'd left in the Comet, Maria had changed into other clothes she had in her car. Glancing over at her briefly, Will again surveyed the sleeveless black jersey that exposed her slender brown arms and clung tightly to her torso like a second skin. Her legs, as smooth and brown as her arms, were bare beneath a short denim skirt. Will had felt edgy ever since Maria's arrival that afternoon, and despite the festive mood in the car he'd found it difficult to relax and join in. He drank several more beers during the drive, but they'd failed to restore his good spirits. He was uneasy, and the

El Bandito was a place that did not suffer ambiguity well. *Why had she come to the house?* He'd wondered. *Why is she here now?* Her presence was unsettling. It upset the balance of the night.

They reached *El Bandito* at nine, and already the parking lot was full. Vehicles, pickup trucks mostly, spilled into the adjacent desert. Lined up at the front of the building was a long line of large motorcycles, and scattered at the borders of the lot and on the access road were the big rigs, two dozen or more.

As they approached the entrance, a group of large, denim-clad men poured out through the door, shouting and reeling like drunken bears. The torrent of noise that erupted from the building suddenly was muted by a bouncer who slammed the door shut behind them, and in the relative quiet that followed the men seemed to recover some awareness of their surroundings. Unfortunately those surroundings included three attractive young women.

The largest, most bearlike and most heavily bearded of the men detached himself from his fellows and came rumbling towards them. Ignoring Will and his other companions, the man planted himself squarely in Maria's path and stared down at her greedily from his towering height. His mouth was grinning, but his bloodshot eyes were slitted and threatening.

"Why, ain't you a fine lookin' piece a' tail!" he bellowed. "C'mere, boys!" he shouted over his shoulder, and then turning back to Maria said, "How 'bout we go for a little ride, sugar?" He gestured toward the row of motorcycles.

His biker friends approached and assembled themselves, their eyes fixed on Maria, the quarry. Will noted that Brian had used this brief distraction to maneuver Becky and Deb to the rear, and already the women were halfway back to the Comet.

Brian himself had slipped off in another direction. Damien and Gene were standing silently side by side, glancing at one another uncertainly.

Maria stood toe to toe with the aggressive biker, holding her ground and seemingly oblivious to his friends moving in on her flanks. She stared up at the huge man unblinkingly. "Fuck off," she said in an even tone.

The man's broad, insincere grin collapsed briefly into a puzzled expression, like a puppy slapped for playing too roughly. Within seconds, however, he regained his swagger and advanced on her menacingly. "You'll be riding more than my chopper tonight, sweet tits," he growled.

As the huge man reached forward to grab her he felt himself abruptly yanked backwards at the waist by a hand firmly clenching his broad leather belt. He spun around to find Will standing before him, and in the next instant he felt the stinging pain of an openhanded slap delivered sharply to his left cheek.

While the biker rubbed at his face and gathered himself, Will spoke. "She said she doesn't want to go for a ride," he told the man. "Now you and your buddies move on."

The man he'd slapped at first turned red-faced with fury, and then in delayed response to Will's words guffawed and shouted to his friends standing at either side.

"Here is one *crazy* fucker!" he informed them. He tilted his head upward, closed his eyes and howled at the moon with savage glee. "We're going to *fuck* you up, boy!" he cried out with conviction, turning his attention back to Will. "We're going to fuck you up *bad*. And this sexy little bitch here, too."

With that the biker drew from a scabbard hidden beneath his short-sleeved denim jacket a huge knife and crouched, ready to spring.

Will felt nothing but an eerie calmness. "Put your knife away," he said, "or I'll take it from you. And then I'll kill you with it."

Will's words produced on the faces of his friends expressions that unanimously conveyed shock and horror. This strategy seemed to them nothing short of suicidal. Will was a a fair-sized guy and tough enough, but the biker had the body of a NFL defensive tackle gone to seed, standing easily 6'8" and weighing roughly 300 pounds.

Furthermore, Will's experience with knife-fighting was presumably non-existent. In contrast, his foe had devoted a fair portion of his adult life to brawls involving weaponry that ranged from his ham-like fists to truncheons, crowbars, chains and the wicked knife he now held purposefully in his right hand.

While Will stood motionless, the biker moved slightly to his right and prepared to thrust. Suddenly an authoritative voice boomed loudly from the outskirts of the group. "Okay, girls," the voice directed calmly but firmly. "Straighten your skirts, and call off your pissin' contest."

Looking up, the assembled saw two brown-clad state troopers approaching, their attitudes relaxed but each with his right hand resting on the butt of a huge handgun protruding from an unbuttoned holster. Taking up the rear was Brian, gently propelling the uniformed duo towards the group like an efficient usher at a formal wedding.

The biker unhurriedly sheathed his knife. Scowling, he stared intently into Will's eyes. "I'll be seeing you again, lover boy," he promised. "Soon."

With that he turned away. He and his friends mounted their bikes and after a few noisy volleys of pointless acceleration exited the parking lot with a deafening roar that faded into silence only when they had vanished from sight down the access road. Once their string of lights no longer could be seen, Will turned to the troopers. "Thanks," he told them.

The taller of the two troopers responded curtly. "Why don't you and your friends get your butts out of here while you still can?" he suggested. "You don't belong here, and only a damn fool would bring his girlfriend here." He nodded towards Maria.

She's not my girlfriend, Will began to protest, but he remained silent. The trooper regarded him sternly for a few seconds more and then spoke to his partner. "Let's roll, Ed. This shit hole only deserves one good deed per night". They walked off together into the darkness, their boots crunching on the gravel.

Will turned to Brian. "Thanks," he repeated.

"De nada," Brian responded, grinning. "Always happy to request assistance from our friends in law enforcement when a fellow citizen finds himself in need."

"They're probably right," Will mused. "The smart move would be to get on out of here."

"Right," Brian replied. *"Absolutamente.* Better to be safe than dead."

"But we *could* have a few beers first," Will suggested.

"Of course we could," Brian affirmed, grinning. "I'll get Becky and tell her the good news of your deliverance. With some gentle persuasion, I'm sure she'll want to celebrate." He loped away in the direction of the Comet.

Gene and Damien already were making their way towards the bar's entrance, leaving Will alone with Maria in the hot, dusty parking lot. They turned towards one another, and she cast him an inscrutable look. "My hero," she said softly.

"Not really," he responded. "I…." As if to cut him off she moved closely against him, head uplifted and lips parted, and lightly placed her index finger on his lips.

At that instant Will heard Brian and the two other young women approaching, Brian leading the way and Becky close behind, still firmly expressing her opinion as to the wisdom of their remaining any longer at *El Bandito*. Observing Will and Maria pressed together, Becky abruptly broke off her protests and stood silent before them. As Will reflexively took a step backward, Brian spoke to break the awkward silence that suddenly had developed.

"All this drama's made me thirsty," he said. "Let's have a cold beer."

He placed his arm firmly around Will's shoulders and guided his friend towards the front door. Becky stepped to Brian's other side, leaving Maria to fend for herself in their wake. She stood alone for a moment and then followed the others into the building.

———

After the initial fracas in the parking lot the bar was anticlimactic. They drank a few pitchers and listened to the house band. Brian danced, expertly, with Becky and Deb, and a man from another table took Maria to the dance floor. Will remained at their table with the other two males. They wished to tease him about his *mano a mano* encounter with the biker, but he simultaneously ignored them and tried not to stare too obviously at Maria while she swayed and spun before him. He found her easily the most attractive woman in the crowded room, and by the looks she attracted from the other men present, he was not alone in his opinion.

Will eventually decided to move to the upstairs lounge to say hello to Belinda. Becky and Deb demurred, professing no interest in watching naked women dance, but Maria insisted on coming along. Brian stayed to keep the two other women company. When Damien and Gene arose and made to accompany them upstairs, Will's experienced an unexpected rush of annoyance. He realized he wanted Maria to himself.

With considerable effort the four of them made their way through the dense crowd, emerging finally into the smaller bar adjacent and then ascending the stairs to the lounge. Belinda was waiting to perform on stage, but when she spotted Will, she turned to speak to a dancer sitting beside her and indicated with gestures that Will should sit and she would join him. One of the peculiarities of their relationship was Belinda's disinclination to dance in his presence.

Despite the large crowd they managed to find a table, and Will struggled to fight down a rising tide of apprehension. *This is not cool*, a small voice within him whispered. Always in the past he'd come to visit Belinda alone. To bring these others with him, to bring Maria, seemed in some way a violation.

Having ensured that her place on the stage would be taken by another, Belinda wrapped a diaphanous shawl around her bare shoulders and walked slowly over to where they sat. Like the Red Sea before Moses, the admiring male crowd parted to grant her passage, but she paid them no heed. Reaching their table, she sat by Will, crossed her long bare legs and drew her wrap more tightly around her. A glass of icewater had appeared at her elbow. She smiled and thanked the waitress, raised the glass to her lips and took a long sip.

Only after she'd set the glass down did she swivel slightly in her chair to address the table, and her casual failure to include Maria in her acknowledgement was like a resounding slap. With an ease born of long experience, she expertly isolated the younger woman, ignoring her in favor of the men.

When finally Will broke in to introduce Maria, she again swiveled in her chair and faced the other woman as if only now aware of her presence. Belinda looked her up and down appraisingly and then took another sip of water before speaking.

"How you do, *chica*?" she asked. "This is the first time you come to the lounge, *verdad*? *Su guapo aqui…*," and she nodded her head to indicate Will sitting beside her, "…your boyfriend here, did he think you would like this place?" She smiled pleasantly.

"She's not Will's girlfriend," Gene corrected her. "She's married to Will's roommate." Well into his third pitcher, Gene was drunk and nearing incoherence.

Belinda smiled again. "*Pues*," she said, "whatever your circumstances, I hope you enjoy yourself." She gazed at Maria for a long moment. "And where *is* your husband, *chica*?" she asked, finally.

As she had throughout, Maria said nothing. Then she arose and walked away from the table.

Belinda watched her exit the room. "Not so much a talker, *esta chica,*" she remarked to no one in particular. Then she, too, arose, but before she left them she leaned down to speak to Will. Her long black hair clustered about her face as if anxious to hear her words.

"If that *puta* really does have a husband, it's with him she belongs," she said softly, her lips by his ear. "Not here. And especially not with you, *guapo.*" Finished, she tossed her mane of hair back between her shoulders and walked away without a backward glance. Within seconds she had vanished into the crowd, and he saw her no more.

———

Will's head was not yet upon the table, but he was beer-sodden, sullen, and decidedly drunk. Feeling at a loss after Belinda's departure, he'd sat drinking steadily with his male companions at their table in the lounge until even they'd abandoned him for more entertaining company. The cocktail waitress was at his side once again and urging yet more alcohol upon him, but his drinking had become perfunctory and joyless.

He shook her off, paid his bill and began to weave unsteadily towards the exit. Halfway there he bumped into Brian.

"What's up, *compadre*?" his friend grinned. "You look like something even the cat wouldn't bother to drag in."

"Fuck you," Will muttered distractedly. He tried to push Brian aside and continue his *hegira* to the men's room, but his friend good-naturedly wrapped his arm around his neck and brought him to a halt.

"Goddammit it, Brian," he protested. "I gotta piss."

Brian smiled. "That's fine, Willie," he said. "But once you take care of business, hustle on down to the parking lot. We're heading home." He released him and headed for the stairs.

The wait for a urinal was agonizingly long, and once in position the act itself was almost as protracted. Finished at last, Will zipped up, bypassed the unspeakably filthy sink that obviously had served double duty as an emergency toilet and re-entered the lounge. He felt considerably better.

Walking downstairs to the smaller bar, he decided against forcing his way through the mass of bodies in the front room and instead made for the fire door that led out through the rear of the building. He knew from experience it was unlocked and, despite its cautionary sign to the contrary, alarm-less.

He stepped out into the dry night air, took a deep breath to clear his lungs and at once found himself face to face with the same giant biker he'd tussled with out front just hours before. The man was puffing at a joint and hideously inebriated, but not so much so that he failed to recognize Will immediately.

"Hey, boys!" he called to his colleagues. "Look who's here."

The other men clustered thickly around him, stinking of stale beer and unwashed denim. In a second they had Will pinned against the rear wall, and their leader's countenance was not promising. He literally spat his words, saliva collecting on his fecal brown beard and mustache, his little pig eyes red with methamphetamine, beer and hatred.

"Give me the fuckin' billy," he commanded, reaching his slab of a hand backward and keeping his fierce gaze fixed on Will. Grasping some type of truncheon that was deposited therein, he shook his huge fist at Will and crowed, "I'm going to beat you to jelly, boy! And then I'm gonna slice up what's left into little pieces."

From the moment he was accosted by his nemesis, Will had become suddenly sober and clear-headed. Yet despite the welcome clarity, he could see no way out of his current predicament. Before him was arraigned a thick wall of hostile bikers, and above him the desert night sky held no promise of *deus ex machina*.

As he readied himself for inevitable annihilation, however, a curious thing happened. As Will watched in amazement, the enormous bear of a man crumpled to his knees and then toppled face forward in the dust, his slow, deliberate collapse like that of a very large inflatable doll punctured suddenly by a very small pin.

As the ogre fell like a curtain descending, behind him was revealed Damien's short, squatty form. The young man held clenched in his right hand the neck and broken remnant of an empty bottle of MD 20/20, a notoriously cheap alcoholic beverage favored by the homeless wino crowd. While initially solemn as he appraised his work, he broke out in a huge grin when he looked up to find Will staring at him.

"Good work, Damien", Will said, "but I think you might have killed him."

Damien shrugged his shoulders. "I don't give a shit," he answered.

Will shook his head wonderingly. "Well said," he replied. "Now let's get the fuck out of here before his buddies activate." The biker's companions inexplicably seemed to have vanished following the collapse of their leader.

Will took what was left of the bottle from Damien's hand and hurled it as far as he could into the surrounding desert, and there followed shortly the satisfying sound of glass profoundly shattering. *That should take care of any finger prints*, he thought. He then grabbed Damien, still gawking at his fallen conquest, and rushed him towards the front of the building.

Fortuitously, the others were were already in the car and waiting. The two stragglers dove into the back seat, and Brian, quick to size up the situation, floored the accelerator with the back door still hanging open. With a prolonged squealing of tires and huge spray of dirt and gravel, they exited the parking lot and pulled onto the paved access road, fishtailing all the way. Will had landed in the back seat face down and feet up. By the time he could disentangle himself from the other three bodies and crane his neck around to look out the back window, he could see a trail of mono-eyed headlights duplicating their route and closing fast.

Glancing in the rearview mirror, Brian caught his eye. "I know," he said. "They didn't waste any time, did they?"

Without another word he suddenly twirled the steering wheel leftward and took the interstate's onramp without breaking speed. The heavy old car protested vehemently and skidded sideways, at one point its front right bumper ricocheting off the guardrail, but Brian soon had the Comet running full steam on the highway and headed south.

Despite his efforts, the string of motorcycles easily navigated the onramp and continued to close the gap. While there was silence from the front seat and from Damien in the back, still too awed by his audacious intervention to contemplate any new danger, Gene began to yelp. Even the preternaturally cool Becky was looking a bit anxious.

"Fuck, man!" Gene screamed. "What are we going to do? Those fuckers'll kill us if they catch us, and they'll gangbang us first." He looked meaningfully at the three women. "And I don't mean just you guys," he informed them.

Continuing to drive at top speed, Brian took one hand off the wheel and flicked off the car's lights. Returning both hands to the wheel he drove on calmly, occasionally glancing in the rearview mirror to gauge the progress of their pursuers.

"What the *fuck* are you doing, man!" Gene shouted. "I can't see a goddamn thing." Will silently agreed. This section of the interstate was poorly lit, and with no cars approaching it was almost impossible to make out any curves or bends rapidly enough to avoid running off the road.

By the way of reply, Brian muttered, "Hang on. This may be a bit tricky."

At these words Gene began moaning, and as all passengers braced themselves Brian suddenly swerved to his right without slowing or hitting the brakes. Instead of sailing off to oblivion, the car rapidly descended an exit ramp nearly invisible in the darkness, slammed through the guardrail as the ramp began to curve and plunged down a shallow bank into the desert. Still not braking, Brian allowed the car gradually to come to rest on its own, its momentum slowed by numerous collisions with small trees, bushes, boulders and the like.

Will noticed that he'd turned off the engine, and when Gene started to open a rear door, Brian spoke abruptly the first words any had voiced since their dramatic exit from the interstate. "Leave the door closed," he commanded. "We got off the main road without flashing our brake lights, and we don't want the interior lights to give us away now."

So they sat in the darkness, and although they were well below the level of the interstate some 50 yards away they soon could discern a long line of motorcycles racing southward on that highway. Brian's gamble seemed to have succeeded. They waited a minute or two more, and then he spoke again. "Even those yahoos aren't stupid enough to keep driving south forever," he said. "Eventually they'll backtrack and maybe check out this exit. If we can get out of here, we ought to head to some place a little less conspicuous."

The Comet miraculously started right up, and with some hasty clearing of brush and rolling of rock they broke a trail back to the exit ramp and proceeded onto the access road. The car's engine made a number of ominous-sounding noises and the front end was woefully out of alignment, but even so Brian could maintain a consistent 40 mph.

He continued south on the access road for a few miles and then turned right at the first intersection, heading westward on Ina Road towards the Tucson Mountains. Deciding that it would be safest to get off the road altogether, they headed for Michael and Will's house located a few miles south of the intersection of Ina and Silverbell.

As they drove slowly down Silverbell, lights still off so as to avoid unwanted attention, Maria pivoted around to face Will from her position in the front seat. "I was so worried, Will," she said. "Thank god you're all right."

Instead of the usual hoots of derision such words typically would have evoked, something in her tone and manner produced an immediate and uncomfortable silence in the car. *Too intimate,* Will thought, trying to ignore the sudden throbbing in his chest and below his beltline.

They drove on in silence until Brian reached the house. "Here we are, boys and girls," he said. "And I think this night's work rates a little party."

———

Their celebration was brief but lively. It was still quite hot, and they gravitated to the pool, shedding their clothes and plunging into the cool water. It was a fine midsummer's desert night. Lightning flashed over the peaks of the Catalinas, but the clear, starry sky above threatened no hint of rain. The beauty of the night, the refreshing water and their successful deliverance from danger encouraged a spirit of giddy abandonment, and their toasts to one another grew increasingly profane and extravagant.

One by one the revelers departed, leaving Will and Maria alone in the pool. For some minutes they circled each other like wary sharks, but eventually they came together, Will seated waist high on the concrete steps at the shallow end with Maria crouched there before him, her brown breasts bobbing at the water's surface, her long hair plastered against her shoulders.

They talked for a while, and then suddenly, as if propelled by unseen hands gently urging them forward, they drifted into an embrace. Her naked chest against his, her round bottom resting lightly on his thighs and her legs encircling his waist, she enveloped him totally. As he entered her he was surprised at the warmth she held within despite having been submerged in the pool's cool waters for so long. She moaned softly in his ear, and her sighs punctuated the deep silence of the night.

When they finished, they walked naked to his bedroom, slept a while and then made love again. She left before sunrise.

Chapter 8

MEXICO

He was shocked by the wind's ferocity. With dependable regularity in the summer months the breeze began to rise by mid-morning, built to its maximum by the early afternoon and died off to nothing by nightfall. But now it was well after midnight, and the wind was whipping the sea's surface into froth.

For some reason the boat would not accept a broad reach, and he'd had to sail more of a westerly course than was prudent in these conditions. A heavy northwesterly gust might have knocked the boat over had he not repeatedly pointed her into the wind and thus avoided taking its full force abeam. Even so, he could feel the boat straining to find a more stable course through the wind-swept swells easily visible in the bright moonlight. She was like a runaway horse spooked by unsure footing.

He gave silent thanks for having taken the time to set the sails just after their passage between the headlands. With the boat so unsteady, the bow was no place to be. It was just then that he happened to glance directly ahead and saw to his dismay that the boom was still clipped to the backstay via a short wire leader. This explained the boat's inability to run before the wind. Worse, the wind's unceasing pressure on the mainsail was being transmitted to the backstay, and the extreme tension on the stay was causing it to bend the mast like a bow.

Left to itself, this unstable arrangement could cause the stay or mast to snap, and in either event the heavy mast, unchecked, would then collapse and with full force upon the boat. Even if they escaped injury and the boat remained afloat, they would be left dependent upon the underpowered outboard. In this sea and with the modest amount of fuel they carried, they'd make no headway against the wind, and if they turned southeast and motored directly before the following swell they could take a breaking wave astern and founder.

He worked frantically to unclip the boom, but the tension exerted upon the leader resisted his efforts. He could drop sail and reduce that tension, but to do so would mean leaving the tiller unattended and the boat helmless in a dangerous sea. He felt close to panic, but in the end all it took was a slight change in course: he pointed the boat a few more degrees into the wind, the sails began to luff and the tension on the leader immediately lessened to the point that it took only a quick, almost careless motion to unsnap the backstay and free the boom. He could almost hear the mast and its stays sigh with relief. He adjusted the sheets, pointed the bow southwest and immediately felt *Celerity* heel to port as she accepted the broad reach.

He was exhausted. This terrible evening seemed interminable. Was it really possible that only a few hours before he'd turned away from the doorway of *El Paraiso*? Now he faced a demanding night as he struggled alone to cope with the surprisingly strong wind.

Keeping one hand on the tiller, he stretched forward to open the port lazarrette and rummaged about until he found the auxiliary medicine kit. After some blind fumbling with his fingers he located the plastic bottle containing tablets of dextroamphetamine, and without hesitation he swallowed two, a 20 mg dose. He'd always appreciated speed's uncanny ability to restore one's spirits and vigor, and tonight, thankfully, proved no exception. Taken on an empty stomach, the disintegrating tablets rapidly congregated in his brain's microcirculation to work their synaptic magic.

Chemically insulated for the present, he enjoyed a brief respite from his apprehension at the danger that seemed to be rising all about them. Standing at the tiller, he listened to the dysrhythmic *thunk* of the bow as it plunged through the swells and felt the spray on his cheek when the larger swells slapped rudely at the starboard hull. Content for now, he sailed on, directing the boat towards the long, narrow peninsula some 80 miles distant.

———

They sighted Isla Estanque shortly after sunrise. The girl was first to pick out the island's triangular silhouette on the horizon. She'd remained below until an hour before, apparently having slept through the night. Now she was standing in the gangway, bracing herself against the boat's unpredictable movements, her hair streaming behind her in the wind.

Instead of the usual early morning glass, the sea's surface was churning with confused swells and whitecaps, and gusts of wind continued to whip the froth off the tops of the waves. The northwesterly was building, a common enough occurrence in winter but decidedly rare during the summer months in this wild corner of the world. Rare or not, he decided they'd best find shelter in the lee of the stormy wind and sea. The ragged angulations of the north-facing ridges on the Midriff's islands bore mute testimony to the power of the storms that could sweep down from their remote origin in the Gulf of Alaska.

He knew Estanque well from a previous voyage. Years ago, under similar conditions encountered during a mid-winter's sail from San Carlos to the eastern coast of Baja, he and his friend had anchored here. Like most islands in the neighborhood, Estanque was volcanic in origin, appearing roughly cone-shaped at a distance, devoid of any permanent source of fresh water and inhabited only by a thin sprinkling of particularly resilient grasses, shrubs, cacti and low trees, along with a small population of rattle-less rattlesnakes. The snakes were said to be present in far greater abundance on Isla de La Guardia, a nearby island lying a mile or so to the north and, after Tiburon, the largest in the Sea of Cortez.

Unlike La Guardia, a long wedge buttressed by rocky cliffs that rose steeply from the sea and so offered few favorable anchorages, Estanque literally seemed to embrace the voyager. On maps it resembled an enormous crab poised to fight, its arms extended from its shell with the claws nearly touching. From its small cone of crumbling volcanic rock extended two low berms that curved towards one another, seeking to meet but falling short by no more than 50 yards. Within the narrow entrance was a shallow bay protected from virtually any weather, no matter its direction of approach. *Estanque* was Spanish for "pond", and this placid cove was aptly named.

He knew from his prior experience that the safer approach to the bay's entrance was from the north. In geologic reality, Estanque was simply a southeasterly extension of La Guardia, and at low tide the southern arm of the smaller island fused with the body of the larger, presenting a reef that would tear the bottom from any vessel of draft.

With their sailboat tucked behind the northern arm and snugly anchored to the bay's fine sandy bottom, he and his friend had spent a pleasant evening at rest, enjoying a dinner of boiled lobster and black beans, drinking many glasses of cheap red wine and listening to the wind above them as it roared down from the north. All was peaceful below the rails, and so they huddled low in the cockpit, relaxing with their backs against the bulkhead and legs extended over the lazarrettes. His friend flipped on the radio, and for a while they listened to the static-laced marine report and the conversations between ships spread throughout the Gulf. Finally they switched over to the tape deck, and the whiskey-soaked poetry of long-dead Jim Morrison competed with the wind. Later he was to recall it as one of the finest evenings of his life, and during bouts of insomnia he would think back to the peacefulness he'd felt as he lay safely just below the touch of the searching wind.

Now he pushed the tiller hard to port, and with the strong wind streaming through the shifting sails the boat rapidly came about. Olivia looked back and called out to him, puzzled. "I thought we were going to that island," she shouted above the wind, pointing towards Estanque's dumpy cone.

"We are," he shouted back, continuing to steer the boat on a northeasterly course. He was tacking to a point that would enable them to clear the headland of the northern arm when they came about once more for the run south on a broad reach with a following sea.

The girl clambered up the gangway's steps and made her way to the stern, careful to avoid the boom that swayed threateningly just overhead. Standing before him, she swayed and staggered as the boat rocked unevenly in the heavy swell. "Then why are we going in the opposite direction?" she asked.

Before responding he pulled her down to a seated and more secure position on the lazarette. He looked up to check the telltales attached to the mainsail and saw them streaming in parallel as they should be. Despite the swells insistently pushing against their hull, they were making good headway, and he calculated they should be in position to come about and make their run within another five minutes.

"Why are we going this way?" she persisted. "There's nothing out there but open water." She swept her hand to indicate the empty horizon ahead.

He checked their position yet again, intent on ensuring he allowed them a distance sufficient to safely clear the rocky fist at the end of the island's curving northern arm. Finally satisfied that they had room to spare, he spoke.

"A storm's building", he told her, his eyes still fixed on the sea ahead. "Hard to know how bad things will get, but it's probably best that we hole up until it blows through. The bay inside that island ahead offers the safest anchorage in the Gulf, and to get to it we have to pass through that narrow opening." He pointed to indicate the gap between the dual headlands.

"With this wind we'd have a tough time beating to that opening from the south, and besides, there's a reef extending out from the southern arm. The tide's in now, and with the high water you can't see it. But it's there, and it's nothing but rocks. Big ones. And sharp enough to peel our hull like a can opener. The tides here are extreme, and with the ebb the water runs over those rocks like a class IV rapids."

He paused a moment to check the tell-tales again before continuing. "Coming at that opening from the north in a wind like this, you have to allow for a lot of side-slip to the east. Caught short, the boat would surf these waves onto the rocks of that northern arm. So we had to tack out to gain the point we need to make our run". He stopped, abruptly, and turned his attention again to the sail set, taking in the sheets a few inches and shifting the boat's course slightly more to the west.

Olivia sat back against the bulkhead, rattled by this sudden torrent of words. Until now the man hadn't strung together more than two sentences at a time, and to hear him speak at such length was unsettling. It was like being in a restaurant and suddenly realizing that those around you who'd been conversing in another language were also fluent in your native tongue. She'd understood little of what he'd said concerning the technicalities of sailing, tides and reefs, but it wasn't this ignorance that disturbed her. She longed to escape Mexico, and his familiarity with even this remote island suggested that his desires might run counter to her own.

He glanced at her briefly as she sat silently beside him. *She's unusual-looking*, he thought. Partly it was that albino hair hacked off just above her shoulders, its dark roots matching her coal-black eyebrows. He guessed her to be eighteen. At most. She was a foot shorter than he, and she couldn't weigh much more than 100 pounds. Her skin was the palest white, but the hairs on her forearm matched the black of her eyebrows. A study in contrasts. Blacks and whites.

Of her character he could judge little. She obviously knew little of boats but nonetheless had exhibited a clumsy willingness to help. Unfortunately she was inept, and he'd decided early on that it would be best to regard her simply as cargo. If he could deposit her somewhere safely without further endangering himself, that was fine. If not, she'd just have to take her chances with him. He needed to devote full attention to the complex question of how to avoid discovery and capture while making his own escape from Mexico. *And then what?* he asked himself.

For now, however, he could delay addressing those particular issues and instead focus on their immediate predicament. When last night they'd departed from San Carlos, his first intention was to put as many sea miles as possible between themselves and the pursuit that was sure to follow discovery of the dead *federal*. Heading due westward under heavy winds and at maximum hull speed, he'd initially considered making a run for Bahia Los Angeles.

"L.A. Bay" was a miniscule village on a flat section of the Baja coast separated by a narrow strait from La Guardia, and the village owed its precarious existence to the fanatical American sport fishermen who traveled there to pursue the schools of yellowtail tuna that abounded in the region.

The town was no more than a ramshackle collection of meager shacks that housed the indigenous population who served the tourists, but it did possess a dirt airstrip. Private planes frequently flew in and out, delivering and retrieving the American pescadophiles. Such a group might be inclined to add a young *gringa* to their passenger list, and depending on the plane's destination, he might buy himself a seat as well. Unfortunately, the tiny village held no secrets, and not infrequently it was visited by *federales* and officials of the Mexican fishing authority eager to extract "fines" – *la mordida* – from the

Americans who fished their waters. No, he'd decided, Bahia Los Angeles was probably not a wise choice.

Further south on the coast were the larger cities of Mulege and Loreto. By virtue of their size, both offered a greater chance of preserving anonymity, but he had visited neither and knew nothing of the difficulties that might be involved in getting away safely once ashore. Yet further to the south, almost to the southernmost tip of the Baja peninsula, were La Paz and its international airport. There were cheap daily flights to Tijuana, and there one easily could hire a cab that would provide transportation to the public beach. From the beach it was a long hike northward through the winding estuary of the Rio Tijuana and across the border to San Ysidro. After that it was easy. He had friends in San Diego who would help him.

But even if this favorable wind held, it would require days of sailing to reach La Paz. By then, his name, an identifying likeness and details of the boat would have been disseminated widely. Capture seemed inevitable should he attempt to buy a ticket and board a plane. Theoretically he could sail on yet farther, bypass La Paz and Cabo, round the cape and by hugging the coast attempt to motor northwards against the wind and swell to Todos Santos. In Todos he could gamble on meeting some sympathetic *gringo* surfers who would take him along on their drive back to the States, but this plan, too, had more than its share of inconveniences and uncertainties.

Unable to reach any satisfactory decision, he'd settled on simply continuing westward and keeping his options open. Given the present direction of the wind and the geographic profile of the southeastern Baja coastline, he could defer any decision as to course until they were well across the Midriff.

Now what appeared to be an impending storm mandated that they simply seek adequate shelter, and Estanque was all of that. They could hunker down until the heavy winds began to subside, and he could use that time to get some sleep, consult his charts and try to develop a plan that held some prospect of success.

They passed through the narrow entrance uneventfully, and after the sea

the waters of the bay indeed were pond-like despite the 40 knot gusts outside the encircling berms. He dropped sail and anchor, paying out plenty of line but minding that the boat would stop short of the rocky northern arm should the wind shift and she swing. Satisfied with their position, he went below and quickly prepared them a breakfast of boiled eggs and instant grits. Olivia refused her plate, and he finished both portions.

Chasing a 30 mg capsule of temazepam with a gulp of orange juice, he settled down on the portside lazarrette and was immediately asleep.

———

He awoke suddenly to the unmistakable drone of a large powerboat. He scrambled to his feet, reached below and grabbed the binoculars from their rack on the interior bulkhead. He glassed the horizon and quickly located the sound's source: just below the southern tip of La Guardia a large sportfishing boat – perhaps 40 to 50 feet in length – was moving at moderate speed towards the southeast. With the binoculars he easily could make out the boat's flying bridge, outriggers and at least five people seated or moving about.

At that distance he couldn't judge whether they were Mexican or *gringos*, but by the odds it was a charter based in L.A. Bay taking a group of Americans out for yellowtail or, possibly, billfish. If the latter, they likely were headed for the seamounts located far to the south, on a course that would take them rapidly out of visual range. While the sport fisher undoubtedly had radar, the rocky heights of Estanque would prevent detection of their small boat.

He put down the binoculars and glanced up at the mast, the most visible evidence of their presence. There was nothing to be done, he decided. Even if he could devise some way to lower heavy metal spar, the fishing boat either would be upon them or far out of eyesight by the time he had it down. All he could do was wait and pray that their attention remained fixed on anticipation of the fish ahead or the mid-morning *cervezas* in their hands.

He glassed them once again and saw that they seemed to have slowed as they motored along through the heavy seas. Fearing their captain might choose the safety of a stopover at Estanque, he willed them to continue on their southeasterly course.

At that moment he realized Olivia had left the boat. To starboard he heard splashing, and looking in that direction he saw her standing chest-deep in the water just off the rock-strewn beach of the northern arm. She'd removed her filthy shirt and was attempting to scrub out its incriminating stains. Beyond her, to the northwest, rose the cliffs of Isla Angel de la Guardia.

Noticing his attention, the girl quickly dipped under the surface, slipped the t-shirt back on and swam to a deeper spot. Treading water, she called over to him. "Is it time to go?"

He shook his head, and she was close enough to the boat to register his response. She swam towards the transom, and, tying it off to a cleat, he tossed her a line. Continuing to float in the water a moment longer, she smiled and exclaimed, "This feels so good!" She looked radiant.

My god, he thought. *The remarkable resilience of the young. Not much more than 12 hours ago there were fragments of a man's organs splattered across her shirt, and half of Sonora is probably howling for our blood. Yet there she floats like she hadn't a care in the world.*

Hand over hand, Olivia used the line to pull herself to the boat and climbed up the ladder he'd set out for her, her wet limbs glistening in the sunlight. As her shivering testified, the water was still cooler than the air, but in a few more weeks its temperature would rise to that of a warm bath, and by October that temperature would recede slightly to a point where it equaled that of the air. To jump into that autumn sea was like falling into cotton. Only the texture of the surrounding physical environment changed.

She found a large towel and wrapped it around her. Sitting, she noted him frown as he stared southward. "What's the matter?" she asked.

"There's another boat out here," he answered, gesturing. "About two miles south of us. A sportfishing charter out of Bahia Los Angeles, most likely."

"So what?" She shrugged, inspecting some small cuts on her toes. "Why would they care about us?"

"If they spot us and identify our boat, they may radio the authorities."

She looked up from her toes, her expression quizzical. "Why would they recognize us?"

No point in minimizing our predicament, he decided. *She deserves to know what we're up against.*

He spoke to her in a level tone. "By now your friends are probably in custody and being questioned," he said. "If so, they've ID'ed both of us, and the authorities will have linked me to this boat. They'll know where I keep the boat, and they'll know more or less when we left last night. The Mexican military, the *federales*, the *policia* and whatever navy they have in the area all may be searching for us. Right now."

Her eyes widened. "What will happen to them?" she asked fearfully. "My friends, I mean".

He looked away, once again glassing the powerboat and noting with satisfaction that it appeared to be continuing on its southerly course. "Unless their parents are very rich, very well-connected or both, they're in real trouble," he answered without lowering the binoculars. "The authorities here don't take well to murder committed by a foreigner, especially when the victim is a federal officer. Even if your friends try to pin his killing on us, things could go badly for them."

"But they weren't guilty of anything!" she protested. "Those men *attacked* us! That so-called federal officer was going to *rape* Anna." She began to sob.

"First of all, Mexican law is different," he told her. "Unlike the States, you're guilty until proven innocent. Worse, it will be the word of foreigners against a Mexican official. And the Mexican courts are very unfriendly to foreigners if the case involves bodily harm or trafficking in drugs. This one involves both."

"But it was only *dope!*" Olivia shouted through her tears. "And they bought it to use themselves, not to sell!"

You are very naive, he thought. Clearly her friends' only hope lay in rapid access to money, and lots of it. That and publicity, especially for the girl. The local and regional authorities might hesitate to take their typical actions if the crime and her capture were publicized widely. Whatever the circumstances, however, he considered it unlikely that any of the three – including the girl – would survive to see a Mexican courtroom. The young men might well be dead already, with Anna still alive but wishing the same fate for herself. This opinion he kept to himself.

The girl continued to cry and slipped down the companionway. He could see her sitting below on the V-berth, her head in her hands. He turned back to track the course of the powerboat, and to his dismay it had changed. Even without binoculars it was easy enough to see the boat smoothly curving to port, and within seconds her bow was pointed north and headed directly towards them. The opposing swell would slow her a bit and make for a rough ride, but even then she could be around the island, through the gap and into the bay within 20 minutes. The boat's captain was likely to know the area well. He'd avoid the southern reef, now just beginning to poke its rocky head above the surface as the tide receded, and he'd know the passage and bay held a depth sufficient to float his vessel.

There was nothing to do but wait. Even with the slight head start they stood absolutely no chance of outrunning the boat, and, besides, to flee now would look suspicious and simply attract more attention. Better for them to stay put and play dumb, hoping these fishermen had heard nothing of the mainland killing and would take them for just another *gringo* couple cruising the Midriff. He called down to the girl, "Better put on some dry clothes," he said.

When there was no response, he swung himself down into the cabin, crouching because of his height. He saw Oliva lying on the berth, curled up in a fetal position. She sat up at his approach and used the backs of her hands to wipe away her tears. "I don't have anything else to wear," she told him. "I ripped my shorts on a metal thing when I jumped in the water." She pointed towards a cleat on the stern rail. "What difference does it make, anyway?" she asked.

He tossed her a bag stuffed with his clothes. "You can find something clean to wear in there," he told her. "That other boat is coming, and it's best we be ready for visitors."

She sat up and stared dully at the bag's contents. "They're all too big," she said numbly.

He pulled out a clean t-shirt and a pair of his running shorts. "Improvise," he told her. "Anything is better than that shirt." He paused. "And try to keep it together. Stay cool, do what I say, and you'll be wearing your own clothes again soon enough."

He left her and returned to the cockpit. As he'd guessed, the powerboat had approached the passage from the north, playing it safe and avoiding the temptation of the shorter route. She'd moved quickly despite the swell and even now was clearing the headlands to make the short run into the bay itself. He told himself to relax. There was nothing to be gained by appearing tense and distracted. Maybe they'd anchor off at distance and leave well enough alone. If they approached, perhaps his Spanish would help. Maybe the girl would provide some distraction.

Regardless, he needed to come up with a means for them to make their exit as soon as possible. If the man at the helm was like other Mexican boat captains, his radio would be tuned to a marine channel or a station that brought in border music. Either way, they would not long remain ignorant of the lurid news from the mainland, and the game would be up.

The problem, he thought, *is how do you explain why you're leaving a secure anchorage to sail a small boat straight into the face of a powerful headwind?*

Just inside the bay the northern arm of the island reflected upon itself, creating a doubly protected small bayou. It was there the powerboat anchored, and although she lay in water only 500 yards away, her captain's view of the sailboat was restricted due to that reflection. As she'd come into the bay he'd seen two men through his binoculars, both Mexican and standing on the flying bridge. Now, at intervals when the wind lessened, he could hear voices speaking and men calling to one another, but the words were indistinct .

An hour passed, and he'd begun to think they would be left to themselves. Just as he was debating whether to attempt a quiet departure under power, however, he saw a dinghy approaching from the fishing boat. She was a 12 foot hard shell that sat low in the water from the weight of her three occupants, all of whom were male and two of whom looked to be of some size. The *hombre* at the tiller of the outboard motored slowly to avoid swamping the boat. Even so, in a minute or less they would be alongside.

He reached into the drawer below his map table and drew out a pistol he'd hidden there two years prior in the unlikely event he'd ever need a weapon for protection. The *federal's* carbine he left in the storage locker for now. As he hadn't handled a gun in years, he quickly reviewed the pistol's workings. Fortunately it was straight-forward, a .38 caliber six-shot with a simple safety mechanism. Satisfied, he thumbed the safety to the on position and stuck the small revolver under a cushion that lay upon the starboard lazarette.

The intruding dinghy bumped slightly against their port hull. Looking over the side, he was greeted by three upturned faces, two white and the other clearly Mexican. The Mexican sat in the stern minding the outboard, a slender man with whipcord muscles, a *mestizo* of the type who said little but observed much. He would be the sportfisher's first mate, the task of ferrying the *gringos* too menial for a captain but the dinghy too valuable to entrust to a simple deckhand.

He saw that the dinghy was a Whaler, an older model but clearly well-maintained and powered by an equally well-kept forty horsepower Suzuki. Japanese-made outboards were popular in Mexico, being relatively cheap and generally dependable, with their parts generic and easily interchanged. From his quick inspection of the dinghy and the mate, he knew this was not one of the low budget charter operations that one so often encountered in this region of Baja. Competition being scarce, many times a charter enterprise involved nothing more than a Mexican fisherman, his brother-in-law and the *panga* they more commonly employed for their subsistence fishing. This mother ship would have powerful twin engines capable of pushing her at high speed and, more relevant to their circumstances, a good radio.

Uncertain as to the niceties of marine protocol, the *gringos* – obviously Americans – were smiling up at him expectantly. Their unsteady postures in the lightly bobbing Whaler proclaimed their nautical inexperience. In contrast, the mate sat easily at the stern, expertly tweaking the tiller, throttle and clutch now and again to keep his craft abreast of the other boat without colliding.

Although he appeared relaxed and indifferent, he could see the mate's lips moving silently as he sought to memorize the registration number affixed to *Celerity's* bow. *Shit,* he thought. *This is no hospitality call.* If aware of the murder on the mainland, the charter captain would send his mate to see whether this was the boat being sought. These two fat Americans were probably just stooges along for the ride, presumably ignorant of the captain's suspicions and intended to distract Will's attention from the true purpose of the visit. Thankfully, due to the intervening rocky berm their hull and its damning identification numbers lay out of the other ship's line of sight. Otherwise her captain simply would have glassed the sailboat and radioed back to Bahia Los Angeles. Perhaps he already had, and this was merely a small adventure, a diversion to entertain the customers while they waited out the storm and the arrival of the authorities.

This last thought made him grow suddenly cold with fear, and he struggled to maintain his composure. Realizing his silence had extended too long, he forced a smile and made ready to speak to the Americans. Before he did, however, he glanced quickly at the Mexican in the stern to confirm that neither he nor the Whaler itself carried any ship-to-ship radio.

"*Buenas dias y bienvenidos,*" he said to the nearer and more obese of the two *gringos.* "Good morning and welcome."

"*Gracias,*" replied the nearer of the Americans in atrociously bad Spanish. He looked to be about 60, and his bald scalp, already sun-reddened and peeling, was badly in need of a wide-brimmed hat. "Are you out for a sail?" the man asked.

He bit back a sarcastic reply and instead answered amiably. "Yep," he told the man. "We left San Felipe a week ago and are on our way to Cabo." Figuring these two for Californians, he'd named the two towns in Baja most likely to be familiar to them. "We got caught in this wind and decided to anchor here until it dies down a bit."

"So did we," the man answered, nodding his head vigorously. "Me and my buddy, Jerry," he gestured with his hand to indicate the other *gringo* in the boat, "we're from Fresno. We were staying at La Costa, got bored, and decided to do some deep sea fishing in Mexico."

La Costa was an expensive resort in North County, a short drive from San Diego. The clientele typically was made up of well-heeled Beautiful People, and he doubted this chubby duo from Fresno had fit in well.

The man chattered on enthusiastically. "We got the resort's shuttle to take us to the border, caught a cab to the airport in Tijuana and bought a ticket for the first flight that would take us to any place in Baja with fishing. We love to fish," he confided. "We wound up on some crappy little prop plane that bumped around forever and finally landed on a dirt strip covered with rocks. I didn't think we were going to make it. Thanks to this storm we've been stuck for three days in that shithole back there." He pointed in the general direction of Bahia Los Angeles. "We were going stir crazy," he complained. "Finally today we convinced the Mexicans to take us out, and now that sonofabitch captain refuses to go any further unless the weather improves."

His companion, Jerry, finally found his voice. "We want to catch a swordfish," he said plaintively. Jerry looked to be a generation younger than his friend, but aside from this they could be twins. Even their attire was similar; each wore a grimy white t-shirt bearing the logo "Born to Fish" stretched tightly over protruding belly, khaki shorts with a beltline riding far below the waist and cheap rubber flip flops. Jerry's were cherry red, and his friend's were bright yellow. Aside from this, they were a perfect match.

Swordfish, he thought disgustedly. These guys would be lucky to retrieve their own bait. Besides, the only big fish in these parts were sharks. Billfishing didn't really pick up until one moved down the coast a hundred miles. He glanced over at the Mexican. The man seemed to be ignoring their conversation, insouciantly resting his elbow on the rail and giving the tiller a small nudge now and again to maintain a six foot distance between the two boats.

Jerry's friend broke the lengthening silence. "How's about a cold *cerveza*?" he suggested brightly.

It was ten o'clock in the morning. *No wonder these guys are fat*, he thought. "*Lo siento*," Will answered, smiling. "*No tenemos cervezas frias. No tenemos hielo.*"

Jerry's friend shrugged his shoulders helplessly. "I don't speak much Mexican," he confessed.

No wonder the world despises us, he thought. "No cold beer, I'm afraid," he explained, smiling to conceal his tension. "We ran out of ice."

The man's face broke into a huge grin. "Don't worry about it," he said. "We've got lots of cold beer and tequila on the boat. Come on over with us."

This was the opening he'd been looking for. To prevent any incriminating message from being radioed out, he needed to get on that boat as quickly as possible, and this portly American was offering an admission ticket. Before he could respond, however, the Mexican in the stern suddenly spoke up. "*No es possible. Vamos a los pescados ahora. Los ventos estan se han calmado.*" It was not possible, he'd said. They were going for the fish now. The wind was down sufficiently.

The man obviously understands English, he thought. He also observed that the wind still blew strongly. Unchanged.

At that crucial moment events took a propitious turn. Olivia suddenly emerged from the cabin and stood before them in the cockpit as if on display. Somehow during the short time spent below she'd transformed herself from a sodden waif into a beguiling young woman. Her exotic white hair, now dry and brushed, softly framed her face, and she'd found some means of coloring her lips and touching up her eyes. She wore one of his t-shirts, black and somewhat oversized, but she'd knotted it in back so it fit snugly and rode well above her midriff. Instead of his running shorts she wore black panties that approximated a bikini bottom. The effect – the makeshift black tankini in startling contrast to her pale hair and skin – was clearly mesmerizing for the two Americans from Fresno currently disconnected from the prurient attractions of American culture.

"Well *hello*, young lady!" exclaimed the older man. "I bet you could use a cold *cerveza* and a couple of tequila shots. What do you say you, me and your tall friend all head over to our boat?"

Aware of effect she was making, Oliva smiled down at the men in the Whaler. She glanced at him sideways. Her glance and his answering nod were brief and imperceptible to the others.

"I'd love to," she gushed. "I'm *so* tired of lukewarm beer, and this boat's getting *way* too cramped." She turned towards their mother ship. "Is that your boat?" she asked the older man. "It looks so *big*!"

"For today that boat is mine, honey," he assured her. "So come on over, and it's 'welcome aboard'!"

"Sounds great," Olivia cooed in response, a hint of seductive promise in her voice and manner. She leaned her arms on the rail, and this new posture served to push her chest forward and more clearly define her young breasts. "What's your name?" she asked.

"I'm Frank," he replied happily. "And that's Jerry." The Mexican in the stern was ignored. "C'mon down and join us."

She immediately pivoted over the railing and began to clamber down the hull of the sailboat, her slender legs dangling briefly while her feet sought the deck. The two Americans in the boat watched her descend, transfixed.

The Mexican arose from his seat at the stern, and the silent reverie of his American clients was broken by his shout of protest. "*No! La muchacha no puede venire.*" The girl could not come on their boat. He stepped forward and made as if to push her back up into the sailboat.

Frank shoved the Mexican away from Olivia. Caught off guard and without a ready handhold, the mate lost his balance and fell hard to the deck, landing awkwardly between the thwarts. Before he could regain his feet Frank's face was inches from his own.

"Listen, you fuckin' spic," he snarled. "We're the ones paying the tab here, and we'll decide who comes on the goddamned boat and who doesn't." Jerry stood beside him nodding vigorously. Meanwhile the girl had dropped quietly to the bow and was adjusting her scanty apparel.

Watching the commotion from the *Celerity*'s cockpit, he'd taken the opportunity to slip the revolver into his waistband, checking to ensure that the butt was well-covered by his shirt-tail. He jumped down to the Whaler's deck in one graceful motion. "Let's go," he suggested cheerfully.

Frank and Jerry settled down contentedly with the girl nestled between them on the forward thwart. The Mexican remained on the deck amidship, just as he'd fallen. Will stepped over him and took the helm, admiring the Whaler's responsiveness.

As they approached the sportfisher, an old Bertram that gave every appearance of being as neat and tidy as the Whaler, he reduced speed momentarily and addressed the Mexican quietly in Spanish, commanding him to take the helm. The man glared but did as directed. Olivia was chattering animatedly to the two men as if she hadn't a care in the world, and Frank's thick arm was draped affectionately around her thin shoulders as he nodded and laughed heartily at something she'd said. The Bertram had swung on its anchor line to point northwest, and the Mexican expertly brought the dinghy up to its stern.

During their last seconds of approach he left the mate at the stern and made his way forward to the Whaler's bow, scrambling around the cheerful trio. In the calm leeward water the boat floated almost motionless, and he had no difficulty grasping the ladder that hung from the Bertram's transom and hoisting himself aboard. The ship's captain stood facing him in the cockpit, regarding him with obvious suspicion. Like his mate, he was a *mestizo*, squat and swarthy. He looked capable of taking care of himself in a fight.

The tall American lifted his shirttail with his left hand and snatched out the revolver with his right. Pointing its short barrel at the captain's mid-section, he addressed the man. *"Hay alguien mas en el barco?"* Were there other men on the boat?

"No," answered the captain, his eyes widening at the pistol's sudden emergence. *"Yo solamente."* They were alone.

Keeping his pistol pointed at the captain, he glanced quickly around him. The four occupants of the dinghy were slowly making their way up the ladder, the *gringos* having insisted that the girl precede them and elaborately assisting her in the effort. The mate stood impatiently behind them in the stern, obviously anxious to speak with his captain. From his vantage point he couldn't make out much of the cabin below or any of the flying bridge above. There could be more crew or passengers in either location. He knew there were helms on both bridges, each likely equipped with a radio.

He told the captain to sit on the port side of the live bait well, and keeping the well between them and his gun trained on the man, he made his way to the helm on the main deck. Beside the captain's chair and tucked neatly in a vertical wooden slot was a baseball bat that fishermen often used to deliver a *coup de gras* to the larger, more aggressive fish they landed.

Grasping the club, he smashed the instrument panel and the radio beside it, taking care to slice with a filet knife any wiring rendered visible by the destruction. Intermittently he looked up from his labors to confirm that the captain remained in his position of passivity, and during one such pause the man spoke to him. *"Gringo,"* he said in slow, heavily inflected English, *"Why la pistola?* Why you wreck my boat?"

He didn't bother to answer and instead looked beyond the captain at the girl and the two Ugly Americans, all scrambling at last over the transom. Where was the mate? The two *gringos* startled at the sight of the gun, and he spoke to them sharply. "Sit down by the captain. Now!"

When they failed to obey, he raised the pistol above his head and snapped off a shot. The gun's report set the nearby sea birds to flight and echoed briefly off the crumbling cliffs of Estanque. Despite his fear, he felt slightly ridiculous, like a bad actor in a straight-to-video action movie. As he watched the Americans scuttle to meet his command, he suddenly experienced another pang of regret that he'd not returned directly to his boat after leaving Guaymas the night prior.

He could see that Olivia had lost some of her previous élan, but he had no other choice. Beckoning, he bade her take the gun, and wild-eyed she plucked it from his outstretched hand as if it were a hissing snake. Trying to remain calm himself, he quickly explained the workings of the gun and directed her to keep the pistol trained upon the three men while he went above to take out the remaining radio. She nodded numbly, staring at the weapon in her hand. He doubted she could bring herself to pull its trigger, let alone shoot a man.

"Buck up," he said softly, smiling at her with a feigned air of confidence. "You don't have to shoot them. Just *act* like you would." He turned and quickly ascended the ladder to the flying bridge.

Using the bat and knife he'd carried with him, he again applied himself to the electronics and, for good measure, swung the bat so hard that it knocked off the wheel. As he moved towards the ladder, he heard two loud splashes, one quickly following the other, and observed from above the two porcine Americans paddling furiously away from the boat towards

Estanque's rocky beach. *Just as well*, he thought. But the captain and his mate were another matter.

He slid down the ladder and immediately saw the girl backed up against the bulkhead, the captain advancing towards her cautiously as she gripped the pistol with both hands violently shaking. In one fluid motion he body-slammed the captain, and the force of the collision carried the other man over and into the bait well. Regaining his feet, he could see the captain was at least temporarily indisposed, gasping for breath and bleeding profusely from an ugly looking scalp laceration.

He grabbed Olivia's left wrist, and as he swung her towards him she inadvertently brought the pistol to bear directly upon his chest. Without hesitating he released her wrist and slapped the pistol from her hand just at the instant the gun discharged, its bullet screaming harmlessly off to the northeast as if to duplicate in reverse *Celerity*'s course earlier that morning. They watched together as the handgun flew overboard, landing in the water with an irrevocable *kerplunk*.

Forget it, he told himself. Again grabbing her wrist, he dragged Olivia to the stern, over the transom and into the Whaler. Simultaneously he set the choke, pulled the starter rope and checked the fuel gauge on the red tank that lay in the engine compartment. *Good*, he thought. *More than half full.* That would help if the wind failed. The motor engaged, and he called to the girl to untie the bowline.

As she did and he was preparing to reverse the small boat, he felt himself struck suddenly in the left shoulder by a giant but invisible fist, its blow sufficiently powerful to lift him off his seat and propel him backwards. Grabbing for the starboard rail with his right hand, he barely avoided tumbling overboard.

As he struggled to regain his position at the stern, he looked up to see the mate standing at the transom of the larger ship. The Mexican held a shotgun, and its two barrels were pointed directly at him. Still stunned, he nevertheless managed to duck instinctively and at once heard the *swoosh* of a second round of buckshot passing inches above his lowered head.

Olivia had arisen from her seat in the bow, now gesticulating frantically and screaming. The mate unlimbered the gun and was busily pushing two fresh shells into the chambers. They had to get moving. Given the Mexican's vantage point immediately above them, there was no place in the Whaler where they could avoid being hit. He noticed that his left hand didn't seem to want to follow his commands, so he used his right to flip the clutch into reverse and turn the throttle to its maximum limit. The sudden acceleration threw the girl to the deck and into the boat's midsection, the same area previously occupied by the mate.

Twenty-five yards astern of the sportfisher he slowed the Whaler slightly, pushed the clutch to forward and returned to full throttle. The engine screamed in protest, but within seconds the prop had halted the momentum of their backwards slide and begun pushing the boat forward and towards the Bertram. He quickly turned the boat sharply to starboard. Even over the engine noise he could make out two more blasts from the shotgun, one following the other in rapid succession. As far as he could tell, no pellets had struck either of them, and at the speed they were traveling they would be well beyond the boat by the time the Mexican managed to reload.

He headed directly to *Celerity*. He briefly considered sticking with the Whaler to take advantage of its greater speed, but it would take time to transfer what they needed over from the sailboat, and he feared they would not have fuel sufficient to bring them to any safe landing along this coast.

When they reached the sailboat, he instructed the girl to climb aboard and then disengaged the Whaler's fuel tank from its outboard. With difficulty he used his one good arm to hoist the tank up to a point where the girl, reaching down, could maneuver it on board. He turned the Whaler about to face the island's rocky northern arm, pushed the clutch to forward and gave the engine full throttle, jumping quickly overboard and taking care to avoid the slashing prop's backwash. There was enough gas left in the engine to propel the unmanned Whaler the scant distance to shore, and at high speed the boat collided with a jumble of pockmarked volcanic boulders and lay suddenly silent amongst them.

Compelled still to rely upon his right arm only, he side-stroked the short distance back to the sailboat and climbed aboard. Hunched over in the stern and panting from his exertions, he forced himself to think. They had to move rapidly. Although the Bertram was immobilized and the Whaler permanently disabled, the Mexicans could swim or wade to the northern side of the narrow passage, the only exit from Estanque's little bay, and from there fire at least several rounds at short range as they attempted to pass through. The girl would be safe below, but even if he hunkered down in the cockpit at the tiller, it was likely the Mexicans' position high above on the rocks would provide an adequate line of fire.

He could aim the boat in the necessary direction and at the last moment join Olivia in the cabin, leaving the tiller unattended with the boat under power, but the currents in the passage were tricky even in the best weather. On a stormy day like today an unmanned helm well could result in collision with one rocky headland or the other. Disaster.

Deciding quickly, he directed the girl to move to the bow and hoist their anchor. Olivia seemed to have recovered since the fracas on the Bertram, and she responded at once. He started *Celerity's* outboard and directed the boat forward at maximum speed as soon as the girl had the anchor clear of the water. Once again the sudden acceleration caused her to lose her balance, and she fell backwards, her rear striking the deck with a resounding smack. The force of the impact caused her to drop the anchor line. The anchor dropped back into the bay, and its line began to pay out rapidly as the boat surged forward. Fearing she'd be too rattled to take rapid direction, he left the tiller unattended and rushed forward to unloosen the proximal end of the line from its cleat. The anchor was no great loss; he had a smaller Danforth stashed in a locker below, and if needs be they could splice together enough line to replace what now lay trailing in the water astern.

He returned to the tiller and approached the passage, intending to hug the southern shore and thus maintain as much distance as possible between the boat and the armed Mexicans on the opposite headland. It was the best he could manage, and the trick would lie in maintaining maximum distance from those who hunted them while at the same time preventing the strong northwesterly wind and swell from pushing their sailboat onto the reef.

They were well into the passage and making good headway when Will heard the unmistakable sound of a powerful boat engine behind them, its increasing volume an all too clear indication that the ship was closing rapidly. He looked in the direction of the sound and saw to his horror that it was the Bertram. Somehow the captain and his mate had contrived to repair the damage he'd done, and now they were in full pursuit. At a maximum speed of 6 knots under power, *Celerity* had no chance of outrunning the sportfisher, and to oppose the Mexican's shotgun he had only some fishing knives and his one good arm. He hadn't time to retrieve the carbine.

As yet unaware of the approaching boat, Olivia was looking southward towards the open sea. Following her gaze he could see that the tide was falling rapidly and running fast over the reef that lay 50 yards to port. The heads of the larger rocks were breaking the surface, and water coursed rapidly between them as if someone had unplugged a giant drain far to the south. The Bertram continued to close. Soon it would be within firing range, and within another minute or two the boat would be directly upon them.

Immediately as they cleared the headlands, they were struck by the full force of the northwesterly wind, which joined with the large swells to urge them southward towards the reef. Risking another thirty seconds, Will steered the boat a bit further to the west and then turned her abruptly turned to port, heading directly for the emerging rocks.

With the current running strong, their hull speed increased perceptibly, and at intervals the boat suddenly accelerated as she surfed down the larger swells. He looked ahead anxiously, searching for a gap where the rapidly receding tide still would leave them the depth they required to clear the reef. He made his commitment, and suddenly they were over the reef and beyond, into open sea. For once he blessed the boat's shoal keel and shallow draft. It made for poor sailing on a close reach, but no full-keeled boat could have passed over that barrier.

Immediately astern, the Bertram continued to streak forward at over 20 knots, and for a second or two it appeared the boat would overtake them. Then there came the terrible grating sound of fiberglass being ripped and shredded by jagged, unyielding rock, and the sportfisher came to an abrupt halt. He circled slowly around to the northwest, carefully maintaining a safe distance between their sailboat and the wrecked Bertram, and they could see the sportfisher settling in the shallow water as the sea poured in a large hole punched through the port hull. Of the Mexicans there was no sign.

Although he shifted the boat to a more easterly course to take them yet further from the island, he was confident they'd escaped. Even if the Mexicans were alive and intact, by the time they ran and climbed to the eastern aspect of Estanque, the sailboat would be far beyond the shotgun's range. The Americans were inconsequential; they'd jumped ship weaponless and at most could serve as passive spectators. For the moment, at least, they were safe.

Chapter 9

ARIZONA

*H*_{ow} *much life has changed*, he thought, *since she first appeared on my doorstep.*

He'd had been attracted to many women over the years, but never had he been so blind-sided by pure animal desire. Every move, every gesture, every remark-all served only to fuel his attraction. When in her presence, he often he felt awkward and uncharacteristically tentative. *Get a grip!* he'd command himself. He was horrified by his lack of control. Estranged or not, this was his best friend's wife, for god's sake, and yet the gravitational pull she exerted irresistibly drew him ever further into a morass of deceit and betrayal.

After her arrival in Tucson Maria had lived for a few weeks with some artists who inhabited a crumbling old compound of small adobe houses at the eastern foot of the Tucson Mountains, not far from Gates Pass. Several weeks after their evening at *El Bandito,* however, she'd moved to an *estancia* on the outskirts of Nogales, a magnificent estate owned by Eddie Andrade, the scion of an old Tucson family.

This arrangement Will found peculiar. Eddie was flamboy-antly gay, and he and his longterm lover, Douglas, had spent years building *una casa grande,* a masterpiece of colonial era architecture whose heavily stuccoed walls, hand-hewn oak plank floors and deeply recessed windows mimicked perfectly the pre-revolutionary *haciendas* of the Spanish *dons* who believed they had conquered Mexico…only in the end to succumb to the country's infinite capacity for assimilation.

To adorn their creation the two men traveled throughout Mexico and the lower Americas, collecting artifacts. The heavy wooden doors that permitted entrance to their courtyard once had graced a long-abandoned church in Vera Cruz. For over a century the bronze bell above the doors had summoned workers to their meals at a *rancho* near Oaxaca. The kitchen's hand-painted Guatemalan tiles were rescued from a home in Antigua over two hundred years old and now scheduled for demolition.

The house was exquisite, inside and out. Approaching it from the long driveway shaded by tall cottonwoods, one was greeted by a pair of enormous Russian wolfhounds who sat regally on each side of the exterior entrance to the courtyard. The arched wooden doors between the dogs were 14 inches thick and stood 18 feet at their apex, with heavy cast iron rings serving as handles. In the courtyard water trickled with a pleasantly tinkling sound from the successive tiers of an enormous hand-carved stone fountain that once had served as a centerpiece for the *plaza* of a small town far to the south in Baja.

Entering the house itself, one walked through rooms whose walls were painted in the deep, rich tones of Mexico. Each chair, table, couch and bench was calculatingly primitive. In every aspect the house and furnishings resounded of good taste.

It was unclear to Will how Maria had come to move there in the first place, and no more discernible was Eddie's reason for allowing her to remain. Was she simply another adornment, akin to the *regalos y milagros* that hung in the hallways or the life-sized wooden *santo* that stood by the front door, eyes cast forever upward in supplication?

"Why Eddie's?" he'd asked at the onset.

"What do you want me to do?" she'd responded. "Live with you in that little cubicle you rent from my husband? Screw you while he sleeps down the hall?" She laughed at his expression and shook her head. "No, *mi amante*, I don't think so," she said. "Our arrangement would hardly permit it. Here I'm rid of the dust and craziness of that hippie-infested compound, and you can come and go as you wish."

'Come and go as you wish', he'd thought later. *What did that mean, exactly? What is it she wants from our arrangement? More go and less come, perhaps?*

It seemed to Will that Maria was drawing away from him, and as he grew increasingly frustrated and quick to rise, she was increasingly evasive. Finally he'd asked her pointblank. They'd been fighting.

"Maria, what is it with you? Do you want to end it with me?" he'd demanded. "A simple yes or no will do".

She'd stared straight ahead before responding, expressionless and eyes half-lidded. Turning on the front seat of his truck to face him, her face remained impassive. "There's nothing quite so complicated as 'a simple yes or no'," she'd answered.

———

To reach Eddie's home one could exit I-10 at its southern terminus and drive three miles westward on the border road, but the *estancia* also was accessible via the scenic but slower two-lane that led from Arivaca past Peña Blanca, winding its way up, over and down the hills that separated Mexico from *los estados unidos*. During daylight hours Will preferred the latter route, but it was 2 a.m., and he simply wanted to cover the distance back to Tucson as rapidly as possible. Now he was speeding past the exit to Rio Rico, a "planned community" whose future seemed perpetually uncertain as one optimistic developer after another picked up the reins from his bankrupted predecessor.

Will was in a foul mood. Yet again his evening with Maria had not gone well, starting badly and ending no better. All they seemed to do now was argue. Her position within the *estancia* remained disturbingly ambiguous, as did her motivation for remaining there. At times, enthroned next to Eddie on the horse-hide sofa in the great room, laughing and drinking from her glass of wine, Maria seemed the *doña* of the estate. Had he not known Eddie to be devoutly gay, Will would have assumed from their easy intimacy that they undoubtedly were lovers.

She spoke of her "work" as if she was painting every waking moment, but nowhere could he see evidence of any such effort. Her conversations with Eddie and his ever-evolving entourage were laced with references to Rivera, Kahlo and a host of more obscure Mexican artists unknown to Will. Those present casually would mention this or that exotic adventure that the group – presumably including Maria – had undertaken since he'd last visited. Will felt decidedly left out.

He accelerated to pass a Crown Vic with Missouri tags that was poking along the otherwise deserted interstate at a safe and sane 45 miles per. As he passed the car he caught an eerie glimpse of two elderly forms sitting rigidly upright in the front seat, hyperextended and immobile. Were they dead, sleeping or suffering the final stages of variant parkinsonism? Regardless, he decided it best to put some distance between them and himself, and for the next few miles he pushed his old truck along at its maximum speed.

Will was beginning to fear that Maria was not the person he'd believed her to be. That their relationship had run its course. That she was moving on, and that he'd be wise to do the same.

And yet. He remembered how they'd fallen into bed together at the old adobe *casita* where she'd lived before moving to Eddie's, too hot with desire to bother removing their clothes or to sweep the ever-present dust from her sheets. He recalled as well a hike they'd recently taken along the cool waters of Arivaipa Creek, Maria uncharacteristically girlish with excitement from her first exposure to the little canyon's unique beauty. It was a hot day, and they'd gone swimming in one of the deeper pools, lying together afterwards on a great, smooth boulder as the sun dried their naked bodies. Later that evening she'd cooked for him, *tacos de carne seca*, in Eddie's huge kitchen, and afterwards they'd made love for hours in her canopied bed.

When at last they'd finished and she lay naked in his arms, his momentary euphoria compelled him to declare, "God, I feel such...*love* for you."

Her reaction was unexpected. She sat upright in her bed, her back supported by a wall of pillows and her expression utterly solemn. "Don't kid yourself, Will," she'd advised him gravely. "Just like everything else, love has a price."

The next morning Maria was silent and morose. When he asked her what was wrong, she'd offered no response. She was brushing her hair before a mirror when he told her he was leaving, and without pausing at her task or turning from her reflection she said, simply, "Goodbye."

The short history of their relationship was punctuated with these and many other episodes of shared passion and simple pleasures alternating with periods wherein Maria abruptly would become inexplicably distant and even hostile. That she could behave towards him with such striking inconsistency - tenderness and generosity alternating with a chilling aloofness – he'd found oddly compelling. At first.

Will could take little pleasure in the happier of his memories now. His perennial optimism had vanished, seemingly for good. That first night in the pool he'd felt himself awash in sensuality. He'd imagined their bodies conjoined, fused together as one organism devoted solely to the most intimate of pleasures two separate beings can share. *After this*, he'd thought, *anything less would be travesty*.

What had followed, however, was a slow descent into just such travesty, a fitful erosion punctuated by occasional encounters that would faintly echo their first night together. For those all-too-few episodes of rekindled passion she typically seemed to require dope as a catalyst. Unable to contain his growing apprehension, Will finally had questioned her about this. She'd replied offhandedly, "I need it to relax."

Now, as on this evening, he'd often leave Eddie's well before sunrise, unfulfilled and bitter with frustration, to drive the empty interstate back to Tucson. He found her behavior unfathomable. She was a riddle wrapped in an enigma, and in his gloomiest and most dispassionate moments of self-examination Will wondered whether it was this very elusiveness that attracted him to her. Now as he felt her receding from him, his fear that she would ultimately forsake him altogether grew in proportion to her mounting indifference.

She'd told him earlier in the week that once when he'd recently called she ignored his message on the phone's answering machine. "I was getting ready to go out with my friends," she explained, "and I knew you'd just harass me because I wanted to be with them rather than wait around for you. I didn't want to hear it."

Angry, he'd asked her what she'd done. "Oh," she replied breezily. "We went dancing at *Dos Pescados*. Eddie, Monica, me, some others." *Dos Pescados* was a discotheque in South Nogales that catered to wealthy Mexican twenty-somethings and a smattering of *gringo* students from Tucson. "We got so trashed we just rented rooms and stayed there," she continued.

Who exactly were these "others"? he wondered. *Who slept where and with whom? More important, why are you telling me this in the first place?* Will literally bit his tongue to avoid questioning her any further.

He'd thought then that he should walk away and spare himself any more of the hurtful words that she launched so carelessly from her provocative lips. Was it believable that her night at the club involved nothing more than an innocent outing with friends? Even if so, what did her avoidance of his call imply regarding their relationship? And even if she had chosen to take his call, would it really have been so unreasonable for him to voice irritation at the prospect of being left behind while she caroused with other men?

And yet, despite his frustration, her indifference and the strained ambiguity that now lay between them, he kept returning. From what source arose this unwelcome masochism? She was, after all, Michael's wife, no matter how frail their marital bonds, and Michael was his best friend. He had pleasured himself with his best friend's wife while that friend slumbered, unaware, in a hospital call room, and he sought to bed her still. Facts were facts. He'd betrayed his friend, and there was no excusing that violation of trust. A Judas now denied his shiny reward.

Chapter 10

MEXICO

Separating mainland Mexico from Baja California, the Sea of Cortez is seven hundred miles long and up to almost two miles in depth. So abrupt and steep is the drop-off in the south that the deep water fish - marlin, tuna, sailfish, wahoo - will pass well within a mile of the Baja shoreline. Most of the few islands in the south are located just offshore. In the north is the Sea's narrowest portion, *La Centura* ("the belt"), the Midriff to *los yanquis*.

At the Midriff a chain of small islands - barren, desiccated mounds of sand and crumbling volcanic rock - extend like stepping-stones to link the mainland with Baja. Estanque is one of the islands in this chain. For centuries the Seri Indians had used *las islas de La Centura* to paddle from their villages on the mainland north of Kino to the eastern coast of Baja, stopping at the islands to rest and collect bird eggs. They are, quite literally, *desert* islands, as rainfall is scarce to non-existent, and only one, Isla Tiburon ("shark island") is known to harbor a freshwater spring.

So remote was their home on the Midriff's mainland coat that the Seri were the last native Americans to be "discovered" by the whites. Not until the Dinwiddie expedition in 1894 was the apprehensive visage of a Seri, one Juan Chavez, finally captured by the white man's camera, and members of the expedition described the tribe as "the most primitive ever found on the West Hemisphere". Even now the Seri remain isolated, receiving few visitors to their hot, arid reservation. Occasionally they venture into Kino to hawk their wares - ironwood carvings and beautifully woven baskets - to the smattering of tourists who visit the town.

The shores washed by the sea are sparsely settled. While fishermen may set up temporary camps from time to time, no humans inhabit the Midriff islands on a permanent basis. North of L.A. Bay the Baja coast is largely wild and unsettled almost all the way to San Felipe - a distance of over 500 kilometers - and accessible only by boat or a single and very bad road that hugs the coastline. There are some small cities south of the Bay - Mulege, Loreto - but for the most part the coast is empty of what passes for meaningful human development until one begins to approach La Paz, far to the south.

The mainland side is not much different; north (*far* north) of Kino and Seriland the only permanent human settlement is a small town, Rocky Point, which attracts tourists from Tucson and Yuma who will abide the area's extreme tides in return for the advantage of proximity to their home cities. South of Kino is San Carlos, and south of San Carlos the coast is more settled: Guaymas and, eventually, Los Mochis are actual cities with train service to points within the interior.

Returning to San Carlos is out, he thought. *Where else to go?* Letting his mind roam up and down the coasts that bordered the sea, he recalled Kino Bay and Peter, its sole inhabitant of his acquaintance.

Decades ago, Peter, a native of Minnesota grown weary of the interminable winters characteristic of his homeland, had quit his job as a machinist, sold his lakeside home and all its furnishings, packed up a few necessities in his rebuilt camper, and with his wife, Bridget, set off southward in search of a warmer clime. For two years they wandered throughout Mexico, Guatemala and Costa Rica, seeking a safe, affordable and congenial place to make their new home. Friends back in Minnesota had recommended San Miguel, but that picturesque old colonial town already had been discovered; grown thick with American expatriates, it was far too expensive. While their nest egg was not small, Peter and Bridget were of long-lived stock, and the money they had – and what little they might add to it – need be conserved.

One by one they considered and discarded the options available, until at one point Bridget even suggested that they turn back north and explore what opportunities might exist on the humid coastlines of Mississippi, Alabama and the Florida panhandle. They persevered, however, and finally one day – after driving many hot and tedious miles through the interior of Sonora – they entered the tiny and obscure fishing village of Bahia Kino. In Kino Bay they found all they'd been searching for: cheap housing, a climate dry and warm, and an expatriate-free community of relaxed, friendly Mexican families who lived simply on the shores of the beautiful, fecund bay. It was - and remained - a well-kept secret, and the town had changed little in the eighteen years they'd lived there.

He and his sailing companion had first met the elderly couple four years prior. Having learned that the town boasted one of the few boat ramps to be found in the Midriff region, they'd pulled their sailboat on its trailer from Tucson to Kino Bay. Enduring a succession of flat tires and unpleasant encounters with Sonoran *policia* over the tedious seven hour drive, they arrived to find that the town's "ramp" was nothing more than a small, deeply scoured concrete slab. It was suitable for launching nothing more than *pangas*, the skiffs used by the local fishermen which, unloaded, drew no more than eighteen inches of water. Even with its shoal keel, their sailboat would never clear the shallow water at the ramp's foot. Discouraged, they bought some bottles of *cerveza fría* at the small *tienda* adjoining the ramp and stretched out in the cockpit of their landlocked craft, drinking and discussing their limited options.

To their good fortune, Peter picked that afternoon to stroll over to the *tienda* to replenish his own supply of *cerveza*. Overhearing the two young men speaking in English, he stopped to exchange pleasantries and share a beer. That one beer extended to several, and they wound up continuing their conversation over a dinner of fish tacos and *frijoles negros* served up by Bridget. The two young men learned much from Peter that evening, including the fact that there existed just north of town a crude but serviceable stone and gravel ramp that might accommodate their boat.

And so it did, albeit with much heart-stopping exertion, and on every trip to the region thereafter the two young men made a point of visiting Peter and Bridget, rewarding their inevitable hospitality by bringing them some small extravagance from the States or treating them to dinner at *El Pulpo Loco*.

He'd been stuck to the tiller now for over six hours, and his thoughts were straying far afield. Hungry despite the amphetamines, he found himself recalling with amusement

Peter's devotion to the dilapidated *restaurante* in "New" Kino, that section of town lying south of the intersection with the highway that led eventually to Hermosillo.

Peter had a special fondness for *El Pulpo Loco*, admiring its rustic charm and the ownership's apparent indifference to commercial success. With few exceptions they were the establishment's only patrons, and the staff would appear flustered but nonetheless pleased by their appearance. Dinner was an elaborately casual affair that would consume most of an evening. Any request for a drink more complicated than *una cerveza* or tequila tended to elicit a prolonged, hushed conversation amongst those on hand – waiter, bartender, cook, owner – and, eventually, a polite invitation for the person requesting the drink to help himself to the bar and its contents.

This worked out well for all parties involved, eliminating as it did the need for any extra effort on the part of the staff or any delayed gratification for the patrons. By the time the food arrived, everyone on hand – patrons and staff alike – usually were gathered at the bar, enjoying pitchers of whatever complicated and highly alcoholic concoctions Peter was inspired to create.

As for the food, the restaurant lived up to its name and tended to serve virtually nothing but octopus caught locally by the fishermen, sold by them to the restaurant and served up *al mojo de ajo* – sautéed in butter and garlic. Occasionally the cook would branch out and substitute ray for octopus, the ray's meat punched out with a cookie cutter to produce circular pieces resembling scallops in their shape and texture. These, too, were prepared *al mojo de ajo* . . . as were trigger fish (with a sweetness reminiscent of lobster), *cabrilla* (sea bass), *camarones* (shrimp), *calamar* (squid) or any other items plucked from the fishermen's nets to appear on the restaurant's single chalkboard menu.

Peter was a good man, he thought. Reliable. And he had a plane: an old Cessna single engine that he flew every few months to Tucson to load up on supplies not available at the local *tienda*. In the manner of many refugees from the American Midwest who had avoided alcoholism, the occupational hazard of expatriate life in coastal Mexico, Peter listened more than he talked. If asked to assist in a desperate and illegal undertaking, he'd make his decision quickly and afterwards keep the matter to himself. If he consented to help, he'd act competently and without delay.

His mind made up, he swung the boat about and pointed her to the northeast. They would run a close reach in the direction of Los Mochis, he decided, then tack towards the west and once off Las Animas turn to make the final run to Bahia Kino. Immediately as he set the boat on her new course, the advancing swells began to knock as if in protest against the port bow. The wind noise increased significantly, and on the close reach in a heavy breeze the boat heeled at least twenty degrees over to starboard. Unsecured items in the cockpit began to slide, and from below, where Olivia presumably was sleeping, he could hear the rattle of metal cups and plates falling to the cabin sole.

After a few seconds she appeared in the companionway and, squinting in the bright sunshine, sleepily asked, "Are we changing direction?" Moving to join him on the stern, she added, "I was sleeping."

She sat beside him on his unwounded side. As it heeled, the boat's angle caused the girl to press closely against him, and after a few minutes of this she slid down and curled up with her back braced against the transom for support. After a few minutes he heard her ask softly, her words barely perceptible above the wind, "How is your arm?"

"There's not much bleeding," he answered. "And I don't have any pain." He didn't bother to add that the latter was a relative thing, that without the drugs he might well be screaming.

"Why are we headed north again?" she asked.

He was impressed that she could identify their course. In the open sea, without landmarks, one had only a compass, the sun and the wind for direction, and thus far she'd seemed ignorant of even the most basic elements regarding a sailboat and its handling. "We're going to try to make it to a little town on the coast north of San Carlos," he answered.

Hearing that name, Olivia raised her head and looked at him with concern. "Why would we go back there?" she asked him. "Won't they be looking for us?"

He tried to decide how much to tell her. "Soon they'll be looking for us everywhere," he said, "if they aren't already. Those guys we left behind will identify us as having been at Estanque, and no one will expect us to reverse course and head back the way we came. Especially with the wind as it is."

As if to punctuate the last, the wind rose yet higher and tipped the deck a few more degrees to starboard.

———

They sailed along in their respective positions for another two hours, Olivia appearing to sleep while he fought to keep the boat on the highest point she'd take. Intermittently he'd glass the horizon, but all around them he could see nothing but empty sea and an occasional seabird skimming low over the swells. At last the girl arose stiffly and went below, leaving him alone at the tiller. He could hear her rustling about for a short while, and then there was silence.

Chapter 11

ARIZONA

It was with a measure of hope that slowly had faded to simple apprehension that Will drove down the I-19. He'd decided to surprise Maria by visiting her unannounced and bearing as a gift an assortment of candles he'd picked up at the Blue Willow. Slowing to take the exit to Pena Blanca, he recalled Maria's distaste for surprises in any form, and not for the first time he considered aborting his mission. *No,* he decided, *I've come this far. Might as well see it through.*

When he entered the house, Maria was reclining on a sofa in the great room, a wine glass in her hand and her bare feet propped on a heavy wooden coffee table. Eddie was standing before her, holding a bottle of wine, and as he turned to welcome Will, a young man entered the room and settled himself closely beside Maria. The man on the couch ignored Will, and Maria herself had offered no more than a noncommital glance. No smile. No word of greeting.

Will felt his entire body immediately suffused with scalding heat. *What the fuck?* he thought. *What is this?*

Eddie thrust a glass of wine in his hand, and Will stood wordlessly until Maria at last looked up at him. "I thought you'd decided to stay in Tucson tonight," she said. Her eyes were shining, but her voice and manner were neutral.

It was an effort to respond. "I changed my mind," he replied. "Maybe I should have called ahead." He nodded, indicating the man beside her. He looked to be in his mid to late twenties. Blonde and blue-eyed, lean and sculpted. Something foreign to his look. *Swedish?* he wondered. The young man remained utterly indifferent to his intrusion.

When Maria ignored his comment, Eddie rushed in to fill the gap. "Oh now, Will," he enthused. "Don't be a pill. You know Maria absolutely adores you." To this also Maria made no response. And in fact, Will was far from sure that whatever feelings she might hold for him could be said to include adoration. Certainly she herself was not endorsing that particular sentiment.

For almost an hour they all sat together, Maria maintaining her position beside the young man while Will and Eddie faced them from separate chairs. The stranger was German, a dancer on loan to the Tucson Met from his home company in Stuttgart. Eddie, with his well-honed talent for recruiting attractive young males to his entourage, had met him at a party held in his restaurant and by the evening's end had invitedthe handsome dancer to stay at his *hacienda* for the weekend. He was a physically impressive specimen but as vacuous as a guppie. At intervals he was given to draping an arm across Maria's shoulders, and each time he did so Will had to restrain himself from lunging to the attack.

They opened several bottles of Eddie's fine red wine, and desiring whatever anesthetic value it might offer, Will drank too much. Despite their host's efforts, conversation lagged. The

German was hopeless, Maria seemed disinterested and Will, still dumbstruck and despondent, found himself sinking into a sullen stupor from the alcohol.

Shortly after Eddie returned from retrieving yet another bottle, Maria arose from the sofa and announced that she was weary and going to bed. She left the room, and in the silence that followed Will unsteadily arose and followed her down the long hall to her bedroom. Her door was open, but he hesitated before entering. He felt unsteady, and it was not just the wine or the peculiarities of the evening. Consequent this affair, he'd lost his equilibrium, emotional and physical. Like a heretofore confident skier undone by the challenge of a forbiddingly difficult run, he'd lost his intrinsic rhythm.

He opened the door and walked into the dimly lit bedroom. At her bedside candles flickered in the darkness, and he could see her easily enough. Lying supine upon the sheets, eyes open, still fully clothed. She reached up, and grasping his wrist she drew him down beside her. When he attempted to speak, she silenced him with her mouth and tongue. Soon all else seemed inconsequential.

———

Afterwards he asked her about the German, and at first she was airily dismissive in response. *Mi amigo nino*, she called him. Her "little friend". Of what consequence was this to him? she'd asked.

"Are you screwing him, Maria?" he demanded. "Because if you are, that would be 'of consequence' to me."

"For Christ's sake, Will," she exclaimed, "he's *gay!*"

"That's not what I asked you," he persisted. "Did you *screw* him?"

She sighed, her exasperation obvious. "So what if I did," she answered flatly. "Suppose I just happened to feel like it, he was handy, and I did. What business is that of yours?"

He'd known it was pointless to question her, just as always it was pointless to seek any confirmation that she cared for him as he did for her. No comfort nor reassurance resulted; such talk simply annoyed her. Generally he'd been successful in concealing his anxieties and projecting an attitude of careless indifference, an insouciance that matched her own. His lapses had occurred most often in the immediate aftermath of their lovemaking, when he was most at ease, tender in his feelings for her and thus vulnerable.

Now was such a time, and her words provoked in him an instantaneous and irresistible surge of anger that demolished his carefully constructed breakwater of restraint. "What is *wrong* with you!" he'd shouted. "What *is* it with you, anyway? Why would any sane man waste *time* on you?"

He paused, trying to collect himself. He could feel himself trembling with rage and frustration. And there she sat. Just *sat*. Breasts unconcealed, the rumpled sheets drawn up to her waist, her hair - still tousled from their sex - streaming down around her lovely, unconcerned face. Her eyes gazed upon his calmly, like a mother who patiently awaits the passing of her child's tantrum.

"You're *broken*, Maria," he declared accusingly. "Broken, or maybe you just never developed. Maybe it's just the way you are. Empty. Either way, there's no loving you. You can't begin to reciprocate."

Her gaze turned cold. "Maybe it's *you*, Will," she retorted, her voice low and dangerous. "If I'm so broken, why are you here? What keeps you coming back?"

He couldn't answer. He felt at war with himself. Lust, revulsion, self-loathing, fear: all were churning within, and no one emotion was ascendant.

"Yes," she said, nodding as if in agreement with her own words. "Perhaps it's you who is 'broken'. Perhaps you fear the loss of that which is not yours to lose. Perhaps you should consider that people are not possessions, toys to be enjoyed and then returned to their place on your shelf. Or beside you in your bed."

With that she tossed to the floor the sweater and jeans that earlier she'd shed for him and drew up the bedcovers. Watching her body disappear under the sheets, he felt a sudden, irrational sense of loss flood over him

She turned on her side to face him and spoke again. "Before damning me for my choices, *compadre*, take a moment to recall those which *you* have made. Who's been fucking his best friend's wife? Before you pity yourself, consider what it is you've done to him." She paused to toss a cascade of hair over her shoulder and reflexively used her hand to clear from her forehead the strands remaining, a gesture now so familiar to him.

"And don't think he doesn't know," she advised him coldly. "He's a hell of a lot smarter than you, Will. He knew about us even before I told him."

"You *told* him?" Will asked, incredulous. "Why would you tell him?"

Her gaze was direct and her expression enigmatic. A slight smile played about her lips. "To hurt him, of course." she said.

Reclining on the bed, the sheet slipping down to expose her breasts, Maria directed her gaze to the saguaro-ribbed ceiling above.

"I required an instrument," she continued. "And of the options available, I decided on you." She turned her head slightly to face him once again. "Happily for me, you've served quite nicely."

"Just what the fuck do you mean?" he demanded.

As if suddenly grown modest, Maria gathered the top sheet about her and shifted on the bed to sit facing him, now reclining against the huge bedroom's exterior wall. "Michael is very bitter," she answered. "He blames me for everything that went wrong in our marriage. He needs to believe it was all *my* fault, and he's tried to convince himself that he loves me no more." Again she presented him her enigmatic smile. "I know better."

As if now finished with him and ready for sleep, she lay back on the bed as before, yawned, and closed her eyes. "Yes, Will, he *knows*," she murmured, "and he is hurt. Over time his wound may fester until it ruins him. I hope so."

With that she turned away from him to lie on her side, drawing the sheet higher and yet more tightly about her until nothing of Maria was visible save for the vague outline of her body and the mahogany-hued hair that spilled out like a stain upon the gleaming whiteness.

There was nothing more to say. He exited the quiet house, climbed into his truck and began to drive northward back to the city. His shift at the hospital began in two hours, and unless traffic was heavy on the southside he'd arrive with time to spare.

Chapter 12

MEXICO

When you get right down to it, he thought, *with serious injuries there's only so much you can do without an emergency department, operating room or intensive care unit.* Specifically, suture material, splints, dressings, epinephrine and an assortment of pain meds will get a person through 99% of whatever treatable mishaps reasonably can be expected to occur while sailing from one point to another. Throw in some antibiotics, a scalpel, forceps, some IV line and a few bags of normal saline (the better to drive home those pain medications). A little common sense doesn't hurt. Thus supplied, in their time he and his sailing friend had weathered successfully an anaphylactic reaction to Portuguese man-o'-war venom, fractured ribs complicated by a small pneumothorax, a third degree burn and numerous lacerations of varying degrees of severity.

This time, however, matters looked pretty bleak. When he could bring himself to inspect the weeping crater that led directly to his right armpit, it was difficult not to give in to defeatism and self-pity. Stained fragments of t-shirt drooped from his wound like the tattered banners of a badly defeated army. Despite the pervasive dryness of the climate, he could feel the wound swell and drip, and his pain increasingly took on the throbbing quality that portends local infection and eventual sepsis. Thus far any associated odor was neutral, but even the dry night air would not conceal the foul transformation likely to come. His mind remained clear, but this, too, would change if the bacterial toxins worked their evil within the blood that fed his brain. He had seen the progression often enough: confusion, delirium, stupor and, finally, coma. The slow fade.

What to do, what to do? This wound badly needed debridement, but his left hand was virtually useless, and with the heavy swell the tiller required the full attention of his right. He considered calling on the girl, who was below and presumably still sleeping off the shock of the day's events, but he felt he could trust her neither with the boat nor the surgical task required.

Finally he decided upon a plan, and he allowed himself another five minutes to rest before beginning the required sequence of small, painful steps. It wasn't much of a plan, but he was at a loss to come up with anything better, and the odds were reasonably good that its successful completion would enable him to survive and hopefully maintain some control over their fate.

He reviewed what was to be done. First he would swallow two 10 mg tabs of dextroamphetamine and wash them down with a warm Coke. As his sympathetic nervous system kicked into higher gear, he would reduce sail by reefing in the main, leave the jib in place for stability and select the least challenging course available to them, even if it meant adding an hour or more to their sailing time to Bahia Kino. Once the boat was as stable as possible, he would use a butterfly to start an IV in the cephalic vein of his left arm; although an angiocath would be more secure and less likely to infiltrate, he doubted his ability to thread even that large vein with one hand and an unpredictably shifting boat.

Although he was reasonably sure that his oral hydration had been sufficient to make up for his blood loss plus the usual fluid requirements, he would run in a liter or two of normal saline just to be sure. To the saline he would add pen G and hope that whatever bacterial invaders had established a beachhead would prove sensitive to this old antimicrobial mainstay. He'd follow the antibiotic with a hefty chaser of intravenous Demerol. Then with any luck he could complete the debridement during the narrow interval between mild euphoria and fumbled-fingered narcosis.

He knocked back the amphetamines and took advantage of the ensuing rush to briskly assemble the other drugs and the equipment he'd need. Although the speed provided a friendly, persuasive push, his arm still hurt like a son-of-a-bitch, and the required movements caused blood once again to ooze from the wound. He dabbed a few of the more prolific bleeders with a crayon of potassium permanganate, gritted his teeth and repeatedly reminded himself that the bliss of the intravenous opiate lay just around the corner.

All finally was in place. He peered ahead into the impenetrable darkness, lit only by the phosphorescent swells breaking to port. He freed the boat from its close reach and allowed her to find her own path in the confused sea. There wasn't much to choose from; the heavy winds had disturbed the normal currents and wave patterns, and no matter the direction taken, their small boat bucked in protest and failed to settle.

Keeping one eye cocked towards his medical gear lined up on the lazarrette cover, he made his way forward in the pitching cockpit and took in a fair portion of the main. The boat still sailed too fast and without the desired stability, but he hadn't the time nor physical resources to replace the genoa with the storm jib. As he reefed in, the sails luffed, flapping wildly in the wind, and the boom swung side-to-side, alternately straining at each of its sheets and snapping the vang.

Exhausted with his efforts and unnerved by the sudden pandemonium that bespoke an unattended rudder, he staggered back to his accustomed seat by the transom and drew the tiller towards him. The sails quieted, the boat settled and all was relatively stable. A wave of nausea failed to pass spontaneously, and he retched over the taff-rail, miserable in his pain and weakness.

Recovering, he managed with his right hand to tie the latex tourniquet tightly about his left upper arm, and he tried to clench his crippled fist a few times to help raise the vein. Even with only one hand, he was able to slip the large-bore #18 butterfly into the vessel without much difficulty. Blood ran from the open port as he struggled to release the tourniquet, and in his rush to plug in the IV line he leaned forward too far, allowing the tiller to escape its position clamped between his left upper arm and chest. At that same instant the crest of a large swell to port collided with the boat's hull. The cockpit shook violently, the boat thrashing about like a rat in the jaws of a terrier. His carefully assembled medical kit flew in all directions, and some items he could hear strike the rail as they flew overboard, irretrievable.

He re-secured the tiller and brought the boat back to its previous course. The bag of normal saline and attached IV line blessedly lay at his feet, and without difficulty he plugged the free end of the line into the butterfly's port and thumbed the plastic clamp to the fully open position. He saw fluid pouring from the bag into the line and knew from the volume of flow that his IV had remained patent during the momentary chaos produced by the collapsing wave.

Now for the drugs, but he could see no vials or syringes within the dim circle of visibility surrounding him. He managed to locate a flashlight duct-taped to the wall of the stern anchor locker and, to his immense relief it produced a strong beam of light when he flipped on the switch. Methodically searching the cockpit by quarters, he found three pre-filled 100 mg syringes of Demerol and three more 1 liter bags of normal saline but no injectable penicillin. Of the surgical kit, only the forceps remained; the scissors and scalpel presumably had abandoned ship.

He could make do with the forceps alone, but he regretted the sudden reduction in his supply of Demerol, and the loss of the penicillin was a critical problem. There remained a bottle of amoxicillin tablets, but he doubted whether the blood levels he could achieve with oral administration would be adequate to deal with what infection already had developed, let alone what might follow. *No choice*, he thought. *You do what you can do.* He freed one syringe of Demerol from its plastic container and injected it into the IV line's access port. The opiate slammed him harder and more abruptly than he'd anticipated, and it took an effort for him to resist its beguiling languor and instead begin the unpleasant task of debriding his wound.

He'd always had a knack for close work, and even one-handed on a pitching deck he deftly cleaned the wound and extracted the shotgun pellets and shards of t-shirt that lay within. The blessed Demerol effectively nudged his pain from consciousness without otherwise clouding his sensorium. *No wonder junkies love this stuff so much,* he thought. The wound bled freely as he probed and pulled, but he paid little heed. He knew that with external wounds it always appeared more blood was being lost than actually was the case, and the saline now pouring into his vein would more than compensate.

After about 45 minutes he felt he could do no more. He dressed the wound as best he could, swallowed 3 grams of amoxicillin and brought the boat back to a north/northeasterly heading. Feeling the first return of the wound's throbbing rhythm, he rewarded himself with another syringe of Demerol and settled back to enjoy what he could of its narcotizing effect. Calculating that they'd probably lost only a few miles of headway during his interlude of autosurgery, he left the main sail reefed. If the wind held they'd make Kino well before the next sunset.

———

He felt his head snap forward, his chin ricocheting off his chest, and swiftly he ascended to the surface of full wakefulness. *How long had he slept?* His eye sockets felt as if they were packed with grains of sand, and his exhaustion was complete, his body a well of physical depletion. He glanced briefly at his arm and chest. The IV bag was empty, and although the butterfly's needle remained securely lodged in his vein, the line obviously had clotted off long ago.

With mounting dread he noted in rapid sequence that the night's darkness was lifting, the jib was free and flapping loudly and the boat was pitching erratically to starboard in the relentless swell, rising and falling helplessly, making no headway and lurching eastward as if shoved repetitively by a giant hand. Peering in that direction, he easily could make out the mainland coast no more than a mile distant. *My God,* he thought. *How had they come to be this far north? Had the winds been that strong?*

He knew the area well. Some combination of sea and wind over the millennia had combined to take a greedy bite out of the coastline, creating an enormous bay that in northwesterly winds was notorious for trapping boats. *Bahia Salsipuedes.* A bay aptly named: "Get out if you can."

Within minutes the boat would slide inside the breaker line, and then it would be only a matter of seconds before she pitch-poled, the mast snapping as she rolled over and over to her shattered demise on the sandy beach. As for its crew, they might survive by jumping overboard, fleeing the careening ship and struggling through the heavy surf to shore, but to do so would leave them with scant prospects. Fugitives afoot on a desert coast, lacking any fresh water or supplies and miles from even the most isolated *rancho.*

Reacting quickly, he started to shout towards the cabin to arouse the girl, but he saw she already was awake, crouching in the companionway only a few feet from him, her face a tableau of white-faced, wide-eyed fear. He turned his back to her, adjusted the Evinrude's choke and yanked the starter rope. Mercifully, the engine roared immediately to life and continued to run as he pushed in the choke and adjusted the throttle. He thrust the clutch into the forward position and the tiller to starboard, praying that the engine would have the power to force the bow to port and so bring the boat about.

But she wouldn't budge. Its belly taught and full from the howling northwesterly wind, the mainsail resisted tiller and prop. It was dicey to drop sail and thus render the boat yet more unstable in such a sea, but he had no choice. He released the starboard main sheet, and the sail, suddenly freed, joined the jib in flapping loudly abeam, two white flags indicating the route to disaster.

Even without the mainsail's opposition, however, the boat would not come about under power. The propeller's shaft was too short, and each time a swell lifted the boat, the propeller sprang fully free of the water and screamed loudly above the wind.

He could think of only one thing left to try, and its chance of succeeding receded with each passing second. He shouted over the roar of the wind and heedless flapping of the unsecured sails, calling Olivia to him. As she crawled her way along the cockpit on her hands and knees, he snatched at the flailing mainsheet with his good hand. Grasping the bitter end, he curled the sheet once around the starboard winch and cleated it off. Feeling her grasp his leg, he pulled the girl to her feet and held her tightly to him against the deck's dysrhythmic undulations.

He had to shout directly into her ear to be heard above the din, and at first when she realized what he wanted of her, she shook her head vigorously and tried to break away. He pulled her back to him, grabbed her chin and stared intently into her terrified eyes. The hippus of her pupils, sequentially dilating and contracting, were a physiologic Morse code bespeaking terror.

He spoke to her plainly, his lips pressed to her left ear and his good arm locked around her shoulders. "You have to do this, Olivia," he told her plainly, "or we'll die." She buried her face in his chest. He could feel her trembling.

"I can't do it with only one good arm," he said. "Just hold tight to the lifeline, move forward slowly, grab that big rope that's tied to the bottom of the jib - that sail on the bow - and bring it back to me." Once more she shook her head and resisted when he tried again to lift her face to his. She continued to tremble, and he could tell that she would collapse to the deck if he released his grip.

"We will die," he repeated slowly. "In less than five minutes the waves will toss this boat – what's left of her – onto the beach. Whether we stay with her or jump off, we'll both drown in these waves."

Of the last he wasn't as sure as he sounded. While he doubted the girl could make her way to the beach, even one-armed he was confident he could manage a side stroke that would bring him to shore intact. But then what? Even to contemplate what might be required was exhausting. And ultimately purposeless.

Now she was sobbing hysterically, her tears lost in his spray-drenched shirt. He tried again to give her an encouraging hug, and having devoted his one functioning arm to her, he lost the helm. The deck pitched wildly, and they fell together, rolling about in the cockpit like lovers maddened by lust, alternately crashing together and then apart as the boat's motion broke their involuntary embrace.

Only seconds were left, and then the slim opportunity would pass. The girl arose and immediately fell – hard - against the starboard lazarrette. She gasped at the sudden pain. An abrupt rising in the wind sent the stays to humming, and with a quick glance to port he saw approaching the huge swells that would seal their fate. Now lying meekly in a passing wave's trough, the boat awaited the wall of water that would send her rolling towards certain destruction on the windward shore now only 200 yards distant.

He looked down at Olivia and then watched apprehensively as she slowly regained her feet and once more began to make her way unsteadily onto the lazarrette and forward to the rail just beyond. One sudden jolt from a colliding swell and she'd be gone, overboard and unrecoverable from this rough sea. Soon she was lost to view in the dim light.

Keeping a steady hold on the tiller with his good right hand, he did what he could to stabilize their wildly careening boat, but still she violently pitched and yawed. He knew that the motion he was experiencing in the cockpit would be amplified ten-fold on the bow. A long minute passed, and then he could see her inching back towards him along the rail, drenched, her face pale with fear, grasping the jib sheet with her trailing left hand as she sought handholds with her right.

To prevent her being struck by the swinging boom and knocked overboard, he took in the mainsheet as much as he dared. Even so, the boom leapt at her threateningly each time the boat slid down the back of a passing swell, delivering a series of sharp, glancing blows to her back and shoulders. Leaving the tiller unattended for an instant, he extended his good hand to her for support. She was reaching for it when the boom struck her yet again, and caught off balance she tumbled heavily into the cockpit. The jib sheet she'd held flew off with the wind.

Within seconds, however, some combination of wind and wave action swung the boat briefly to port and snapped the jib's clew back towards him. Seizing his one and only chance, he grabbed at the sheet as it whipped by his face, and even as the effort caused him to pitch forward and his head to strike the deck face-on and painfully, he could feel the familiar braided line secure within his right hand. Quickly he looped the jib sheet one turn clockwise round the winch and began to pull. Once the jib was sufficiently full and finally quiet, he cleated off the sheet and sprang to the tiller, pushing it hard to starboard. He glanced at the girl, sprawled face-down on the deck, exhausted by her efforts and the hammering she'd taken from the boom, lying motionless in her sodden t-shirt. *That was brave,* he thought.

The jib now full, the boat's bow came down and her movement, uncontrolled but seconds before, settled into a steady forward course. This was all well, but they still were losing ground to shoreward due to sideslip. The boat's shoal keel was insufficient to the task, and even with both sails up and the outboard assisting, she could not be induced to come about. The net loss of forward progress would lead them quickly now to the destruction that awaited in the impact zone.

It was a desperate maneuver, but what else was left? He pulled the tiller sharply towards him to begin what even the most incautious sailor would characterize an uncontrolled jibe. The rudder bit into an encouraging swell, and the boat began suddenly to move to starboard. As the boom snapped from right to left and the boat paused, he feared for an instant that they'd simply surf down a following wave to their end. A last ride into the beach like a longboarder at the end of his session.

The boat continued to turn, however, and suddenly they were headed due south, running on a broad reach with a following swell. Coaxing the boat, keeping the sails filled and telltales aligned, he was able to make 10 points or more towards the west, away from the grip of the boat-swallowing Salsipuedes. To the south there were still the protruding headlands to clear, but they lay two or three miles distant. If the boat held together in the heavy gusts, he was confident they would reach safe water in the open sea.

He made a few minor adjustments in the sail set and then turned his attention to the girl. She was obviously still terrified, unaware that their immediate danger had passed. He was able to speak to her without shouting; sailing now with the wind they were rewarded with near-silence. "We're going to be all right," he reassured her. "We'll need to head southwest a bit, back in the direction we came, but we can turn around once we're well clear of this bay."

Although Olivia huddled against the bulkhead not six feet from him, he was surprised when he barely could make her out in the dim light of early morning. What seemed to have required hours had been completed in only minutes. The sun had not yet risen above the hills that lay just beyond the shoreline. The sky was thick with mares' tails, almost overlapping one another like the scales on a fish. Normally such clouds were a delight to the sailor, a harbinger of fine, steady winds, but only dumb luck - and the girl's unexpected courage - had prevented that wind from mercilessly destroying their boat.

She'd failed to answer or acknowledge him in any way. "You don't need to be afraid", he said, not unkindly. "You saved us. The boat's fine. We're fine. Go below, and put on some dry clothes."

Still she made no response. She hugged her knees to her chest, and her face was buried in her arms. Her thin shoulders were trembling.

You're full of it, he thought. *Your brachial plexus is shot to shit, the arm is probably infected and a good portion of what in Mexico passes for the agents of law enforcement is hunting your hide. You should be crying, too, amigo..*

He scouted around a bit and found his auxiliary medicine kit in the stern anchor locker. Inside was another bottle of dextro-amphetamine tablets, and he chased down 10 mg with a gulp of lukewarm water from the plastic bottle that had rolled around the cockpit along with them as they'd wrestled together in the bay of Salsipuedes. *Not a bad substitute for coffee,* he thought. *Definitely more kick.*

He tried to recall when he'd last eaten, and it seemed to him that years had passed since his breakfast of the morning prior. But the speed killed what appetite he'd developed from his early morning exertions, and he contented himself with occasional swigs of water, an automatic response motivated less by thirst than by the knowledge that he must continue to make some effort to compensate for the fluid loss inevitable in the pervasive dryness, fluid loss compounded by the persistent oozing from his shoulder wound and what undeniably now was fever signaling infection.

They were making a steady five to six knots to the southwest and were clearing the headlands easily. While later it would brutalize, the rising sun felt warm and restorative against his face. The boat slipped easily through the following swell.

Chapter 13

ARIZONA

It was a typical Sunday evening, empty of portent and giving no indication of the changes that would occur before the next sunrise. The house was quiet. Will was on call, midway through a shift that had begun early that morning and would extend for yet a few hours more. Even then, if custom held he would follow his stint at work with a nocturnal run along the Santa Cruz and, afterwards, a visit to the Wrangler for jalapēno cornbread washed down with a cold pitcher of beer. He habitually kept his running gear, a pair of jeans and a clean shirt in his truck for such occasions. Although he would protest loudly to the contrary – and in fact had done so on numerous occasions when the topic arose – Will's habits were as predictable as those of the roadrunner who lived in their brush pile.

True, his habitual predictability had lessened of late. Since taking up with Maria, his eccentric yet consistent patterns of behavior had swerved to become erratic. Many nights he disappeared after work without a word to anyone, returning the next morning red-eyed, sleep-deprived and uncharacteristically irritable. Michael knew he was driving regularly to Nogales to visit Maria at the Andrade estate. The drive was at least 90 minutes each way, and Michael knew all too well from past experience that nights spent with Maria rarely offered much in the way of restfulness. Will had not slept at home the night before nor stopped by in the morning before his shift. Probably he'd driven directly from his tryst to the hospital.

Regrettably, Maria's intrusion had altered their relationship. When they were together at home, Will alternated between furtive avoidance and an awkward forced cheerfulness. Michael easily could sense his friend was appalled by his hypocrisy, and he suspected that a tortured confession was in the offing. That would be as embarrassing as it was unnecessary.

Three weeks prior Maria had ambushed him in the hospital's parking lot as he was walking to his car. *I have something important to tell you*, she'd said ominously, and his obvious indifference to her subsequent revelations concerning her sexual liaison with his room-mate had infuriated her. She'd nearly run him down as she exited the lot.

It was a beautiful evening. The sunset glowed in its familiar shades of orange and red, and the sharp, jagged outline of the Tucson Mountains made a dark silhouette in the foreground. A full desert moon later would rise above the saddle between the Catalinas and the Rincons. The dry, hot air of the afternoon had begun to cool. Trying to shrug off the melancholy he'd felt descend when he considered the issue of Will and Maria, he decided to forego the old Saab and savor the night by riding his scooter to work.

He walked over to the pen that held Will's two geese. As was their custom, they greeted his pleasantries with exaggerated hostility, extending and lowering their long necks and hissing vehemently. Michael had bought them for Will as a birthday joke, and to everyone's surprise the two downy goslings survived into adulthood and appeared to be thriving. From the start they were thoroughly irascible and aggressively misanthropic. Will seemed to find them amusing, and despite their unrelenting animosity and total lack of appreciation for any efforts undertaken on their behalf, he would see that their bowls were full and pen clean even when his truck's battery was dead, his bills unpaid, and his clothes unlaundered.

Michael hissed back at the geese briefly and then walked away, shaking his head. Within the makeshift carport the previous owner had thrown together out of old posts and plywood scraps sat his ancient Vespa. He wheeled the scooter out into the dirt driveway, sat astride it, turned the key and pushed the starter button. Despite weeks of disuse, the engine caught at once and responded encouragingly when he gave it some throttle. Remembering his helmet, he briefly considered and then rejected the notion of retrieving it from his bedroom closet.

At the end of the driveway he stopped the scooter to inspect once again the fading sunset and the lights of the sprawling city below. From the outset he'd admired this dusty hot land for its peculiar beauty. Of his friends, only Brian and Will also had seemed to appreciate the intrinsic oddness of the place, and the three of them had taken pleasure in exploring every peak, canyon, honky-tonk and *taqueria* they could manage within the limited time permitted by their schedules. In particular, they had fallen hard for the wildness of Sonoran Mexico, that incredibly arid land bordered by a vast sea.

Now he feared Brian had become an addict, and Will . . . well, Will was entrapped by a drug of a different kind. True to form, Maria was drawing those who stand too close into a vortex of deception and despair. Michael needed to bring an end to the misperceptions that reigned, but he was congenitally averse to direct confrontation.

He sighed involuntarily. *Bastante*, he thought. Enough. We will talk, and then Will can do as he chooses. At least he will do so knowing the truth.

Reaching into his knapsack, he pulled out a notebook and pen and wrote: *Will. How about breakfast at the Willow? Mike.* The Blue Willow served a great plate of *huevos rancheros*, and when the weather was fine, you could eat outside by the fountain in the courtyard. One on his way in to the hospital with the other headed home, they'd met there for breakfast regularly in the past.

He stuck the note in his shirt pocket He'd leave it on the seat of Will's truck for him to find when he finished his shift. He knew where the truck was parked, and Will never locked his doors. He needed to go now if he wanted to arrive at the ED thirty minutes before his shift actually started, as was his custom; he found the overlap helped ease the transition from having one doctor in charge to another. His thoughts had strayed to Maria, however, and even in the abstract her presence was not to be easily dismissed. He sighed once again, glum at the prospect of confronting Will with the truths that circled about Maria like flies on carrion.

He shrugged without knowing he did so and began to motor out onto the irregular oval of dirt and gravel that passed by their house. This street, colorfully named Hills-O-Gold, intersected with Silverbell Road after meandering through the sparsely settled neighborhood for a few hundred yards. He turned right on Silverbell and began to pick up speed, the night air cool on his exposed face and head.

———

At that same moment Dooley Gulledge was driving disconsolately northward on Silverbell towards his parent's home in Marana. What had begun as a promising afternoon had turned out badly for Dooley, and his mood as desolate as the parched banks of the Rio Santa Cruz, the deeply cut dry wash that bordered the *barrio* and ran with water only when filled by the heavy monsoon rains of mid-summer. The *barrio* occupied much of Tucson's southwestern quarter, and on St. Mary's Road, a main artery within the quarter, stood the small block home of Dewey's sweetheart, the lovely Felicia Montijo.

Felicia and Dooley were both seventeen and classmates at Salpointe High. Early during their junior year they'd decided they were passionately in love, and that their love remained unconsummated over the ensuing months reflected both Felicia's Catholic strictures and the difficulty Dooley had experienced in finding a time and place appropriate to his attempting a breach of those strictures.

Today had seemed to offer the long-awaited opportunity. During the hours immediately after school Felicia's house was uncharacteristically quiet, her loud and noisy flock of younger siblings having decamped with their mother to visit grandparents on the eastern edge of the city. As always, Felicia's father was at work, minding the counter at his small *panaderia* downtown.

Left blessedly alone, they'd quickly gotten down to business on the living room sofa. Dooley happily was investigating some previously unexplored regions of his beloved's partially clothed body when the front door suddenly opened, and the bright Tucson sunshine rushed in to fill the darkened room.

Felicia's father was not tall, but he was a solidly built man and endowed with surprising strength. Within seconds Dooley felt himself immobilized within the unyielding grip of the older man, plucked from Felicia and hurled unceremoniously through the *casita*'s front door. He rolled painfully down a small flight of brick steps and finally came to rest at the base of an unyielding saguaro cactus. As a denouement to the whole discouraging experience, its spines had punctured his right cheek. Behind him, Felicia's loud wailings were muffled abruptly by the door's slamming.

He gathered himself up and plucked from his cheek the few spines that hung there. Fortunately for him, unlike the beaver tail cactus and virtually all species of cholla the saguaro preferred to retain its spines when assaulted. He'd just completed that task when the front door flew open to reveal Mr. Montijo standing at his threshold, still obviously enraged and now bellowing in Spanish.

"Si no te vas de aqui ahora mismo, le voy a dar de comer tu cuerpo a mis perros!" he shouted. *"Y no tu vienes aqui otra vez, bastardo!"* Go now, he commanded the boy, or he would feed his body to the dogs. Although the Mexican's thick frame nearly filled the doorway, Dooley could see Felicia standing behind him, fully dressed now and weeping.

He understood little Spanish, but Mr. Montijo's tone made it clear that he was presently unwelcome and likely to remain so. The man made a threatening move towards him, and Dooley ran to his car, an '87 Firebird. In a parting gesture of juvenile defiance, he accelerated rapidly as he reversed out the short driveway, his rear tires spinning wildly and spraying gravel throughout the Montijo's scruffy front yard.

Once well clear of St. Mary's Road and the Montijo house-hold, he stopped at a convenience store and used his older brother's suspended driver's license to buy a six pack of 16 ounce Bud and a pack of Marlboro Reds. Parked along the Santa Cruz, he drank the beers one after another and smoked most of the cigarettes before climbing back into his car at sunset to drive home.

His car was his pride and joy, and normally he would have taken much pleasure in navigating Silverbell's long straight-aways and sudden, stomach-dropping dips, but tonight he was too morose to enjoy the ride. He felt sodden from the beer, dulled rather than intoxicated. His face burned from the cactus spines and the humiliation he'd suffered at the hands of Felicia's father, and when he considered how hopeless were the prospects for his relationship with his beloved, it took an effort to fight back the tears. Dooley hadn't cried since he was eight years old and his brother snapped the tail off his pet mouse.

———

Mr. and Mrs. Howard Slubacher of Amana, Iowa, had expe-rienced a difficult day. They'd set out that morning in happy anticipation of spending the morning at "Old Tucson", an ancient tourist trap located in the broad valley to the west of Gate's Pass. Instead they'd become hopelessly lost and driven for hours in the penetrating desert heat and glare, more or less circling the tiny town of Ajo ("garlic"), Arizona, a speck on the map amidst the vast, discouraging landscape of the Papago reservation. They'd stopped repeatedly to ask directions, but what little information they could derive from the Papago they encountered was vague or unintelligible.

Finally back on track, they now sought to recover something of their ill-spent day by enjoying the celebrated "Authentic Chuckwagon Dinner" at Li'l Abner's, a steakhouse on the fringe of the city that featured good beef grilled over mesquite, outside seating at picnic tables and an appropriately hokey "cowboy band".

Departing the Best Western on Miracle Mile and bedecked in their recently acquired cowboy finery - heavily embroidered shirts with pearl snap-buttons, imitation turquoise bolo ties, black jeans (Generous Cut) and wide leather belts with huge silver-plated buckles - they now were driving northward on Silverbell towards their destination. The sun was setting behind the Tucson Mountains to their left, and Mrs. Slubacher exclaimed repeatedly at the spectacle, each time reminding her husband to keep his eyes on the road when he attempted to sneak a glance.

They'd driven their Buick 88 all the way from Iowa. A veritable land boat in its great length, broad beam and tonnage, the vehicle's cotton-smooth ride and air-cooled interior were a balm after the difficult day. All signs boded well for a pleasant evening, and their bickering of the afternoon had transformed into the companionable rapport characteristic of a long-married couple who prefer predictable outcomes and no surprises.

—

As Dooley's initial humiliation transformed gradually into an impotent rage, his driving became increasingly reckless. In his mind's eye each roadrunner that scurried across his path or armadillo that lumbered dully along the pavement took on the sneering form of Mr. Montijo, and he took pains to convert each into blotches of fresh road kill. He was more successful with the armadillos.

Sliding around a curve thirty miles above the posted limit, he came suddenly upon an enormous white sedan that crept along cautiously at low speed, obstructing his passage. He laid upon his horn, the extended blasts resounding loudly in the quiet desert night. When this action elicited no response from the car ahead, he flashed his lights repeatedly and maneuvered his car such that its front bumper nearly touched the other's rear

———

Distracted by his wife's concern that they'd passed Li'l Abner's "way long ago" and were once again destined to become lost in the open desert ("and at this time at night!"), Mr. Slubacher was slow to detect Dooley's hostile presence astern. When at last he heard the honks above the comforting roar of the air conditioner and saw the headlights flashing angrily right on his tail, the elderly man set his stubborn Iowan jaw, clamped his hands yet more firmly on the enormous steering wheel and resolutely drove onward.

His wife beside him suddenly realized what was transpiring and began to screech. "Pull over to the side! Let him pass, Howard!" She craned her neck around to peer fearfully at the crazed individual pursuing them. Mr. Slubacher ignored her imprecations. His generation of Iowan men did not respond to aggression by stepping aside – witness the "Korean War Veteran" imprinted on his license plate – and he had no intention of accommodating the driver behind him

———

Dooley pounded the steering wheel repeatedly with his fist and cursed loudly. By some adolescent alchemy his rage at being frustrated in his quest to win Felicia's heart and other bodily parts had been transferred to these Iowan snowbirds who blocked his way. Without hesitation he pulled into the left lane of the narrow road and accelerated powerfully to blow past his foe.

———

Lifting the hair from his scalp and caressing his face, the dry desert air rushed over him as Michael drove southward on Silverbell. To the west, over the mountains, were the last streaks of a sunset so glorious that briefly he considered stopping to savor its remnants while he had a smoke. He already was running behind schedule, however, and he knew Gina Parks would take offense at a tardy arrival.

As he rounded a bend in the road and started down a short decline, he saw something puzzling ahead: a mile distant and closing the gap rapidly were four headlights facing him and spread across the road. He wondered briefly whether it might be one of the giant earth-movers that perpetually chewed at the land between Silverbell and the interstate, intent on transforming an admittedly undistinguished stretch of desert into yet another depressing sprawl of Del Webb homes, each with its tiny lot denuded save for a lone mulberry tree. The origin of Mr. Webb's apparent infatuation with the unattractive and ecologically misplaced mulberry tree was obscure. Possibly the humble tree catered to the preferences of a midwestern clientele nostalgic for the green-leafed trees of their homeland and yet weary of cold winters.

But present circumstances were such that he hadn't the time to dwell on more abstract matters like the mulberry trees. He could see now from the mismatch of the headlights that they represented two cars more or less in parallel, the one in his own lane traveling faster…but not fast enough to regain the opposite lane before it would collide with Michael's scooter.

He himself was traveling too rapidly to brake to a stop, and besides, a landscaping operation had temporarily removed the road's eastern shoulder, leaving in its place an abrupt drop-off of about eighteen inches. To make matters worse, the approaching vehicles were now so close that he doubted he had time sufficient to clear the path of the slower car and then risk jumping the drop-off. To his right was only a thin shoulder of gravel that separated the pavement from the encroaching desert. Given his scooter's light weight, a head-on-collision with the faster vehicle would certainly claim one life – his own – but the fate awaiting him beyond the thin shoulder was at least marginally less certain . His decision made, he accelerated and turned his scooter sharply to the right.

———

The Slubachers failed to observe Michael's spectacular exit. Mr. Slubacher was too intent on dueling with the young whippersnapper in the vehicle beside him and steadily was increasing his speed to avoid being passed. At the moment Michael left the road Mrs. Slubacher's face was buried in her hands. At intervals she would interrupt her weeping to beseech her husband to stand down. As for Dooley, he barely registered the sudden appearance of the approaching headlight and its equally sudden disappearance.

Shortly thereafter, Mr. Slubacher finally gave in to his wife's pleading and slowed down to allow the boy to pass. The Iowa couple recovered from their experience and eventually managed to find the elusive Li'l Abner's. Both were impressed by the massive steaks placed before them.

Dooley made his way home to Marana. His telephone conversation with Felicia later in the night was marred by his difficulty comprehending her whispered words and a sudden intrusion by Mr. Montijo. In contrast to Felicia, her father's speech was loud, distinct and unambiguous. Dooley's anger wilted into desolation, and he went to bed that night a boy grown sadder but no wiser.

———

Airborne for only a few seconds, Michael could feel himself separating from the scooter at the apex of his short flight, and he did not fully lose consciousness even when his body slammed hard against the *caliche*. Stunned for a moment, he recovered to find that he lay on his back and that, oddly, he felt no pain.

He tried to shift his position and quickly realized that aside from some shoulder shrug he'd lost the ability to move his limbs. *So I'm quadriplegic*, he thought. Although he sensed no neck pain, he assumed he must have suffered a cervical fracture and dislocation with spinal cord compression and possible contusion. Given his retained shoulder shrug, what appeared to be a bit of deltoids function and his continued ability to breathe, he judged the level of his cord injury to be between C5 and 6.

His disability was inconvenient. Being lighter than his scooter, he'd been flung about 20 yards further into the desert. By raising his head he could see that its tank had exploded upon impact and that even now a fire was building rapidly in the dry underbrush. An ever-expanding circle of flame extended from the brightly burning carcass of his scooter, and its advancing edge was steadily approaching.

Michael being Michael, he evaluated his situation calmly and objectively. Even with high dose intravenous steroids administered acutely and immediate surgical intervention, it was unlikely he'd regain any meaningful use of his arms and legs. In any event, such treatment was unlikely to be forthcoming soon. As quadriplegic life held no attraction for him, he decided it was just as well that he die now and forego the extended preliminaries that would attend a prolonged hospitalization and dreary months to follow in a skilled nursing facility. While death by fire was no picnic, he did have the advantage of being insensate from the clavicles down, and there was a good chance that smoke inhalation would render him dead or at least unconscious before the flames reached his face.

Things could be worse, he concluded. All in all, it was as good a place to die as any. His mind was clear, and he had his vision. The sunset now had nearly passed, but he could lie there and for one final time enjoy the star-filled sky of the sweet desert night. He wished he could smoke a last pipe as he waited, but one couldn't have everything.

He inhaled the bitter scent of burning creosote bush. Again raising his head, he could see that the flames were now just beyond an old mesquite that stood 30 feet from him. As the fire moved hungrily forward, he watched the mesquite's branches

199

suddenly ignite in unison. Its brightly illuminated limbs were reminiscent of the olive trees that lined the entrance to the Westward Look resort, their branches heavily festooned with twinkling white Christmas lights.

He'd taken Maria there once while they were still together, a poorly paid resident seizing the opportunity to treat his wife to a university-sponsored dinner at an otherwise unattainable restaurant. During the dinner she'd left the table repeatedly to visit the women's bathroom for a snort of coke or crystal – he couldn't recall now which had been her drug *du jour* at the time. The drug made her flirtatious, and at one point she vanished for an extended period with one of the anesthesiology residents. When they'd finally returned she was leaning into the young man, her face upturned towards his and both laughing hysterically. By their behavior and her wrinkled dress, Michael assumed Maria had felt compelled to share various of her favors.

It was not long after that evening that he moved out, taking his personal belongings and only enough money to rent a room from a friend. He left the balance of their checking account to Maria, and she'd immediately cleared out the account and moved on. To Vancouver, apparently

He looked up and saw the fire was almost upon him. He tried for a moment to rock his body side to side on the chance that he might roll himself to a less exposed position, but his immobile limbs resisted the action. His note to Will burned along with his clothes when the fire at last took him.

———

Weary from lack of sleep and depleted by his confrontation with Maria, Will struggled through his twelve hour shift. As he reviewed MRIs, placed central lines and tested reflexes, he tried unsuccessfully to expel her from his thoughts.

Night came at last. Will heard one of the nurses in the ED mention that a brush fire had broken out along Silverbell Road, but the she was vague on details. He started to call home but then recalled that Michael was probably on his way to the ED himself.

Finishing with his last patient thirty minutes later, he searched around for his room-mate and was surprised to learn that he was more than an hour overdue for his shift. The doctor he was to relieve, a cardiothoracic surgery resident named Gina Parks, was a rangy, acne-scarred brunette from New York whom Will briefly had pursued in years past. Dr. Parks was angry, and she was threatening to call the ED chief to complain.

"Where the fuck is he?" she demanded of Will. "Rob and I have plans, and I'll be damned if we're canceling them just because your buddy can't be bothered to show up on time." Rob was her live-in boyfriend. What she saw in the snarky runt was a mystery to Will.

Will spoke to her soothingly. "Mike's never late, Gina, and he never forgets a shift." he said. "Something's got to be wrong. Just give me a few minutes, and I'll make sure you get out of here."

Obviously unmollified, Gina strode off on her long up-state New York legs, her black mane of hair tick-tocking in synchrony to the rhythm of her agitated gait. Ignoring a brief pang of unrequited love, Will called their house. No answer. He paged Gene, on back-up call that night for general surgery. After the requisite amount of begging and promises of restitution, the diminutive Texan reluctantly agreed to cover the ED, and Will released Gina to her boyfriend's dubious attractions.

He hit the metal disc that opened the saloon-like doors of the ED and walked out into the night. He found odd the juxtaposition of Michael's absence and the news of the Silverbell fire, and he intended to have a first-hand look. He climbed into his truck, wove through the crowded physicians' parking lot and eventually began to make his way westward on Speedway. He turned north on Silverbell and at once began to worry.

The horizon ahead was surreal, the sky glowing unnaturally bright and intermittently lit by upward fluctuations in its shimmering intensity. Increasing his speed, he drew closer and came suddenly upon a thicket of bright yellow fire trucks and police cruisers with revolving blue lights. The desert to the west of Silverbell was ablaze, the fire encompassing dozens of undeveloped acres within the former ranchland that some said belonged to McCartney and others claimed for Ronstadt. Two cruisers parked sideways and sitting nose to nose were blocking the road. He pulled onto the narrow shoulder, parked his truck and walked past the cruisers towards the cluster of fire trucks, eerily distinct in the harsh glare of a battery of powerful klieg lights. Their shiny yellow metal contrasted sharply with the enveloping desert night.

A policeman called out to him to stop and, fighting down his growing unease he forced himself to turn about and approach the man with his best facsimile of a calm, professional demeanor. He'd taken the precaution of bringing along a traditional doctor's bag, and pointing to it he explained to the officer who confronted him that he was a physician summoned to assist the fire medics. Despite his jeans, casual shirt and otherwise undoctorly appearance, the officer let him pass, and he walked unhindered the last hundred yards to the center of activity.

A fireman stood by one of the trucks, his face soot-stained and sweat-covered. Will identified himself and asked, "What gives?"

The fireman swiped at his face with a filthy towel and shook his head negatively. Clearly exhausted by his recent efforts, he answered telegraphically. "Don't know. Brush fire. Started close by the road. Probably set. Maybe squatters."

Tucson's ambience and climate lent well to encampments of the wandering homeless. The patch of desert adjacent to the county hospital was especially popular with those recently discharged from the psychiatric service and anxious to seek early readmission, but this quiet stretch along Silverbell, empty but within walking distance of the interstate and its exits, ranked highly as well.

Pointing towards the ambulances, Will asked, "Anybody hurt?"

"I don't think so," the man answered slowly. "Not much out there but creosote bush and mesquite." The fireman's eyes were closed, and he braced himself against the truck to remain upright. "Swallowed a bit of smoke," he explained. "It's a real mess in there. That creosote bush puts off fumes worse than tear gas."

Will wished him well and picked his way through the crowd to find an ambulance. He had to fight through a brigade of reporters and cameramen from the local radio and television stations. That they invariably were granted such special access to all human mayhem and natural disasters had always seemed to Will an odd ordering of priorities, but in America a microphone conveys as much official respect as a resuscitation kit, especially if accompanied by a camera. He noted with passing interest that the attractive blonde from *News 10 at Nine* sported an impressive set of implants.

Eventually he reached an ambulance and learned from the EMT crew that the fire was coming under control. No source for the blaze had yet been identified. He borrowed a cell phone and called home. No answer. He then called the ED and asked for Gene. While waiting for him to come to the phone, Will watched a ghostly trio of firemen emerge from the thick smoke, their black forms back-lit by the strangely glowing sky. As they passed by, Will noted their silence and grimly set faces.

He put away the phone and approached them. "How is it in there?" he asked.

One fireman stopped, looked him up and down and demanded, "Who are you?"

Will identified himself, and the fireman relaxed and apologized. "I thought you were another one of those reporters," he said. "Buncha fucking vultures." He began to cough heavily and turned his head aside to spit. Recovering, he continued. "There's a body in there," he said, "and what looks like a little motorcycle. Not much left of either."

Will tossed the cell phone to its owner and immediately vaulted past the three men. Ignoring the shouts of protest and warning his action provoked, he sprinted across the road and into the smoldering desert. The acrid smoke seared his throat, and his eyes began to tear uncontrollably, nearly blinding him. He ran by the charred remnants of bushes and small trees, and in his haste he stumbled over a twisted pile of blackened metal and pitched forward onto the unyielding ground. Rubbing his eyes clear as best he could, he could see the metal object was Michael's scooter, recognizable by the partially melted metal logo tag and the flecks of white enamel that yet clung to the charred remains.

He pulled himself to his feet, his clothes, face and hands blackened by the sooty desert and the wreckage of Michael's scooter. Around him denuded branches of mesquite and creosote bush cracked and popped like gun fire, and in the distance he could see the firemen struggling to control what the flames chewing at the withered underbrush.

The landscape that lay between the firemen and where he stood resembled what he'd always envisioned when he read of World War I's battlefields. The *caliche* was uniformly black, and smoke wafted from the very soil itself. Here and there were scattered the charred trunks of the larger mesquite and *palo verde*, presiding forlornly over the ruined landscape like the shattered masts of a defeated armada. Of the endless low waves of dense vegetation that had blanketed the desert floor, nothing remained but fragile casts of ash that collapsed and dissipated with the slightest stirring of the night air. Will's eyes continued to tear, and in the darkness it was easier to make out the distant firemen than what lay immediately adjacent.

Suddenly from the gloom there emerged four firemen carrying a litter. Upon it had been placed a red body bag that outsized its contents but nonetheless bulged awkwardly at various points. The bulges evidently had defied any attempts to zip up the bag snugly, and its opening consequently lay agape. Will made to speak, but his parched throat produced only harsh, guttural sounds that communicated no meaning or purpose. The firemen brushed past him, weary and intent on their task. He could do no more than trail behind, his eyes fixed upon the incongruous red bag, bobbing along like a pennant lifting to a fresh breeze.

205

Finally the party reached the road and an ambulance. The firemen wearily lowered the litter and leaned back against the vehicle to rest. Identifying himself as a physician, Will asked one of the bearers, "Is it a man?"

The firemen removed his hat and brushed the sweat from his eyes with the back of his hand. "Hard to know," he replied. "It's human."

"May I take a look?" Will asked. The fireman looked startled. "I'm a doctor," he explained. "And I may know the person."

The fireman shrugged. "Be my guest."

Will tugged the zipper downwards, and suddenly freed of the tension produced by the corpse's limbs fused akimbo, the bag fell open easily. He knew at once it was Michael. Despite the ruin, despite the absence of hair, face or a single recognizable feature, he had no doubt. He sank to his knees and rested his forehead against his filthy hands.

The firemen shifted uncomfortably, and one spoke. "Do you know who this is, doc?" he asked gently.

"Yes," Will answered, finally. "I know him."

———

The fire was extinguished shortly thereafter, but the desert continued to emit hot snapping sounds throughout the night. By morning the road was open to traffic, and those who lived on the outskirts could make their way into the city and to their various jobs. As with travelers everywhere confronted with the spectacle of a disaster not their own, they paused on their way to gawk at the devastation.

Events unfolded quickly. Michael's body was taken to the morgue at the university hospital, and following behind in his truck Will had called Maria. In a tone clearly hostile she'd cut him off and hung up. He gave the police her name and telephone number, but their calls went unanswered, and an officer from the Nogales department who was dispatched to the Andrade home radioed back to report that no one had responded to his loud knocking. It was left to Will to make a formal identification of the body for the police report.

He was surprised when the police dismissed him, apparently satisfied that the death was accidental and that there was no need for further investigation. Somehow, irrationally, he'd assumed he would be charged and held in custody. He drove home numbly, avoiding the southern portion of Silverbell and approaching their house from the north.

What to do next? he wondered. Michael's parents were elderly, and Will decided to spare them an unholy call in the night and instead convey his terrible news in the morning. Beyond that he could think no further. The geese hissed as he walked past their enclosure, and he opened the door to a house dry, dusty and silent. He considered but rejected calling Maria once again. What was the point?

———

Following Will's notification, Michael's parents had sent one of his older brothers, a Jesuit priest, to collect his remains and return them for burial in St. Paul. Will flew to Minnesota for the funeral and returned on an early flight the following day. Brian accompanied him and, odd though it seemed to Will, remained for an entire week after he left, staying with Michael's parents. Maria never appeared, either before the funeral or at the service in St. Paul.

A few weeks after the funeral Will gave notice that when the new academic year began in July, he would not be returning for the third and final year of his fellowship. During the remaining weeks of the academic year still in session he ceased working in the lab, turned over his equipment and data to a pleasant oncology fellow from Pakistan, and reduced his clinical activity simply to showing up for his appointed nights and weekends on the call schedule. Away from work he spoke to no one save Brian. From Maria, he heard nothing. When he called the *hacienda*, Eddie could tell him only that she'd left suddenly and without notice.

He would never see her again.

Chapter 14

MEXICO

They'd turned north once again and then east to make their run into Bahia Kino on a broad reach. The wind remained steady but had lessened perceptibly over the last few hours. If it continued to drop they would need the outboard to reach the mainland by nightfall.

There were two approaches to Kino, and as he sat at the tiller he weighed the merits of each. The southern approach was via a small estuary on whose northern shore was situated *El Pulpo Loco* and its rough marina, reduced to derelict status by years of winter storms and human neglect. Once in the estuary they would be visible only from the air or other boats that similarly drew little water and were making specifically for that destination. To reach the secluded estuary, however, would require that they motor past the marina, and despite its dilapidation there could be someone about to mark their passage. Besides, even if they motored by unobserved, their anchorage would put them miles from the road back to Old Kino and Peter's *casita*. He doubted he was capable of walking that distance, especially as a portion – a long portion – would be over untracked desert.

The northern approach would take them into the small bay where was located the makeshift ramp he and his friend had used to launch this same boat on so many of their trips across the Midriff. As he knew from Peter and prior visits to the area, the ramp was little used and the bay seldom visited. Along with its other deficiencies, the ramp's location on the bay's southern shore left it exposed to swells kicked up by northwesterly winds such as the one they'd been experiencing, and to launch or retrieve a boat with the sea breaking on that steep, rocky ramp was too much even for the Mexican fishermen and their sturdy *pangas*. They preferred instead to use the concrete ramp beside the *tienda*, the one pitched too low to accommodate a sailboat.

A rocky, deep-rutted but passable road led one mile from the ramp at the bay to the northern terminus of the asphalt road that ran through Old Kino. If they could find anchorage somewhere close to the ramp, he thought he could manage the walk back to town and to Peter's. If the old man was home, he'd ask him to fly them across the border.

Satisfied with his decision, he lolled back against the stern rail and made a conscious effort to relax and forget for the moment that he was, in fact, a wounded fugitive whose freedom – perhaps even his survival – might be measured in hours.

He thought of the first trip he'd made here. Heading west across the Midriff from Kino, he and his friend, the boat's co-owner, had hove-to on the open sea that first night to get some sleep. When they'd awakened in the early morning, the sea was flat, and a dense fog had gathered around them, reducing visibility to zero.

Bemused by the appearance of fog in such a dry climate, they sat together in the cockpit, drinking coffee and waiting to see if the breeze would come up. After an hour had passed with no discernible change in the conditions, they grew impatient and decided to motor southwest towards Baja, directed by their hand-held compass. As he'd leaned over the transom to lower the outboard, however, the compass fell from his shirt's breast pocket and struck the water with a irrevocable *plunk*. Even now he could recall that sound precisely.

They both watched as the compass slowly spiraled bottomwards. According to the *Baja Sailing Guide*, the sea in their present location was over a mile deep. So fine was the water's visibility that with ease they could track the first thirty feet of the small compass's long descent. Lacking any wind and the option of motoring now removed by the loss of the compass, they once again settled back to wait.

More time passed, and they began to hear about them a sound like the loud expulsions of wet breath. It was a pod of gray whales, and so close to the boat they passed that at intervals the two men could feel their spume spattering lightly against their faces like a misty rain. The effect was surreal: the sailboat encased in fog on a dead calm sea, the whales arching to raise their blow holes above the water's surface. He'd been excited by the whales' appearance but also apprehensive. Recalling what the boat's previous owner once had told them, he remarked, "It's a good thing she's unsinkable, isn't it?"

Reaching into his jacket for his pipe, loading the bowl and methodically tamping down its contents, his friend said nothing for a moment. He lit his pipe, inhaled and expelled a few clouds of rich-smelling Bugler tobacco before responding.

"Let me tell you a story," he suggested. And he went on to recite to his increasingly unnerved friend the tale of a couple whose large ketch had gone to the bottom ninety seconds after its hull was cracked by a whale off the coast of Chile. They'd spent the next 132 days at sea in a small life raft until finally they were picked up off Mazatlan. Whether their relationship had survived the long period of enforced intimacy was unknown.

Story finished, his friend tapped his pipe against the hull to rid the bowl of its remnants and poured himself another cup of coffee. Watching his friend fill and light another bowl, he'd silently reflected upon the story at length and was decidedly relieved when the pod of whales left them to continue on its way south. Shortly thereafter the fog began to dissipate, and a light northeasterly breeze arose, allowing them to proceed in roughly the same direction taken by the whales.

The conditions today couldn't be more different, he thought. The wind was high and from a different quarter, the seas were running and his friend . . . well, he was at best present only in spirit.

He glassed the horizon to the northeast and thought he could make out the low brown hump of San Esteban. The island lay roughly ten miles to the northwest of Kino and was famous for its chuckwallas, ferocious-appearing but harmless reptiles that apparently could thrive on little beyond rock, sand and heat. A smaller island, Turner, lay directly west of Kino, but it was too small to sight at this distance.

He pointed the boat towards the south end of San Esteban. Given the side slip eroding their headway, this course eventually would place them just north of Kino. He glanced at his watch. It was now 7 o'clock. With sunset at 8 and assuming this wind held, he calculated they would arrive in the vicinity of Kino with enough twilight remaining to pick out the bay's entrance. He'd drop sail to reduce their visibility and motor on in darkness to seek a decent anchorage.

The wind died off shortly before sunset, and he was forced to resort to the Evinrude to cover the last few miles to Kino. The swells remained large despite the wind's absence, and he worried they were consuming too much fuel. The notoriously inaccurate gauge oscillated back and forth around the half-full mark, but lifting the tank he could tell this reading was overly optimistic. He hoped there would be enough left to accomplish what would be required.

The lights of low-lying Old Kino twinkled along the shore for a mile or two. To the south a long stretch of darkness was broken by the clustered lights of the condominiums, but even with the binoculars he could see no indication of *El Pulco Loco* or the marina just beyond. Motoring to a point just north of the lights, he found it easy enough to locate the entrance to the bay, and passing the headlands he could make out the *tienda*, festooned as always with strands of Christmas lights.

Once inside the bay it was difficult to find an adequate anchorage. The shore fell away steeply, and the bottom in the shallower water immediately offshore was rocky. To make matters worse, they would be forced to anchor on the bay's windward shore. To anchor to the north, in the lee of the wind, would triple the walking distance to Peter's, and he was not up to the long swim that a more direct route would require. Ten o'clock came, and then eleven, and still they motored back and forth, pausing at intervals to drop the hook and test its hold.

Finally they found a patch of sandy bottom at a depth of about thirty feet. The anchor seemed to bite, and paying out the chain and a copious length of line to optimize the scope, he placed the engine in reverse and backed up gently until the rode was taut and the boat would move no more against the hook.

Satisfied at last, he called Olivia back from her position on the bow and indicated she should sit beside him. He explained to her that she should remain with the boat while he went ashore to seek out his friend in town.

At first she was resistant. "You're not coming back," she said, fearfully. "You'll leave me here alone on this boat and go back to the U.S. alone." She folded her arms across her chest and ducked her head.

"I'll be back," he said. "I'm going to ask my friend to fly us to Arizona tomorrow in his plane. I've got nothing to gain by leaving you behind, and, besides, I'm going to try to save my boat. I've got to come back."

"Do you promise?" she asked.

"I promise," he said.

He finished lacing up his shoes, a task made difficult by his one-handedness. Rising, he told her, "I should be back in a couple of hours. If I'm not, it may mean something's happened to me. If I'm not back, wait here until tomorrow night and then walk down that road to my friend's house." He described Peter and his *casita*. "If for some reason I haven't gotten to him, tell him you know me and what happened in San Carlos. He and his wife are good people, and they'll help you out." He took a moment to scribble out a note: *Peter: This girl's telling the truth. She's all right. Please help her.* He signed it.

By the time he'd finished writing she was crying again and refused to take the note from him. Sighing, he went below and left it on the galley's countertop. Back in the cockpit he stepped up on the lazarrette and hopped over the rail into the warm bay. Side-stroking towards shore with his good arm, he looked back at the boat and saw the girl's pale face, peering anxiously after him through the darkness.

The night air was so dry that all wetness had left his clothes by the time he reached the *tienda*. Peter's house, a small pink block building, sat 100 yards further south on the town's only street. Approaching the *tienda*, he crossed to the opposite side of the road and tried to remain in the shadows. There appeared to be some trucks parked in the vacant lot next to the store, but in the darkness he could discern no more than vague outlines. Suddenly the *tienda*'s door opened, and the light pouring out illuminated two white-helmeted soldiers emerging into the night. They were carrying cardboard boxes, and they moved towards the vehicles parked in the lot.

The trucks' headlights came on, and in the intersecting lines of illumination he could count six other soldiers moving about, some with automatic weapons strapped to their backs. In a moment the trucks were loaded and rumbling away in the direction of New Kino. The area once again was dark and silent.

To be certain, he waited a few minutes, crouched down behind a roadside bench, and soon he could hear snatches of conversation penetrating the silence. Crawling out of the shadows for a better look, he saw two young soldiers at their post in the vacant lot beside the boat ramp and *tienda*. Their carbines were slung casually from their shoulders, and they chattered in Spanish as they gazed out seaward.

Shit, he breathed silently. The soldiers' presence here could mean only one thing, and his plan would have to be adjusted accordingly. They were lucky to have made it into the bay undetected, and he had little doubt that the southerly approach through the estuary was guarded more closely.

With the soldiers' backs to him, he picked his way slowly down the street to Peter's home. Its interior was dark. The *casita* was a small, one story building of cinder block with a heavily stuccoed exterior. It sat like a bunker on a slight rise overlooking the town's sole thoroughfare, and a bank of windows over the sleeping porch attached to the building's front provided a fine view of the inner bay and Isla Turner westward in the distance.

As he stealthily approached the darkened house, he could see that Peter's ancient Ford pickup was parked in the carport at the end of a short, inclined driveway paved with crushed oyster shells. His *panga* was adjacent to the truck, on its trailer. So *far, so good*, he thought. For his sporadic flights to Tucson Peter typically drove his truck to the dirt strip outside of town where he kept his plane, and unless he was in the air or out fishing, he usually could be found at home.

He circled to the rear of the house and tapped on the kitchen door's glass window, striving to make himself heard above the roar of the window unit that cooled the bedroom but careful not to attract unwanted attention from passersby below or the soldiers across the road. Tapping again and waiting for a full fifteen minutes without apparently arousing anyone, he was about to leave when the door suddenly swung open.

Peter stood barefoot before him in the threshold, easily visible in the moonlight and clad in faded jeans and a T-shirt. He could see from the lines in his face and the stoop of his shoulders that the man had aged considerably since they'd last met, but the gaze of his bright blue midwestern eyes was as keen and direct as ever. If he was surprised to see the younger man, he gave no such indication. He also kept the lights of his house extinguished.

Silently he bade his visitor enter, immediately shutting the door and locking it once both men were inside the kitchen. Wordlessly he opened the icebox, extracted two cans of *Tecate* and then walked slowly from the kitchen through the darkened living room to the enclosed porch beyond. He followed the old man through the house and sat on the edge of a wicker chaise. Peter settled himself in his customary position by the window in a swiveling leather desk chair. A telescope and set of expensive binoculars fixed atop a tripod were perched on either side of the chair. These Peter employed to track the comings and goings of the boat traffic within the bay and the human traffic in the town below.

Bending forward, he extended a *cerveza* to the younger man and said simply, "If we keep the lights off, no one on the street below can see us." He took a long, swallow from the upturned can.

"Then you know?" the younger man asked.

Peter sat back in his chair and rested his feet on the window ledge. "I know you're in trouble," he replied. "I know this whole damn town is full of *cholos* in uniform who'd like to punch your ticket. And I know there's a *federal* in San Carlos who somehow got shot with his own rifle...and nobody seems to think it was suicide."

He took a deep breath and exhaled slowly, his fears confirmed at last. Although there'd been precious little reason to support it, he'd maintained a lingering hope that the incident had remained a local affair and his fear of coordinated pursuit thus illusory. That first shocking view of the *soldados* at the *tienda* should have squashed that hope effectively, but the sudden despair he now felt informed him otherwise.

He began to tell Peter the entire story, starting with the *yanqui muchachos* and finishing with his surreptitious entry into the *lagunita* north of town. Except for arising once to retrieve two fresh beers from the kitchen, the old man listened without interrupting. When he'd finished, Peter asked him a short series of simple questions. Were drugs involved? Had the charter boat captain or his mate been seriously injured? Who was the girl?

In the younger man's answer to the last Peter apparently found some inadequacy. For the first time in their conversation he seemed disconcerted, even agitated. Shaking his head, he stared at his guest for a moment and asked, finally, "Where is Mike?"

"*Muerto,*" Will answered.

Peter's sad old eyes widened, and he continued to stare at the younger man.

"Not here," Will told him. "Before. In Tucson. A scooter accident."

"A *scooter* accident!" Peter exclaimed. He seemed stunned by the news. *"How?"*

Perhaps it was his anticipation of what the coming day would bring, but Will spoke at length and without reservation. He told him of Maria. He described in some detail his feckless behavior, and how passion for the woman had led him to betray his best friend. He told Peter that it seemed now to him his life had involved nothing more than a series of random events and empty accomplishments, punctuated at last by a mistake whose consequences were irrevocable.

When he'd finished, Will took a long pull at his *cerveza*, and both men stared out the window at the black sea beyond. At last Peter broke the silence. "What do you plan to do?" he asked.

After Will had answered him, at length and in detail, the old man shook his head definitively in protest. "This is foolishness and worse," he said, his voice rising. "I'll have no part of such nonsense." As if to emphasize his refusal he turned away to stare resolutely at the darkness beyond the window.

"There's no other way, Peter," Will said quietly. "I've considered it from every angle. If you don't want to be involved, I'll understand. But if you want to help, this is the only way. Otherwise they could link me to you, and at the very least you and Bridget would be deported and lose your home. And you know it could go a lot worse than that."

The old man sat a long while and pondered silently before he spoke. "All right, William," he said. "I'll be there at sunrise, and I'll do what you want. But we both know that if Mike was here, he wouldn't like it." He frowned at the younger man.

"Michael's *not* here," Will replied. "Michael's dead. And so he doesn't get a vote. This is the best I can do, Peter, and I'll appreciate any help you can give me."

They talked a bit more, adding more details to the plan Will had contrived, and then Peter unfolded himself from his swivel chair and arose, stretching. "You better get on," he said. "Dawn's only a few hours away, and I know I could use some sleep. You should get some, too. After you're finished canoodling with your girlfriend, that is." He scowled as if pained by his own reference to the girl.

Will smiled. "She's no girlfriend of mine, Peter," he said.

"Then you're even more of a fool than I thought," the old man countered. He looked at Will grimly and said no more before leading him back outside, into the darkness.

———

At the boat the Olivia's impatience sequentially gave way to apprehension and, finally, panic. Hours had passed, and the man still had not returned. He'd been lying, she decided. He had no intention of coming back for her, and yet again she was to be left alone. Bitterness fought with her anxiety. *Why is it so easy for others to leave me?* she wondered.

The middle child of three children born to a middle-class family in Dumas, Texas, what parental devotion was to be found in their emotionally barren home had devolved to her older brother, while her younger sister had enjoyed the considerable extramural success that seems the birthright of any pretty teenage female born in a small Texas town: cheerleader, boyfriends, dances, corsages.

Her parents were devout Baptists, and their religious views and cultural mores were of a decidedly conservative bent. They had little time or patience for a child whose personality was coursed by deep veins of impiety and rebellion. She was pretty, but not so strikingly so as her sister. As a female, she was to her parents intrinsically undeserving of the same attention due her brother. In short, she'd been dealt a poor hand, and the results were predictable.

Her school performance deteriorated in proportion to her advancing age, and at 17 she dropped out and left home to live in a seedy two-room Amarillo apartment with three other teenage itinerants of similar backgrounds. It was a dreary existence, involving a series of tedious, low-paying jobs interspersed by periods of unemployment when she spent her days scavenging for the barest of necessities.

Then one night at a impromptu party thick with drug-induced revelry Pico and Josh had suggested she accompany them on a vaguely conceived excursion to Mexico, and she'd considered the invitation a kind of deliverance. There were nothing and no one to keep her in Amarillo, and the boys genuinely seemed to desire her company. Only hours prior to their intended departure, however, Anna arrived on the scene, and everything changed.

Anna had a look and seductive manner Oliva could never hope to match, and the boys were correspondingly enchanted. While not discarded altogether, increasingly she felt like a piece of baggage tossed in the trunk to be retrieved only at erratic and unpredictable intervals. As they drove deeper into Mexico, she considered bailing out, but she had little money, spoke no Spanish and was afraid to hitchhike alone.

So Olivia had gone along with the others, and now she was alone on a tiny boat in the middle of nowhere. She'd been uncertain as to her feelings towards this man with whom she'd fled. While she found disturbing his long silences and terse, unsmiling demeanor, he seemed kind enough.

Now she knew she hated him. Like all the others, he'd abandoned her, leaving her literally out to sea. Her thoughts were as black as the enveloping night, and the panic she'd felt earlier was collapsing into abject despair. She stared down at the filet knife that she'd fetched from the galley for self-protection. She considered its sharp edge and the possibilities it held.

Suddenly she heard a splashing astern that stood out discordantly from the natural sounds of the night. Grasping the knife, she hurried to the transom and peered down over the rail into the dark water below. It was the man, and with some difficulty he was hauling himself out of the water and up the stern ladder.

In a moment he stood dripping before her in the cockpit, and she surprised him by wrapping her arms tightly around his neck as she commenced sobbing. He reflexively took a step backwards, but she refused to loosen her grip. At last he managed gently to remove her arms from his neck and, seated on the lazarrette, stripped off his shirt, wrung it out and hung it on the lifeline. Even absent the sun, the humidity was so low that the shirt would be dry within minutes.

The girl gasped when she saw his naked left shoulder. Even in the pale moonlight it was obvious that the bruising was extensive, and the wound itself gaped open like the mouth of a drooling idiot. Swollen, discolored subcutaneous tissue strained at the margins of the wound, and his exertions in the water had caused new bleeding. When he turned his head once to the right, she thought she could see glistening white cords shining from the depths of the wound, and, revolted, she looked quickly away.

Olivia sat beside him on his right and asked, "How is it? Does it hurt very much?"

He'd observed her staring at the wound, and her obvious horror helped to confirm his concern that the maiming of his shoulder was irremediable. The first few hours after the shooting he'd held out some slight hope that the brachial plexus – the complex intersection of nerves that supplied the arm - was simply bruised and concussed by the blast and might recover, with restoration of the lost function in his arm. While debriding the wound, however, he'd seen the free ends of the severed nerve trunks emerging from his mangled flesh like angry snakes. The severed trunks would not rejoin. Ever.

Thus far the oral antibiotics appeared to be holding sepsis at bay, but even if he avoided that complication and survived, the limb gradually would evolve into a withered, useless and quite possibly painful appendage. As irrelevant as an appendix.

Well, he thought, *after tomorrow it's not likely to make much difference one way or another.*

He shifted his position to face the girl more directly. "My arm's partially paralyzed," he said briefly, "but that shouldn't make any difference in what we need to do to get out of here." Shifting to that topic, he told her, "I saw my friend, and he's agreed to fly us across the border in his plane. He'll pick us up on shore tomorrow at sunrise, and we should be in Arizona in time for breakfast." He briefly described his near-brush with the soldiers in town and subsequent visit with Peter.

She looked up at him dubiously. "Won't they stop us from taking off?" she asked. "And how will we get past them to the airport in the first place?"

These were good questions. Blandly he explained to her that he intended to create some type of diversion that would draw attention away from their route of escape. "By the time they realize their mistake," he said, "we'll be long gone."

"Won't they just come get us in Arizona?" she persisted. "Or make our government send us back?"

Another good question. "No," he improvised. "We have no extradition agreement with Mexico. Once we're back in the States, we're free." He still worried about this a bit, but Peter would take pains to insure the girl remained anonymous and under wraps until matters died down. As inevitably they would.

To forestall any further questions he asked her, "Where are you from? I've never asked you. I can tell from your drawl that it's somewhere in the South, but I can't place it exactly."

"I come from a little hick town in north Texas," she answered. "Dumas. Dumb Ass. Not far from Amarillo. In the Panhandle."

"Is your family there?" he asked.

"Yeah, my family's there, but that doesn't matter," she replied. "My parents were glad to see me leave. They think I'm a loser."

Will pondered her words. "Maybe they're the losers," he said at last.

There were another two hours before sunrise. The night was dead silent; the bay's surface had stilled, and even the lapping of the small wavelets against the hull had ceased. He decided to get some sleep.

Chapter 15

THE SEA

Will awoke after an hour of restless dozing. Olivia lay motionless, still obviously asleep, her breathing slow, deep and regular. He arose quietly and went below, searching about for whatever might prove useful for the task ahead. He paused to swallow another 10 milligrams of dextroamphetamine.

Rummaging around in an aft locker, he found an old life ring the previous owner had left behind with the boat. The "ring" was in fact a horseshoe-shaped mold of flotation material encased within a yellow coverlet that could be unzipped and removed. The bright color was a problem, he thought, obviously chosen for its visibility in a choppy sea.

Remembering, he opened a drawer in the galley and extracted found a half-empty can of dark green spray paint he'd used once years ago in an attempt to transform the ugly yellow stripe beneath the gunwales into something more visually pleasing. He shook the can for a full minute, the small metal ball within rattling rhythmically in the darkness. Despite the obtrusive noise, the girl slept on soundly just a few feet astern from where he stood.

Shaking completed, he stepped back up into the cockpit. Holding the horseshoe at arm's length, he sprayed the coverlet thoroughly, and once finished he was pleased with the result. With its new color the ring would be difficult to spot even if by luck one were to come directly upon it. Briefly he considered using the paint to camouflage his face, but upon reflection it seemed to him dramatic and probably pointless. *Must be the speed talking*, he thought. From the lazarrette he fetched a diving kit-bag with a waterproof coating and zipper and forced himself to think what items might be so crucial as to warrant their inclusion in the bag's limited space.

From its hiding place wedged between the interior bulkhead and bunk he drew out the plastic zip-lock bag that held his cash and papers. He added a pocket knife equipped with various handy attachments, a six inch filet knife, a spool of high-test nylon fishing line, some matches, a small handheld compass, a tube of sunblock and a handful of high-energy chocolate bars. He tried to cram in a folding cloth hat, but it wouldn't fit. In its place he substituted a thin t-shirt that he could fashion into some sort of protective headgear.

Without adequate water he knew there was no chance for survival. He filled four plastic water bottles and placed them in a mesh diver's bag. *It's not much*, he thought, *but if's not enough I'm probably a goner anyway*. He threaded a short length of quarter inch line through the handles of the zippered kit-bag and the mesh bag holding the water, knotted the two bags and secured the line to a surfer's leash whose velcro band he would attach to his ankle once in the water.

Finished at last, he looked over his gear a final time and was satisfied. Stowing the lot in the starboard lazarrette, he lowered the cover, sat down heavily and lay back against the rail. Despite the speed, in a moment he was deeply asleep.

———

He awoke to bright sunshine and the repetitive honking of a car horn. Suppressing a sudden wave of panic, Will glassed the shore and immediately located the honking's source: Peter, standing beside his pick-up, his arm extended through the window to reach his horn and looking impatient. *How long has he been there?* Will wondered. He'd overslept, and he hoped the consequence would not prove ruinous.

He awoke the girl. "Time to get up," he told her. "We need to get moving. Now."

As she went below to gather her scant belongings, Will started up the outboard and leaving it in neutral went forward to deal with the anchor. He struggled to raise it. The hook appeared to be snagged on the bottom - probably on a rock - and with only one good arm he hadn't the strength or leverage to free it. There was little chance he'd require the anchor again. Swiftly he drew out his diving knife from its scabbard and cut the line.

He scrambled back to the cockpit and flipped the clutch to forward. The boat's sudden acceleration sent Olivia tumbling back down the galley steps, and he could hear her gasp as she hit the cabin sole.

You all right?" he called to her. *This would be a bad time for an injury*, he thought. He began to maneuver the boat to starboard, drawing parallel to the point where Peter was standing ashore. The water was fairly deep here, but her swim would be a short one.

Olivia emerged from the cabin looking pale and shaken but otherwise intact. "I'm okay," she told him. "Just a little scared." She even managed a faint smile.

He nodded to the port rail. "Over you go," he said told her. He'd reduced speed and reversed to bring the boat nearly to a halt. *Celerity* rocked gently in the early morning swell.

"Whhaat?" she stammered. "What do you mean, 'over you go'? What about you? I'm not going if you aren't. No way." She stood before him defiantly, arms crossed tightly over her chest.

"Oh, I'll be along shortly," he assured her. "I just need to leave the boat some place where she'll be less conspicuous." He nodded again towards the shore some twenty yards to their left. "Get going. I'll catch up with you at Peter's."

She stepped up on the rail but then hesitated, turning to look back at him doubtfully. "I don't believe you," she told him. She began to cry.

Will let go the tiller, took a step towards her and gave her a solid push. He heard the splash as her body hit the water, and when he was sure she was clear of the hull, he turned hard to starboard and steered the boat towards the open water to the west. Looking back as he approached the bay's neck, he could see the dust rising from Peter's truck as it disappeared over the rise on its way back to town.

———

Although he'd fully anticipated their presence, the sight of the great gray ships at anchor no more than a mile abeam caused his stomach to turn over and set his heart to hammering. They were three in number, and with their bows set to the north-westerly breeze and their hulls aligned in parallel they formed a neat if lethal triangle. Each dwarfed his tiny craft, and with their powerful engines he'd absolutely no chance of outrunning them, no matter how high the wind.

His plan — his hope — was to exit this smaller bay undetected, under power with sails lowered, turn to starboard and then make a few miles north before raising sail and thus stimulating pursuit. If he were lucky and had judged the distances correctly, he could jump ship at a some point sufficiently close and paddle in to the rocky shores of Tiburon.

Tiburon, the largest island within the Sea of Cortez, lay some 20 kilometers north of Kino Bay. What to do if he made it to shore he'd yet to work out, but at least the island had the advantages of size, with an infinity of places for concealment, a freshwater spring at its northern aspect and close proximity to the mainland: a narrow passage separated the island from the vast emptiness of coastal Seriland, and at low tide one could almost walk its entire width.

While admittedly vague on specifics, it was the best of the plans he'd been forced hurriedly to form, and at this juncture second thoughts were superfluous. Given their proximity, it seemed to Will inconceivable that those on the large ships anchored well within range of his naked eye would permit his departure to go unobserved, but as he passed beyond the headlands and turned north he could detect absolutely no sign of human activity when he glassed their decks.

He continued to motor north, and after 30 minutes — three miles of northerly progress towards the big island — the ships remained as inert as before. He raised as much sail as he had aboard and pointed *Celerity* on a more easterly course so as to catch the freshening breeze. The boat's speed increased slightly, but more importantly the sails filled and billowed; he was confident that whoever was standing watch on those big gray ships could not help but notice this gleaming white signal.

But he continued on his way for another hour, and still there was no sign of pursuit. The southern headlands of Tiburon now were looming before him, and with his binoculars he could make out the large ships apparently still at anchor off Kino.

This he hadn't anticipated. If anything, he'd worried that the Mexicans would spot him attempting to depart in the early morning and immediately run him down. Now he seemed to be eluding them entirely, and to do so would mean sacrificing the diversion he'd planned and a corresponding decrease in the odds of Peter escaping safely with the girl.

He stood at the stern and glassed the ships once again. Still no motion. *For God sakes*, he thought, marveling at his pursuers' lack of diligence. *Are they all still asleep?* There was nothing else to be done, and so he jibed to bring the boat about and reversed his course.

With the motor engaged, the following swell and the boat on a broad reach, he made good time. In less than an hour he was so close to the ships as to worry once more that he hadn't the head start he would require to avoid capture. As he pondered this from his position at the tiller, he again glassed the nearest cruiser and saw at once that he'd been spotted. Faintly in the distance he could hear an alarm beginning to sound, and through the glasses he could discern crewmen on all three decks hustling to their stations. His heart pounding, he immediately reversed course once again.

After 10 minutes had passed he glanced back and saw to his relief that only now had the ships managed to weigh anchor and ponderously turn their noses in his direction. To reach a position where he could jump ship undetected and swim safely to Tiburon's shore he needed to make at least another five miles northeastward, and rapidly he calculated the probability of achieving this.

The ships now beginning their pursuit lay roughly five miles to the south: his head start. He was making about five knots, and under full power those ships easily could quadruple his speed. *Doesn't look good,* he concluded. If the Mexicans were quick in getting under way, he'd have another 15 minutes at best before he'd be forced to abandon the sailboat, and that would still leave him an awfully long swim to the island. Even so, if the tide was running with him, he'd probably make it. If not…

Suddenly he heard a muffled explosion some distance to the south, and within seconds he heard the brief scream of a projectile passing overhead, followed immediately by an eruption of water 200 yards to port. For a full minute all was silent save for the droning of the Evinrude, and then the same sequence of *Boom! Scream! Kersplash!* was repeated. He looked back. The lead cutter had closed the distance between them, and shortly its crew would be able to detect his every above-deck movement with their high-powered binoculars.

This is it, he thought. Without hesitation he grabbed his gear and the flotation device, turned the boat hard to starboard and using the mainsail to shield him, dropped quickly over the port rail and into the sea. The wind was up, and he watched *Celerity's* stern recede rapidly as she moved eastward. He felt no regret at their parting. As far as he was concerned, she couldn't remove herself too quickly from where he now floated.

Sitting astride the horseshoe-shaped float, he watched the cruiser alter course to match the sailboat's new heading. He attached the line leading to his gear bag securely to his right ankle and noted to his satisfaction that the weight of its contents nicely balanced the float's buoyancy. Without making any effort he could keep his head above water, and it would be simple enough to submerge if the cruiser came close or to ascend a bit if a large swell threatened to swamp him.

Given the sea's unsettled surface, he'd be difficult to spot even if they happened directly upon him, and from the look of things they were in hot pursuit of his empty boat, now but a flash of white sail intermittently visible against the sere hills of Tiburon.

For the moment he was safe…but then what? His boat obviously was done for. He couldn't remain where he was for long; the water in his dive bag was sufficient for thirty-six hours at best. The Baja coast lay an impossible distance to the west, and his only chance of making landfall was Tiburon to the east-northeast. He guessed his present position to be about four miles north of the island's southernmost extremity, but the dry, rarified air made distances on the Sea of Cortez notoriously difficult to judge.

More important was the direction of the current. The tides were swift and extreme throughout the gulf, especially here at the Midriff, where the sea narrowed and deepened. At peak tide the current could run up to eight knots, and at such times it was pointless to sail against it. One could be running on a broad reach with a strong wind filling the sails and still lose ground to the tide's relentless pull. To swim against the tide would be exhausting and no less pointless.

He perceived quite clearly that his only chance of reaching Tiburon lay in the hope that the tide was on the rise and that its current would carry him sufficiently close to the island that he could kick into shore before the ebb. If luck was against him, a falling tide would drive him southward into the open sea, and there he would float until he perished.

On numerous occasions in the past Michael had cautioned him to factor in the currents when plotting a course, and Will had taken to buying a tide table at the marina before each of their departures. On this trip, however, circumstances had denied him that opportunity, and his approximations of the times for high and low tides were likely to be inaccurate. Yesterday at Estanque the tide had begun to drop around noon, and with a change occurring roughly every six hours that would suggest he was now in the midst of a falling tide. He hoped he was wrong.

The Mexican naval ship was miles away from where he was bobbing in the sea, ever increasing its distance from him. Soon they would overtake his sailboat and, detecting his ruse, double back to search the waters. He had little worry that they'd find this successful. He knew from experience how difficult it was to detect at close hand even large objects floating in calm waters, and the heavy swell and its whitecaps would make their task near-impossible. While this was the Midriff, the narrowest section of the long sea, there was still a lot of water surface about.

Of far greater concern to him were the tide and the direction of the current it induced. Lacking any reliable reference point, Will was unable to judge whether his drift was northerly towards Tiburon or southerly into the void, into the oceanic waters that dwarfed this sea. The vast Pacific. What had Jeffers called it? *Half the planet...the unsleeping eye of the earth.* There was absolutely nothing he could do to influence the issue, and so he turned his mind elsewhere.

Sharks. As a rule he didn't worry much about those wilder aspects of the natural world that many found terrifying – grizzly bears, lightning storms, rattlesnakes, and the like – but in his present circumstances he couldn't entirely suppress his anxiety. For one thing, he knew this area was lousy with sharks, and that sharks would pass beneath him was inevitable. He could only hope they'd find his dangling white limbs of no interest.

———

The hours passed. *You're running out of tomorrows*, he told himself, *and this time there will be no second chance.*

As a diversion he tried recalling happier days. After all, he reasoned, these might well prove to be his last hours, and was it not better to dwell on the best of life rather than the worst?

He recalled one particular restaurant. *La Roca*, in Nogales (the Mexican side). His hands down favorite. It was an oasis of charm and serenity located on an obscure alley just a block beyond the grimy chaos of Nogales's main thoroughfare. The restaurant was built into a hillside, and one wall of the main dining room was composed of solid rock, its many niches holding candles that flickered provocatively in the dimly lit room. The ceilings were high, the walls were painted the familiar deep colors of Mexico and all the furnishings – tables, chairs, paintings and mirrors – were antiques from the colonial period.

The restaurant was magnificent, the food superb and the service meticulous. Often when Will and his friends would come the white-coated Mexican waiters outnumbered the patrons, but their respectful attentiveness never cloyed. The fact that they'd treated many of the waiters, kitchen staff and their family members back at the university hospital assured their welcome.

They would spend hours at the restaurant - drinking, dancing, eating and drinking yet more - and when the bill finally arrived, its total was ludicrously low. Will's favorite waiter was Ramon. He'd treated the young Mexican's mother, wife and aunt. When Will questioned the accuracy of the calculation, Ramon would only smile and shake his head. Often the tip they left exceeded the bill itself.

He thought of the fine days spent surfing. That first clean right at Torrey Pines, years ago. The ride had seemed endless as he cut up and down the wave's face, always just ahead of its breaking crest. He'd returned to his friends sitting on their blankets and anticipated applause, but it turned out no one had been watching. The experience was his alone.

Other good memories? There were many. That first ascent to Finger Rock with Michael and Brian. The wintertime view from the Mogollon Rim. Those sunset cocktails with Sally. A long-distant Christmas day with his brother. A collage of time well-spent.

———

For a long while after this he simply drifted and tried not to think at all. He watched a flock of sea birds pass overhead on their late afternoon journey to the feeding grounds of Kino Bay, and he envied them their thoughtless mobility. He took a sip of water and tried to ignore how little remained in the plastic container. He was grateful for the sun's descent, both for the colorful sky it produced and for the cessation of its relentless assault upon his exposed face and head. Despite his having fashioned a makeshift turban out of his tee shirt and dunked his head frequently below the surface, his face and scalp felt scalded, and an annoying pain was pounding persistently at his temples. This last was a sure indication of his inability to maintain an adequate fluid balance, no easy feat in the sunlight and heat of July even when one carried a sufficient supply of water.

Seized by sudden impulse, he opened the valve to the plastic container and sucked down what water remained. It was far from enough, and within minutes his lips were as dry as before and his throat thoroughly parched. He worried that should the time come, he'd lack the saliva to swallow the small handful of pills he'd doubly sealed in small plastic bags and stashed in his pocket before jumping overboard. Amongst the tablets were oxycodone and alprazolam, and while ingesting the lot might fail to kill him outright, it was sufficient to promote a dense stupor and with it a brief, unresisting descent into the sea's embrace. For at least the hundredth time he checked his pocket to ensure the pills were still in place. *If it comes to it*, he thought suddenly, *I could chase them with seawater.*

That to arrive at such an obvious solution had required any effort whatsoever seemed to him clear evidence that his ability to reason was succumbing to the effects of dehydration, and he wondered whether he'd remain conscious long enough to experience the visual hallucinations that could accompany extreme volume depletion. Perhaps he wouldn't need the pills after all. Perhaps his dry brain would simply produce a comforting apathy, an immunity to emotional and physical duress. Perhaps he would die like Jack London's reckless trekker who in the end contentedly froze to death.

———

The sun continued to drop towards the sea. *Who will mourn me?* he wondered. He felt sure the Mexican authorities would spare no effort in publicizing their violently successful prosecution of the murderous, drug-crazed American… yet another victory in the struggle to cleanse their land of *yanqui* depravity. His parents were dead, and his brother had died when he'd driven off the road in a remote section of east Glacier Park. His father had two brothers and his mother a sister. One uncle had died in his car on a patch of icy road in northern Virginia, and he'd had no contact with the other in over fifteen years. His aunt had died when he was still in college. He was *de facto* an orphan.

Who, then, would mark his passage? Becky and Brian perhaps, the latter if he'd managed to avoid overdose or violent death at the hands of a disgruntled dealer. There had been other friends, but of that group there was but one whose concern for him might even now provide some comfort. That friend was dead, however, incinerated to a blackened cinder.

What of Olivia? Once safe, would she find a happier course? For what he'd done he felt neither satisfaction nor regret. He was here, and she was there. That was enough.

And Maria? Whatever their relationship had been - an ill-founded caricature of love or simply a spasm of lust - with it had come much death. He counted the bodies: the *federal*, the three hitchhikers, and, of course, Michael. Now would be added a sixth.

It was nearing nightfall. From his passive and persistent movement – slow, clockwise circles – he concluded the current must be accelerating in concert with the changing tide. But was it rising or lowering?

Grown weary with straining to gauge his position relative to the island's distant coastline, he paddled about to face westward. The turquoise sky had softened, and the light now cast upon the water had muted to a golden tone. From this he calculated that the sun must be setting behind the Sierra San Pedro Mártir of the Baja peninsula some 100 miles distant, placing the time somewhere between 7 and 8 o'clock.

My bell is tolling, he thought. *And just me to hear it, me and my own lonely consciousness.*

He watched the light slowly fade and thought of the numberless beaches strung along the far coast of Baja and of the happy times he'd spent there. *If it was to be an abbreviated ride,* he thought, *at least it was a good one.*

While there was still light enough to see he reversed his direction to face eastward once again. Even in the gathering darkness the silhouette of Tiburon's lumpy southern headlands were easily discerned…but diminishing. This time there could be no question. Gradually he was drifting away from the island, moving inexorably further south. South to the great ocean. South towards those waters whose name is peace.

Part II

Happy were he could finish forth his fate
In some unhaunted desert most obscure
From all society's love and hate
Of worldly folks, then might he sleep secure...
In contemplation spending all his days...
That, when he dies, his tomb may be a bush
Where harmless robin dwells with gentle Thrush.

William Cowper
The Task

Chapter 1

BAJA

Lying on his board, he gazed westward, but the marine layer remained so thick as to make it impossible to see the incoming swells until they were almost upon him. He paddled about to face inland. The fog totally obscured the beach, and he could approximate its location only from the sound produced by the larger waves as they crashed upon the rocky beach.

The Mexicans had named the cape Punta Bandera, and decades before the central government in La Paz had encouraged the development of an *ejido*, a rural fishing and farming cooperative, on the mesa above the beach. But the poor fishing, scarcity of fresh water and infertility of the soil had combined with the unfavorable weather - incessant winds and frequent heavy fog - to discourage those farmers and *pescadores* who strove to make for their families a home in the unfriendly environment. Now all that remained of the *ejido* were a few dilapidated shacks huddled together on the bluff and a scattering of tomato plants that had defied the inhospitable elements, bearing mute testimony to the ceaseless efforts of the farmers and their families long departed.

On those rare winter days of sunshine, blue skies, a southerly swell and an offshore wind, the surfing here was sublime. The great point extending into the sea curled slightly northwards to form the unnamed *bahia* where now he floated, and its headland sliced those incoming southerly swells to produce head-high, undulating waves that broke left across the entire extent of the bay's wide mouth. Like most right-handers who had come to surfing relatively late in life, he preferred a right-breaking wave, but it was hard to find fault with a seemingly endless ride down the glistening face of this perfect left, accompanied only by the gray dolphins who hung suspended as they, too, surfed the translucent wedge of onrushing water.

Because it traversed an uneven bottom littered by huge submerged rocks, the right-breaking wave to the south of the point unfurled raggedly and usually could not be surfed. He'd tried those rights on a few occasions, when the waves appeared deceptively alluring, and his second attempt had cost him his board and nearly his life. On his first ride of the morning the wave suddenly had fallen apart beneath him, and the powerful forces released by its collapse had pushed him deep and dangerously close to the rock piles below. Attempting to ascend, he found his leash had wrapped around a gnarly fragment thrusting upwards from the sea floor, leaving him tethered twenty feet below the surface.

To save himself he released the leash's Velcro collar that was attached to his right ankle. Streaking to the surface, he hungrily drank in the blessed air, pausing every few seconds to dive beneath an incoming breaker. Despite the rocks, crashing waves and roiling water, he felt no real danger now that he was unfettered. Those who spend much time in and on the waves know their power is too great to be opposed directly; when confronted by a towering wall that is poised to break, one's safest course is to oppose all instinct and head for the bottom, allowing the wave to pass above. By using this technique he knew he gradually could make his way beyond the breaker line and the point itself. He then would swim parallel to the shore and northward, eventually turning east to bodysurf the swell into his home bay.

But the board was trapped. It remained tethered below when he'd released the leash and ascended. In the relative calm between the oncoming waves he dove down to where he'd been momentarily caught, but despite the surprisingly good visibility he could see nothing but rocks and sand. Afraid that continuing the effort would sap him of the strength required to reach the safety of his bay, he finally gave it up and began the long swim home.

He mourned the loss of the board. It was not his best ride. He had three others he preferred, and, in fact, had chosen it, his oldest board, to use that day in anticipation of just such a mishap. Even so, the board's loss troubled him. It was a gift from a friend, a perpetually friendly and universally liked Hawaiian who had owned a surf shop in the Pacific Beach sector of San Diego before he emigrated to Mexico. The board had been Glenn's first, from his boyhood in Makaha, and he'd kept it over the decades as he'd matured from a young Ohahu grommet into one of California's finest amateur surfers. He'd always felt the board Glenn had given him held within it something of the *mana* of old Hawaii, and that the positive spiritual force it conveyed may have vanished from his life forever haunted him more than the material loss.

Those were the thoughts that came to him as he lay bobbing in the fog, trying blindly to anticipate the next decent set. *I spend too much time alone*, he thought. All this concern about karmic influence came from living like a hermit. He should head down to Todos, stay a few days with Glenn and tell him the story over a couple of beers and a platter of tacos. He was long overdue for some companionship.

He could feel the tail of his board rising as the first swell of a new set arrived. He began to paddle as that swell passed beneath the board, and looking behind him he saw that the next wave was well-formed and could be taken. He felt his speed accelerate as the wave caught up with the board, and after thrusting a few more times with his arms he sensed that sudden fusion between water and fiberglass that produced a ride.

He rose to a standing position in one quick, fluid motion, his left foot forward and pressed slightly downward on the outside rail to force the board's edge into the wave and turn it further leftwards. He had "caught" the wave, but the process of setting up a decent ride was just beginning. The face was steep, and for a second his board broke free of the water entirely on the drop before it merged again with the moving wedge. He rode the wave's face downwards almost to its base before carving again with the outside rail to ascend back to the midsection.

There he remained, hurtling northward, the wave's crest tumbling as it trailed just behind his right shoulder. In the fog he could see nothing but the board at his feet and of the wave only the portion that lay immediately ahead. The velocities of the board and wave were nearly equal, and given the silence of the ride and the fog's obscuration of any reference point he felt himself motionless. Almost as if he simply stood upon the sea. This inevitably would end, but the when and where of that end were lost in the fog ahead.

———

The long ride had taken him within 50 yards of the beach, and instead of paddling back out for another he decided to pack it in and walk home, the board tucked under his good arm. Despite the fog, the morning chill and a building breeze, he soon felt overheated in his spring-suit and stopped to unzip, dropping the suit to his waist and baring his upper torso.

The ocean temperature along this coast rarely ascended above the low 60s. When he first came to the area a year prior, he'd invariably worn a thick full-suit in all but the warmest weeks of late summer and early fall, and he'd often wished for a hood, gloves and booties. With time, however, he'd grown acclimated to the cold water, and the short-armed, short-legged spring-suit represented his only concession even during the winter months. When the water temperature rose above 65, he usually forsake a wetsuit altogether. The water was blindingly cold upon entry, but the energy he expended while paddling out quickly warmed him.

His home was the largest of the shacks abandoned by the *ejiditos*, and as the months passed he'd added new features to increase its comfort and appeal. With lumber salvaged from other shacks he'd built a roofed platform off the front that served both as an observation deck and a sleeping porch on those rare nights when the late summer heat made it intolerable to remain indoors. From a large metal barrel he fashioned a woodburning stove, and a rusty length of cast iron pipe served as its flue.

The climate of coastal Baja was hard on flying insects. The windows he constructed were consequently unscreened, but he added heavy wooden shutters for use on cold nights or during storms. A makeshift flagpole protruded high above the shack's slanted roof line, and at its apex fluttered one of various specimens from his eclectic collection acquired in La Paz and Todos; Tonga, Tuvalu, Mauritius, Kiribati…islands all. As with his adopted home, land masses dominated by oceanic water.

It was a rough dwelling, but comfortable. Its best feature was the view from its position on the bluff, overlooking the beach and sea. Each night when he was not surfing an evening session, he would sit on his deck and watch the red ball of the sun vanish slowly behind the marine layer or, in the drier months, sink directly into the sea.

Obtaining fresh water had presented no particular obstacle. Those who had lived there before him had sunk many wells, and more than a few still yielded potable water. Thick planks of plywood served for his roof, and for reasons both aesthetic and practical he'd cemented upon them a layer of thin flat rocks removed from the tomato fields by the *campesinos* and stacked in huge piles along their borders.

Within the rock façade he created a series of channels such that all rainwater striking the slanted roof was directed into a pipe that led to an old bathtub he'd retrieved from another shack. Mounted five feet off the ground upon a platform built from salvaged blocks and scraps of lumber, the tub served nicely as a cistern, and from it extended three hoses. One led to a wood-fired boiler in the event he desired a hot shower; for simply rinsing off the salt, another led to a small length of pipe capped by a shower head that itself was mounted head high on the shack's outer wall; and the last snaked through a hole he'd carved in the shack's wall to supply water to his sink. Clamps affixed to each hose controlled the water's flow.

Food, too, was simple enough to obtain. For one, there was an abundance of tomatoes. Over the years natural selection had thinned out the weaklings, leaving a few strains of hearty survivors that he felt certain must be unparalleled in the tomato kingdom for their resilience and self-sufficiency. This versatile red fruit, tasty and rich in ascorbic acid, could be eaten whole like an apple, diced and pickled with chunks of fish and mollusks to produce *ceviche* or blended with whatever spices and onions he could scrape together to make would enliven even the blandest dish.

He cultivated a small *salsa* garden in a raised bed that lay against the leeward wall of his shack, an area protected from the salt-laden on-shore breeze that frequently built to shutter-rattling dimensions. He'd obtained seeds from a variety of sources, and coppery-scented cilantro and certain *chiles* grew easily enough when spared the salty breeze and coaxed along with the nitrogen-rich ashes from his stove.

Protein was more of a problem. Although he occasionally would arouse himself to prepare a bouillabaisse, fishing bored him, and the results typically seemed not to justify the effort required. During the months of late summer and early fall the sea just beyond the rocky ledge was alive with spiny lobster, and it was child's play to free-dive ten feet, pluck a bug from the sandy bottom and deposit his catch in a mesh diver's bag tied to his ankle. After a week or so of gorging on the sweet flesh of the *langostas*, however, he would begin to dream of eggs, beef, chicken . . . anything but more lobster. Then in early November the lobster herd would respond to some signal apparent only to its members, vanishing virtually overnight and not to be seen again until the following September. Previously sated, by December he missed them terribly.

Throughout the year he could gather mussels from the rocks at low tide, but a steady diet of mussels also grew tedious. He considered trying to raise a few chickens and planned to discuss this proposition with his friend, Jose the bartender, when he next made the trip into town. Until then, he had to make do with whatever protein the sea offered and he was willing and able to harvest, using *las frutas del mar* to supplement the beans, rice and pasta that formed the mainstay of his diet.

In procuring the last he was dependent upon the *tiendas* and *mercados* of the town, and such dependence made him uneasy. Even now, after a year and the long distance he'd traveled, he felt conspicuous when compelled to appear in public places. Despite his Spanish, his black hair and his sun-darkened complexion, that he was *de los yanquis* was all too evident. For one thing, he towered above those he passed on the street, and despite the time he'd spent on this long peninsula and the care he'd taken to assimilate, every gesture of hand or inflection of speech marked him as foreign.

He was winded from his exertions in the surf, the walk back in the soft sand and the effort of picking his way carefully up the path that led to the top of the bluff. Now he lay sprawled on the rude wooden chaise that he'd nailed to the deck to prevent its being blown into the tomato fields by the wind.

His thoughts turned to weather and how much it seemed to influence human behavior. The peninsula of Baja was long but quite narrow, barely sixty miles across at the point where he now lived. And yet the people of the Pacific coast were as different from those who lived on the Sea of Cortez as were the Chinese from Icelanders. It seemed to him that their distinct differences in behavior must reflect the widely divergent climates of the two coasts. This section of the Pacific Coast was often damp, foggy and rather cold, and in his estimation those who lived and worked immediately seaside were notable among the Mexicans he'd known for their sullen reticence, absence of hospitability and general indifference to others. Especially strangers.

This attitude changed dramatically as one moved inland, where the fog dissipated, temperatures soared, humidity plunged and water became ever more scarce. As he continued eastward to arrive finally at the settlements along the great narrow gulf that separated Baja from mainland Mexico, the traveler would find the indigenous people exponentially more welcoming, friendly and hospitable to outsiders.

Take Turtle Bay, for example, about forty miles north of his current home. In that small coastal town there was a *cantina* he'd finally ceased to patronize due to the unpleasant reception he invariably experienced. If a stranger dared enter and request *una cerveza*, he was left to drink his beer alone amidst a hostile silence.

In contrast, a stranger need only approach the open-air beachside *cantina* in Puertocitos, a fishing village some fifty miles north of La Paz, to be invited inside and, despite all protests, treated to bottles of cold *cerveza* and then invited to fish the next day by every *pescador* present. Like as not, at some point during such evenings a plate of succulent fish tacos would appear magically at the stranger's elbow, and when finally it came time to call for *adios y la cuenta*, the response was *a esta invite yo*. You are our guest.

Perhaps it was time to return to that sunnier, friendlier coast, he mused. *Hard to know, so hard to know.* Aside from the newspaper published in La Paz, *los periodicos* of southern Baja were literally provincial in their perspective; events occurring north of San Loreto or beyond the coastlines were considered to be of little importance. War could break out between the U.S. and Iran, and the newspapers of the region would ignore this irrelevance in favor of a report concerning the *autobus* accident on *Calle* 89 or the local cultivation of a squash that bore the visage of the Blessed Virgin.

It was consequently impossible for him to determine how precarious his situation remained. Over a year ago, he'd left his home and job in Tucson to seek…what? Solace? If so, Mexico had proven to be a poor choice of destination. He'd prevented a rape, watched a *federal* murdered ten feet from where he stood and then rescued a young girl who'd been in great danger. For his troubles he'd become *un fugitivo*, avidly pursued by the Mexican authorities. During the initial days of his flight he'd suffered a gunshot wound to the shoulder that left his arm permanently weakened.

When he'd last enjoyed regular access to the La Paz paper, stories related to the murder and ensuing manhunt had continued to appear sporadically in its pages. In the last related article he'd read was a statement from Hermosillo's equivalent of an American district attorney blandly reporting that two American males held in custody, both accomplices in drug-smuggling and the murder of a Sonoran *federal*, had died in the prison's hospital of wounds sustained while attempting to escape. Of the young female apprehended with them there was no mention.

The official went on to explain that two remaining members of this murderous *yanqui* gang were likely dead, but he assured his constituency that all appropriate agencies remained in a constant state of vigilance on the remote chance that they might yet survive. He ended by imploring the residents of the Sonoran coast and surrounding regions to report immediately to the authorities any information they might possess concerning these *assassininos*.

The story ran for three columns on an inside page and was accompanied by his photograph and a remarkably inaccurate artist's rendering of Olivia. The photograph was an old one, taken by friends he'd been visiting in Santa Barbara. In that photo he was holding his goddaughter, and both were smiling at the girl's mother as she snapped the picture. He and the woman's husband often had surfed together that summer, and his hair was bleached to light brown by the sun. Taken with the changes invoked by the decade that had passed, the thick mustache he'd grown and his far darker complexion, he doubted that any stranger or casual acquaintance could connect him with the man depicted in the newspaper. Still, he was impressed by the effort the authorities must have made to track down the obscure photograph.

He looked seaward. The fog had begun to lift, and now he could see the shore break, green waves rising and trembling briefly before their crests collapsed into flashing white water that rushed furiously up the rocky beach. The swell was building. He could hear the sonorous *boom!* of the waves as they crested and plunged against the resistant sea at their base, and he knew in time the bluff itself would begin to shudder perceptibly with their impact.

No, he'd no method of determining with accuracy how fresh the murder case remained in the hearts and minds of the relevant authorities. He shook his head ruefully, marveling at life's randomness and the magnitude of the bad luck he'd experienced. In the absence of any personal motive, he'd placed himself in a situation wherein he was a witness to murder, and such were the circumstances that there existed no means of proving his own innocence. Without doubt, those boys in the Hermosillo prison had died under torture, and he was just as certain that before succumbing each had pointed to him as the triggerman. His fate had been clear to him from the very moment he watched life fade from the eyes of the slain *federal*.

He leaned back heavily in the chaise and watched a perfect wave break leftward across the bay. *It is as it is,* he thought. *One was ill-advised to delve deeply into Mexico expecting justice. A dry well can yield no water.*

Chapter 2

THE MIDRIFF

Since abandoning ship when the Mexicans fired upon his sailboat, for fourteen hours Will had floated in the sea. Thirsty beyond all endurance, he'd begun to contemplate drowning himself when he looked eastward and found that he appeared to be drifting ever closer towards a hump-shaped black silhouette in the darkness. Unless he was hallucinating, that hump *must* be the southern headlands of Tiburon. *But how?* he wondered.

Earlier during the twilight he'd seen that he was being carried away from the island by the outgoing tide, ever southward towards the distant Pacific. But the dark silhouette, growing ever larger and more distinct, was no hallucination. It was - *que milagro* -Tiburon.

He concluded that as the tide swept southwards, the configuration of the island's southernmost extremity must produce a clockwise eddy current that had gathered him up in its embrace and was now propelling him steadily landward. Elated despite his exhaustion, he was inspired to begin kicking so as to speed the process.

Even with the current assisting it was another hour or more before his feet touched bottom and he staggered ashore onto a tiny shingle beach of stone and sand. He collapsed at once, crawling the short distance from the water's edge to the sheer cliffs that framed the beach.

Resting his back against the cliffs' unyielding stone base, he glanced about him. It was very dark, but with the moon now directly above him and moving westward there was sufficient illumination to confirm he'd made landfall at a tenuous location along the island's southwestern coast.

The beach clearly was dry at low tide only. Well above him on the cliff's face he could see plainly a distinct highwater mark. If he stayed where he was much longer, the turning of the present tide would deliver him once again to the sea. His options were distinct and limited: either scale the cliffs here or re-enter the water and drift south in search of a more hospitable beach.

He was very thirsty. As he knew all too well, the island's only permanent source of fresh water, *agua dulce*, was located on the opposite end of the island. Even if he reached the island's interior, he would have to traverse many miles of rough terrain to reach the lone spring. He'd neglected to include shoes, sandals or reef walkers in the bag he'd carried with him overboard, and he knew from prior experience how cruel these rocky, cactus-strewn Midriff islands could be to one so careless as to wander barefoot beyond the sandy beaches at their periphery.

He tried to put aside his anxiety and rationally assess his predicament. The first priority was water. He knew he'd never make it to the spring, and yet if he remained where he was he'd be swept back out to sea and dead from drowning or dehydration within another forty-eight hours. That it would rain within that period was extraordinarily unlikely. Despite the blustery winds they'd experienced while sailing to Estanque and then northward, there'd been no hint of impending rain since he'd crossed the border into Mexico a week prior.

As to act otherwise was likely to prove suicidal, Will determined to make his way up the bluff. Perhaps on the relatively flat land above he would find a *tinaja*, a natural cistern resulting from the accumulation of rainfall within the depression of a weathered rock. Although only a few hours of darkness remained and his footing would be hampered by the lack of visibility, he decided to start out straight away. He feared that the effort required to gain the plateau above would prove beyond his capacity if attempted with the sun up and heat rising.

He stood for a moment to allow his head to clear and then began to walk slowly northward on the rocky beach towards a ravine that looked as if it might offer the easiest route to the top. When he reached the near edge of the ravine and peered through the darkness at what lay within, he found that the luck which produced the eddy current had not yet deserted him. For there below, at a point where the ravine's sandy bottom heaved up to form a berm that rose well above the high tide line, lay three men and a boy - *pescadores*, undoubtedly - all swaddled in blankets despite the warm night and apparently fast asleep. It was inconceivable that these fishermen would fail to have with them abundant food and water, and so ravenous was his hunger and terrible his thirst it was all Will could do to restrain himself from leaping at once into their camp to tear at their belongings.

Instead he descended into the ravine as quietly as he could, and once there he crept noiselessly in the sand to avoid awakening *los pescaderos*. To his dismay, he could find no evidence of any provisions. If they were contained within the blankets of those who slumbered, he would be hard-pressed to extricate what he sought and escape undetected.

Then he saw it. Shining in the bright moonlight where the mouth of the arroyo gave way to the beach was a *panga,* the long, open-decked and durable boat favored by the Mexicans who fished these waters. Those now sleeping had dragged their *panga* well above the water's edge and used a length of sturdy line to secure its bow to a large boulder.

When he looked inside the boat, Will almost fainted with relief. Arranged neatly in the stern were a number of plastic jugs that contained fresh water, and tucked away in the bow was a waterproof bag that, unfastened and opened, proved to contain tortillas, *queso blanco* and tins of potted meat. Will lowered himself to the deck, taking care to conceal himself from any who might gaze down towards the *panga* from their campsite above. Bracing his head, neck and shoulders against a strut, he used his trembling right hand to open one of the jugs and tried his best to drink its contents slowly and quietly.

That effort proved impossible. His dehydration was far-advanced, and in rebellion against the sudden profusion of liquid his stomach reflexively emptied. He stifled his retching with an oily rag he found draped across the transom by the *panga's* outboard engine, waited a moment for his nausea to pass and then tried again. This time he was successful, and after drinking two liters of the indescribably delicious water, he wolfed down a tortilla filled with cheese and tuna from one of the small tins.

He still felt ill, and there remained the matter of his wounded shoulder, but the resolution of his thirst and hunger restored his spirits as well as a portion of his strength. With his view to the east obstructed by the island's bluff, it was difficult to estimate how much time remained before sunrise, but in any event he knew *los pescadores* were early risers. It would be wise to depart as quickly as possible.

He placed four full jugs of water on the sand beside the boat but decided to keep for himself all of the food. Even without a radio, these men were likely to be rescued later in the day by their neighbors from Bahia Kino who would be fishing this coastline in their own *pangas*. At worst, they could cross this narrow southern extremity of the island, wade the shallow channel that separated Tiburon from the mainland and soon reach a settlement of the *indios* who inhabited Seriland.

Will untied the *panga* from the boulder, stowed its line in the bow and as quietly as he could pushed the boat over the down-sloping beach and into the water. The tide was still on the ebb, and the current was swift. Using one of the oars as a crude rudder, within thirty minutes Will had maneuvered the boat to a point below Tiburon's southern headlands and at least three kilometers from where he'd left the slumbering *pescadores*.

He knew his shoulder was infected and badly in need of treatment. Abandoning stealth, he put down his oar and pulled the starter rope. The *panga*'s outboard engaged immediately, and he found its fuel tank to be well more than half-full. The boat skimmed gracefully through the water as he directed her eastward, and within another fifteen minutes he had reached the mainland.

———

Desemboque was the only village *of* any size within the vast triangle of desert known as Seriland, and some years prior Will had volunteered to work several weekends at a makeshift clinic located on its northern outskirts.

The "clinic" was a twenty-foot square cube with walls of cinderblock and a roof fashioned from scavenged two by fours and scrap metal. The building lacked an exterior door or any coverings for the windows, but given the dry, hot and endless summer characteristic of the region, such amenities were superfluous. At midday, with the desert sun fiercely beating down on that metal roof, the building's interior was more suitable for baking potatoes than practicing medicine, and patients consequently were seen outside, under a *ramada* of cactus ribs and ocotillo branches. A tiny closet served as the clinic's pharmacy, and although it was locked after hours, anyone who possessed even a passing familiarity with the clinic - staff, patients, patients' families - knew the key could be found under a certain flat rock.

Will doubted that either the facility or its security protocol had changed in the two years that had passed since his last visit, and he knew the closet contained the antibiotics and IV equipment he now so badly needed. It would be a long walk - twenty kilometers in and then back again, he estimated - but with food and water now at hand he thought he could make it. Assuming the effort did not accelerate his infection.

With the knife he'd stashed in his dive bag before jumping ship he cut two segments from the *panga's* bowline and used them to transform the sack he'd stolen from the fisherman into a crude backpack. Having an adequate supply of water was essential if he was to survive his trek, and water was heavy and burdensome to pack. He decided to carry four of the plastic jugs with him to what he'd approximate as the halfway point, cache two of the jugs there and count on refilling his two remaining jugs at the clinic. This would allow him about six liters for his hike through the desert, plus whatever he drank while at the clinic.

Both to avoid the hottest portion of the day and reduce further the already low risk of detection in this empty land, he planned to depart in the early evening, arrive at the clinic around midnight and then be back to his starting point by sunrise. The moon would be near-full, and its light should be sufficient to illuminate his way.

Beside the water jugs in the *panga*'s stern he'd found a pair of rubber boots. They were several sizes too small and undoubtedly would raise blisters, but he used his knife to cut slits in the fabric that would allow some ventilation and a bit more room for his feet.

The *panga* was a problem. Unlike Tiburon, this was a flat desert coast, and even scanning in both directions with his binoculars Will could see nothing - no rocks, no dune, no shrub - that offered any prospect of concealment. To mitigate the disaster that would result if the boat was taken in his absence, he decided to bury whatever food and jugs of water he'd not be taking with him at some distance from the *panga*.

In his debilitated state it took him four trips to move his provisions, but at last he managed it. Secure in a deep pit covered by an innocent-appearing plank of weathered plywood, one amongst many similar bits of debris strewn along the beach, were three jugs of water and a few tins of food. Enough to enable him to survive for the several days he would require to travel on foot to Kino Bay should the boat be missing when he returned. To return to Kino would obviously be dangerous, but given his current circumstances it was prudent to have another option should his primary plan fail.

Exhausted from his efforts and feeling generally ill, he tilted *the panga* on its side, used an oar to prop up the boat and spent much of the daylight that remained napping in the shade he'd created. The narrow channel remained quiet, devoid of human activity. Given its shallow depth and sterile, sandy bottom, fishing in the channel was poor in comparison to what was available in the deep water off Tiburon's western coast. And with its heat, aridity and unprotected exposure to sun and wind this shoreline seldom was used by local fisherman for their temporary camps.

At last the sun began to set. Will turned the *panga* over and heaped sand around and upon it in an attempt to camouflage its hull. He marked the boat's location relative to a prominent outcropping on Tiburon across the way and planted in the sand precisely one hundred paces south of the buried provisions a length of pipe he found on the beach. He finished off the last swallows from a jug of water and put it aside. Shouldering his makeshift backpack and glancing at the compass he held in his right hand, he set off in a northwesterly direction.

———

The journey was uneventful. Will found the clinic without difficulty, and indeed nothing had changed. Under the same flat rock he recalled from years past was the key to the tiny pharmacy. Rifling through the drawers within, he extracted a bottle of betadine, various types of tape and dressings, what he required to start and run an IV, aspirin, oral and injectable penicillin and, in case the bacterial culprit was resistant to the penicillins, a week's supply of injectable vancomycin. Except for the items he was pilfering, he left all exactly as he'd found it, locking the door behind him and placing the key back under its rock.

Once he was well away from the clinic he stopped and dressed his wound in the moonlight. He considered administering his first intravenous dose of penicillin, but he was anxious to return to the *panga*. Instead he injected the antibiotic intramuscularly into his hip and, washing them down with his precious water, swallowed six 500 mg capsules of amoxicillin from a bottle he'd decided to toss into his makeshift backpack along with the rest. It was better than nothing.

When he arrived back at his starting point, all was as he'd left it. There were still a few hours remaining until sunrise, and he thought it best to get underway immediately. Despite its isolation, his current location was too exposed. Along the perimeter of Tiburon there were an infinity of places to hide until he was fit for more extended travel, and one in particular was known to him from previous visits to the region under more peaceful circumstances.

Sorry now that he'd taken the precautions, Will laboriously transported the buried provisions back to the *panga*. As he pushed the boat into the water and engaged its engine, he could see on the eastern horizon the first linear glimmering of dawn. Fighting down his anxiety, he twisted the throttle and, accelerating quickly, pointed the *panga's* bow towards the dark lump that was the southernmost extremity of the island.

It was still fairly dark when he cleared the southern headlands and turned north to parallel the coast. Passing the spot where he'd left the fishermen stranded, he pushed on for another ten kilometers in search of a specific indentation within the heavily crenellated coastline. His concern mounted. It was growing light, and soon there would be *pescadores* about.

News traveled quickly in Bahia Kino, and within hours everyone in the fishing community would know of the stolen *panga*. Even worse, Will thought, the chronology of events was such that he himself might well be considered the likely thief. If so, there soon would be more than indignant *pescadores* on his trail.

Finally he saw just ahead the small bay he'd been seeking, and gunning the outboard he turned the *panga* abruptly rightwards to enter its narrow mouth. Within the bay the shoreline doubled back upon itself to form a second and smaller body of water - a bayou of sorts - that was impossible to see from the gulf side even at close distance. The entrance to this bayou was yet narrower than that of its parent bay, and only a boat of shallow draft like the *panga* could clear the jumble of rocks littering its bottom.

Beyond this portal the bayou was roughly circular in aspect. Steep rocky bluffs barred any access from the island itself, and on its seaward side a gently curving berm of rock and sand separated its waters from those of the sea beyond. The berm itself varied in height from about fifteen feet where it fused with the sheer stone cliffs of the island to no more than three feet where it tapered down to serve as the northern lip of the bayou's mouth. At the base of the berm was a crescent-shaped sandy beach that sloped to meet the water, and at its widest point there was a section that lay well above the tide line.

It was there that Will made his camp and a field hospital of sorts. As before, the overturned *panga* provided both shade and a comfortable sense of containment, and the soft warm sand served satisfactorily as his bed. For three days he lay quiet, arising only to relieve himself or ascend the berm to search the waters beyond. Once or twice he saw what appeared to be fishing boats well off in the distance, but nothing more. Otherwise he slept, intermittently dosed himself with intravenous penicillin, changed his dressings and relied on his stolen provisions for sustenance.

By the third day his fever was gone, and the wound itself was much improved. Some granulation had begun at its margins, and whatever discharge he could express was no longer purulent. By the fifth day he was feeling so well that he discontinued the intravenous treatments and switched to oral antibiotics. During the hottest part of the day he began to swim in the bayou's clear, cool waters. Binding his knife to a staff of driftwood, he fashioned a spear and stalked the larger fish that loitered amongst the submerged rocks.

His long series of near-misses was at last rewarded, but instead of eating the fat *cabrilla* he speared he saved it for bait. From the tackle he'd taken from the fishermen and using empty water jugs, he fashioned three fish traps. The results were impressive. The cannibalistic bottom fish of the bayou avidly snapped at the flesh of their predecessors, and with minimal effort Will soon was gathering in as many fish as he desired. When his diet of sashimi grew monotonous, he sliced off strips of meat and hung them to dry. In the hot, dry climate the filets cured quickly.

Dimming his pleasure at the success of the fish trap was the realization that each empty jug signaled an increasingly serious shortage of fresh water. With virtually no chance of rainfall, soon he would have to search out the fabled spring at the island's northern interior. If he left the bayou, however, he would eliminate any chance of connecting with Sally.

He was lying on the sand in the shade cast by the *panga* and mulling over the issue of fresh water when in the left periphery of his vision he sensed a flicker of motion alien to the setting. It was not a bird, nor was it the spray from an exceptionally large wave striking the exterior face of the berm and rising briefly above it.

Instinctively flattening himself upon the sand, Will peered intently in the direction of the perceived motion and watched the upper portion of a bare mast move silently into the bay and towards the mouth of his bayou. Moving quickly, he dragged the *panga* to a less conspicuous spot behind a jumble of boulders, gathered up his knife and the last jug of water, now half empty, and scrambled over the berm to its seaward face.

After a moment he raised his head slightly to scan the bayou. He saw that the masted vessel was a small catamaran, the only type of sailboat that could maneuver through these waters without running aground. In deference to the bay's challenging passage the mainsail was reefed, and the forestay bore no jib.

Glassing the boat, Will saw only one person aboard: a deeply tanned young woman in a yellow bikini, her long brown hair pulled back in a ponytail. Fine-tuning the focus, he trained in on the woman's face. It was Sally, a welcome apparition, absolutely incongruous in this wild place of rock, sand and sea.

He knew her well. They'd dated sporadically throughout his residency, and even during the period of his obsession with Maria and the dark time that followed they kept in touch. While with Michael's death his interest in socialization had largely ended, he'd found Sally's company not only tolerable but comforting.

They'd meet at some quiet bar to share a pitcher of beer. She asked no difficult questions, and she seemed no more inclined than him to offer much in the way of personal information.

She worked as an ICU nurse at Tucson Medical Center. Appreciated by the male staff for her striking good looks no less than for her professional competence, Sally was also notorious for her solo excursions into the unpopulated northeastern reaches of the gulf. At least once every month she would trailer her catamaran to an obscure beach on the mainland coast north of Kino and then leap-frog from point to point along the coast and between the Midriff islands, pausing at intervals to camp. It was she who'd told him of this obscure and well-protected bay, and twice when he'd sailed to Baja with Michael they'd used it as an overnight anchorage. He knew this beach to be one of Sally's habitual campsites, and he'd hoped if he remained here long enough their paths might intersect.

And so they had. As he watched, the young nurse expertly tacked upwind and glided to a stop on the sand. She tied off what mainsail was still exposed to the wind, secured the boom, and used a bowline to drag the boat farther up on the beach. She stood in the sunshine for a moment, facing the bayou, and as Will watched she plunged into the aquamarine water.

She dove repeatedly and would remain submerged for up to a minute or more. During one such submersion Will scrambled out of his hiding place in the rocks and stood on the beach waiting for her to reappear. She surfaced about twenty-five meters offshore and, treading water, addressed him without the slightest indication of surprise or apprehension. "I saw the *panga* when I sailed in," she called over to him, "but I didn't see you. You must have been hiding." Her tone was matter of fact.

"What are you looking for?" Will called back. She'd swum closer to the beach, and while only her head and shoulders broke the surface, so clear was the water that he could see her torso and legs lit by the penetrating sunshine.

"You can usually find mobula rays here," she told him. "They like to lie on the bottom and bask."

She rose, waded through the shallow water to the beach and then stopped. "Turn around," she directed him.

When at last he turned back towards her she wore a t-shirt and board shorts she'd presumably extracted from a large water-proof duffel that lay on the sand next to her catamaran. "They're good to eat," she told him. When he looked puzzled, she added, "The rays. They're good to eat."

She walked past him, sat down cross-legged upon the cata-maran's port hull and began to comb out her long, thick hair. When she'd finished, she walked over to her discarded bikini, rinsed it thoroughly in the bayou and then tied both pieces to the catamaran's forestay to dry. Will glanced uneasily at the bright yellow fabric fluttering conspicuously in the onshore breeze.

She looked at him closely. "You're in some real trouble, aren't you?" she asked.

He saw little point being evasive. "Yeah," he answered.

Sally leaned over and busied herself with brushing the sand from her long, muscular legs. "Everyone thinks you're dead," she told him. "They say you killed a cop in San Carlos and then drowned in the gulf when the Mexican navy caught up with you."

He sat down beside her. "Well," he replied, "I'm not dead." She made no response to this. "It was a *federal*," he continued.

"Not a cop. And it was someone else who shot him." Briefly he summarized the events of that fateful night.

As she listened to his words she gazed steadily out at the bayou, and when he finished, she turned her head to face him. She spoke calmly, her brown eyes clear and untroubled.

"I love it here," she said off-handedly. And by this he took her to mean not just the small bayou but the entire Midriff region. "You don't come across many people, and I like that. Most of those you do run into are decent enough." She paused, as if considering. "But there's some bad ones, too."

She nodded in the direction of the mainland. "Two years ago one of the girls I work with was camping with her boyfriend on the coast. In Seriland," she said. "A bad idea, really. They shouldn't have been there in the first place. A bunch of drunk Seris came to their campsite. They raped her and stabbed the guy in the stomach. Both of them lived, but they don't come to Sonora anymore." She resumed gazing at the sparkling water before them. "I keep to myself when I come down here," she concluded. "I stick to the uninhabited places. Islands, mostly. So far I've been lucky."

"I hope your luck holds," Will told her. "Things can get pretty complicated when it doesn't."

She'd nodded her assent, and he recalled later that they'd sat together for a long time without speaking.

———

For Will the ensuing week had the quality of a dream. While it was impossible to forget the unhappy circumstances which brought him to Tiburon, he marveled at the good fortune which had delivered Sally, *dea ex machina,* to this tiny beach. For reasons practical and otherwise, she was for him the perfect companion. She was entirely at home with their surroundings. Her wilderness skills easily equaled his own, and with her nursing background and skilled hands she could do a far better job than he at cleansing and dressing his wound; under her expert care the healing process visibly accelerated.

Although she was a strong, independent and utterly self-reliant woman, she projected femininity of a sort he'd not experienced in a very long time. Her manner typically was reserved, but she could be playful and even mischievous. She was patient with his moodiness. If he grew morose, she'd manufacture an entertaining diversion. If he needed solitude, she'd preoccupy herself with some small task.

The days passed. They awakened early, not long after sunrise, and following a quick swim they'd fire up her camping stove to boil water and scramble eggs. Mixing the eggs with *carne seca,* cheese and chopped *jalapenos,* Sally would spoon the blended product into one of the homemade tortillas she'd brought from Tucson and serve him a plate of breakfast tacos as he reclined on the catamaran's trampoline, sipping at a mug of hot tea.

After a leisurely breakfast they'd occupy themselves with the numerous trivial chores that attend camping. When those were completed, they'd don masks, snorkels and fins to embark upon small expeditions within the bayou devoted more or less equally to sight-seeing and food-gathering. They took turns with Sally's spear gun, hunting the largest fish that favored the deeper water and submerged rocks at the bayou's narrow mouth, or they'd glide over the bayou's sandy bottom to search out the small rays that clustered there. Sally was right; cut into circular fragments and sautéed in olive oil, the meat of the mobula was indistinguishable in taste and texture from that of the sweet-est scallop.

In the afternoons, during the hottest portion of the day, they alternately lounged in the shade of the *panga* and swam in the bayou to cool off. Towards sunset, after their last swim, she'd redress his wound, and together they'd prepare a meal that included whatever they'd managed to spear, stab or hook in the bayou that day. Afterwards they'd sit atop the berm and have cocktails made from containers of fruit juice and a plastic bottle of precious vodka that Sally had stashed in her duffel. When the sunset's spectacular colors faded, they'd return to their campsite and lie together on a blanket spread out upon the sand, the star-filled night sky above them.

———

As the days progressed and he continued to recover from the physical and emotional trauma he'd endured over the preceding weeks, Will could feel himself finally beginning to relax. What's more, he was enjoying himself, and he could sense at last some waning of the emptiness that had descended upon him conse-quent to Michael's death. For the first time in many months he felt something approximating hope.

At Sally's urging he began to consider the possibility of accompanying her when she returned to Tucson. *If the Mexican authorities believe me dead,* he told himself, *then this whole mess may just blow over.*

When he told Sally that he feared he'd be placing her in danger, she assured him that the risk involved was minimal. She told him the border crossing she used was both remote and unguarded. There was no one there. Ever.

And then, just as Will had decided to leave with her, there occurred in rapid sequence two events that seemed to slam shut the door on any hope of his soon returning home.

———

He was ascending the berm in anticipation of their sunset cocktail hour when above the sounds of the sea birds and breaking waves he heard the unmistakable droning of a boat engine. After ducking quickly behind the berm to conceal himself, he cautiously raised his head to peer between the piles of rocks at the sea just beyond. What he saw immediately produced a reflexive acceleration of his heart rate.

It was a patrol boat, Mexican, with uniformed crewmen standing fore and aft and glassing the shoreline with binoculars. Will glanced back at their campsite and was confident nothing beyond the berm would be visible to them. On the day Sally arrived they'd taken the precaution of stepping the catamaran's mast.

He scrambled down the berm to intercept Sally and alert her to the danger. *If that boat turns into the bay*, he was thinking, *we're in serious trouble.* Although the patrol boat drew far too much water to pass from the larger bay into their bayou, from almost any angle within that bay their campsite could be easily detected.

He grabbed Sally's arm and in a few short, hurried sentences told her what he thought they should do. She nodded assent, and breaking away from one another they rushed to accomplish their respective tasks. Will packed the smaller of Sally's two camp stoves, a tiny unit made for backpacking, two jugs of water, his knife and binoculars, a compass, a change of clothes for them both and his mesh diving bag. Sally rapidly gathered up a full jug of water and a sack containing their remaining tortillas and a round of *queso*.

Thus equipped, they scampered over the berm to where its seaside face merged with the sheer rock cliffs above. They used the binoculars to monitor the bayou's *boca*, but after twenty minutes of anxious scanning there were only the usual birds: the cormorants, "fish hawks", perched upon the rocks, and the seagulls soaring above or placidly afloat in the water. Gripping the binoculars, Will carefully inched his way up to the apex of the berm and to his vast relief observed that the patrol boat was now well off to the north, presumably continuing its search.

Acutely compounding Will's dismay at the unexpected appearance of the patrol boat, not fifteen minutes after it passed by they saw approaching from the south a small plane flying at low altitude. Frantically they hastened to camouflage their campsite, the catamaran and the *panga* as best they could. Similar to the patrol boat, the plane passed directly overhead and continued unhesitatingly on its northerly course.

Clearly this changed the situation. The authorities obviously were not convinced Will had drowned, and their search for him persisted. No such effort would be made consequent to the simple theft of a *panga* and a few provisions.

———

Despite this unfortunate development, Sally still pressed him to escape Mexico with her. Her pick-up truck had off-road capability, she said, and there were open to them hundreds of unmarked trails that would circumvent any checkpoints positioned on the few major roads and deliver them safely across the border.

Will thanked her, but his decision to abandon that option was clear and irrevocable. As remote as the region was, to travel the open waters back to her truck and then drive for two hundred miles through the desert provided too many opportunities for calamitous misfortune. The potential consequences were far too grave to allow this generous young woman to share in the risk. He was adamant.

"Then let's swap boats," she suggested. "With the *panga* I can be back at my truck in five or six hours and off for home straight away. If I leave the boat at the beach where I'm parked, someone will find it within a few days. If the people looking for you find it, they'll think you're on the mainland and headed for the border." Noting his obvious skepticism, she added, "And if you take the *panga*, you won't be able to get much of anywhere without more fuel. Trying to find fuel could be dangerous. Maybe impossible."

She stared at him solemnly. "My cat's small, but she's sturdy," she told him "With a good wind behind you, you could make the Baja coast in a few hours. And if you stayed in sight of land and ducked in when any weather blew up, you could sail that boat all the way to California."

She smiled. "And when you get there, you can give me back my boat." He'd learned from her days ago that she planned to leave Tucson. After accepting a job at the same hospital in San Diego where Will had interned, she'd bought a small cottage in Hillcrest.

———

Eventually he'd agreed to the exchange, and now they were standing on the beach, facing one another and preparing to part. She was returning to Tucson. He would strike out for La Paz, re-provision there and then round the cape. He had an old friend who lived in Todos Santos, and once back in Tucson Sally would contact that friend to advise him Will was headed his way.

She passed him a scrap of paper. "It's my new address," she said. "Keep it with you, and I'll see you when you get to San Diego."

He embraced her, and she raised her face to his. They shared a long kiss, and when they broke off, she looked up at him intently. There were tears in her eyes. "Be safe, Will," she said.

He helped her push the *panga* into the bayou and watched as she guided the boat into the larger bay. Climbing up on the berm, he waved to her as she entered the gulf and headed westward. She picked up speed, and soon even with the binoculars he could see nothing moving upon the sea.

Chapter 3

THE MIDRIFF TO BAJA

Sally had been right. Accustomed to the slow, steady plunging of a monohull, Will was amazed by how swiftly the catamaran skimmed before the wind. True, the boat side-slipped alarmingly if he attempted to tack, but fortunately there was a lot of west in the characteristic northerly breeze.

Fearing detection from both sea and air, he'd waited until sunset to hoist sail and depart Tiburon. The lack of visibility at night posed little problem; until he reached the Baja coast, there was no chance of his inadvertently running aground. His course would take him well below the most southerly of the Midriff islands, and the portion of the gulf he would traverse was a mile or more in depth.

About an hour after sunrise he glided ashore at an empty beach on the Baja coast that he calculated to lie more or less halfway between Bahia Los Angeles and Mulege. Taking stock of his provisions, he could see that water once again was to be his greatest concern. While he could supplement his food supply with whatever he gathered from the sea, there remained onboard only eight liters of fresh water. He could refill the jugs in Mulege or Loreto, but he was loath to show his face in any town or city still so close to the Midriff. On the other hand, even with favorable winds he feared that eight liters might not suffice for the voyage to La Paz.

But the winds *were* favorable, persisting even into the night, and by sailing under darkness and sleeping in the shade for much of the day Will reached La Paz just as his water gave out. Arriving well before sunrise, he beached the catamaran just north of a large marina. From all the sleek luxury yachts present, he assumed the facility was intended for use by tourists rather than the Mexican fishing fleet or other commercial interests.

He dropped sail but left the boat rigged and his gear tied down in case a rapid departure was required. Carrying a blanket, he walked to a small dune complex fifty yards inland from the beached catamaran. Exhausted, he spread his blanket on the sand, lay down and fell immediately asleep.

———

Awakening at sunrise, he placed his knife and the small vinyl folder containing his money and papers in the waistband of his shorts, concealed beneath his oversized t-shirt. Deciding that the boots he'd found in the *panga* on Tiburon would only serve to make him more conspicuous, he walked barefoot across the expanse of sand towards the marina.

At the marina he eventually found a cab that took him to the city's downtown. He bought a pair of *huaraches*, and for the next hour he simply walked around to take in the myriad of shops, restaurants and people. After the solitude of Tiburon and the gulf, La Paz seemed to him as densely populated and frenzied as Manhattan.

He bought some cheap clothes and a backpack at an open-air market and a newspaper from a street vendor. Hungry, he entered a nearby *taqueria* to have an early lunch. Seating himself at a small table with his plate of fish tacos and a soda, he unfolded the paper and began to read.

To his chagrin he discovered on an inside page a more youthful image of himself gazing back at him. It was from a photograph taken by friends in Santa Barbara six years prior, and somehow that obscure snapshot had made its circuitous way to this paper. Beside his photograph was an artist's rendering of Olivia that presumably was based upon descriptions provided by the Mexicans they'd encountered on Isla Estanque; he doubted that the surviving *federal* from San Carlos would have had much to contribute. The sketch was a poor likeness. With its grim scowl and hollow cheekbones, the visage of the female on the page suggested a far older and malevolent version of the ingenuous teenager Will had rescued.

He turned his attention back to his photograph and wondered whether the likeness was sufficient to enable his identification by a stranger. The article accompanying the photograph and sketch was discouraging. The author's chief source appeared to be an official highly placed in the *frontera's* office of criminal justice. Although the man was based in Hermosillo, the capital of Sonora, his strident words had extended across the gulf and southwards to distant La Paz.

Buried within the bombastic declarations of unwavering determination was one valuable but worrisome item of information: the justice official reported that recent evidence had emerged to suggest the American chiefly responsible for the heinous murder in San Carlos might be alive and at large in Mexico. If true, the official vowed, the drug-smuggling *yanqui* murderer would be apprehended and brought to justice. He ended by urging all citizens of the region to contact the authorities immediately should they possess any information regarding this dangerous fugitive.

Will put the paper aside and gazed out the restaurant's dusty window at the street beyond. He hoped that this "recent evidence" had not resulted from any mishap befalling Sally. It was not inconceivable that she'd been caught while en route from Tiburon to her truck on the mainland, with the stolen *panga* linking her to Will.

His heart sank at the possibility. She was a clever and resourceful woman who was not easily intimidated, but in Mexico the wheels of justice crushed the strong and weak alike. Regardless, there was nothing to be done for it now, and whatever the source of this new "evidence" - if there *was* any such evidence - this article's existence was proof enough that neither the murder in San Carlos nor he, Will Rawlins, had vanished from the public consciousness.

His appetite gone, Will arose from the table leaving the tacos untouched, shouldered his pack and began the long walk back to the marina. *Best not to take a cab,* he decided. *And best to get underway at once.*

———

It was after he rounded land's end and began to point northwestward that the catamaran's deficiencies became all too apparent. Will's desired course led him straight into the prevailing wind and the endless swells that pushed relentlessly southwards. When he attempted to tack, the boat bucked and heaved like a balky horse, side-slipping badly and making little headway.

After an hour of futile struggling, he abandoned any hope of sailing north to San Diego by leapfrogging along the coast. The wind he faced now was relatively light. Were it to build significantly, as inevitably it would, he'd have no recourse but to turn about and run southward before it, praying that his rigging could withstand the stress.

Disappointed, he pushed the tiller to port, let out some sail and headed due east on a broad reach. As the minutes passed he found the wind and swell were progressively decreasing consequent to the modest protection offered by a westerly angulation of the coastline. He used this respite to resume tacking, and eventually he managed to make enough headway north that with his binoculars he could see ahead the bay of Todos Santos. After another tedious hour of tacking back and forth he at last drew even with the town and turned to starboard to point his bow directly towards a beach.

Ironically, after the long sea voyage from Tiburon it was to be here, in these last few minutes of his journey, that he almost came to ruin. Not for nothing is Todos Santos a favorite destination of California surfers, and that afternoon the surf was big. The catamaran's hulls performed like two long boards yoked together in parallel, and with her sail full the boat streaked towards shore.

To avoid broaching Will had to keep the bow pointed directly at the beach and hope no following wave broke directly on his stern, but even in this he failed. The combined forces of the wind and the right-breaking waves were too much for the boat's rudder to resist, and as he drew closer to the beach the catamaran abruptly broached hard to starboard while descending the face of an especially large wave.

Now positioned parallel to the oncoming swell, she didn't last long. A breaking wave tumbled the catamaran, spilling Will into the water and leaving him trapped beneath the trampoline as the boat was driven shoreward by the onrushing surf. Quickly, before another wave caught the boat, Will dove to the bottom and allowed the catamaran to pass above and beyond him. As always, there was that paradox: struggle against the sea and risk extinction; give the sea its due and survive. On the bottom, well beneath the turbulent chaos above, all was quiet.

He waited to surface until another wave had passed. Treading water, he looked shoreward for some sign of the boat, but all he could see were the shoulders of unbroken waves rolling inexorably towards their collapse within the shallows. Turning seaward to assess the approaching waves, he positioned himself accordingly and bodysurfed easily into the beach.

There he found the catamaran, its mast snapped off cleanly at the foot but otherwise intact. Sally's neoprene bag containing his money, papers and meager store of provisions appeared intact, still firmly lashed to the boat's frame. He himself was somewhat worse for wear. Somehow during the boat's overturning he'd taken a blow to his left shoulder, and although his wound had not reopened, his pain was far worse than he'd expect from a simple contusion. He felt suddenly depleted. He'd save Todos Santos for later, he decided. Better now to rest.

He did what he could to secure what was left of the rigging, lay out in the sunshine what few sodden articles of clothing he possessed and then reclined on the still-intact trampoline, his good right hand gripping his knife. Once all was arranged, he sat and watched the waves roll in.

He slept throughout what remained of that day and the night that followed. When he awoke the next morning, he was ravenous with hunger. Slipping on his t-shirt, now dry, he shouldered his duffel and began to walk across the sand towards the town beyond.

Once he reached the streets there were few people up and about, and most stores were closed. After penetrating deeper inland and walking southward on a major thoroughfare for a few blocks, he turned into a narrow alley that led to a side street. Midway down the block he found the small *taqueria* he knew from years past. On its window were painted the words *Las Ollas*. The Waves.

The humble restaurant featured a surfing motif. Boards of all vintages were mounted in horizontal arrays on three of the walls, and on the fourth was painted in bright acrylic hues a mural of *la bahia del Todos*: a trio of surfers all facing out to sea and watching the fine sets that rolled beachward.

The *restaurante* was empty, and he seated himself at a corner table facing the door. After a moment a heavy-set Mexican woman of indeterminate age entered the room from what was presumably the kitchen, smiled at him and spoke. *"Quieres el desayuno?"* she asked.

He requested coffee and a plate of *huevos rancheros*. Nodding as if in agreement with his choice, *la mujer* left the dining area, vanished into her kitchen and soon re-emerged carrying a large aluminum canister brimful of coffee and a heavy porcelain mug. Both the rapidity of the service provided and the presentation of the coffee itself were somewhat atypical. Whatever the size or grandeur of the *restaurante* involved, dining out in Mexico was almost inevitably an unhurried affair, and the concept of a "hearty breakfast" washed down with multiple cups of coffee was as foreign as a snowstorm.

Will had just poured himself a second cup when the restaurant's door flew open and a small group of youngish men walked in, laughing and talking loudly. All were deeply tanned and similarly dressed, wearing an assortment of t-shirts, shorts and sandals.

To his relief he saw his friend was amongst them. Glenn was a native of Hawaii he'd known in San Diego, a devoted surfer who'd run a board shop in Pacific Beach before relocating permanently to Todos. The man's gaze swept over Will sitting alone at his table in the corner, but he gave no sign of recognition.

Will had finished his plate of *huevos* and was sipping at another cup of coffee when Glenn passed his table, ostensibly on his way back from *el bano*. Without pausing or shifting his gaze from the restaurant's door directly ahead he spoke briefly and in a low tone. "Meet me outside," he said. He continued on his way.

After he paid for his breakfast and walked into the sunshine he found Glenn parked at the curb, motor running, seated behind the wheel of an ancient and dust-covered pick-up truck. It was identical to those driven by the *campesinos* of the region save for the surfboards protruding out the back of its bed. He was alone.

Will bent down to speak with him through the open window, but Glenn cut him off. "Get in," he said curtly. And as soon as Will had closed the passenger door, the Hawaiian began to drive.

Glenn lived several miles beyond the northern outskirts of the town in a pleasantly dilapidated hillside shack whose porch afforded a fine view of the large bay below. During the drive to his home there was time for Glenn to apprise Will of his current status as fugitive. The news was not good.

"There aren't many details in the paper," Glenn told him, "but from what I've read and heard from people who live in these parts, the local, state and federal authorities are busy looking for a tall American male who shot and killed a *federal* in San Carlos a few weeks back." He glanced over at Will, sitting beside him.

"The guy deserved it," Will replied, "but I wasn't the one who did the shooting." Briefly he described the circumstances.

Glenn nodded. "Bad luck," he said. "What's strange is all the attention this is getting. Normally the authorities here in Baja wouldn't give a crap about some *federal* getting jacked in a flyspeck town far away on the mainland." He paused for a moment, slowing his speed to allow a vanload of surfers to pass.

Will told Glenn about the article he'd read in the La Paz paper. He mentioned the particularly vehement declarations attributed to the district attorney.

The Hawaiian groaned. "That guy is a major kook," he said. "He's determined to be governor, but he's such a pathetic loser that even his own party refuses to support him. Unfortunately the press loves him. He keeps them supplied with outrageous quotes."

"Given all the fuss he's making," he concluded, "someone could ID you. "You need to keep yourself clear out of sight. Even Todos won't be safe."

Will sat silently as Glenn navigated the bumpy dirt road that led to his hillside shack. *What now?* he asked himself.

As if reading the other man's thoughts, Glenn grinned, took his right hand off the steering wheel and reached over to give Will's neck an affectionate squeeze.

"Leave it for now, bro" he advised, not unkindly. "Try sleeping in a bed for a change, drink plenty of cold beer and at the ebb tide tomorrow we'll surf the best right break in Todos."

He stopped in front of the two story wooden building draped with trumpet vine and festooned with the vibrant bright hues of bougainvilla, "Get your head straight at Casa de Glenn," he told Will. "And by and by your way be clear."

——

Will spent the next three weeks enjoying the Hawaiian's hospitality. Mornings they spent surfing a consistently fine break that somehow had resisted discovery by the locals and itinerant *gringos* alike. So accessible and consistent was the wave that even with his injured left arm Will could manage to paddle the short distance out and catch as many rides as he desired.

Often they were accompanied by several of Glenn's friends, fellow expatriates from SoCal. Casually expert surfers clearly comfortable with the remoteness of Todos and the anonymity thereby conveyed, they provided pleasant company but asked few questions. After the evening sessions they would sit and relax on Glenn's rickety deck, drinking beer and listening to the rhythmic crash of the waves below

It was a comfortable life, but ever nagging at Will was the knowledge that his continued presence posed for Glenn a dangerous and potentially fatal risk. Todos was relatively isolated, and Will took pains to avoid any public exposure, but even here in the southern extremity of rural Baja secrecy was not inviolate.

But where to go? To attempt now to return to the States seemed premature, but to remain in Mexico conveyed its own burden of inconvenience and peril. Will queried Glenn and his friends at length, and after many *cerveza*-fueled conversations on the deck one of Glenn's friends had recalled the abandoned coastal *ejido* to the west of Guerrero Negro.

"It's no paradise," the young man reported. "It was cold and foggy the whole time we camped there, and the surfing to the south of the point is sharky. But it's definitely high on privacy."

So Will had bartered the damaged catamaran for a 150cc scooter in decent condition, collected some supplies and after another week of respite set out with Glenn to set up his homestead between the sea and the fields of abandoned *tomates*. The Hawaiian helped him unload his scooter, tools and provisions, and before they parted Glenn had given him three boards, including the old blue longboard he'd used himself as a boy growing up in Makaha.

As he watched Glenn drive away after, he'd no inkling that this isolated speck of coast would serve as home for the next two years.

Chapter 4

ELENA

Continuing to watch the sets sweep in, Will thought to himself that his shack and bay might prove difficult to leave. He'd come to this place a desperate and discouraged man, and it was not time alone that had brought him peace and restoration. The surfing had helped, most definitely, and to return to the waveless shores of the Mar del Cortez would create a void in his life that he'd be hard-pressed to fill.

In time the fog vanished entirely, and the marine layer receded towards the horizon. Judging it to be mid-morning, he decided to prepare for the journey into town. He needed to pick up a few necessities – beans, white gas for his lanterns, matches and the like – and while there he discretely would seek news related to his status as *un fugitivo*.

For transportation he had the Honda scooter he'd procured in Todos Santos before moving north. Although to his surprise the motor function in his proximal left arm had slowly improved to the point where he could use the limb to paddle out even in heavy surf, he had almost no grip strength and was totally reliant on his right hand for any activity involving precise hand and finger movement. Fortunately the scooter was simple to drive and had a reliable foot break.

He used bungee cords to attach a plastic crate to the rear fender, and the apparatus was sufficiently sturdy to hold about 40 pounds of groceries or hardware. The scooter burnt almost no gas or oil, and it was perfect for the unpredictable back roads of Baja. If he came upon a section washed out by flash floods, he could maneuver the scooter upstream or down until he found a crossing point. If a dune of sand had drifted across the road, he could simply walk the scooter over it.

His financial situation remained secure. When he'd abandoned his boat two years prior, he'd taken care to stuff into his diving bag a waterproof plastic box containing his papers and $2,000 in cash. Of that money over half remained, and his needs were few. Tequila was cheap, and at home he rarely allowed himself more than the indulgence of a single shot with a slice of lime to toast the sunset. Although he had a definite fondness for *las cervezas de Mexico*, he saved his beer-drinking for the bars in town. Unlike America, where a draft at a decent bar could exceed a store-bought six pack in cost, enjoying a bottle of *cerveza fria* in a Mexican *cantina* cost little more than drinking that self-same beer at home. Besides, at his shack he had no way to keep beer cold.

The day was warm, and so he showered without firing up the boiler. Pulling on a clean cotton shirt, he winced at the sudden jolt of pain in his left shoulder and chest that even this simple action produced. The shotgun round he'd taken during the first days of his flight from the Mexican authorities initially had rendered the limb nearly useless. With time the weakness had diminished, but the pain persisted.

He slowly buttoned his shirt with his one good hand, carefully shaved off two day's worth of beard and made a passing attempt to trim his moustache. His hair had grown longer than he cared now to wear it – he felt it further emphasized his foreignness – but little could be done about that until he found time to visit the *barbareria*. To conceal his blue eyes he wore a pair of dark glasses distinctly Mexican in style. Although even with his dark complexion, mustache and nondescript clothing he may not have passed as Mexican in the revealing bright sunlight of midday Baja, when seated in the darkest corner of a poorly lit *cantina* the effect was convincing.

Despite all his precautions, he always felt a vague sense of dread when he ventured into town. Its name itself was unsettling. *Guerrero Negro*. Black Warrior. Named for an American ship that, overloaded with the oil and carcasses of slaughtered gray whales, had foundered and sunk in the nearby waters. An odd choice in a placid land where towns most often were named for some distinguishing geographic feature (the relative abundance – or scarcity – of fresh water nearby, the character of the water itself), a saint or some other Biblical reference. *La Bufadora* ("blow hole"). *Santo Tomas*. *Agua Caliente* ("hot water"). *Todos Santos ("all saints")*.

But he'd kept a low profile during his infrequent visits and thus far had experienced nothing to justify his apprehension. Those who identified him as American likely took little notice of the fact. *Gringos* frequently paused in the town for gas, food and beer while en route to nearby Scammon's Lagoon to watch the whales and their calves. Surfers were common as well, often frequenting the town's *cantinas* in search of *cervezas frias* as an antidote to the inescapable heat and aridity. It was the recurrence of his presence that was unusual, and for that reason he limited his visits.

By his cheap wristwatch it was just past noon. If he left now, he could complete his errands and enjoy a *cerveza* or two with Jose. Jose was owner and proprietor of *El Tecolote* ("The Owl"), a humble *cantina* of unpainted cinderblock walls and bare concrete floor that he favored for its obscurity and relative lack of patronage. Unlike the flashier *cantinas* that lined the busiest block downtown and offered meals, loud juke box music and a full bar, *El Tecolote* squatted alone on a forlorn side street and provided its patrons only *mescal*, *cerveza* and quiet solitude in compensation for their pesos. Within its dark interior he'd seldom found more than three or four others, the customers usually *campesinos* of Indian caste who solemnly lifted their glasses in silence or at most murmured softly amongst themselves.

It was a far cry from the rowdy surfer bars of Todos Santos, and it served the peculiar circumstances of his situation. And after the enforced solitude of his shack by the bay, any company, however tepid, was welcome.

Within the walls of *El Tecolote*, "tepid" was an appropriate descriptor. The omnipresent Jose was the living, breathing epitome of a laconic Mexican male, and while one might think that the paucity of his clientele and the paltry revenue such modest patronage generated would induce a man to feign some enthusiasm over the arrival of a new customer, that man was not Jose. A short, squat, muscular *mestizo* with a bowl-cut mop of graying black hair, a mustache to match and an ageless face, he was capable of standing for many long minutes behind his bar, polishing the same glass with the same dirty rag, completely impervious to the needs of his customers.

For Will, however, he made an exception, and the American was never quite sure what he'd done to deserve such deference.

Although the content of their conversations rarely ranged beyond observations regarding the weather or the ever-declining value of the peso, such was Will's social isolation that even these spare exchanges he found rewarding.

And then there was the girl.

———

It was only by the slightest of chances he'd met her, on a hot and dusty afternoon in Guerrero Negro two months prior. After he'd finished shopping for provisions, he found *El Tecalote* to be uncharacteristically closed. Not quite ready to return home, he'd taken the pack containing his provisions and walked back the way he'd just come.

She swept by him as he stood debating whether to enter one of the bars that fronted the town's main street. With her lithe body, chin held high and brown hair flowing freely down her back, she was like a visitor from another planet. When she moved by him and on down the sidewalk, he observed with appreciation the suggestive undulations of her soft, round rump snugly encased in a pair of fawn-colored suede jeans that seemed to have been tailored precisely to her dimensions. Her look and attitude contrasted sharply with the other women she passed briskly on her way, a uniformly lumpy group heavily swathed in layers of clothing despite the day's heat, their hair hidden beneath drab scarves that recalled the *babushkas* of Stalinist Moscow.

As he watched her walk from him, she turned suddenly to enter the largest and most brightly illuminated of the *cantinas* that lined the block. *El Papagayo Azul*. When she failed to emerge, his curiosity compelled him to walk over to the *cantina*'s open doorway and peer in.

She was sitting alone at the near end of the long wooden bar, a glass of water sitting untouched before her. With her slim legs crossed, erect posture, fine features and uplifted chin, she presented a regal affect: the tawny-skinned queen confidently ensconced on her humble throne. The attitude of insouciant self-confidence she projected was distinctly unusual to observe in women living anywhere but in Mexico's most cosmopolitan cities, and Guerrero Negro was not to be included on that short list. For an unaccompanied woman so young and attractive to enter a bar dressed as she was, with her hair visibly loose and flowing, was an open invitation to unwanted male attention, the dimensions of which quickly could escalate beyond the simply annoying.

He paused for another moment, continuing to watch her. *What the hell*, he decided, and stepped into the *cantina*. He sat three stools down from her at the bar and ordered a beer. It was almost six, well past the five o'clock threshold he maintained for the sake of ritual rather than prophylaxis against the alcoholism that afflicted so many American expatriates in coastal Mexico. The sun would not begin to set for another two hours, and, besides, he was now so accustomed to the route that led back to his *ejido* that he felt no unease when traveling it at night. In fact, given the invisibility that the darkness bestowed, he'd come to prefer it.

Despite the loud, raucous American music issuing forth from the jukebox, the *cantina* was deserted save for the girl, a bored bartender and himself. Although he missed the obscurity that represented the primary attribute of Jose's establishment, there was no mistaking the rare experience of having an attractive female so close at hand. And this *cantina* appeared safe enough. Relaxing, he decided it would serve as an adequate haven for drinking a few beers, after which he'd climb on his scooter to return home well in advance of the *yanqui* surfers and whale-watchers who tended to descend upon the strip for a long night of post-prandial drinking and carousing.

As he sipped at a second beer, Will watched the young woman's reflection in the mirror. Finally he turned on the tall stool to face her. "*Disculpa,*" he asked. "*Puedo invitarte una copa?*" Might he buy her a drink?

She stiffened at his words, and her reply was immediate. "Do you believe you are in some manner acquainted with me, *senor?*" she asked, addressing Will's reflection rather than turning to face him directly. "If so, you are mistaken." Her tone grew more hostile. "I have observed you staring at me in this mirror," she added. "To do so is quite rude." Her English was perfect, with only the barest trace of a Spanish inflection.

He sat for a moment and gazed back at her reflection silently as if considering how to reply. She was even lovelier than he'd first perceived. Her hair, the color of dark honey, fine cheekbones and light skin bespoke a strong infusion of Castilian blood, but the plump, pouting lips were those of *los indios.*

"I'm afraid it is you who is mistaken, *senora,*" he told her at last. "I'd not noticed you until now."

Somewhat to his surprise she briefly dropped all trace of *hateur* and laughed. Then, collecting herself, she replied, "*Es verdad. Por lo menos*, you are a very rude man. *Claro.*"

"No," he answered, "Not rude. Merely honest." He followed this with another swallow of the deliciously cool beer.

"I see, I see," she mused. "How do you Americans say it...'a spade is a spade', no? Allow me to reply in kind." Now she turned to look directly at him, and her gaze was steady. "I have no interest in your drink," she said evenly. "Nor in you." Dismissively, she turned away as if to contemplate the street outside the *cantina*.

Will finished his beer, arose and walked over to sit on the stool beside her. "Please excuse my having intruded upon your privacy," he began, addressing her slim back. "I spend too much time alone, and I'm afraid I've forgotten what few manners I once possessed." He paused. "*Como recompensa*," he continued, "may I buy you that drink?"

She turned and gave him a cool, neutral look. "You seem a man not altogether lacking in social grace," she said at last. "What could explain your seclusion? Perhaps a consequence of your intrusive behavior, and not its cause?"

Will glanced at her sharply, but she'd pivoted on her stool to face the window. After a moment she sighed and then turned back towards him, resting her forearms on the bar. He could sense nothing suspect in her manner. The young woman seemed indifferent, *no mas*. And yet...

She'd rolled up the sleeves of her blouse to the elbows, and on her slender wrist was a silver watch, simple but elegant. As she noted the time, she remarked, "My friend was supposed to meet me here, but she is late. We made plans to have a cocktail, tell each other our troubles and then go to dinner." She paused and looked at him appraisingly as if considering his offer. "Yes," she decided. "I suppose I could accept a drink from you. *One* drink. *Solamente*."

Will called to the bartender for another beer, and in rapid Spanish the young woman ordered some complicated-sounding mixed drink that involved gin. Time passed, the friend did not appear, and despite her declared intention the first drink led to another. When she insisted upon paying for their second round and began rifling through her purse for the *pesos* required, he took advantage of her distraction to inspect her more closely.

She'd left unfastened the top two buttons of her white linen blouse, and from the angle his height provided he had an unobstructed view of the tops of her small, round breasts and the lacy beige bra that held them. Her eyes were deep brown, of a hue that matched her hair, and she had long, graceful fingers. When she spoke, her speech was clear and precise, but the richness of its tone caressed the ear. *My God but she's lovely,* Will thought. Although she conveyed the reflexive poise of one older and more experienced, he guessed her to be barely into her twenties.

With the second drink she relaxed and became more animated. She nudged his leg with the toe of her sandal, nodding at his backpack. "What do you carry in that old bag?" she asked. "Just your dirty socks, or something more dangerous? *Mas peligrosa?*" She folded her arms on the bar and leaned towards him, searching his face with mock seriousness.

"Just provisions," he answered. "*Nada mas.* Soap. A bottle of tequila. A box of wooden matches. Some *frijoles* and tortillas."

"*Frijoles y tortillas!*" she exclaimed in mock horror. "Are you but a poor *campesino?*" Her smile was dazzling.

He returned her smile. "No," he said. "I came down here to surf, and I'm camping on the beach."

She gave out an exaggerated sigh, batted her long lashes flirtatiously and feigned a swoon. "*Ay, un surfista! Me gusta los surfistas,*" she gushed. She drew yet closer and gave him another long, appraising look with her luminous brown eyes. "But are you not rather old to be a - *como se dice?* - 'surf bum'?" she asked.

He nodded. "Probably so," he answered. "And aren't you rather out of place in Guerrero Negro?"

She laughed and nodded. "Verdad!" she agreed. *"Sin duda."* Without doubt.

Just as he'd been pleasantly surprised by her physical appearance, he found appealing her casual manner and willingness to banter with him, a male stranger. Such behavior was common and accepted on the border and in the cosmopolitan cities, but they were now deep in a portion of Mexico distinctly unsophisticated. In Guerrero Negro only *una puta* - a prostitute - would publicly invite the attention of a man not within her innermost circle, and this young beauty looked nothing like the garish whores he'd seen sitting at the bars of the busier *cantinas*.

But soon he learned that she was far from her natural environment. Perhaps after her weeks of cultural isolation she was simply relieved to have an opportunity to dress and behave in her accustomed manner.

The friend failed to arrive, and they drank and talked for a full two hours. While in their conversation they discussed nothing of great consequence, there was an easy communication between them. She seemed a good listener, and the observations she voiced were notable for their humor and insight.

Her name was Elena, she told him, and she'd grown up in Guadalajara. Two years prior she'd graduated from *la universidad* in Mexico City with a degree in marketing. After a prolonged period of fruitless searching for a job suited to her education and interests, she'd finally found employment as the manager of a resort hotel in Cabo San Lucas that was undergoing extensive renovation following the ravages of Hurricane Jimena. While she awaited the hotel's re-opening she was staying in a *casita* owned by relatives. She was economizing, she told him, saving money in anticipation of buying a condominium just down the beach from her workplace. She liked her job, the liveliness of the resort atmosphere and the natural beauty of the sunny coast.

Guerrero Negro was very dull, she confided…especially after her years in *La Ciudad* and, more recently, immersed in the frenzied nightlife of Cabo. In this hot, dry and highly conservative city a young woman was expected to remain locked up in her house, she complained, venturing out only to purchase groceries at *el mercado* or to attend mass. Local custom dictated that during these infrequent public appearances she must keep her hair tightly bound and her body concealed beneath voluminous dresses of an unfeminine cut. Loose, flowing hair and more feminine attire were considered provocative, an open invitation to malicious gossip and unwanted male attention. This was especially so if the woman was to walk about unaccompanied.

"Our culture is one with our religion," she mused. "The Catholicism introduced by the Spanish. By Spanish *men*." She paused and gazed at him gravely, her chin resting in her hand. "Here as in much of Mexico," she continued, "it is difficult for a woman to speak and act as she wishes in a culture designed by men."

She and her girlfriend had determined to stage their own small rebellion, and tonight was to have marked its inauguration. They would *dress* as they pleased, *go* where they pleased and *do* what they pleased! But now it seemed that her girlfriend had cast aside her resolve, and Elena was left to carry on the rebellion alone.

It was just past eight, and the *cantina* was filling up. Will glanced around at the *yanquis* who now crowded the bar and was preparing to take his leave when Elena asked suddenly, "Would you like to have dinner?"

He gazed back at her without responding, and it seemed to him her expression was entirely guileless, indicating nothing more or less than what was offered. Seeing him hesitate, she explained, "My house is only a few blocks from here. You may as well eat before you return to your beach, and I bought too many *tamales* today to eat them all myself."

Why not? he thought. *I'm tired of having only myself for company. Why refuse this bored and beautiful young woman?*

"All right," he told her. "I accept. My scooter is parked around the block. I'll get it, and we can ride together."

"No, no," she demurred, shaking her head. "I am a woman living alone, and it would not do for my neighbors to see me arriving home with *un hombre norteamericano*. I will walk home, and you may follow in a short while. Please park your scooter some distance away, and use the alley behind my house to come to my back door." She described her *casita* and how to find it.

When she arose from her stool and walked out of the *cantina*, the young *yanqui* standing beside him, a surfer by his look, spoke to him with good-natured envy. "What a babe," he said. "You are one lucky dude."

Smiling but offering no reply, Will shouldered his backpack and walked out into the darkness.

———

As Elena had indicated, the house was only a few blocks east of the *cantina*, one of a dozen or so similar structures built of block and stucco that were clustered together on a short street that rapidly gave way to the open desert. Unusual for Guerrero Negro, all were in good repair and sat on small, well-kept lots. Nowhere were visible the usual piles of trash, stacks of castaway tires and decrepit vehicles that hadn't moved under their own power for many years.

The interior of her home was equally neat but rather spartan in its furnishings. In the kitchen and sitting room there was only such furniture as one would require for functional use: in the kitchen, a small round table and two chairs, and in the sitting room a love seat, an end table and a lamp. All appeared to be new. The walls were entirely free of photographs, paintings or other decoration, and within the two rooms the only concession to color was a burgundy rug that lay before the love seat. She'd told him earlier that her uncle, *un abragado* in Guadalajara, had bought the property as an investment, hoping to rent the *casita* to *touristas* intending to view the gray whales in the nearby lagoon. The *casita* appeared to have seen little use.

Shortly after he'd arrived she bade him sit for a minute on the loveseat while she went off to another portion of the small house. As she left him, she called back over her shoulder that he was welcome to a beer from the refrigerator. Looking within, he found it well-stocked with *cereveza Mexicana* and little else. Searching the drawers for a bottle opener, he found a corkscrew, several knives and a set of inexpensive flatware. The *talavera* tile counter of the kitchen was populated only by a glass pitcher and a small pile of cloth napkins folded neatly. All seemed typical of a sparsely appointed Mexican rental.

He finished the beer quickly, and with it following those consumed at the *cantina* he found himself in need of a toilet. Searching the *casita's* sole hallway for a bathroom, he entered a room whose door was ajar and found that he'd intruded upon Elena in her bedroom. The room contained a small fireplace, and within it a fire was burning. Aside from a shaft of light cast from a closet, the fire provided the room's only illumination.

Elena was standing between the fireplace and a large bed, her back towards him. She'd removed her blouse and lacy beige bra, and from the waist up she was naked. Before he could discreetly exit she turned towards him, and her eyes widened with alarm. Hastily she retrieved her blouse from the bed and held it before her chest to conceal herself. Despite the brief exposure and dim light, he had seen her breasts were as fine as his surreptitious glimpse at the *cantina* had suggested. The orange glow cast by the fire accentuated the angular beauty of her face framed by the honey-brown hair cascading over her shoulders.

"I'm sorry," Will told her. "I was looking for a bathroom."

"Yet another intrusion," she observed, but she was smiling as she spoke. "The bathroom is over there." She nodded towards the space he'd taken to be her closet.

When he'd finished and was exiting the bathroom, he found her now fully clothed, a sweater having replaced the blouse, sitting on the floor before the fireplace. She appeared tense, and the smile she gave him was insufficient to conceal her anxiety. "Perhaps we can sit here and enjoy the fire for a moment before we eat," she suggested, her voice faintly tremulous.

"I'd like that," he'd told her, and after he'd settled himself next to her they sat together in silence, each staring at the flames. He was acutely aware of her proximity, her knee touching his, the soft rhythm of her breathing, her scent. Aroused, he turned and drew her face to his.

She returned his kiss briefly but then broke off their embrace. "No," she told him. "I cannot." But her voice held no conviction, and her parted lips seemed to belie her words.

He kissed her again, and this time her response was more passionate and prolonged. They continued to kiss, and as he stroked her she began to moan softly. Slowly they undressed one another, pausing at intervals to caress the flesh revealed.

Months later, all he could recall of this, their first time together, was how she shuddered as she arched to receive him. And how he'd awakened afterwards to find her lying on her side, her back to him, at the far edge of the great bed.

———

Following that first night, they'd developed a routine of sorts. At first he continued to come to town only once a week, on Fridays, and when he did, he would return to *El Tecolote*, drink a few beers and wait for the evening's darkness to arrive. Then he would ride his scooter to Elena's neighborhood, park a few blocks from her house and walk the rest of the way. Invariably she was there, and always her greeting was enthusiastic. They'd talk, make love by the firelight and fall asleep naked in each other's arms. They arose early, and before he departed she would prepare him a breakfast of *huevos y tortillas de harina*.

As the weeks advanced his visits to town became more frequent. Acutely aware of her alluring proximity, at every sunset he fought the temptation to go to her, and in this he was ever less successful. Now it was not unusual for him to make the trip to Guererro Negro as often as three or four times each week, often arriving, unheralded, long after dark.

While they rarely made formal plans to meet, she was always home in the evening when he'd come tapping softly at her back door, and her pleasure in seeing him was evident. Occasionally he would ask her to meet him at *El Tecolote* on a predetermined night, but aside from this and their initial meeting at *El Papagayo Azul*, their time together was spent solely within the tiny house.

Elena expressed no dissatisfaction with the arrangement. When he'd questioned her on the point, she'd shrugged in response. "How better to spend our time together in this dusty old city?" she asked him. "Attend mass, perhaps? Shop at the market? I doubt you'd find either a pleasant diversion. The former is dull beyond imagining, and the latter is hardly picturesque."

They were lying on her bed, naked beneath the single sheet that covered them. It was a warm night, and there had been no fire. "Perhaps you have tired of me and our activities, *surfista*?" she suggested. "Perhaps this wave has become too familiar?" She rolled over to lie upon him, her hair a shining cascade that encircled them both, her body sealed to his. She smiled down at Will.

"No," he'd responded. "This is what I want." He embraced her more tightly, and in synchrony their bodies began to move together.

———

Her *casita* was clean and comfortable but…*sterile* was the best adjective Will could think of to describe it. It was as if the absentee owners had ceased halfway in furnishing the little house, satisfied that the sparseness of its furnishings would be sufficient for the whale-watching clientele they anticipated.

The cupboards and shelves *de la cocina* contained the minimum equipment required to cook, serve and eat a simple meal. One drawer held the set of cheap flatware and a filet knife. In a cupboard were a couple of sauce pans and a cast iron skillet, a few plastic bowls, some plates, a green glass pitcher, two large coffee cups and a motley collection of unmatched glasses. That was all.

Her refrigerator seldom held more than milk, juice and a few eggs. Exploring the tiny pantry one morning, he found only a sack of coffee beans, a half dozen cans of *frijoles negros* and some jars of salsa. She appeared to keep on hand only the ingredients required for the *huevos rancheros* she often prepared for his breakfast, including the excellent tortillas she bought fresh every day from the old woman who stood by the *supermercado*. When he questioned her regarding her meager larder, she was breezily dismissive. "Oh," she laughed. "I never eat."

Although Elena dressed simply, even he could appreciate that her clothes and footwear were of excellent quality, and he never saw her wear the same outfit twice. And while he was no expert on women's lingerie, the seductively cut bras and panties she favored had clearly not come from the conservative shops of Guerrero Negro. More likely they'd been purchased in a trendy Cabo boutique, he decided. Like the grey whales in the nearby lagoons, she was only a visitor to the region.

With time she was ever more at ease in his presence. They spent many hours simply talking, lounging on the floor before her fire, sitting at her kitchen table or lying beside one another in the great wooden bed. Along with the trivialities related to

303

her day-to-day life in the town, she spoke to him freely of her childhood, her family, and her hopes for the future. She aspired to owning her own business, she told him. Perhaps a restaurant, perhaps a small but elegant seaside hotel. Even more important to her, however, was a happy marriage, and she made no secret of her desire for children.

It seemed to him that he held no place in the future she envisioned, for even as their relationship deepened she made no reference whatsoever to its potential endurance. Will found his exclusion somewhat disconcerting, an unwelcome reaction he struggled unsuccessfully to suppress. *You fool,* he told himself. *You cannot afford the luxury of attachment. Confine your hopes to survival.* He suffered nonetheless. At some point in the not so distant future she would be leaving Guererro Negro - leaving *him* - to return to a far more glamorous life in Cabo. That she had someone waiting for her there was hardly inconceivable.

As the weeks passed Elena became more inclined to ask him questions of a personal nature, and for the most part his answers were necessarily vague. When they'd met, he'd simply told her his name was Brian and that he came to Mexico to surf. He subsequently explained that he lived in San Diego and worked at a job which afforded him the flexibility of spending extended amounts of time in Mexico whenever he wished. He did describe for her at length the details of his coastal refuge, but he never invited her to visit, and she never requested to see his home. He was relieved. So deeply ingrained now was his sense of himself as *un fugtivo* that he reflexively preserved his anonymity. And never did he consider telling Elena the circumstances of his involuntary exile or the events which provoked it.

Her affection for Will appeared genuine, and her passion was evident. He reveled in her attention and the simplicity of their relationship. His feelings for Maria, the ultimate source of his fugitive status, had cut deep, but through that relationship had coursed a corrosive current of guilt and deception. With Elena there were no such complications.

And yet there remained about the young woman something faintly elusive, something more complicated that lay just beyond the compelling charms of a beautiful and intelligent young woman. There was something at the periphery of her behavior that now and again would flit briefly into view and then vanish just as quickly. Always he'd been observant, but his experience as a man pursued had made him acutely sensitive to his physical surroundings and the behavior of those who existed therein. He found it impossible to identify the source of his misgivings, but the unease itself was undeniable.

Reading, he would look up from his book to find her regarding him with a fey expression that held equal measures of appraisal and concern. At such times she'd break off her gaze abruptly, moving on as if engrossed in her task of the moment. There were also those mornings when his departure would produce in her an attitude of distress that she could not entirely conceal, and not even his promise of returning that same night was sufficient to restore her calm.

Finally, there was the matter of Jose. Elena accepted without question his preference for the humble *cantina* over the livelier establishments on the main thoroughfare, and on an evening every week or two she would meet him there for drinks before they returned to her home. Although she was pleasant when she greeted him, Jose largely ignored her. For some reason the *cantina*'s proprietor seemed to have taken poorly to her. When the two men were alone, Jose continued to converse animatedly with Will on their usual topics, but with the young woman's appearance he would lapse immediately into a taciturn silence and move away to the opposite end of the bar.

Elena seemed unconcerned. "It is his behavior towards you that is unusual," she told him. "To all others he is *como un hombre rico con los secretos pero sin deseo a compartir.*" He was like a man rich with secrets that he refused to share.

Chapter 5

ABDUCTION

The cool night air was invigorating, and when he reached the main highway and accelerated, he could feel his anticipation rise as he drew ever closer to the city. Although he'd been with the young woman just two days before, so acute was his eagerness to see Elena that not for the first time he experienced a pang of regret for the vulnerability she'd provoked in him. He knew all too well that in his circumstances the slightest misstep could result in catastrophe. To compound the odds inherent from simple bad luck by actively engaging in behaviors even so modestly public as those involving Elena was to invite that catastrophe.

Accelerating yet more, he dismissed the unwelcome tug of apprehension. So keen had grown his desire that the risks involved seemed to him trivial when weighed against the pleasure. Glancing down at his watch, he saw would arrive at the *cantina* well before they'd arranged to meet. *Good*, he thought. He'd take the time to enjoy a few cold beers, engage Jose in conversation and perhaps glean from the *mestizo* some hint of the basis for his apparent hostility towards Elena.

As his visits to the *cantina* had grown more frequent and regular, he'd begun to take the precaution of parking his scooter behind an abandoned and derelict *casita* across the street. Picking his way through the overgrown and heavily littered lot in front of the building, he crossed to the *cantina*, entered through the open doorway and immediately sensed something was amiss.

Instead of offering up his usual greeting, Jose remained silent when he glanced up briefly to register Will's entrance. Eyes downcast, he continued to polish the glass in his hand with a cloth that itself needed cleansing, and he remained at the far end of the bar, leaning against the wall.

As his eyes adjusted to the dim interior light, Will could see the *cantina* was almost empty of customers. No *campesinos* sat at the bar engaged in their usual monosyllabic conversation, and none of the small tables nearest the bar was occupied. To his immediate left, however, in a corner beside the doorway, he saw seated about a table three men dressed similarly in black. Their imposing size dwarfed the chairs on which they sat. All were wearing jackets and, despite the room's dimness, sunglasses whose lens were of the darkest shade.

Be they plainclothesmen here in an official capacity or something else, Will knew at once he was in great danger. As casually as he could manage, he turned about and began to make his exit. Swiftly, the man seated closest to him sprang up to block his way and, grasping Will's upper arm firmly, asked, "Why do you leave the *cantina, senor*? Why not come join us for *una cereveza*."

Will tried desperately to remain composed. "*Gracias y muy amable,*" he replied, thanking the stranger for his invitation. "*Pero es necessario que yo voy a la casa de una amiga.*" Unfortunately, he was on his way to the house of a friend.

The man who held him flashed something between a grin and a grimace. "But I insist, *mi amigo,*" he informed Will. He inspected the ornate watch on his left wrist. "It is but early *en la noche*," he declared. "Surely there is time for a drink *con los hombres*? *La chica* can wait for but a little while, no?"

Will thought quickly. He doubted the three men were agents of the government acting in an official capacity. If they were, they'd simply have arrested him without any preliminaries. But if they were rogue agents or simply criminals, even now Elena could be walking towards grave danger. He needed either to warn her or to draw these men away from the *cantina*. But how?

He glanced briefly at Jose, still standing against the wall and polishing the same glass with a studied indifference to the events transpiring before him. As if he could feel Will's eyes upon him, he looked up, stared back at the American and gave a barely perceptible nod toward the cash register located midway down the bar.

Will understood immediately. In the past Jose had spoken of the weapon he kept concealed in the unlikely event any disturbance arose within his sleepy *cantina*, and once he'd shown Will the short-barreled .410 he kept on a shelf just beneath the register. The odds were long, he thought, but whoever these men were, it would not do to be taken by them. Moreover, there was Elena's safety to be considered.

He abruptly drove his right heel down hard against the man's instep, and when the Mexican released him he vaulted over the bar and, crouching low, scrambled to the register. Shotgun in hand, he rose up slightly to survey the situation. What he saw was not promising.

All three men had drawn impressively large pistols from shoulder holsters hidden beneath their jackets, and one was pressing the barrel of his weapon firmly against Jose's right temple as he held the unfortunate man in a chokehold. The man who'd confronted Will had recovered, and both he and his other companion had their pistols trained directly upon him.

"It is useless, *mi amigo*," he advised Will solemnly. "You die, the old man dies. Better to live, *yo creo*."

Will carefully placed the shotgun butt forward on the bar top. "*Con los manos arribos*," demanded the gunman, "make your way around the bar. Slowly."

Will complied, and Jose was released. They cuffed his hands behind his waist, and then with their large, muscular bodies uncomfortably close around him the three Mexicans walked him out the door and towards a sleek black sedan parked at the south end of the block. The sun was long set, and although it was now slightly past seven o'clock, Will was grateful to see no sign of Elena approaching.

They tossed him into the back seat, and at once the sedan was underway.

———

Who are these men? he wondered. *Where are they taking me? And why?* They clearly were not *policia*…or, at least, *policia* acting in an official capacity. If not *policia* or something similar, who were they, and what could they possibly want with him?

For almost an hour they'd kept him on the floor of the back seat, one man at the wheel and the other two sitting in the back with their feet casually planted on his body. As they turned left off what Will presumed to be the main north-south highway and onto an unpaved road, they allowed him to rise and sit between them. His new position was not much improved over the one prior. Such was the girth of the two men flanking him that despite the seat's width their meaty thighs and torsos pressed upon him from each side.

The only conversation thus far had involved an occasional brief instruction to the driver delivered tersely in Spanish by his initial captor, presumably the trio's leader, who was sitting to his right. As the car drove slowly westward on the increasingly primitive road of dirt, sand and rock, Will searched his mind for a way to escape his situation.

The gunman to his left was beginning to nod off. At first he tried propping his head against the window, but the irregular jolting produced by the road's rough surface was not conducive to sleep. Before slumping down to a more comfortable position that further compromised Will's meager space, he'd removed his sport coat and placed it on his lap. Beneath the coat lay his shoulder holster with a large revolver nestled within, and the holster' strap was unfastened. With each bump in the road the weight of the pistol caused the butt to slip further from its position in the holster. Eventually it slipped quietly from the man's lap to the sliver of seat that separated them, coming to rest just inches from Will's cuffed hands. Tantalizingly close.

Fighting down his impatience, Will slowly and surreptitiously pulled the handgun towards him with the tips of his fingers. Glancing at the man to his right, he saw that he was napping as well and had noticed nothing. Even so, he feared that any attempt to lift the gun up and off the seat would attract the others' attention, but no one stirred when he at last hooked the trigger guard with his index finger, lifted the gun and with what force he could muster awkwardly pressed it to the small of his back.

In tiny, inconspicuous increments he used the fingers of both hands to maneuver the weapon slowly down and into the space between his waistband and sacrum. He could feel himself sweating profusely from the effort required to accomplish the task, and he slowly slid himself leftwards against the still-sleeping man to put himself in line with the cool sea air rushing in through the driver's open window.

The driver caught his movement in the rearview mirror and muttered something to the man sitting to Will's right. The man awoke immediately and swiveled around to inspect Will with suspicion. *"Por que usted tan sodado?"* he demanded. Why was he so sweaty?

Will stared back at him, expressionless. *"Por que estoy tan asustado?"* he suggested. Because he was frightened?

The Mexican chuckled and turned to address the driver. *"Nuestro amigo Americano es un hombre muy bravo. Mira a que el hace las chicas bromas"*. He said the American must be a very brave man to be making his little jokes.

The driver nodded. He said that this *yanqui* might well require all of that bravery, for he was going to meet a man whom many had found *no tan amable*. Not so pleasant.

His companions smiled grimly and nodded in agreement. The thug sitting to Will's left then spoke. *"El Santo. El Uno Obscuro. El jefe nuestro,"* he said softly, as if reflecting upon his own words. The Saint. The Dark One. Their boss.

Less than a minute later the driver turned left onto a long driveway of crushed shell and parked before *una casa grande*. The man to his right pulled him out of the car. Will worried that the sudden movement might jostle the pistol loose from his jeans, but by squirming a bit and feeling with his hands he confirmed that the weapon remained snugly in place.

He stood there still handcuffed as the other men exited the car, and at precisely that moment the man who'd been sitting to his left began shouting to his companions. He was standing beside the sedan, his holster, now empty, in his outstretched hands.

Will instantly sprinted towards a large bed of dense green shrubbery that lay between the westernmost corner of the house and the driveway. He could hear footsteps pounding behind him, but even without the use of his arms he knew he could reach his intended destination before they could seize him.

Launching himself through a wall of scratchy limbs and thick foliage, he rolled once, flicked the pistol deep into the underbrush with his still-cuffed left hand and then rolled back towards the two men who were now almost upon him.

Gripping his armpits tightly, they dragged him out into the open lawn. His left axilla screamed with pain, its damaged and hypersensitive nerves protesting the rude treatment. Once they had him upright he two men shoved him back towards the house, and an authoritative male voice suddenly called out from the portico.

"Bastante!" the unseen voice commanded. *"En la casa. Y pronto."* He told the men to desist and to bring Will inside. At once.

He'd taken advantage of his scant time beneath the canopy of shrubs to survey what he could of the *hacienda* and the surrounding grounds. There was a door in the rear of the building that gave way onto a short walkway of stone and concrete leading to what was obviously a parking area. Within that area he could see two vehicles: a sedan seemingly identical to the one he'd just exited and a large black SUV with high clearance that almost certainly possessed the capacity for fourwheel drive.

His kidnappers half-dragged him up the exterior steps, into the great house and down a long, high-ceilinged hallway. As they passed by one of the doorways that lined the hall, Will briefly glimpsed a spacious, dark-paneled room whose walls were lined with bookshelves containing hundreds of volumes. Obviously the *don's* library.

At the end of the hall they descended two short flights of stairs, and Will's sore limb protested violently against each successive step. At the bottom of the stairs was another long hallway with walls of rough stucco painted a bright white, presumably to compensate for the lack of windows and the dim illumination provided by a series of sconces set at regular intervals along the way.

Unlike the attractively stained and polished wide wooden planks of the main story above, the floor here was of clay tile. Midway down the hall the three men stopped before a tall, formidable-appearing wooden door with wrought iron hardware. Unlocking it, they silently directed Will inside, still cuffed, and behind him he heard the door slam shut and the lock immediately engage.

Rising to his feet, Will tried to ignore his pain and get his bearings. The spacious room was windowless and under-furnished for its size but nevertheless attractive. The heavy wooden bed, bedside table and dresser were elaborately carved and looked to be both old and of superb quality. A single lamp was set upon the table and provided the only illumination. Adjoining the bedroom was a good-sized bathroom nicely set off by colorful Mexican tiles and containing a pedestal sink, toilet and shower.

Whatever the room's attractions, however, there was no escaping the fact that he was a prisoner locked in a cell. His hands still bound behind him, Will felt with his fingers for the watch he wore on his left wrist, but it was gone – presumably a casualty of the scuffle outside. When he'd last checked the sedan's digital clock as they were turning into the *hacienda's* long driveway, it was just after nine.

He spent some minutes inspecting the door and its lock more closely and conducting an ultimately fruitless reconnaissance of the room and bath looking for some type of weapon. With nothing better to do, he lay down on the bed to rest, but in a moment the door swung open, and two new men unknown to Will strode in purposely to begin a their own search of the room.

They were dressed in a manner almost identical to that of his kidnappers, and they, too, were powerfully built. The taller of the two beckoned Will to rise and proceeded to frisk him efficiently. When the man had finished, he pushed Will towards an empty corner of the room, and there he stood while he watched the other black-clad *hombre malo* go silently about his business.

Search completed, the man who'd frisked Will glared at him intently. "Where is it?" he demanded in heavily accented English. "*La pistola.* Where is it?"

"*No tengo una pistola,*" Will replied. "If I did," he added in English, "I'd have shot you with it when you entered."

His interrogator sneered at this, but Will doubted he'd understood the English. To his surprise, the man suddenly spun him around, unlocked his cuffs and then turned back towards the door to call out, "*Entrade!*"

Immediately upon his command there crept into the room a small, bent man of ancient visage who was dressed as a formal manservant. Eyes downcast and manner utterly servile, he carried in his left hand a pair of black shoes polished to high sheen and in his outstretched right a small packet neatly wrapped in brown paper and twine. Over his arm was draped a pair of gabardine trousers and a long-sleeved shirt of white linen.

"*En la cama*," the frisker barked impatiently, and the old man carefully placed all that he carried on the bed. "*Y vaya ahora. Andele!*" the frisker commanded. The withered old man exited the room as noiselessly as he'd entered.

The frisker turned his attention back to Will. "*El jefe* wishes that you dine with him," he said tonelessly. "*Han sus ropas.*" He nodded towards the articles on the bed. "*Tienes cinco minutos. No mas.*" Motioning to his companion, both men left the room, and once again he heard the lock engage.

Unwrapping the package, Will found socks and underwear that appeared to be new, and he noted that the trousers and shirt appeared to be precisely of sizes that would fit him. When the Mexicans returned in five minutes as promised, Will was sitting on the bed, and he remained dressed as before.

Observing their prisoner still in his t-shirt, jeans and running shoes, the frisker angrily unleashed a string of Spanish profanity and advanced on Will as if to strike him. His companion, however, lay a restraining hand on the other's beefy upper arm, and the two then conferred briefly in the hallway outside the room. A decision apparently having been reached, the frisker reentered the room, commanded Will to stand and again cuffed his hands behind him.

The two thugs directed Will back along the route he'd traveled to his gilded cage, and when they reached the floor above, they delivered him into an expansive room so dimly lit after the brightness of the hallway that it took his eyes a moment to adjust. When they did, he saw in the center of the room a heavy wooden table with a single chair at each end, all appearing similar in age and design to the intricately carved furniture of his cell. Upon the table was a candelabra, and the light cast from its tapers provided the room's only illumination.

Seated at the end of the table nearer the door was a slim, darkly attractive Hispanic man of about forty lounging casually in his chair, smoking a thin black cheroot and gazing out one of the room's several large windows at the darkness beyond. *The much heralded el jefe,* Will concluded. *El Santo, pero El Uno Obscuro tambien.* If this man was any kind of saint, he was indeed likely to be a dark one.

The Mexican seated at the table turned his head and silently regarded Will for a full thirty seconds. He then swiveled in his chair to face the two men crowding the doorway. "Remove the handcuffs," he said quietly and with only the barest trace of accent. "And then leave us."

The frisker looked unhappy at this but complied. After the two men had left, the Mexican beckoned Will to sit at the table's opposite end and spoke to him in the same quiet, even tone he'd used to command his men.

"Allow me to introduce myself," he said. *Me llamo* Manuelo Arivada. Please be seated." He inclined his head slightly as if in deference to Will and then gave him an appraising look. "Was the clothing I provided not to your taste or size?" he inquired.

"I don't want your clothes," Will answered. He remained standing beside the indicated chair with his arms slightly flexed at the elbows and his legs, concealed by the table, tensed and ready to spring.

"Please be seated, Dr. Rawlins," the Mexican repeated. "While I understand your anger and sympathize, I believe you will find it to be misplaced. As for the clothes, I simply hoped to make you more comfortable."

Will ignored the man's use of his name and stared back at him, unblinking. "You're the one who should be feeling uncomfortable, *hombre*," he informed the man. "You've kidnapped an American citizen, and I suggest that you release me now."

As he spoke, he glanced at a bookshelf immediately behind the Mexican and saw upon it a collection of bayonets that presumably were antiques, relics from battles waged long ago. He considered rushing the man, snatching one of the lethal-appearing blades and transforming his host into hostage.

The man they'd referred to as *El Santo* followed his glance, smiled and shook his head slightly. "This room is intended for dining and conversation, Dr. Rawlins," he said. "Not for violence." He paused to puff at his cheroot and then reached beneath the table before him. Suddenly in his hand there was a large revolver. Casually inspecting the handgun, he continued, "It would be pointless to terminate our dinner prematurely."

"You're making a terrible mistake," Will repeated. "You've mistaken me for someone else. My name is Brian McCoy. And I'm not a doctor."

The Mexican shrugged. "As you wish," he replied, indicating again that Will should sit.

Giving up for the moment, Will sat down. *And the condemned shall eat a hearty meal*, he thought.

From a second door that apparently linked the hacienda's *cocina* to the formal dining room there suddenly emerged the same old man who'd brought him the clothing. Belying his apparent fragility, he bore in his hands a heavy silver tray upon which rode an elegant ceramic soup tureen. With the tureen's matching ladle he served first Will and then his master, filling their bowls with a pumpkin-colored soup.

"*Gracias, Diego,*" Arivada told the servant after he'd completed his task, and the old man bowed slightly before turning to vanish from the room. "In English I believe it is called squash blossom soup," the Mexican proclaimed. "Is it familiar to you, Dr. Rawlins? or Brian, if you prefer."

"I know the soup," Will replied curtly, fighting the impulse to seize the bowl and drain its contents all at once. He'd not eaten since breakfast that day, and despite his predicament he was famished.

The soup was delicious, as were the courses that followed. Raw oysters, roast quail, *chili con queso, carne tampiquena* and, for dessert, a small dish of *flan*. Each course was accompanied by a different wine, and although Will avoided the whites, the reds were all excellent.

The meal had been notable for an absence of conversation, but now *El Jefe* chose to break the long silence. "I've saved the best for last," he told his captive guest. "*Un porto.* It is the finest port. Sent to me by colleagues who live in the Douro valley of Portugal. Do you know it, Doctor Rawlins?"

Across the surface of highly polished and exquisite ironwood Will stared back at his interrogator. "First of all," he answered blandly, "I have no idea why you continue to refer to me as 'Doctor'. Second, I do know Portugal and the Douro. Lastly, I couldn't care less about your precious '*porto*'." It was hard to tell at the distance, but he thought he could detect in the Mexican's face the briefest flicker of annoyance.

"How unfortunate," the man replied. At that moment the server, Diego, re-entered bearing yet another tray, this one smaller and laden with two stemmed glasses of cut crystal and a matching decanter filled with liquid the color of venous blood. With exquisite care the old man placed a glass beside the two diners and with his eyes fixed upon his task carefully poured into each a generous portion from the decanter. Finished, he positioned the tray next to his master, bowed to both diners and prepared once again to depart the room.

The dark slender man reclined gracefully in his chair and lifted his booted feet to rest them upon the massive table. Igniting a wooden match with a flick of his thumb, he lit another thin black cheroot he'd pulled from his shirt pocket and began to draw at it slowly with obvious contentment. First directing his gaze at an exhaled plume of smoke, he then glanced over at Will amicably. "You've been so quiet, my friend," he observed. "Was the food not to your liking?"

"If it was dinner I wanted, I could have eaten in Guererro Negro," Will answered flatly. "Why am I here?"

Instead of responding, the other man lifted the crystal glass and held it to the light. "*Porto*", he said. "Of a memorable vintage and rendered with the most meticulous care. It comes from a small Portuguese village near Pinhao. Normally the few bottles produced are sold only to the finest restaurants of Lisbon, Madrid, Paris and the like, but the vineyard's owner is an old friend for whom I've performed some small favors." He took a sip from his glass. "*Magnifico*," he pronounced.

He saw that Will's glass remained untouched. "Drink," he urged. "Perhaps it will lighten your mood."

"I don't care for port," Will replied. "Too thick. Too sweet."

Manuelo Arivada returned his feet to the floor, swiveled lightly in his chair and addressed Will directly. "*A veces* a man must drink whatever the glass brings him," he said. "Myself, I've drunk the bitter *sidra* poured from pitchers held far above the glass while I sat with my Asturian hosts in Llanes. With my Japanese associates in Kyoto I've drunk chilled sake from wooden boxes held precious by their families for generations. In the mountains of this land I've drunk the fiery *aquagardiente* from a bottle passed hand to hand by the *campesinos* who shared my campfire. I disliked them all - the *sidra*, the sake and the *aquagardiente* - but I drank all three with evident pleasure, and no one observing me was the wiser."

"You, my friend," he concluded, nodding towards Will, "might find it advantageous to do the same with the glass I now offer you."

Will stared silently at the man for a few seconds and then slowly emptied his glass onto the white linen tablecloth before him. The blood-colored wine spread slowly towards the table's edge, and the repetitive *plop* of the thick droplets striking the wooden floor resounded within the cavernous room.

The Mexican appeared unconcerned. He resumed his earlier posture, boots on the table and chair tilted back, and he addressed his next words to the darkness gathering at the window.

"Perhaps I have been too oblique," he said softly. "It is a mistake easily made when one converses with *norteamericanos*, a people so direct. Please allow me to begin again." He paused to puff silently at his cheroot and took another sip of port.

"In these days of electronic surveillance and communication," he said, "it has become exceedingly difficult to lose oneself, even in a land so sparsely populated and antiquarian as the one in which we both now find ourselves. To *remain* lost is yet more difficult."

Now he turned once again to face Will directly. "You, my friend, currently find yourself in a situation where it would serve you well to remain lost . . . if not forever, then at least for a very long time. *Claro*. To attempt to do so without assistance will prove tedious at best and, more likely, fatal."

Expressionless, Will stared back at the other man. "I have no idea what you're talking about," he responded.

Arivada smiled softly at this and leaned back in his chair. "I believe we may be wasting time," he declared. And then suddenly his black eyes turned cold, and his hands were clasped and resting on the table. He leaned forward over them as he spoke.

"You are a wanted man, Will Rawlins", he said intently. "Very much wanted, *verdad*. Myself, I care nothing for what crimes you have committed, but, believe me, in Mexico your life is forfeit. And you can be sure that if I found you so easily when I had the need of it, even the corrupt and incompetent agents of our government eventually will do the same."

Will remained silent at this. The Mexican produced another cheroot, lit its end and began again. "To return to your homeland is pointless," he said. "Even if you could avoid capture in the process, with time, and no matter where you flee, you will be caught and returned to Mexico to face what passes in our courts for justice."

"I've done nothing wrong," Will replied nonchalantly.

His host shook his head slowly back and forth at these words and sighed. "The dead *federal* in San Carlos would not agree," he said quietly. "And his *compadre*, witness to the crime, certainly will not agree. All of the other witnesses are dead or have vanished. You fled the scene of a murder, a murder wherein illegal drugs were involved, and during your escape you threatened innocent Mexican civilians at gunpoint."

He again shook his head sadly but then broke into a sudden smile. "No, my friend," he said brightly. "Guilty or not, you have 'done' a great deal, and if you are caught you will pay most dearly."

"So what?" Will answered. "Why should you care what happens to me?"

The Mexican ignored Will's question. "I possess the means to enable you to *live*," he said, staring at Will gravely. "I can provide you with sanctuary."

"I'm living now", Will answered. "I don't need your help."

The other man smiled. "Living alone in a shack even the *campesinos* considered unfit would not seem to represent much of a life," he ventured. "To exist alone, a lost soul stranded on the banks of the River Styx."

Will gazed levelly at the Mexican before responding. "How and where I'm living suits me just fine," he replied firmly. "Regardless, these issues are not your concern, and I demand that you release me immediately."

Leaning forward, the Mexican spoke to Will lightly but earnestly. "My friend," he said, "you are in no position to make demands of *any* sort. I'm offering you a most comfortable refuge, and I believe it would be wise for you to concentrate on this opportunity rather than wax nostalgic for your windblown shack amongst the *tomates*."

The two men paused in their conversation as the elderly server unobtrusively crept back into the room, refilled his employer's glass from the decanter and attempted to suppress his dismay at the sight of Will's port congealing on the tablecloth and the floor immediately below.

Arivada smiled at the old man's obvious discomfiture. "Perhaps our guest would prefer a different beverage, Diego," he suggested.

At this the servant turned to face Will and raised his eyebrows inquiringly.

What the hell, Will thought. "*Una cerveza fria, por favor*," he told the old man. "*De la clase no esta importa*."

The servant responded with a slight bow and left the room, returning shortly with a chilled beer glass that he proceeded to fill from a bottle of *Stella Artois*. Not a beer commonly encountered in Mexico. Will took a long, slow swallow, savoring its pleasing bitterness.

He looked up from his glass to find his host again staring at him intently. *Here it comes,* he thought.

The Mexican once again began to speak. "Both I and those in my employ require a physician, ideally a surgeon. For reasons which need not concern you, our circumstances here are such that it is preferable to have this physician immediately at hand. Happily, you meet our requirements. Accept this position, abandon your shack, and you shall live here in comfort and safety. Both you and any woman you desire."

He paused. "There is something else," he said. "Something more…personal. I have a brother. Enrique. Much younger than I. Born to my mother some years after my parents moved to this place and when my father was quite old. Just seven years before his passing. His wife, our mother, joined him in death but a few months thereafter. Given the circumstances, for Enrique I've served as much as father as I have brother."

He broke off to pour himself another generous measure of *porto* from the decanter. "A year ago," he resumed, "Enrique began to behave in a manner most uncharacteristic. He'd been a quiet boy, remaining so as he reached adulthood. Reserved. One whose emotions and feelings were not easily discerned." He gazed at Will absently for a moment, as if still puzzled by his memory of the events he described.

"With little or no provocation he would become suddenly enraged, shouting and using profanity of the coarsest sort. And then, just as suddenly, he would be himself once again." He shook his head. "He began to complain of odors. Unpleasant odors-a *burning*, he described it-undetectable to others. Previously meticulous in his personal habits, he ceased bathing unless forced to do so and took to wearing the same clothes day after day. Previously circumspect in his behavior towards women, he began to act in a manner most lewd, openly propositioning even the wives of our acquaintances and attempting to grope them in full view of their husbands."

Classic, Will was thinking. *Classic frontal lobe disinhibition, with some olfactory seizures thrown in. Could be a dumbbell meningioma, but more likely a glio.* He waited for the man to tell him what he knew would come next.

"One day," the dark Mexican said, "just as he was complaining again of the burning odor, he had what now I know to have been a *grand mal* seizure. It ceased after a minute or so, but he remained unresponsive to my words and breathed wetly and loudly in a manner most concerning. We transported him to the hospital as quickly as was possible. From there he was transferred to Mexico City, and after much testing we learned he had…"

"…a frontotemporal brain tumor," Will interrupted. "Glioblastoma mutiforme."

The Mexican smiled thinly. "It is gratifying to find that my faith in your medical competence was not misplaced, Dr. Rawlins," he said.

Will ignored the other's use of his name; there seemed little point in continuing the subterfuge. "I assume the doctors in Mexico City advised you that your brother's tumor is incurable and inevitably fatal," he said. "If so, they're absolutely correct. There is nothing to be done that will help your brother in any meaningful way. Nothing can cause his malignant tumor to vanish. No one can help him. No one."

Manuelo Arivada - the boss, the saint, the Dark Man - leaned towards him from the far end of the long table, resting his weight on his forearms. "Ah, Dr. Rawlins, but you are too modest. I believe that *you* can, assuming that you are properly motivated. In fact, I am sure of it." He leaned back in his chair. "And that is why I'm so very willing to help you."

Chapter 6

BAJA

He slept poorly and was awake when they came for him. As once again he was trundled upstairs by burly men clad in the now-familiar black, he worried that his fatigue might impede his attempt at escape. *There's no help for it,* he thought. *It is as it is.*

After they'd ascended the stairs, awaiting them in the hallway was an enormous *mestizo* who bore a striking resemblance to one of the men who'd accosted him at *El Tecalote* the evening before. The man was several inches taller than Will and outweighed him by at least one hundred pounds, the latter an attribute suggesting tremendous power rather than slothful obesity.

Visibly annoyed and speaking in rapid-fire Spanish, the huge Mexican directed one of the three men escorting Will to cuff his hands behind his back. He advised the other two that they would accompany him in conveying the *yanqui medico* to the hospital and that *el jefe* had proceeded them in the SUV by thirty minutes. He wished to visit with his brother before the others arrived, he explained.

They walked through the kitchen, out the back door that Will had observed the evening before and onto a small stoop from which three steps led to the walkway and vehicles beyond.

As they sorted themselves out after exiting the kitchen, Will darted suddenly away from his captors, leaping off the stoop and making for the canopy of shrubs where he'd hidden the gunman's *pistola*.

So taken by surprise were the others by his actions that even with his arms pinned behind him Will had sufficient time to dive under the canopy, roll to the spot where he'd concealed the weapon and maneuver the pistol beneath the waist of his jeans. Purposefully he'd worn the white linen shirt his host had provided, leaving the long tail of its hem untucked and hanging low.

Putting up only minimal resistance, he allowed the Mexicans to retrieve him from the shrubbery.

"*No mas!*" shouted the enormous *mestizo*. "*Vamanos ahora a la ciudad. Andale!*"

"*Si, Hector,*" the men responded in unison. Glancing at his watch, "Hector" directed them to put the *yanqui* in the car. Before he'd departed, *el jefe* had given him precise instructions and a strict timetable, and now already they had some minutes to make up. For this or whatever blessed reason, neither he nor the other men bothered to frisk Will as they pushed him into the backseat. There he sat wedged between Hector and another of *El Santo*'s foot soldiers while a third sat alone behind the wheel.

At its junction with the unpaved road, the *hacienda*'s long driveway was flanked on both sides by steep, rocky hillsides and obstructed by a high, arched gate of wrought iron that opened electronically. With the sturdy gate closed, the entrance was impassable to any vehicle. Just before the driveway's terminus was a whitewashed *casita* that appeared to serve both as gate-house and home to the estate's groundskeeper and his family.

A bevy of brown-skinned, black-haired children and teenagers were running and chasing each other on the grass surrounding the small house, and in its doorway stood a lean Mexican whose black hair was streaked with gray. The man's face was devoid of expression as he watched the car pass, and he made no gesture of greeting nor farewell.

The three Mexicans in the car remained silent, and as they drove slowly eastward on the heavily rutted and unpaved road Will grew worried that no opportunity would arise for him to use the weapon he'd taken such pains to obtain. Hemmed in and trussed up as he was, the most he might accomplish in his present position would be to free the pistol from his jeans and shoot one of the men beside him. With the other two undoubtedly armed and able to react quickly, that maneuver would gain him nothing.

Quickly he devised an alternative plan. As they began to ascend and descend a series of small *arroyos*, Will recalled that on the journey in last evening they'd come to a particularly deep, broad and treacherous ravine that the driver had managed to negotiate only by skillful maneuvering and, even so, with obvious difficulty. He estimated they'd arrive at that ravine in no more than fifteen minutes, and so he turned to Hector on his left. Complaining that handcuffs were biting into his wrists, he asked that they be removed. If the nerves were damaged, he said, it would reduce his surgical aptitude. Did Hector wish for *el hermano del jefe* to die on the operating table? he asked.

Hector glared back at him suspiciously but nevertheless then drew a set of keys from the breast pocket of his coat, jerked Will's hands roughly towards him and unlocked the cuffs. Returning the keys to his pocket, he reached beneath his jacket and withdrew a shiny Glock. With a menacing look, he thrust the pistol's muzzle firmly against Will's ribs and muttered, "*Sus manos en sus piernas. No mueva. Entiendes?*" Will was to place his hands on his thighs and keep them motionless.

Fifteen minutes later the opportunity he sought presented itself. The road descended steeply into an *arroyo*, and a broad swath of soft sand had to be crossed before the vehicle could ascend the opposite bank. Arivada had driven the SUV over this ravine earlier in the day. His tracks in the sand were easily discerned, and Will was pleased to observe they seemed to cut quite deep.

Unlike the SUV, the low-lying luxury sedan was ill-suited for traversing the *arroyo*. Although Will expected the driver to take some type of precautionary measure, either speeding up while the car was still on solid ground or slowing his speed and shifting the transmission to low, the man simply plowed into the sand. The car became immediately stuck.

In Spanish Hector angrily instructed the driver to accelerate, a maneuver Will was confident would serve only to exacerbate their predicament. Indeed, the furiously spinning wheels sank more deeply into the receptive sand.

Hector cursed softly under his breath and then ordered the man sitting to Will's right to get out of the car and assist him. Leaving Will alone in the car with the driver, the two gunmen proceeded to lift and push the heavy sedan from behind as the driver intermittently floored the accelerator in response to Hector's shouted commands.

It was futile. The car had become hopelessly stuck in the sand trap. Clad in their heat-absorbing black garb, Hector and his companion now were sitting on a large, flat-topped rock, sweating profusely in the bright morning sunlight. Presumably intending to report this mishap to his *patron*, Hector was extricating his cell phone from the same pocket which held the keys to the handcuffs when Will flung open the door and from his seated position snapped off two shots in rapid succession.

The first whizzed harmlessly past his large target, but the second caught Hector full in the belly. The big man crumpled ponderously to the ground. When the driver turned around to gape at him, Will struck the man a nasty blow across the face with the pistol's barrel and then turned his attention back to the remaining Mexican outside.

That man had reacted more quickly and appropriately than the driver, but even as he was slipping his pistol from its holster beneath his armpit Will was out of the car and had his own weapon trained directly on the man's torso at a distance of no more than ten feet. When the Mexican persisted in his effort, Will dropped his aim slightly and blew apart the would-be gunman's left knee. The man dropped to the sand, howling.

Walking over to where he lay writhing in the sand, Will removed the man's pistol and tucked it in his waistband. He returned to the car, opened the front door and dragged the inert driver out to deposit him prone upon the sand. Satisfied that the man would not soon regain full consciousness, Will then loped over to Hector's inert form and with effort rolled the huge man onto his back. He saw an entrance wound in the left abdomen and a gaping exit wound at the left flank. There was a fair amount of blood in the sand, but he suspected the internal bleeding was more serious. Regardless, Hector was no longer a factor.

He added Hector's pistol to his growing arsenal and withdrew the cell phone from the man's coat. On Hector's belt was a pager, and when Will inspected the device more closely he could see the device included a transponder. Arivada would know their general location, and he likely knew also that their transit to the hospital had ceased. Will used one of the abundant rocks lying about to smash the pager and then tossed it into a jumble of uprooted shrubs.

He returned to the driver. The man was still unconscious but now moaning slightly. He cuffed the driver's hands behind his back and used Hector's long belt to bind the man's ankles.

Searching about, he found in the wash a fragment of old fence post that he used as a crude shovel to dig out the loose sand from around the tires. After depressing their stem valves and deflating the tires considerably, he climbed behind the wheel, shifted the sedan's automatic transmission to its lowest gear and slowly drove the vehicle across the sand onto the solid ground just beyond.

He left the motor running and climbed out of the car to walk back to where the three Mexicans lay in various attitudes within the sandy wash. Of them, only one was fully conscious, and despite the pain from his ruined knee, the man glared up at the *yanqui* balefully, his facial expression one of pure animal hatred. *If I had any sense,* Will thought, *I'd kill each of these men where he lies. To leave them alive can only lead to trouble.*

Turning away, he walked back to the car. Once behind the wheel he left the sandy arroyo behind him and drove eastward a short distance until he came upon a faint dirt track that entered the road from the north.

He continued to drive eastward on the road for another mile and then at a relatively flat area turned left into the scrubby coastal desert. After picking his way carefully through the rocks and underbrush for ten minutes, he turned southward and drove until he reached the dirt track at a point about two hundred meters from its union with the main road. Hoping this maneuver would assist in confusing any pursuit, he proceeded to drive slowly northwards on the track as it meandered its way northward along the desert plateau.

———

Initially Will had no particular plan other than to put as much distance as possible between himself and the pursuit certain to follow upon discovery of his escape. After two hours of driving, however, he calculated he'd gained no more than ten kilometers due to the road's poor condition and its tendency to wind about like a wanderer lost in an unfamiliar land. *How appropriate,* he thought. He also worried that he would be easily visible from the air, and although the clear blue sky was now absent of small planes or helicopters, he feared it was only a matter of time.

What to do, what to do? he pondered yet again. He hadn't the food or water needed to abandon the car and trek overland to a presumably safe public destination. Although he knew there to be small *ranchos* scattered about the plateau, they were few, far between and difficult to locate in this hardscrabble land. Small indeed was the chance that he'd stumble upon a hospitable *campesino* who would provision him.

Glancing down at the gas gauge, he saw that the sedan's tank was well over half full. He decided to search out a suitable place to camouflage the vehicle for now and then resume his journey after sunset, traveling at night with the headlights off and the bulbs of the brake lights removed. That still left unanswered what route he should take and his ultimate destination, but for now this limited plan would have to suffice.

Just off the track to the right he found a place where he could park the car in an area rendered near-invisible from ground or air by a thick clustering of shrubs and stunted trees. As he maneuvered into the area branches screeched in protest against the luxury vehicle's once-pristine exterior, now heavily coated with dust.

Will was arranging desiccated brush over the hood, windshield and any other uncovered surface that might reflect the bright sunlight when suddenly the silence was broken by repetitive loud bursts of *mariachi* music. It was Hector's cell phone, and for a moment Will debated the pros and cons of answering. When at last he pressed the answer button and raised the phone, *El Santo's* voice filled his right ear.

"Dr. Rawlins," said the Mexican calmly, "you must return at once. One of the men you have shot appears to be dying, and he urgently requires your attention."

"So what?" Will answered. "So one of your thugs dies. Why should I care?"

There was a long pause on the other end, and then finally Arivada spoke again. "You have refused to treat my brother, and now you refuse to use your knowledge to save the life of a man whom you yourself have shot. What manner of physician are you?"

Will laughed. "Whatever manner of physician I am," he replied, "I'm not so stupid as to return willingly to you."

Again there was a pause on the other end. "Then perhaps you will return if presented with new circumstances, Dr. Rawlins," the Mexican suggested. "With me here is the man who long has attended to the gardens on my estate. You may have seen him as you departed this morning. His name is Tomas, and good Catholic that he is, he is father to six children. Return now, or I will kill this man with the pistol I hold in my hand."

"If you want to kill your gardener," Will responded, "then kill him. *You* trim the fucking hedges."

"Very well," Arivada answered, his voice still calm. His words were followed immediately by the sound of three gunshots fired in rapid succession, and in the background Will could hear the sound of a woman screaming. For reasons unrelated to the apparent murder he'd both provoked and witnessed via cell phone, he felt a reflexive surge of apprehension.

El Santo returned to the line. "Through your obstinacy, Dr. Rawlins, there are now six children rendered fatherless," he said gravely. "Should this leave you unmoved, then perhaps something more personally relevant will enable you to recall your professional responsibilities."

There was a brief exchange of muffled, unintelligible voices, male and female, and then suddenly it was Elena. She was sobbing uncontrollably as she spoke, and in the midst of his dismay it occurred to Will that he'd never before heard her cry.

"Brian," she managed at last to tell him. "He *shot* him. Everywhere there is blood."

"Are you all right, Elena?" he asked her urgently. "How did they find you? Why are you there?"

His voice seemed to calm her. Her sobbing diminished, and she became more coherent. "*Estoy bien*," she replied. "Unhurt.

Untouched," she added with emphasis. "They took me from my home just hours ago. They would not tell me why."

Then for a moment she was sobbing and again unable to speak. "Brian!" she cried through her tears. "You must not return. He will kill me anyway. Just as he killed this innocent man whose body now lies on the floor. He...."

Someone evidently removed the phone from her hand. Then it was the Mexican speaking again. "*Su novia* is quite mistaken," he said evenly. "Her death is of no more interest to me than your own. What I desire is for you to administer to the man you shot and then attend to my brother. Once these matters are accomplished, you may do as you choose. Your companion, unharmed, will be free to join you if that is what you wish."

Will didn't believe a word of it, but he could also feel the trap closing tightly about him. The evening prior he'd remained awake after the long dinner and considered Arivada's offer. What was the likelihood that this criminal would keep his end of any bargain? Even if he did, the prospect of serving as house physician for what was presumably a cartel was hardly appealing. Besides, the man's brother was certain to die in any event. Will would be seen to have failed. *For me there can be only one outcome,* he'd concluded. *To avoid that outcome, escape is imperative.*

With Elena his captive, however, the Mexican clearly held the trump card. As if to confirm this the man then added, "Of course you may refuse to comply." There was a pause. "But if such is your decision," he remarked casually, "I fear *su novia* will suffer for it. Most assuredly."

Will sighed silently. "Where do you want me to go?" he asked dully. "What do you want me to do?"

"Go quickly to the hospital in Guerrero Negro," Arivada responded. "A man's life depends upon your expediency." He hung up.

Chapter 7

BAJA

Hector, you're one lucky thug, he'd thought after opening the man's abdomen to inspect the damage within. His bullet had ruined the man's spleen and fractured a rib upon exiting, but the other internal organs were untouched. Although his experience in performing splenectomies was limited, it was a relatively simple procedure.

In this surgery he was assisted by the hospital's only physician, a Dr. Villalobos, who appeared to be in his early sixties. Although the man was clearly wary of Arivada, he displayed neither the obsequious fawning nor fearful bumbling that the Mexican chieftain had inspired in the hospital's administrator and nursing staff. Furthermore, he was adept and at ease in the OR, so much so that with him assisting the operation was completed, skin to skin, in little more than twenty minutes.

As they were changing in the small dressing room adjacent to the OR, Will remarked upon the other's proficiency. "I should have been assisting *you*," he said to the surgeon. "For that matter, you could have managed just as easily alone. The man was bleeding out from a lacerated spleen. Why wait for me?"

Dr. Villalobos shrugged. "Ask your friend who waits for us outside," he suggested. His English was perfect. "You did well enough," he added.

Will smiled. "That man waiting outside is definitely no friend of mine," he replied. "So how did you come to be so good with a scalpel?"

"I trained in general surgery at the *universidad* in Mexico City, and following that I completed a fellowship in trauma surgery at Baylor," the man replied, drying his hands on a towel provided by the scrub nurse.

Will gave out with a soft whistle. "That's a lot of training for a guy in a dusty one-doctor hospital," Will observed.

Dr. Villalobos smiled grimly. "It was hardly my intention to live and practice in Guerrero Negro," he answered. "Manuelo Arivada, the so-called '*El Santo*', is all-powerful in this region, as was his father before him. He can exert significant leverage when it pleases him to do so." He completed knotting his tie and then resumed speaking.

"I was born in a small town nearby, and although I was fortunate to leave my impoverished home to attend university and medical school, it was in large measure the father's power and influence which enabled me to do so. With the father's death and his son's ascension...*pues,* let us say simply that my family's health and longevity depended upon my returning to work in my birth place."

Will sat down on the small wooden bench to lace up his running shoes. "What's with this *El Santo* guy, anyway?" he asked. "Where'd he come from, and why would he choose the outback of Baja for his home?"

The doctor sitting beside him sighed with deep-rooted exasperation. "*Quien sabe?*" he answered. "Some say that his father was a *politico* from Sonora. *Un gobierno,* at one time. That *El Santo, el uno obscuro,* is the bastard son of this governor who took as his mistress *una chica* of fabled beauty. That the mother was descended *de los Yaquis, los indios* who labored and perished in the mines of Diaz. Others claim she was of the Tarahumara *indios* who long have lived in the *barranca* country of the north."

"*Dicen que* that father eventually attempted to cheat those yet more highly placed and so fled Hermosillo to escape prison. Or worse. He left behind his official family and, along with his criminally acquired wealth, brought with him to Guererro Negro his mistress and the boy. He used his riches to buy a vast tract of land and to build the home wherein his son yet resides. The state and federal governments apparently were too preoccupied with their own mischief to bother giving chase to the father, and so in peace and luxury, however isolated, he lived out his remaining years."

Through the dressing room's sole window they could see the light fading outside. "We must go," said Dr. Villalobos, arising.

"But what of *El Santo?*" Will persisted. "I gather he didn't just stay back at the ranch with mom and dad."

"No," the Mexican agreed, shaking his head slightly. "Would that he had. After graduating from law school at your Georgetown University he is said to have traveled to the Caribbean and South America to apply what he'd learned from his professors, as well as from his amoral cesspool of a father. Shortly thereafter he reappeared in Guerrero Negro, and over time he accrued great power through bribery, blackmail, trafficking in *las drogas* and carefully applied acts of extreme violence. The last were notable for their clear message: do as I command, or you and those for whom you care will suffer most dearly. Now he holds all who live here in thrall, dispensing charity to the ignorant poor with one hand and cruelty to those who oppose him with the other." He grimaced. "*Un santo. Pero un santo de muerte.*" A saint, but a saint of death.

"Why did you come back?" Will asked. "And why stay in such a place?"

Slowly, with resignation, as if the act itself were metaphor, the doctor closed the locker door before him. "Why?" he repeated. "My parents and sisters continued to live here after I left to undertake my medical training. When I'd completed that training, my purported benefactor summoned me to return to Guerrero Negro and to establish my clinical practice here. Six days after I declined his 'invitation' I found on my doorstep a neatly wrapped box that contained my mother's fourth finger. Her wedding ring was still upon the finger." He smiled grimly. "I suppose one could say that I choose to live and work in Guererro Negro for the sake of her remaining fingers."

"But now my family is gone," he said softly, as if speaking to himself. He shifted his gaze from the closed locker door to look up at Will somberly. "Shall we go examine our patient? he asked. "He of the brain tumor?"

There seemed nothing to say that would serve any good purpose. Will mutely followed the man out of the dressing room and through the saloon-like doors of the OR back into the main hospital.

After reviewing Dr. Villalobos's case summary and the patient's imaging studies, the condition of *el hermano del jefe* was pretty much as Will expected. Although he remained fairly alert, he exhibited a mixed aphasia, left gaze preference and a dense right hemiparesis. He'd max'ed out on dexamethasone; any temporary improvement the steroid could produce already had occurred, and the potential for further benefit from it or any other drug was nil. The young man remained on a high dose, but at this point it was likely to serve only as a catalyst for promoting infection or metabolic aberrations. If stopped suddenly, however, he quite likely would die from the effects of acute steroid withdrawal. How that outcome might influence their chance of escaping this predicament alive and intact was unclear but not likely to be positive.

Will was considering and discarding this option of abrupt steroid withdrawal while he cursorily checked the man's right plantar response. As he stroked his sole with the contoured end of an old "tomahawk" reflex hammer, the patient's great toe hyperextended, the other four toes flared and there rapidly followed flexion at the knee which briefly lifted the covering sheet up off the bed. At this evidence of obvious movement in a limb where for many days only paralysis had been observed there was a general exclamation of surprise from the small group gathered behind the two doctors: three nurses, the hospital director and Arivada himself.

"Don't get excited," Will told them curtly. "It's only a reflex. *Un reflexivo, nada mas.* It means nothing." Having finished his examination, Will conferred briefly with Dr. Villalobos in the hallway outside the brother's room, and when he turned away he saw Arivada impatiently awaiting his impression.

"Your brother will die within the next six weeks," he told him. "And probably sooner if you persist in this idiotic notion of my operating on his brain. He lives now only because Dr. Villalobos has provided expert medical support." Even as he spoke, Will questioned the wisdom of giving voice to his pessimism. *If I tell him his brother's a goner,* he thought, *what becomes of my stock price?*

The Mexican's countenance darkened, and for a moment he looked away. When he turned back to face Will, his expression was grim. "I do not accept this prognosis, Dr. Rawlins," he told the American. "I know of your research involving a new therapy for brain tumors. A treatment that utilizes the body's own immunity to destroy such tumors. You must operate upon Francisco as soon as possible and then begin this therapy. You will remove as much as you can of his tumor, begin your treatment, and he will live."

Will was stunned. Using tissue cultures, he'd indeed conducted research involving immunotherapy for malignant brain tumors. The so-called therapy paradoxically had seemed only to stimulate the growth of tumor cells, and he'd concluded that the specific technique he'd developed was, literally, a dead end. After publishing a brief report in an obscure medical journal he'd begun to try another approach. Then had come Maria and the rest, and he'd abandoned his research altogether. How in the world had this man unearthed such a trivial nugget from his academic past?

"That research has no relevance to your brother's tumor," Will retorted. "The treatment didn't work. Immunotherapy aside, even if I could remove his entire tumor and he survived the operation, your brother would be no better off neurologically than he is as you see him now. What is gone will not return. He would be utterly dependent on others for dressing, eating, bathing and even using the toilet. I suggest you consider him and what *he* would want. Preserving him to sit in a wheelchair full of his own shit is not what I'd consider a gift of love."

Arivada's black eyes radiated anger, and it was clear his rage was barely suppressed. This clearly was a face some unfortunate few before him had beheld just prior to their painful demise. *Too bad,* thought Will. *But this fucker is hardly deserving of a more compassionate presentation. Let alone sympathy.*

His eyes never leaving Will's, Arivada called to a lackey standing behind him. "*El yanqui medico, a la casa. Y el otro, toda la noche con mi hermano y su amigo aya con el Doctor Villalobos tambien. Toda la noche, y con ojos abiertos.*" He told his man to take Will back to the *hacienda*, to have Dr. Villalobos remain in the hospital all night to attend to his brother and to leave one of the gunmen behind to watch the doctor closely.

His orders delivered, the dark, slender man turned from Will without comment and stalked out the hospital's front door to the street.

———

The drive back to the *hacienda* was notable for a complete absence of conversation or any repeat of the violent action that had marked his journey into town just hours prior. Will was anxious to see Elena, but the men who led him handcuffed into the house ignored his queries regarding her whereabouts. They shoved him face down on the bed in his room, unlocked the cuffs and quickly departed, taking care to shut and lock the heavy door behind them.

There he remained, alternately napping and struggling to devise some new plan, until two hours had passed and the door suddenly opened. In strode the man Will now thought of as Little Hector, a mineraturized version of the giant he'd shot and nearly killed, trailed by two more black-clad gunmen.

With his hands clasped behind his neck Will continued to recline on the vast bed, looked up at the man cheerfully and asked, "How's it going, Little Hector? Do you miss the big guy, or is it a rush to be the one *giving* orders for a change?"

The man sneered down at him uncomprehendingly, drew back his coat to reveal the holstered pistol below his armpit and motioned for Will to arise.

"No good, *amigo*," he told the man. "No matter how many guns you have, you won't get anywhere these days without being multi-lingual." He continued to lie on the bed.

Fifteen minutes passed, Will reclining and the three Mexicans clustered silently around the bed, when from the doorway a stern voice commanded, *"Andale! Ahora!"* It was *el jefe,* Arivada, leaning against the doorframe with his arms folded at his chest and glaring at the men inside. *"A la biblioteca,"* he instructed Little Hector in a somber tone. *"Ahora!"* He turned away and stalked off down the hall, a man accustomed to having his orders obeyed.

Little Hector's hostility towards his prisoner was palpable. He was unnecessarily rough in reapplying the handcuffs, and as the quartet ascended the first flight of stairs he raised one foot and gave Will a solid kick that sent him sprawling forward. Unable to brace his fall, Will landed hard against the unyielding thick clay tiles. He was not too stunned by his fall to take the opportunity to twist his body abruptly sideways, taking Little Hector's legs out from under him and causing the man also to fall solidly against the stairs.

When both men regained their feet, the Mexican withdrew his pistol and leveled it at Will's chest. Fearful of further aggravating their boss, his two companions moved quickly to pin Little Hector's arms behind him and in Spanish urgently advised him to gain control of himself. Acquiescing but plainly unmollified, Little Hector returned his *pistola* to its holster, and they proceeded without further event to the room that served as *el jefe's* library.

Arivada was sitting behind a massive wooden desk, beautifully carved and its surface highly polished. He looked up at his three retainers with visible annoyance and in an even but ominous tone commanded Little Hector to remove Will's cuffs and leave the room promptly with the other two gunmen. "*Pero vengaqui en dos horas,*" he said firmly. "*Tu solo.*" He wished Little Hector to return in two hours. Alone.

In contrast to its purple hue when earlier his face had been suffused with rage, Little Hector's scar now shone bright pink as he blanched at his boss's last words. His air of hostile arrogance evaporated as he stumbled from the room.

Arivada watched the three men leave, sighed and then shifted his gaze to Will standing before his desk. "Be seated," he said, indicating the chair opposite him. His tone was neutral and his face expressionless. Gone was any vestige of the elaborate courtesy the Mexican had afforded him the evening before. Now his host was all business.

The Mexican gazed at him thoughtfully. "You've had a busy day, Dr. Rawlins," he observed. "Shooting and then saving the same man within a period of only hours must…"

Will broke in. "Where is Elena?" he demanded.

El jefe made a slight, dismissive motion with his hand. "The young woman is quite safe, I promise you," he replied. "Quite safe. Unharmed. Very much alive."

"I want to see her," Will demanded. "Now."

The Mexican appeared to ponder this before replying. "If I have her brought here briefly to join us, will that reassure you?" he asked.

"No, it won't," Will told him. "I want Elena with me until you release us both."

He sensed annoyance in the Mexican's immediate reaction to his words. A brief flicker about the eyes.

Will pressed on. "And I want her with me in the OR when I operate on your brother," he said.

"Why do you wish this woman to be with you in the operating room?" Arivada asked. "She knows nothing of that which is medical, let alone a process as intricate as the surgical removal of a brain tumor."

"I want her with me," Will repeated. "Elena. Or else I don't operate."

The cold, reptilian stare Will had witnessed earlier that day now returned. "'Or else'," Arivada repeated. "Can you really wish to experience the consequences of this 'or else', of your failing to comply with my request? A request, may I emphasize, that offers you the opportunity not only to survive but also to cease living as *un fugitivo*. To live instead in safety and comfort.

An offer I continue to extend in spite of the regrettable behavior you've exhibited."

"I want her with me," Will repeated.

Presumably considering his request, the Mexican waited a long moment before he responded. "After returning to your room," he said finally, "you will be provided with both dinner and the woman. While not so elaborate as the meal we shared last night, the former will be quite adequate. As for the adequacy of the woman, that is beyond my capacity to ensure."

Again he paused. "And although she may remain with you tomorrow when you perform surgery upon my brother," he continued at last, "allow me to advise you that anything less than an excellent outcome from the operation could produce much discomfort for you both."

This said, they sat in silence together for a full five minutes, Arivada gazing out the window at the night beyond and Will impatient to return to his room and Elena. Just as Will was preparing to arise, *el jefe* turned back to face him and resumed speaking. His expression was solemn.

"I've known few physicians in my life," he said, "and most of them only as a result of my brother's illness. Many of them were from this country, and all, with the notable exception of Dr. Villalobos, have seemed to me, in one way or another, unsatisfactory. When, irony of ironies, I learned that an American neurosurgeon accused of murder was so close at hand, I used my sources to learn more of you professionally. Of your surgical proficiency and your research. I also called certain associates of mine in Arizona to learn something of what you were like as a man."

Who in the world could this man know in Tucson who would have any such knowledge? Will wondered. Aloud he said, "Your informants misled you. While I'm a neurosurgeon, I have no particular expertise in operating on brain tumors, and my research produced no positive result. Besides, Jesus Christ himself couldn't successfully remove your brother's tumor."

The man appeared to ignore his words. "I understand that when one becomes *un medico*," he mused, "he takes an oath. A vow, if you will. A vow that he will provide care whenever care is needed, and that he will do no harm." His gaze was now intense. "Did you not take this oath, Dr. Rawlins?" he asked.

Will said nothing.

"One might argue that you shot those men today in a moment of desperation," Arivada continued. "And that you did so with no intent to inflict mortal injury. Because for a physician it is a moral imperative to prevent such an outcome."

His elbows on the desk and hands clasped, the Mexican leaned forward to address Will yet more directly. "I do not believe this of you," he said quietly. "Whatever happened involving the *federal* in San Carlos, your actions today clearly indicate who you are and what serves to motivate you: passion and survival. If you conceive a passion, you will undertake what is necessary to fulfill that passion. If you have concerns as to your survival, you will kill. As simple as that. *Verdad.*"

He leaned back and shrugged. "So we are not so different, you and I," he concluded. "Not *santos*, certainly, but instead men whose attributes permit them to survive and to indulge their passions. You will be content here, I believe. *Muy contento.*"

"We are in no way the same, Arivada," Will replied disgustedly. "You *choose* violence. Whatever acts of violence I've committed were forced upon me by circumstance. By chance alone, or by the evil of others."

El Santo smiled grimly. "*Los vientos*, eh? *Vientos de mal*," he replied. "Winds of evil. How convenient."

He arose from his chair and strode quietly from the room, leaving Will to sit alone and contemplate his words.

—

Much later that evening, long after he'd been served a modest dinner of *pollo con arroz*, the door flung open, and as if catapulted Elena hurtled into his room. Even before she came to rest lying sprawled on the floor, the door slammed shut, and the lock engaged.

He rushed over to where she lay, stunned but quite conscious, and helped her to the bed. "Are you hurt?" he asked anxiously.

Using both hands to pull her disheveled hair back from her face, Elena attempted a smile. "No, my love," she replied. "I've been kept in a room much like this one." She glanced briefly around at his room and its contents. "I was trying to sleep. And then *de pronto* the door opened, and I was seized by two men."

She paused before continuing, and when she did her voice was barely a whisper. "I thought they had come to have their way with me. *Para violarme.* I tried to free myself from their hands, but they were too strong. *No habia la violacion.* Instead, they dragged me here and threw me at you *como un saco del grano.*" Like a sack of grain. Again she tried to smile.

Will could not take his eyes off her. Despite her bedraggled appearance and obvious distress, he was struck yet again by her beauty. So glad he was to see her that for a moment he could forget their desperate situation. For a moment there was only her, Elena, his beguiling ally.

She was quick to restore him to reality. "Why did they bring me to this place, Brian?" she implored. "Why am I here? Why are *you* here?" Agitated, she clutched his arms and searched his face intently.

Briefly he recounted for her the story of his abduction from the *cantina*, the brother's glioblastoma and *el jefe's* mistaken belief that he was capable of curing the brain tumor.

He described his attempted escape and his subsequent contribution to saving Hector. While telling of these events, he was struck by the rapidity with which they had occurred. *Little more than twenty-four hours ago I was walking through Jose's doorway,* he reflected. *Feeling fine. Inconspicuous. Excited at the prospect of seeing this same woman who sits here beside me. Things have changed a lot in a short time.*

Even now, with all that had happened and the heightened intimacy of their current circumstances, he was hesitant to reveal to Elena what really accounted for his presence in *El Santo's hacienda*. In Mexico. In her life. *But look the mess she's in because of me,* he thought. *Doesn't she deserve to know the truth?*

Aloud he said only, "I'm so sorry, Elena. It's only because of me, because of your connection to me, that you've been dragged into this." *So pointless,* he told himself, *to have permitted this relationship to develop. So much better for her had I just kept walking when she passed me on the street.*

Will hugged her tightly and then lifted her up, placing her gently on the bed and lying beside her. Almost at once she fell into a deep sleep, but he remained fully awake. The conversation with Arivada had unsettled him no less than the events of this strange, chaotic day. In particular, he wondered how accurate was the Mexican's assessment of his character. His capacity for violence.

Years before he'd been assaulted by a man in Mexico. It was during his first winter in Tucson. On a whim, he and a friend, Dean, had decided to use their free Saturday afternoon to roam the Mexican side of Nogales. By the time they'd driven the sixty-odd miles south and parked Dean's old beater in a lot on the American side, both of them were pretty well toasted from the beers they'd drunk on the trip down.

They walked from the lot across the border into Mexico, and after they emerged from their third *cantina*, both were stumbling along unsteadily, conversing happily and slurring their words. It was growing dark.

As they gamboled towards no particular destination, they were accosted on a street corner by a short young man who, except for his clothes – ill-fitting blue jeans and a long sleeve dress shirt that had seen better days – would have looked more at home in the Amazon basin than on a Nogales street corner. He had a thick mop of straight black hair cut in bowl shape, with his bangs horizontal and just brushing his eyebrows. His face was nut brown and smooth-skinned save for a sparse gathering of long black hairs on his upper lip that approximated a mustache.

As they passed, he called out softly to Dean. "Hey, senor," he asked. "Would you like to fock my seester? She is sixteen years only and almost a virgin."

Almost a virgin? His proposition was straight out of the movies, a cliché as old as a fossil.

"Why, *sure*," Dean answered immediately. The he looked down at the filthy sidewalk, his expression despondent. "But I have no money," he admitted.

The diminutive Mexican shook his head in protest as began to wheedle. "Please, senor," he said, smiling. "You are American. *Muy rico*. She will fock you good for ten dollars only."

Dean shook his head sadly. "I have no money," he repeated. "*No estoy rico*." Suddenly his face brightened. "But I have *los zapatos tan buenos*," he said, pointing down at his aged running shoes.

The Mexican looked skeptical but finally shrugged. "*Bien*," he said, and motioned for Dean to follow him through a dark doorway cut into the dilapidated building beside which they stood.

Dean cheerfully took off to follow the pimp, and Will, rushing to catch up, grabbed his arm and brought him to a halt. "What the fuck do you think you're doing, Dean?" he asked. "This guy probably has a couple of his buddies inside all set to steal your wallet and beat the crap out of you. Even if there is a girl, I doubt you'll find she has much to offer besides a little something for you to take back to Julie." Julie was Dean's current girlfriend.

Dean just smiled at him, weaving a bit as he spoke. "Relax, dad," he said. "Nobody's going to beat the crap out of me, and the last thing I'm looking for is a roll in the rubble with some Mexican whore. I just want to check it out. It'll make a good story."

And then as Will watched, Dean stepped across the threshold and into the darkness beyond.

He leaned against the building's exterior wall and waited, feeling increasingly apprehensive and far less intoxicated with each passing minute. Unable to stand it any longer, he walked over to the entrance and called out, "Dean. Are you all right?" Silence was his only response, along with a faint scrabbling that ceased almost as soon as it began. *Fuck*, he thought. *I don't like this.* Now there was only silence.

He had to go in; there was nothing else to be done. *I wish I had a light,* he thought. *And some kind of weapon.* Even his Swiss army knife would do, but it was back in Tucson. Back where he wished they'd remained themselves.

The first room he entered was large and empty, its concrete floor littered with shards of plaster that had fallen from the ceiling above. It became progressively darker as he cautiously picked his way further into the building, and when he rounded a corner and entered a second room the light gave out entirely.

As Will fumbled through his pockets, searching for a box of matches he'd picked up earlier in their *cantina* to *cantina paseo*, there emerged from the darkness the same scrabbling sound he'd heard from the building's entrance. Only louder. Gradually the sound evolved into that of footsteps that clearly were drawing nearer, and dropping to a crouch he willed himself to remain completely silent. The footsteps stopped, and despite the invisibility and sudden quiet he could sense with certainty that there was another person in the room with him.

All at once the beam of a flashlight cut through the darkness, and in its backglow he could make out a dark human shape. Immediately the shape lunged forward as if to embrace him, and in the shifting light Will could discern the shape belonged to a short, dumpy young man who held a flashlight in his left hand and what appeared to be a knife in the other. He was

Mexican, and as if to emphasize the desperate intensity of his work his eyes were wide with fright.

Reacting quickly, Will slammed his right knee into his assailant's soft upper abdomen, just below the diaphragm. As the Mexican doubled over, gasping for breath, Will snatched the knife from the man's right hand and picked up the flashlight he'd dropped. The knife was about eight inches long and, except for its finely-honed blade, identical to the hundreds they'd seen that day in the front windows of the various tourist shops they'd passed.

Still gasping, the man lurched clumsily forward, fell to his knees like a supplicant and slowly lifted his arms to encircle Will's thighs. Reflexively Will struck him a hard blow to the head with the cheap plastic flashlight, and the man collapsed to the floor.

Will dropped the flashlight. Gripping the knife with his right hand and the Mexican's shirt collar with his left, he wrenched the unconscious man upright and braced him against the wall. In one motion Will drove the knife deep and then upward below the lower margin of the man's sternum, just to the right of the xiphoid process and directly into the heart's left ventricle.

Relaxing his grip, he allowed the Mexican to fall limply to the floor. The discarded flashlight illuminated the rapidly expanding pool of bright red arterial blood that extended outward from beneath the man's prone body.

Will picked up the flashlight and quickly scanned the room. Save for the unconscious man on the floor and himself, it was empty. To his right a doorway led into a third room, and as he moved towards it he could hear voices arguing loudly in Spanish from within. He peered around the doorjamb, taking care to keep the flashlight directed behind him, and saw that within the far wall of the room there was an open doorway that led to the street.

Night had come, but the light cast from the streetlamps outside provided enough illumination for him to perceive Dean facing the original mop-top *mestizo* and two other men. Dean stood between the three men and the exit door, and without hesitation Will rapidly skirted the perimeter of the third room and stood at his friend's side. Dean stopped in mid-sentence and looked at his friend curiously. Whatever he saw caused him to remain silent.

Will faced the three men, shined the flashlight directly into the eyes of Mop-top and brandished the knife at all three. Its blade was coated to the hilt with congealed blood. He hoped none of the men carried a gun.

Wordlessly the two Americans backed slowly towards the exit that led into a dark, deserted alley. Just beyond were the lights and crowded sidewalks of *Avenida Revolucíon*. As they sprinted towards that busy street, Dean shouted back over his shoulder, "*Vayan con dios*, motherfuckers!" Just as they were reaching the street, Will hurriedly wiped the knife's handle with his tee shirt and tossed the weapon onto a flat rooftop.

Looking back, they could detect no sign of pursuit, and they stopped before a brightly lit door front to take stock. Looking him over once again, Dean said gravely, "Thanks for caring."

"*De nada*," Will replied. Following Dean's gaze, he looked down at his shirtfront and jeans and saw they were heavily soaked with blood. "I hurt somebody pretty bad back in there," he explained.

Dean stared back at him, expressionless. "Then it's probably best we hustle on over to the States."

Pooling what money remained to them, Dean bought Will a pale blue cowboy shirt with snap buttons, a pair of cheap linen trousers that resembled the bottoms of a scrub suit and two cheap Mexican blankets. Will waited in a dark corner and then changed behind an overflowing dumpster. His blood-stained clothes they placed in the bottom of the shopping bag, covering them with the blankets. Without incident they strolled back across the border, walked to Dean's car and drove home.

Later that evening they drank a last *cerveza* as they watched Will's incriminating clothes turn to ash in the flames of Dean's outdoor fireplace. Afterwards they never spoke of their excursion to Nogales, and as the years passed his memory of that violent night grew hazy. There were even times he could convince himself that he'd no choice but to plunge the knife. Or that the man had survived his horrific wound.

As he lay in the great bed with Elena sleeping peacefully beside him, however, Will knew the anonymous Mexican had bled to death on the floor of that dark room.

Chapter 8

BAJA

At his second viewing of the hospital it appeared to Will, if anything, even more dismal in aspect. It occupied the middle third of a squat two story building that extended the length of the block, and the building's drab olive exterior was badly in need of a new coat of paint. Or at least a good washing.

The hospital was flanked on its left by a *zapateria* and on its right by a *mercado* that long ago had closed its doors to business. The hospital's single glass door had been crudely brushed-painted white, and its exterior was filthy with dust. Stenciled upon the door in inconspicuously small black letters were the words *Hospital y Clínica*.

The hospital's sad facade served only to emphasize the pointlessness of what was being demanded of him. Will stopped before the entrance and turned to address *El Jefe*, who was standing just behind him with two bodyguards.

"Really, *amigo*, you've got to be kidding," he told the Mexican. "Let me repeat, Christ himself couldn't excise a glioblastoma in this shithole." He looked once more at the filthy door with its sad lettering and laughed disgustedly.

El Jefe clearly failed to share his mirth. "The people's Christ was not a neurosurgeon," he replied calmly. "And I can assure you that all you require to perform this operation is immediately at hand."

Will gave out an exasperated sigh. "Can you not hear me?" he demanded. "This is not going to go well for your brother. *No es posible.*"

El Jefe gave a brief, dismissive gesture with his right hand. "From your performance yesterday, however unfortunate its precipitating circumstances, I'm all the more confident you will succeed in the task before you."

"That was a *splenectomy,*" Will retorted, "and a splenectomy performed on a strong, healthy man. Any damn fool can take out a spleen."

"We waste time here," the Mexican replied, indifferent to Will's protest. Staring at the taller man with his cold black eyes, he continued in a tone soft but heavy with portent.

"Should this end poorly," he told Will, "I will assume you simply failed to do your best. As such, your elimination, and that of *tu amante*, will transpire no less painfully than that of the so-called Savior whose name you invoke. I would advise you to anticipate neither redemption nor resurrection. This is no Biblical *cuento de hadas*, my friend. No fairytale."

Having so spoken, he pushed open the hospital's humble door and beckoned Will inside.

———

They made an odd group, the six of them, as they waited in the small OR for the patient to arrive. All were masked, gowned and gloved, including Little Hector. The thug stood by the two Mexican scrub nurses, each of whom nervously darted her dark eyes fearfully at the gunman from time to time as if to confirm he was no mere apparition. Elena stood as far apart from the rest as the space in the small room would allow, her face hidden behind her mask and her long hair tucked beneath a yellow paper cap. She'd not spoken nor moved in the minutes since Will had whispered into her ear a few urgent sentences as they stood together washing at the scrub sink.

Will was standing beside the Mexican surgeon, Villalobos, who was to serve as his assistant and *de facto* anesthesiologist should the scrub nurse assigned to that task encounter any difficulty. It was far from optimal, Doctor Villalobos had admitted in his perfect English, but the hospital's sole nurse anesthetist had fled the town upon somehow learning what was to be required of her.

After greeting the Mexican crime boss and apprising the man of his brother's present condition, Villalobos had asked that he and Will be left alone for a few minutes to discuss how the upcoming surgery best should be conducted. Immediately suspicious, *El Jefe* was at first reluctant to accede. Apparently concluding that he had no real choice, he eventually shrugged and left the antechamber, taking with him the others. Elena included.

The Mexican doctor wasted no time on preliminaries. "I have a plan," he informed Will abruptly. "The area containing the scrub sinks is immediately adjacent to the OR. At either side of that area are the dressing rooms, one for the men and one for the women. Beyond the scrub sinks and the exterior doors is the room where the families of patients wait while surgery is performed. Nothing within those doors – the scrub area, the dressing rooms or the OR itself – is visible from the waiting area."

Before continuing, he glanced up to confirm that no one could be eavesdropping. "I've told *El Jefe* that for the sake of avoiding post-operative infection no one must pass through those doors while surgery is in progress. This he did not like, but I insisted. As a compromise, it seems that one of his men will remain with us in the OR, but his master and the rest will be sequestered beyond."

Will interrupted the man. "Why do you want to help us?" he asked. "Arivada is sure to kill you if he finds out."

"*No lo creo*," Villalobos replied dismissively. "I think he still will require my services. In any event, this man already has taken my life. Because of him my family lived always in fear. Now they are dead and beyond his reach. It is time finally to seek some measure of revenge."

He paused. They could hear footsteps approaching. He had much left to tell the American, and there was little time.

Villalobos began again, speaking rapidly. "In the men's dressing room is a small window that looks out upon an alley, and that window is now unlocked. During the surgery we will create a diversion and so remove the man guarding us. You then must hasten to the dressing room, gain the alley and turn left towards the street at the hospital's rear. Once there, cross to the opposite side and continue running to the south."

He paused again. Looking up, they could see that *El Jefe* and the others were almost upon them. "Enough," he said urgently. "There is but little more, and that I will tell you as we operate."

Finishing, the surgeon looked up to receive *El Jefe* with an expression of detached professionalism remarkable for its complete absence of guile.

―

"...*y otra vez, el bazo es como trescientos y tres milimetros de la corazon.*" Villalobos was telling Will that the spleen was located about 303 millimeters from the heart. This was nonsense, but to monitor their intraoperative conversation Little Hector had demanded the two physicians speak only in Spanish.

Rapidly they'd improvised a code. In this case, "spleen" was the room kept by the doctor for liaisons with his women, and "303" was its address on the street at the rear of the hospital. In similar fashion they'd quickly agreed upon a diversion that should allow Will sufficient time to escape without openly incriminating his surgical co-conspirator.

By camouflaging a key Latin word or phrase within a sudden rush of Spanish, Villabobos had even managed to communicate the make and location of his car. Again resorting to Latin, he emphasized that all main roads exiting the town were certain to be watched closely following Will's escape and that by no means should he undertake his departure from Guerrero Negro until well after sunset.

All seemed settled between them save for the issue of Elena. She'd remained silent and near-motionless at the end of the table for the duration of the surgery thus far, the skin and fascial incisions unnecessarily prolonged so as to permit the two men sufficient time to confer. At intervals Will could see Villalobos briefly dart his eyes towards the young woman, look back briefly at Will and then seem to grimace under his mask, but neither from these actions nor his necessarily obscure speech could he deduce what, if anything, the other wished to convey.

Does he worry she won't be able to manage the dressing room window?
Will wondered.

Earlier at the scrub sinks Will hurriedly told Elena that
Villalobos had devised a plan for them to escape. He told her
she should be on the alert for a sudden diversion during the
surgery, and that when this occurred she should follow him
rapidly to the men's dressing room. She'd stared back at him, her
eyes expressing alarm, but said nothing.

An hour had passed since Will made the initial incision, and
still the bone saw used to accomplish the craniotomy lay idle.
The two scrub nurses were beginning to look puzzled, and even
the gunman was fidgeting at his position against the wall where
he'd placed himself as far from the surgical site as possible. *Good,*
Will thought. *All the better if he's squirrely about blood.* When he
looked up from the incision site, Villalobos nodded briefly. *Let's
go,* he was indicating.

To the horrified wonder of the scrub nurse assisting the two
surgeons, Will neatly and deliberately sliced through the wall
of the patient's left middle meningeal artery. A pulsatile geyser
of bright red arterial blood erupted immediately, spraying both
surgeons' gowns. Keeping his gloved hands on the patient,
Villabobos twisted about to call out urgently to the gunman.
"Su jefe. Aqui. Muy pronto!" he shouted. *"Hay un complicacion
muy grande!"* He told the bodyguard to fetch his boss, that the
brother had suffered a severe complication.

The man edged doubtfully towards the operating table, recoil-
ing when he spied the white sheets now shining crimson in the
bright surgical lights. At that instant Will allowed his finger to
slip from the lacerated artery, and the geyser resumed erupting.
With this the gunman fled from the room to do as bidden.

There was no time for any farewell beyond a hastily exchanged *vaya con dios*. Propelling Elena before him with both arms, Will glanced back as they rushed from the room. There he saw the elderly surgeon calmly repairing the laceration while his nurses stood forlornly with their arms at their sides.

The dressing room was closet-sized and its single window proportionately small. As Villalobos had promised, the window was unlocked and partially open, but fearing the time expended in squeezing through such a narrow space would delay them unduly, Will used a metal folding chair to smash out the window's glass and most of its wooden frame.

His heart was pounding, or was that the sound of feet rushing their way? He stripped off his mask, gloves and gown and bade Elena do the same. Using a gown to wrap her hands, he boosted the young woman up to the shattered window and literally pushed her through the opening. As he did so, Elena's scrub top rode high and her bottoms low, and he saw tucked in her lacy black thong both a slim cell phone and a pager identical to the one he'd found attached to Hector's belt during his ultimately unsuccessful escape at the sandy wash.

There was no time to act upon this new and disturbing information, but as he raced down the alley with Elena at his side he realized with a jolt that this could be what Villalobos had been attempting to communicate. That all along his "*novia*" had been serving as particularly attractive bait.

When they emerged from the darkness of the narrow alley and onto the sunlit street behind the hospital, Will looked quickly both ways. The street was quiet, its sidewalks nearly deserted in the heat of midday, but from any of the cars parked along its length one of *El Santo's* men could be watching.

There was no choice. If there remained any window of time for escape, that space was narrowing rapidly. Taking Elena by the hand and noting her subtle resistance to his lead, he ducked low, sped across the exposed street and kept to the shadows as he quickly navigated the blocks that led to the doctor's second story apartment. Now running behind her, urging her on, Will stooped down briefly to retrieve from the gutter a short segment of heavily rusted steel rebar. Rising up, he saw an elderly woman staring at him from the doorway of a tiny *mercado* across the street. Quickly she turned and disappeared inside.

With an old skeleton key Villalobos had slipped him during surgery, Will unlocked an exterior door that opened to a dark, narrow stairway. Pushing Elena ahead and locking the door behind him, Will rushed up the stairs and down the dusty hallway to the door marked 2C. The same key opened this door as well, and when he flicked a switch on the wall just inside, an ornate overhead fixture illuminated a single large and sparsely furnished room.

On the floor was a black shag carpet, a relic of the '70s. The drapes, the bedspread, and the upholstery of an overstuffed arm-chair all appeared to be of satin and were crimson in hue. The bed was oversized even this expansive room, and beneath its shiny bedspread was a set of black sheets, similarly satin. The walls were bare save for a faded and highly stylized print of an Aztec warrior and his maiden, and on the bedside table was an old desk lamp.

While Elena was struggling to catch her breath and distracted, Will quickly slid under the mattress the piece of heavy steel bar he'd scavenged from the street and the .38 Villalobos had slipped him in the dressing room before the sham operation.

He straightened up and quickly paced the room's perimeter, taking special note of the tiny closet just inside the entryway. He observed that the door to the room opened to the inside, away from the closet.

As he surveyed the room, Will felt an overwhelming bitterness. His circumstances over the past two years had been of the type that rewarded clear-eyed rationalism, but in that instant he found himself awash in conflicting emotions that collided like the swells of a confused sea. On the one hand he feared for his life, as well as that of the quietly courageous doctor who'd provided the tenuous refuge of this modest room. At the same time he felt rising within him an uncontrollable rage directed at the young woman whose hands now grasped his right arm.

He glanced down at her. Elena. So lithe, lovely and seemingly sincere. *Can this be true?* he wondered. *Is she really just a faithless whore who's been playing me from the start?* A transponder within the pager she carried even now could be guiding those who sought them, and if she was left alive to tell what she knew, Villalobos was certain to suffer a miserable death.

So what am I supposed I do? he asked himself bitterly. *Just kill her now with my bare hands?*

And then he heard the sound of many footsteps approaching rapidly down the hallway. He needed a plan, and as always there was so little time.

He grabbed Elena's shoulders and spun her about to face him. "Whatever happens," he told her urgently, "we must stay together. Don't allow them to separate us." He couldn't fail to note the fleeting look of uncertainty his words produced.

"Of course, my love," she replied. "But is it truly them?" She gestured towards the door and the hallway beyond. "How could they have found us so quickly?"

How, indeed? he thought wretchedly. *You're good at this, Elena. Really good.* Aloud he spoke, "I don't know. Just follow my lead, and let me do the talking."

Just then the door burst open, and filling the space were Little Hector, fresh from the OR, and two other men, all crouched low and pointing the barrels of their shiny pistols at the room's two occupants.

Little Hector frisked Will expertly but left Elena to one of his companions. Will observed how superficial was her inspection compared to his own. Despite his brief patting and prodding, the gunman "missed" the pager concealed beneath her thin scrub pants, and his examination excluded her breasts, buttocks and genital area. From this last Will concluded she was no mere *puta* of the streets hired specifically to lure him. Such treatment would suggest that she held a position of some importance in *El Jefe's* organization. He mentally filed the observation.

The thick wall of bodyguards clustered about the doorway parted, and in strolled their boss as casually as if he were entering the home of an old and trusted friend. Although he was the smallest man present, with his aura of barely restrained menace *El Santo* dominated the room. He stared at Will for a moment before speaking, and his gaze was cold.

"You continue to live only because my brother as yet survives," he said finally. "Your friend, Dr. Villalobos, was kind enough to repair what damage you'd done, and tonight he will watch over his patient most carefully." The Mexican paused for a moment before resuming.

"Tomorrow, of course, is another matter," he declared offhand-edly. "The good doctor will pay most dearly for assisting in your regrettable attempt to abandon your professional responsibility."

Will decided to chance an aggressive response. "*Tu eres un tonto*," he told the Mexican.

He watched *El Jefe's* face closely as he spoke, but the man's expression betrayed no reaction to his words. His cold black eyes simply continued to glitter.

"I made no commitment to you or to your brother's care," Will continued, his tone harsh. "You kidnapped me and made me your prisoner. You chose to ignore me when I told you, honestly, that your brother is soon to die, surgery or no. Murder all the innocent people you want, *hombre*, but it won't change a thing."

Arivada's only response to Will's diatribe was a thin smile. "Ironic that you of all people should speak of innocence, Dr. Rawlins," he remarked mildly. And then he shrugged.

"But this is irrelevant," he said. "In the morning you will perform the operation that was intended for today, and having proven so vividly that you are not to be trusted, you will perform the surgery alone but for the hospital's two nurses. All of us," he gestured to indicate himself and the gunmen who flanked him, "will be immediately at hand to observe you at your work."

Will thought quickly. "I can't remove the tumor without a surgical assistant," he protested. "I need Villalobos."

"No, Dr. Rawlins," *El Jefe* replied, shaking his head slowly from side to side. "Because of your actions, the doctor's life is forfeit." He then nodded briefly at one of the bodyguards, and the man grasped Elena's arm.

"And you will spend this night alone, my friend," he said. "So that you may concentrate upon the task before you, we will remove all distractions. Including your lovely young companion."

Will made his decision. As there was nothing he could do for Villalobos, he would concentrate on saving himself. "Leave her here," he demanded. "Permit us a last night together. If not, just kill us now. If you take her away, there will be no surgery. *Te lo promento.*"

Will could see his words had discomfited the other man. *El Santo* stared silently at the floor for a full thirty seconds before turning abruptly to exit the room, beckoning his men to follow. "*Bastante*," he exclaimed to no one in particular. Then addressing Little Hector, he told the man to leave Elena with the *yanqui*, to post a man at their door, and to meet him downstairs.

The door closed, and suddenly they were alone. Before Will could begin to speak Elena stepped forward, clasped her arms around his waist, pressed herself against him and looked up at his face beseechingly. Tears spilled from her eyes.

"*Please*," she pleaded. "No more plans. Please just give him what he wants. I beg you. Please. I'm…I'm…". She buried her face against his chest, and her body shook from her sobbing.

Will smiled bitterly. *What is it you want, Elena?* he wondered. *What's your stake in this? Money? That condo on the beach in Cabo? Maybe the bossman himself?*

Aloud he said, "Don't worry, *chica*. I'm fresh out of ideas. All I've managed to do with my brilliant plans is get two innocent men killed." He was referring to the gardener and to Villalobos, although now he suspected the former might remain very much alive.

As she wiped the tears from her eyes, the young woman's relief at his words was evident. "*Gracias a Dios*," she murmured. "Perhaps even now we can escape *este aprieto imposible.*" This horrible predicament. "*Unidos, mi amado*". Together. "*Por siempre.*" Always.

"*Ya lo creo,*" he replied, smiling. But his thoughts were dark.

Composed now, Elena placed her hands on her slim hips and looked about the room. "The owner's taste in interior decorating leaves something to be desired," she said wryly. "*Tal vez un burdel.*" It resembled a brothel.

That's speaking rather unkindly of a man who soon may be sacrificing his life for us, Will thought. But he said nothing.

She walked over to the bed, briefly lifted a corner of the satin coverlet and then released it with obvious distaste. "One wonders what type of woman would come to such a room."

Indeed, Will thought. *But surely none so beautiful nor treacherous as you, Elena.*

———

For some hours they lay beside one another on the great bed, each still fully clothed in their scrubs. Elena seemed to doze, but Will remained fully awake. From time to time he lifted the shade of the room's only window to survey what he could of the street below, and although the block appeared quiet there could be no doubt that Arivada had his men in place. Watching.

Towards sunset Little Hector abruptly entered without knocking, his ham-like hand clutching a paper sack that contained two soft drinks and a few tacos. Tossing the sack on the bed, he gave Will a brief but malevolent glance and announced, "*La Comida Ultima.* How you say…The Last Supper?" Laughing at his own joke, he left the room and locked the heavy door behind him.

Will glanced over at Elena, now sitting with her legs drawn up and her back braced against the bed's padded headboard. Her face was set, her expression unfathomable. "Let's eat," he suggested, sorting through the sack's contents.

She turned and looked at him intently, her eyes shining with purpose. "Brian," she implored him, "promise me again that you will do what *El Santo* commands." Her tone was so earnest, and her plump lips trembled with emotion. *Damn but she's good*, he thought.

"Promise me!" she insisted. "Please, no more plans. *Mi amado*, promise me that you will do as he asks. He will kill you otherwise, and if you die I have no wish to live."

Will smiled and gently stroked her smooth cheek with his hand, his thumb pausing to caress the lips he'd come to know so well. "*Ay, chica*," he reassured her. "My only plan now is to get some sleep, try tomorrow to remove that poor's man's tumor and then hope Mr. Bossman is so grateful that he decides to let us go."

Once more her relief at his words was palpable. They shared the humble dinner, and by the time they'd finished it was quite dark outside the window. He judged it to be about 9:00.

Elena arose from the bed, stretched her arms above her head and yawned. "I feel *mugrienta*," she informed him. Grimy. "I'm going to take a shower." As she stood at the door of the tiny bathroom she paused one last time to confirm his intentions. "Do you mean it, Brian?" she asked. "There will be no more of your plans? You will do as Arivada wishes?"

"Sure," he replied absently from the bed. "*Bastante*. Enough is enough. *No mas*."

She looked at him appraisingly for a long moment, and then, apparently satisfied, walked into the bathroom and shut the door behind her. Once he'd heard the shower running for a full minute, Will moved quietly across the room and placed his ear to the cubicle's thin door, but there was only the sound of the rushing water.

———

When she emerged from the shower, Elena was clad only in a white towel so undersized that even with her hand holding its two ends together much of her otherwise naked brown torso was left unconcealed. In the lissome young beauty's other hand were her scrubs and undergarments, and these she tossed to the floor by the bed. That hand now free, she used it to sweep her long thick hair back across her shoulder and stood there before him, striking a provocative pose.

"I feel so much better," she said softly. "Ready for bed, but not quite ready for sleep. Not quite ready just yet."

She let the towel drop to the floor, kneeled before him where he was sitting at the foot of the bed and placed his hands on her breasts. Moving his hands over her naked skin, she closed her eyes, placed her lips to his ear and whispered, *"Amante, mi amante. Hombre querido. Por favor. Ahora."*

He allowed her to undress him, and soon they were naked together beneath the sheets of the unfortunate doctor's bed. She was unrestrained in her passion, and as afterwards he lay there waiting for her to sleep Will reflected upon the act just completed. *Either you're just not as good at reading others as you thought,* he told himself, *or you have a particular blind spot for women and sex.* He'd detected no hint of subterfuge in her responsiveness, and he took it as a lesson to be remembered that women were just as capable as men of yielding to lust in the absence of any personal attachment.

Her breathing became deep and regular, and when he nudged her and whispered her name, she made no response. Quietly he eased himself off the bed and crept across the room, pausing to gather up the clothing she'd deposited on the floor. From its weight he knew he carried more than her scrubs and underclothes.

He closed and locked the bathroom door before turning on the light, a single naked bulb. So low was the ceiling that he'd almost snapped off the bulb with his head upon first entering, and so cramped was the little bathroom that he avoided attempting to turn around for fear that the noise he produced might awaken the sleeping woman.

He'd expected to find the pager/transponder, but there was also the sleek cell phone. To his surprise, Elena had left the phone electronically unlocked. Checking her recent calls, he saw that her last was made at precisely 9:04 pm that evening. He reviewed her list of contacts and found it contained only five names. The first was "MA", and its number matched that of her last call. MA. Manuelo Arivada. *El Santo* himself. Presumably she had called him to confirm that the *yanqui impetuoso* was tamed at last.

He stood there for a moment, pondering. *What is Elena to the Mexican boss?* he asked himself. Why she'd been used to entrap him was obvious. Arivada's men could have snatched him up at any point, but Will's evolving devotion to Elena had provided the leverage required to ensure his compliance. Could that table be turned? Could she now shield his escape? Knowing she was at his mercy, would the Mexican perhaps hesitate to kill him outright?

He dressed quietly and sat on the toilet to tie his shoes. Pausing as he exited the bathroom, he could hear that the young woman's respirations were still slow, deep and regular. Quietly he moved across the room and extricated his two weapons from beneath the mattress. In the bathroom he'd attached Elena's beeper/transponder and cell phone securely to the waistband of his scrub pants, positioning them inside, against his skin, to reduce the chance of them being torn loose during the action to come. He sat carefully down on the edge of the bed for a moment and reviewed his plan.

Finally satisfied, he drew back the covers from Elena's naked form and nudged her to wakefulness with the barrel of the pistol he held in his right hand. "*Wake up, mi camaradita cachonda,*" he whispered to her. My lusty little comrade.

Even in the dim light cast from the bathroom he could tell immediately from her expression that she understood all that was happening. When she opened her mouth to speak, he jabbed the gun's barrel where not so long before he'd caressed her tongue with his own.

"Make one sound, and I'll put a bullet through your head," he whispered intently. "Believe it, *chica,*" he added. I've got nothing to lose." She stared up at him, wide-eyed. "Nod your head if you understand," he told her. She nodded.

Withdrawing the barrel from her mouth and shifting to press it against the angle of her left jaw, he resumed his whispering. "In a moment you and I are going to walk to that door.

You will stand before the door while I position myself in the closet. Once I nod to you, you will turn on the overhead light, knock on the door and call to the guard outside. You will tell him there's been a problem and ask him to come quickly. Then you will step back three paces. When the door opens, you will continue to face the door, naked, and make no attempt to cover yourself when the man enters. All of this time my pistol will be aimed at your head, and if you fail to do as I've said I will kill you without hesitation. Nod if you understand." She nodded. Tears were streaming down her cheeks, dripping to land on her naked chest.

Gesturing silently with his pistol, he directed Elena to arise, and now pressing its barrel firmly against her back he propelled her towards the door. When she was in position, he broke contact, but before entering the closet he gave her a meaningful look and used the long iron bar he held in his left hand to tap the pistol's muzzle and then point at her forehead.

He gave her a brief nod from the closet and used the rebar to indicate the light switch. She flicked the switch, and suddenly the previously darkened room was harshly lit by the cheap fixture overhead. When she hesitated, he motioned to her urgently with the rebar in his left hand and trained the pistol yet more carefully upon her head with his right. She turned from him to give the door a few sharp raps and then called out, *"Hay una problema muy grande! Venga, por favor! Andale!!"* She stepped back three steps from the door.

There was the sound of a key being turned, and then the door opened slowly. Whoever it was, he remained standing in the doorway. Jammed against the adjacent wall within the closet Will could see nothing but Elena standing just before him, her arms at her side and, as he'd instructed, making no attempt to conceal her nakedness. Fearing she'd betray him with a word or glance, Will extended his arm as far as he dared so that she might see the pistol still aimed directly at her head.

"*Que lo quieres?*" a low voice rumbled. When the young woman made no reply, the man took two steps forward.

As the Mexican stood there gaping at Elena's nakedness, Will leapt from the closet and dealt him a vicious blow to the forehead with the rebar he'd shifted to his right hand, the pistol now grasped with his left. The man collapsed soundlessly in a heap, and keeping the pistol trained on Elena, Will knelt to examine him.

Satisfied that the Mexican would remain disabled for the time required, Will rose to his feet and addressed the young woman. "Put your clothes on," he told her. "Quickly." His tone was curt. He tossed the piece of rebar he'd used to fell the guard under the bed - he could see no further need for it - and checked the rear pocket of his scrubs to insure it still contained the doctor's car key. Shortly after they first entered the room Will had separated the key from the one required to open the door, placing the former under the mattress with the rebar and sidearm.

Even now, Elena made another attempt to dissuade him. "Brian...*Will,*" she pleaded. "What are you doing? You promised there would be no more plans. *Mi amante*, you will get us both killed."

He shook his head. "Game's up, *chica,*" he told her. "But I'll grant you, you make one hell of a whore. Now get dressed."

She began pulling on her scrubs. As she slipped on her boots she looked up at him with a face that held both grief and resignation. "You have it all wrong, Will," she told him. "*Soy contigo.*"

I'm with you. "And Manuelo has no interest in killing you. He wants only for his brother to live."

"Great," he replied. "Now hurry up."

He'd worried that a second gunman would be stationed down the hallway at the head of the stairs, but the corridor was empty. Elena stumbled on the steps and nearly lost her balance as he pushed her along from behind. When they reached the door that opened to the street, he motioned for her to stand behind him. Pausing a few seconds to gather himself, he grasped Elena's right hand with his left, pulled her against him and burst through the door.

A thug dressed in the now-familiar uniform of a form-fitting, short-sleeved mock turtle dickey, shiny black trousers and highly polished black loafers was leaning against the outside wall to the right of the door as it opened. Serendipitously, the heavy door ricocheted off his face, and the force of the collision knocked him to the ground.

Regretting that he wore only his dilapidated running shoes, Will kicked him full in the face as hard as he could and then, half-dragging Elena behind him, turned left and began to run down the sidewalk towards the next block. To the corner where Villalobos had told him his car was parked.

This street appeared deserted, but as they rushed along Will suddenly heard behind them voices shouting out in unintelligible Spanish. In the next instant two shots were fired, and Will, un-hit, was grateful for the lack of illumination. Ahead, however, was a single street light on a pole, and he cursed softly to himself when he saw beneath it the doctor's enormous Pontiac Bonneville, gleaming brightly in the small cone of light.

There was no help for it. Jamming the pistol in his waistband, snatching the key from his pocket with his right hand and using his left to grip Elena, he rushed across the empty intersection to the car. Once beside it, he crouched low to unlock the door. Swinging the door open, he maneuvered them both behind it just as the gunfire resumed. Bullets slammed into the barrier of metal now shielding them.

And then, as he was preparing to push the young woman into the front seat, she inexplicably stood and immediately caught a round to her left face. There was a brief explosion of bloody spume and particulate matter - bits of bone, cartilage and teeth - and Elena collapsed to lie inert, half in the car and half out.

Taking care to keep low, Will man-handled his gunshot companion towards the passenger's side of the front seat, slipped behind the wheel and started the engine. As he pulled out into the street the phone at his belt began to sound. It was a fragment of some classical piece that he faintly recognized but couldn't place.

Before responding to the call he glanced over at the young woman sprawled motionless across the seat beside him. The upholstery and floorboard were soaked with her blood, and while Will knew head and scalp wounds were notorious for looking more serious than they really were, he feared such was not the case here.

Even with the blood and her long hair matted within the wound, he could see the bullet had shattered both mandibles into fragments, and so large was the exit wound that her mangled and lacerated tongue was exposed to its very root. She might survive, he thought, but even the most painstaking cosmetic surgery could never repair the torn and devastated landscape of her once-lovely face.

He answered the phone, and before the caller could utter a word he began to speak rapidly but distinctly. "Make any attempt to follow me, and the woman dies," he said. *"Entiendes?"* On the other end the only response was silence, and after a second or two Will pressed the phone's "end call" button. *Probably pointless,* he concluded. Elena's value to his nemesis was difficult to calculate.

Anxious to avoid attracting the attention of *la polica*, whom he assumed must be in *El Santo's* pocket but perhaps not yet aware of the circumstances, Will drove slowly with his lights on to the town's limits. Once at its southern boundary he turned eastward on an obscure side road, accelerated to ninety and turned off the car's lights. Once he'd traveled about ten miles, swerving frequently to maintain control on the curves of the narrow road, he stopped and carefully placed the beeper/transponder on the roadside.

Doubling back to the road's origin at high speed, he stayed on the main highway only until he found a short segment of dirt track, heavily rutted but navigable, which he knew intersected with the road leading to his *ejido*. After turning onto the track and driving a few hundred yards beyond the main highway, he stopped the car, snapped on the overhead light and turned to examine Elena.

She remained unconscious but still breathing. The blood flow from her wounds had lessened only slightly, and its color was a brighter red than would be associated with venous injury only. If a major artery had been severed and then failed to contract and thrombus spontaneously, hypovolemic shock was a real possibility. Delicately he probed the entrance wound with his fingers, but such was the tissue destruction he could find few anatomical landmarks. He saw no obvious arterial bleeders.

Turning away, he rested his forehead against the crenellated steering wheel and tried to think. He could not bring himself to leave her by the roadside to die. Whatever had motivated the young woman's actions, she deserved better than to bleed out lying in the dirt. Despite the potential consequences, he found it impossible to abandon her completely.

He backed up a few yards, turned the big car around, and returned to the main highway. He began to drive southward rather than towards the coast as he'd initially intended. There was a town forty kilometers south of Guerrero Negro, and in that town was a small medical facility with a *cuarto de emergencia* that was staffed 24 hours a day. While they would lack the capability to provide much more than first aid and intravenous fluids, perhaps the staff there could stabilize her to the point where she'd survive an ambulance transfer to one of the hospitals in La Paz or Cabo.

As he sped down the highway with the car's headlights extinguished, he once again heard the brief burst of classical music from the phone at his waistband. Fumbling in the dark, he managed to get the phone to his ear and answer, "What is it?"

The voice on the other end was immediately recognizable. *El Santo*. "To flee is pointless, Dr. Rawlins," the Mexican said evenly. "We know your precise location, and even as we speak my men are but minutes away."

"Really?" Will responded. "Then tell me, *hombre*, just exactly what is my present location?"

The man on the other end ignored Will's question. Either he's bluffing, Will concluded, or they're heading for that transponder lying beside the road.

"Return immediately to the hospital with the woman, and I will spare her," Arivada resumed. "You have my word."

Will laughed involuntarily at this. "Your word doesn't mean much to me, *amigo*," he told the man.

There was silence from the other end, and Will could envision the man mulling this over. "The girl is irrelevant," *El Jefe* declared at last. "But if you proceed, you most certainly will die."

There was no point in continuing, and Will worried that his pursuers might track him via the phone. "*Adios*, Manuelo," he replied, ending the call. Pulling off the road briefly, Will found a large rock and used it to pound the phone into tiny fragments.

Back in the car with Elena slumped against the door, bleeding and unconscious, the words of Friar Laurence's counsel to the love-struck Romeo came to him abruptly and unbidden. *These violent delights have violent ends.*

He drove up to the unprepossessing *clinica* and left Elena in the car, taking care to position her head low in an attempt to preserve her cerebral blood flow. When no one responded to his shouts and pounding at the door, he hurled the same rock he'd used to destroy the phone at the *clinica*'s large front window, and it collapsed with a loud shattering of glass. He could see lights turn on soon thereafter.

First to the door of the facility was a woman who looked to be in her fifties, a swarthy *mujer* swathed in a colorful shawl the size of a bedspread, her appearance and bearing more typical *de los campesinos* than a healthcare provider.

"Hay un medico aqui?" he asked her, fighting to suppress his mounting agitation.

"No," she replied. *"No lo tenemos. Tecnicos medicos solamente."* There was no doctor on site. Only medical technicians. *"Hay un hospital en Guererro Negro,"* she suggested.

"Hay conmigo en mi coche una mujer quien tiene una herida muy seria." He was nearly shouting now. *"Un belazo."*

As much from his manner as the mention of a serious gunshot wound, the woman recoiled and made as if to close the door in Will's face.

He shoved her aside roughly and strode through the doorway. At the end of the hall in which he now stood he saw a dimly lit room that contained an examination table, a small white refrigerator and some cabinets that appeared to hold medical supplies.

He turned to the frightened woman. *"Hay los otros aqui?"* he demanded. When she nodded her head in the affirmative, he told her to have the others extricate Elena from the car and, if they had one, to use a gurney to bring her to the room beyond. She hastened off.

As he waited for Elena to be transported to him, Will canvassed the refrigerator and cabinets and selected such instruments and materials as might be of use: bags of saline, IV kits, various dressings, scissors and several pairs of forceps and clamps. While he was sorting and arranging all that he'd selected, two young Mexican males clad in white wheeled into the room a gurney upon which lay the unconscious Elena. She was as pale as the sheet that covered her. The woman who'd answered the door was nowhere to be seen.

They transferred her to the exam table, and as the two Mexican *technicos* looked on silently, Will rapidly started two

IV's and began to run in the saline at a wide open rate. It was no easy task; her superficial veins had collapsed, and for one of the IVs he'd had to make a blind stick that luckily found the internal jugular. After ensuring that the IVs were running well, he checked her blood pressure: 60 palpable. Even her carotid pulse was difficult to find, and her heart rate was 130. She'd lost a lot of blood.

He'd just removed one of the pressure dressings he'd applied to stop the active bleeding and was beginning to probe the wound below when he heard the sirens. *Of course,* he thought. The woman *called* la policia *to report my maniacal intrusion.*

In rapid fire Spanish he commanded the two young men to continue administering saline at the highest rate possible. He told them they should transport her to a more appropriate facility at once, but not to the Guererro Negro hospital. The doctor there was dead, he told them. *El es muerto.* Although they gave no visible indication of comprehending while he gave his instructions, he could see them moving quickly to her side as he exited the room.

Seconds after he'd begun to speed back northward on the main highway he could see in his rear view mirror the lights of the police cruisers as they turned into the clinic's lot.

———

After leaving Elena, Will continued to drive towards Guerrero Negro. As he approached the southern outskirts of the town he threaded his way through a labyrinth of back streets and alleys to arrive finally at Jose's *cantina.* The building's interior was dark, and the surrounding area appeared deserted, but to be certain Will circled the block three times.

Reasonably confident that he was unobserved, he turned the Bonneville off the pavement, drove through an empty lot overgrown with tall weeds and parked the car behind a huge pile of rubbish at the lot's rear periphery. He walked back to the street and tried unsuccessfully to spot the vehicle from a variety of perspectives.

Satisfied at last that it would be difficult to detect the car even in bright daylight, he jogged over to the corner opposite the *cantina* and pushed his way through the weeds and debris of the lot upon which squatted the crumbling *casita* behind which he'd hidden his scooter just three days before.

Three days. It seemed an eternity. From beneath a stone lying beside the kickstand he extricated the scooter's spare key and gave brief thanks for having taken that precaution.

Traveling slowly, he exited Guerrero Negro the same way he'd entered, and within minutes he was driving southward for the second time that evening, his headlight extinguished. Nearly soundless. Well-nigh invisible.

Now what? he asked himself. It was almost 2:00 am, he was exhausted and all roads in the area undoubtedly were patrolled by *El Santo's* men. He calculated that the turn-off to his *ejido* lay another ten kilometers distant, but to remain on the main highway for the ten minutes required could prove fatal.

There were several old dirt tracks that exited the road he was traveling. They meandered all over the coastal plain, but most linked up with his road eventually. He decided to exit off onto the next of the tracks, get a few hours of sleep and then reassess when his mind was clearer.

Chapter 9

BAJA

He awoke well before dawn, hungry, thirsty and sore from sleeping on the hard, rock-strewn *caliche*. Anxious to reach his home before daylight, he climbed back on the scooter and threaded his way carefully along the barely discernible dirt track that led to the *ejido* road.

The sun had risen well above the sere inland hills when he arrived at the eastern boundary of the old tomato fields. Skirting the coastline and his shack, he rode southward for several hundred yards to the high ground, to a point from which he could look back upon his home while remaining concealed behind a mound of lava rock.

At first he wished for his binoculars, but as the sun rose yet higher in the cloudless sky he could see quite clearly the entire *ejido* spread out below him. All that moved were the soundless waves and the relict tomato vines bowing before the onshore breeze. It made for a beautiful scene - the field, the bluff, the beach and ocean - and he was saddened by the knowledge that this no longer would be his home.

He motored slowly down to his shack and hurriedly began to collect what he wished to take with him. *It's quiet now*, he thought, *but they'll be coming*.

Having paused to drink deeply from the plastic container of *aqua dulce* he kept on the table in his kitchen and to wolf down two tortillas wrapped around a chunk of *queso blanco*, he loaded a backpack with three liters of water, some non-perishable food, a few articles of clothing, a favorite knife, wooden matches and his aluminum mess kit.

From behind a loose adobe brick in the wall he removed a plastic bag containing his money and papers, slipping it, some sunglasses, a second knife and his binoculars into the backpack's side pockets. He used two bungee cords to secure the pack and his sleeping bag to the small rack behind the seat of his scooter. Tucking the .38 more securely into his waistband, he climbed aboard and made ready to depart.

Just as he prepared to accelerate, however, out of the corner of his eye he spied an incongruous slash of pale blue bobbing in the ocean, in the turbulent area between the beach and the point where the incoming waves began to fall apart in the shallows. What surfers refer to as the impact zone.

Stepping off the scooter and removing his binoculars from the pack, he glassed the water. It was Glenn's board or, at least, a fragment of that board. Compelled by an irresistible urge, he raced down the trail leading to the rocky beach, waded through the shallow water and snagged the broken shard of fiberglass.

He slipped the fragment of surfboard under the cords, drove his scooter to the southernmost extremity of the tomato field and then turned left. Just before he reached the far corner of the field, Will turned right and slowly descended down into a long, narrow arroyo that ran perpendicular to the coast for a mile before terminating at a wide, sandy wash. The wash ran dry most of the year and extended for miles in either direction, paralleling the main highway that ran north to Guerrero Negro and south to Todos Santos. Its distance from the highway varied between five and ten kilometers according to the path it cut through the rugged coastal terrain.

It had been months since the arroyo had experienced rain, and the sand at its bottom was deep and soft. He had to dismount frequently to push his scooter through the sand or to maneuver around the scrub and piles of rock that had tumbled down from the eroding banks of the miniature canyon. At first he despaired of his slow progress, but there was no sign of pursuit, and as the hours passed he concluded there was nothing to be gained by hurrying. Where he toiled at present was likely to be a safer haven than any destination that lay before him.

In fact, he had no clear idea of where he should go. Once he reached the broad wash he would decide in which direction to turn, but beyond that he'd given little thought to how best to proceed. Although Will's relevance to *El Santo* would vanish with the brother's imminent death, the Mexican struck him as the sort of man who would not be content to allow an adverse score to remain unsettled. If he were to survive, Will concluded, continued flight and concealment would be required.

———

At last he reached the wash, and as much to delay making any decision as for comfort he stopped and carefully lay his scooter down. He sat for a while in the sand with his back resting against a large, smooth boulder and finished a modest meal of plain flour tortillas and water. The sun lay low. He judged it to be around 6:00.

He sat and pondered his options. The coastline immediately north of Guerrero Negro was unknown to him, but if he journeyed far enough he knew he'd eventually come to San Quintin and its namesake bay. An otherwise nondescript town, the adjacent coastline was blessed with beautiful beaches and dunes where he'd camped many times to windsurf on the shallow bay or to surf the point break at the bay's mouth.

While San Quintin would do as a temporary refuge, for the long term it was insufficiently isolated. Although he'd once camped there bayside for a week and not encountered another human the entire time, it was not unusual to see a van or pickup truck loaded with *yanqui* surfers cruising the beach on their way to town or back to their oceanfront campsites, as well as clusters of Mexicans digging for clams. Compared to his *ejido,* it was a veritable resort.

If nothing else, however, San Quintin offered the comfort of familiarity. Will was confident that with the scooter he could find some niche in the oceanside bluffs of the peninsula, hidden from prying eyes and offering at least a few days respite. Time simply to rest and contemplate his future in the absence of any immediate threat.

It was to be San Quintin then, he decided.

————

Concerned that even the low drone of his scooter might carry in the still night air, Will had decided to wait until morning to depart. He made camp in the wash, on a patch of soft sand partially encircled by a berm of boulders, uprooted vegetation and large clods of *caliche* that had been deposited there by a muddy torrent born of some long-ago thunderstorm.

He arose at dawn to drive the remaining seventy-some kilometers to San Quintin. He spent several pesos to fill the scooter's tank at the town's sole Pemex station and then set out for the bay. Although years had passed since his last trip to the area, he quickly found his way, and soon he was on the track that led to the peninsular bluffs.

As he rode, Will recalled how years before he and his brother had collected sand dollars on the oceanside beach beyond the bluffs ahead. Afterwards they'd used them to decorate a Christmas tree adorned only with similar gifts supplied by the sea: garlands of cowrie shells, ornaments made from small pieces of driftwood and the like. His brother had died the following summer, and after that Will had little interest in Christmas trees.

Similar to his recently abandoned home at Punta Banda, the peninsula's headland resembled a slightly crooked index finger, its tip the point which could generate the right-breaking waves that drew surfers. Using its hand throttle to navigate the steeper portions, Will walked his scooter up the peninsula's eastern face and then after crossing the apex began to descend towards the beach below. He quickly found an ideal location halfway down the seaside bluff: a small, sandy pit his scooter could access but well away from the trails favored by surfers and beachcombers.

Surrounded on all sides by heaps of rocky soil thick with scrubby vegetation, his pit was well-concealed. Even knowing its location, Will found it difficult to spot when he circled the perimeter at a distance of less than a hundred paces. It was a foxhole of sorts. Along with the attribute of invisibility, the sand within would make for comfortable sleeping, and the view was superb: never-ending lines of blue swells breaking upon the sandy beach below.

He glanced wistfully at the fragment of fiberglass still strapped to his scooter and wished for a board. There was a lot of west in the swell, and some epic rights were peeling off the point at the peninsula's terminus. Straining to see more clearly, he could make out a few black dots bobbing in the ocean just outside the break line. He extricated his binoculars from his backpack and glassed the area. Sure enough, the black dots were surfers, and he watched with envy as at intervals one would arise to take an incoming wave and streak down its face for a full thirty seconds.

For now, however, it felt good simply to recline in his bowl of sand and let the sun bake the fear and weariness from his bones. He closed his eyes.

Part III

CAZADOR

Man…is nature dreaming, but rock and water and sky are constant. [All] the rest's diversion: those holy or noble sentiments…the love, lust, longing: reasons, but not the reason.

Robinson Jeffers
The Beauty of Things

He sat at his desk smoking quietly, admiring the sunlight that shone in through the library's tall windows and reflected off the rough-hewn planks of the room's oak floor. His ancestors had fashioned those planks. From the forests high in the Barranca del Cobre *they had selected the finest trees, felled them by hand with their saws and axes, used hammer and chisel to divide the trunks and then with great effort dragged the heavy sections of log to their village to be milled. They were* indios, *native to the inaccessible mountains and by their isolation free of Spanish blood. They were a hard people, and necessarily so. They were also passionate beneath their stolid exteriors, indifferent to conflicts not their own but relentlessly devoted to avenging any wrongs that they themselves should suffer. Their blood ran strong within him. And, soon enough, he would have his own revenge.*

Chapter 1

THE FUGITIVE'S RETURN

He sat in an inconspicuous spot and observed the endless stream of people push through the turnstile. All races and ethnicities were represented, but most were Mexican, white or those who could claim both lines in their heritage. He'd watched carefully for hours, but he'd seen nothing of potential concern in the monotonous behavior of those who wore the brown tunics of the U.S. Border Patrol. Not once had any of the uniformed men paused to glance a second time at a passing face, let alone pull a pedestrian aside for closer scrutiny.

It seemed too easy. He'd long anticipated this day, the one particular moment when he might pass from exile back into his homeland. *Surely there's more to it than this*, he told himself. *Can it really be this…casual?*

Yet again he inventoried his appearance. Although still deeply tanned, he was now clean-shaven, and a barber in Rosarito Beach had trimmed his sunbleached brown hair to a respectable length. He wore a simple white shirt, its long sleeves rolled up neatly to a point just above the elbows, a brown belt and a pair of scuffed loafers without socks. His jeans were American-made and modestly stylish. In short, aside from a certain air of reserved watchfulness and the manner in which the third, fourth and fifth fingers of his left hand remained persistently in partial flexion, he looked like a typical southern California surfer entering the early years of his middle age.

This was not altogether subterfuge. He was indeed both a surfer and now well into his thirties. Relevant to his apprehension, however, was the unfortunate fact that under Mexican law he was wanted for the murder of a Sonoran *federal*. For three full years he'd lived in Mexico as a fugitive from justice or, at least, what served for justice in the land of *narcocultura* and *la mordida*. Complicating matters further had been his unfortunate encounter with Manuelo Arivada, the powerful cartel *jefe* who dominated southern Baja.

Will had spent the first months of his involuntary exile seeking a safe refuge, the next year in an abandoned *ejido* on the Pacific coast west of Guerrero Negro and most of the last two years in Todos Santos, an hour's drive northwest of Cabo San Lucas. In that time he'd suffered a gunshot wound to his left shoulder, an abduction, and a near-fatal betrayal by a woman he'd believed himself to love. He'd pulled a trigger on two men with full intent to kill, but one survived his being shot, and the other…nothing. Along the way he'd grown weary of the fugitive's life: always hiding, always looking over his shoulder, always striving to remain inconspicuous.

At first in Todos he'd lived with Glenn, a surfing expat from Hawaii by way of San Diego whom he'd met and befriended years before when both had lived in Pacific Beach. Eventually, however, his fear that he'd contaminate Glenn's peaceful existence with the fallout from his own troubles led him to lease a tiny apartment in town.

The apartment was bleak, but its obscure location on a lightly traveled back street in the midst of a poor neighborhood offered the benefit of anonymity. When the heat, isolation and claustrophobia became more than he could bear, he'd go spend a few days with Glenn at his hillside shack two miles north of town. To his eternal gratitude, the Hawaiian invariably made him feel welcome.

Most days he would arise before dawn, unchain his scooter and with a board tucked snugly under his crippled left arm ride from his apartment to one of the many point breaks scattered along the coast. More often than not he had the waves to himself. There were fewer Mexican surfers in those days, and at sunrise the Americans were either sleeping off their hangovers or on the water at locales better known.

This, the surfing, and the occasional visits with Glenn had helped to counteract his pervasive sense of *ennui*, but even so it was hard for him to ignore the fact that virtually all that marked his passage was a deep tan, his vastly improved performance on left-breaking waves and his ever-dwindling financial resources.

It was this last that finally precipitated Will's decision to return to the States. What money he'd brought with him three years ago was almost gone. He had virtually nothing of value left to sell, and his situation with respect to the Mexican authorities was such that to seek employment was out of the question. Thanks to the cheap rent and a diet consisting primarily of beans, rice, tortillas and fish, he'd managed to stretch his thin finances, but even with further belt-tightening he'd have been hard-pressed to last more than another month. Glenn, ever hospitable, would have taken him in and provided support indefinitely, but, as before, he was unwilling to place his friend in danger.

Although he saw and heard nothing of Manuelo Arivada, he worried that for reasons known only to him the Mexican *narcotrafficker* might simply be biding his time. Todos Santos lay well south of Guerrero Negro and Arivada's *estancia,* but secrets were not easy to keep even in that sparsely settled corner of the world. Arivada had experienced no difficulty in locating him at the remote *ejido* where he'd felt so secure. Perhaps in time *El Santo Obscuro* would descend upon him.

And so he'd sold his last remaining board, his scooter, and what few other odds and ends he possessed to trusted friends and used part of the money to purchase a bus ticket to Tijuana. Glenn drove him to the station, where they said their goodbyes. He'd felt both dismal and apprehensive as he sat in his seat at the back of the bus, watching as the eternally unfinished Mexican building projects of Todos gave way to the scrubby coastal desert.

Although Will had carried with him a cheap plastic suitcase, he did so primarily to avoid attracting attention during the long journey. The bag contained only some toiletries, a single change of clothes and – he'd been unable to resist – a long, finely honed diver's knife encased in a plastic scabbard and hidden within the folds of his one spare shirt. He wished for a handgun, but in the unlikely event that his bag was searched, to have been apprehended in Mexico as a foreigner possessing an unregistered firearm would have precipitated certain disaster. The meager papers he carried – his passport, an expired Arizona driver's license – were more liability than asset, as even at the most primitive *oficina de policia* the papers rapidly would have led to his identification as a notorious fugitive wanted for murder.

Even in the States, he wondered, would he be able to use these documents and his social security number safely? He had little knowledge of international law, and during his years in Mexico it had been impossible for him to obtain any reliable information regarding whatever extradition policy the two countries shared. For all he knew, any attempt to use his true identity in his native land would result in his being apprehended and eventually deposited in a Mexican kettle filled with *agua tan caliente.*

At the depot in Tijuana he'd changed his clothes and strapped the knife to his lower leg, hidden underneath his jeans. The jeans were a loose fit. He now carried only a hundred and seventy-five pounds on his six-foot four inch frame. In a trash barrel he deposited his suitcase and the clothes he'd worn on the long bus journey. Taking a cab to the border checkpoint, he'd intended to walk across at once and catch the trolley to downtown San Diego, but instead he found himself frozen, sitting for hours on this same grimy concrete bench beneath a pedestrian overpass, watching the long line of people snake through the turnstile.

Will glanced up at a clock that hung on the wall of a nearby shop. Four-thirty. If he didn't start now, it would be dark by the time he made his way to his friend's home in Hillcrest, assuming she still lived there. Better to arrive in daylight so as to cushion the shock of his appearance.

He'd carefully considered the stateside options available to him before settling on Sally. For one thing, he trusted her. She was a level-headed, independent and quietly self-confident ER nurse who was well-acquainted with the circumstances that had precipitated his Mexican predicament. Even more pragmatic, she'd specifically invited him to visit her if he managed to return to the area, and her house was a short walk from the trolley station.

At last he arose from his bench, exhaled deeply and willed his heart to cease beating so rapidly beneath his thin linen shirt. Looking carefully in both directions, he stepped off the sidewalk to cross the street that separated him from the border checkpoint.

———

His passage across the border had been anticlimactic. The guard glanced at him briefly. He seemed to take note of Will's blue eyes, but he said nothing and bade him pass through with a barely perceptible flick of his wrist.

Once across and officially in the States, Will fought the impulse to sprint from the checkpoint and instead walked slowly to the nearby trolley station. He paused at a kiosk to buy his ticket from a lovely *senorita* who smiled at him from her seat within the bright red booth. Although she was much younger – eighteen, he guessed – something about the girl reminded him of Maria. Perhaps it was her enigmatic smile blossoming from those full, pouting lips. He wondered whether she was a Mexican national who crossed the border at will, her days spent in this tiny booth and her nights *en una casita* crowded amongst thousands like it on the scabrous hillsides of Tijuana.

The ride north on the trolley was as uneventful as his crossing. He sat alone on his seat by the window and watched San Ysidro merge into Imperial Beach and then the city itself. His eyes had grown used to the sparseness and simplicity of Baja, and San Diego seemed to him very crowded. Too much, somehow. An overabundance.

It was unseasonably cool for an early October evening, but the mostly uphill walk from the trolley station to Sally's cottage on Hillcrest's mesa warmed him. He labored up Hob Nob Hill and relaxed his gait as he strolled along the mild undulations of First Avenue. He turned right on Front, a block south of Mercy Hospital, where he'd served his internship a decade prior. Much in the area had changed since his last visit, but much also remained as it had been. In the distance to his left he could see the darkened window front of El Cuervo, a venerable *taqueria* that presumably still served delicious cheese quesadillas and soft tacos stuffed with *carne asada*.

Concerned that he might appear too conspicuous if he continued on the heavily traveled street, he turned right, down one of the intersecting avenues, and passed a series of gay bars. For reasons presumably steeped in tradition and cultural geography, these bars catered to male patrons, while the bars located just beyond Sally's neighborhood were exclusively and aggressively lesbian.

As he passed it, he recognized one of the bars for its unique entrance, a doorless frame from whose trellis hung long strips of black leather cut into sections about half a foot wide. *Was this some type of signal?* he wondered, akin to those carved on trees and fence posts by wandering hobos during the Depression? Did the leather mark the bar as a haven for a rougher sort of clientele?

After he turned left on Robinson it was only another mile to the address Sally had given him when they'd parted in Mexico. *A good thing,* he thought, as it rapidly was growing dark. *But I probably should have called.* Three years had elapsed since they'd last spoken with one another. What if she'd moved, and whoever answered his knock at the back door mistook him for an intruder and called the police? What if she was married? How would her husband take to the abrupt and uninvited presence of a male stranger who happened to be fleeing a murder charge in Mexico?

He cursed himself for his recklessness but was reluctant to take the time to retrace his steps and search out a phone. Soon it would be entirely dark, and whatever the current circumstances at her home, he still felt that a nocturnal appearance was unlikely to be received as well as one softened by the receding daylight. And so he continued to step along briskly.

When Will reached the address, he was instantly relieved. Although there was no name on the mailbox, from within the cottage he could hear a cacophony of barking and howling.

He smiled. Although she could project an air of cynicism, he knew Sally to be a hopeless sucker for abandoned animals - and particularly so if they also were injured, large, ugly and utterly resistant to house training. This soft spot extended to cats as well. Whenever he'd visited her Tucson home in years past, he could be sure to find an enormous new mongrel that happened to be blind, a three-legged Siamese pregnant with kittens, or some other sad specimen from the underworld of domesticated pets whose grounds for abandonment were all too evident.

The gate leading from an alley to the bungalow's back yard was locked, but he easily scaled the wooden fence and dropped noiselessly to the ground on the opposite side. The kitchen was lit, and, through its broad window he could see Sally standing at the sink. He crouched beside a large tree and waited for ten minutes, but no one else appeared. Finally, and regretting once again his failure to have called in advance, he tapped lightly on the back door and softly called her name.

A full minute passed, and then suddenly the door opened, presenting Sally framed by the interior light that streamed out and illuminated the concrete stoop upon which he stood. Her face registered recognition and disbelief. They both stood motionless and silent for a moment before she stepped to him, her face crushed against his chest and her arms embracing him tightly. He held her and stroked the back of her head lightly.

At last she released him. "I can't believe you're *here*," she murmured wonderingly, her eyes never leaving his face. "After all this time," she continued, "I thought surely you must have died."

Will smiled. "Well," he answered, "the fact is…I'm alive."

Sally's eyes were dry now, and she looked at him appraisingly. "Are you still on the run?" she asked simply.

"Yep," he answered.

"Then you'd better come inside," she replied. She turned, and he followed her across the threshold.

Chapter 2

SAN DIEGO

Will spent the next few weeks trying to acclimate to life back in the States. At the same time, he had to avoid becoming so relaxed as to commit some indiscretion that could produce disaster. He'd not lived in this city for many years. Even so, and despite the large transient population always moving in and out like the tides, there remained clinging like limpets to their rock a hard-core community of natives – especially *surfing* natives – who had never left and never would.

Between medicine and the beach, he knew a surprising number of these individuals, and he consequently avoided the hospital campuses and nearby beach communities. When the pull of the sea grew irresistible, he drove north with Sally to Torrey Pines Park, and they'd hike south to an isolated spot midway between the park's entrance and Black's Beach. He missed surfing, but he had no access to a board or sufficient money to buy one, and at this point he was reluctant to impose yet further upon Sally.

Not that she seemed to mind his presence in her life. They'd rapidly established a rhythm that seemed to suit them both. She worked as a nurse at the hospital four blocks away, and while she was gone during the day Will would attend to her menagerie, the housecleaning and the shopping. He'd always liked to cook, and now he often spent hours visiting various specialty markets and preparing intricate dinners.

With no better way to repay Sally's hospitality, he undertook any small home repairs that were within his range of capability, built and planted wooden flower boxes and lay a brick sidewalk from the alley gate to her kitchen door. In the evenings when she came home from work they'd share a bottle of wine on the patio underneath the willow-like green branches of the California pepper tree that dominated the back yard, and she'd tell him the small details of her day. In turn, he gradually pieced together for her the fragments of what had happened to him since they'd parted on Tiburon, and she would shake her head in amazement at the adventures he described.

After some weeks had passed they became lovers. There was no drama to it. Sally simply left her own bed one night and slipped quietly between the sheets to lie beside him. The sex that ensued was slow and languorous, like a dinghy adrift on a sea kissed by soft breezes, gently rising and lowering with the passing swells.

———

Will's deepening affection for Sally was tempered by misgivings that restrained him from openly reciprocating the feelings she seemed to have for him. Apparently condemned to exist in the shadows, how could he speak to her of a future together? He knew all too well the limitations that complicated the fugitive's life. Like a potentially lethal virus he carried with him an ever-present threat that that complicated every action, every decision.

In the past he'd avidly pursued relationships with two other women, both of Mexican descent. He'd come to understand that his insensible passion for the first, Maria, had little to do with what love must entail. How can one love another who is wholly incapable of loving?

His subsequent relationship with Elena had been no less disturbing. He'd allowed himself to become entangled with a woman whose commitment was worse than feckless. Her love for him was feigned, a bitter tea steeped in betrayal. She had delivered Will into the cruel hands of Manuel Arivada, and only by the narrowest of margins had he avoided a violent death.

What flaw must lie within his psyche, he wondered, to have drawn him to these women who used him so mercilessly? While the heart's yearnings clearly could prove difficult to comprehend, the origins of his own passion seemed to Will to lie beyond all reasoning. He'd found that the price paid for such ignorance could run high, and it appeared inevitable now that his misguided indulgences of the past would cost him a lasting relationship with someone more deserving of his commitment.

For Sally was a very different type of woman. She was strikingly attractive, with her angular face, auburn hair and feline green eyes complimented by a trim figure that drew admiring glances from other men when they were out in public together. More to the point, she was honest and kind, and he had come to realize that no one ever had cared for him as much.

She was intelligent, funny and generous. She was tidy and neat without being obsessive. While she was drawn to the wild places, she could maneuver with grace in the most urban environment. She was equally at ease in a sweatshirt and jeans or a clingy black cocktail dress. That she was unequivocally devoted to him was obvious. What could he offer in return? No job, no money, no prospects. Nothing but the possibility of disaster lurking constantly in the background.

He had a trusted friend, Patrick, whom he'd met in Tucson and known for many years. Until moving on to a desk job in Washington, Patrick had served as a field officer in Tucson. Not long after returning to the States Will had called him to discuss his situation, and Patrick promised to discreetly investigate. When Will called him back in a week as they'd agreed, his friend's tone was solemn and his information sobering. Will's case remained open, he said. Wide open. The Sonoran court had charged him with murder and possession of illegal drugs with intent to sell. Both the FBI and the DEA were involved, and at Washington's behest they were cooperating with their Mexican counterparts. If apprehended in the U.S. he would be immediately extradited to stand trial in Hermosillo.

"Get a lawyer," he advised Will. "A good one."

"Why bother?" Will protested. "I don't have a card to play."

Patrick said nothing. Will's assessment of his plight was all too accurate.

"What if I brought in Arivada, the cartel boss I told you about?" Will asked. "Would that get the Mexicans off my back? or at least get me on the right side with our government?"

Patrick's reply was equal parts dubious and noncommittal. "Bringing in a cartel boss is not what you'd call a one-man job," he said. "Get a lawyer, Willie. No matter what the gambit, you're going to need one if you plan to deal with the Feds."

So fall turned to winter and winter to spring. Will continued to dwell with Sally and share her bed. In their conversations they talked of everything but a future together, and their silence on that subject became an ever-widening crevasse dividing them. Despite her cheerful demeanor, he sensed there was growing in Sally a faint malaise. *Maybe you should go*, he told himself a thousand times. *Better that you just go.*

———

Gradually he'd come to tell Sally most of what had befallen him during his years of involuntary exile in Baja. She found his story incredible. "You say you shot two of Arivada's men," she asked him. "Did you ever actually kill anyone down there?"

In the backyard under the pepper tree Will had constructed a circular terrace out of old Mexican brick he'd found for sale in the southside *barrio*. As had become their custom at sunset, they were sitting on the brick terrace under the tree, inhaling its fresh, spicy fragrance, and before answering Will paused to pour into each of their glasses another inch of wine from the bottle they shared.

"When I shot that first man at the arroyo, I suppose I hoped the bullet would kill him," Will answered. "As things turned out, I wound up removing his spleen and saving his life. Although I guess one could make a case for murder by my having abandoned Arivada's brother on the OR table, he was a dead man regardless. And Elena? Whether or not she survived her wound is anybody's guess, but it wasn't me who fired the gun."

Will intentionally had limited his response to those three years in Sonora and lower Baja. He saw little point in burdening Sally with the saga of his knife fight in Nogales. What was to be gained by informing her of that dark shadow-world where violence reigns and death comes so easily?

Chapter 3

INTRUSION

He was thinking of Sally as he sat alone on the sea wall at the south end of Mission Beach, watching the sun melt into the Pacific on an atypically clear, warm and dry June evening. A Santa Anna had blown in the day before, its desert winds driving the marine layer far off to the western horizon. Soon enough the front would weaken and die, to be replaced by the usual June gloom, but today he'd taken advantage of the spectacular weather to run the six miles from their Hillcrest cottage to this point on the beach.

Those whom he'd known in years past lived only two miles to the north, just beyond the terminus of the same sea wall, densely congregated within a two block radius of one another and endlessly rotating between the apartments and small houses clustered therein as the rents and other circumstances dictated. They were creatures of ritual, their lives given over to surfing, and except as needed for work or other unavoidable contingencies they rarely ventured east of the nearby interstate that paralleled the coastline. As long as he stayed off the waves, even at this short distance to the south there was little chance of his encountering anyone who might recognize him.

A good-sized swell was moving in, and he watched as one particularly fine wave backlit by the setting sun broke slowly from right to left, its action dictated by the rock jetty that rose from the beach's southern end, jutting into the ocean and marking the entrance to Mission Bay. Once again he lamented his lack of a board.

When years prior he departed San Diego for Arizona, he'd left an 9' Tony Staple's tri-fin in a friend's keeping and had used it many times when he'd traveled back to Pacific Beach for a weekend or vacation. Retrieving that particular board would require reconnecting with his friend, and it would be more prudent to buy another instead. He longed to begin surfing again, and he was well familiar with the enticing breaks along the coastline that ranged from San Onofre south to Sunset Cliffs.

If he did return to the waves, he would need to so quietly . The surfing community was tightly knit and its members well-known to one another. Newcomers were noted and their actions observed. Any change in the day-to-day rhythm that disturbed the *chi* of the community – its cohesiveness – was frowned upon and actively discouraged.

During the time he'd lived there Will had appreciated the community for its insular attitude and devotion to tradition, but now he saw that those very attributes could prove a liability. No matter how unobtrusively he returned, he would be conspicuous, and although nothing had arisen in these past eight months to provoke concern, he was troubled still by a conversation he'd had with the attorney Patrick had recommended. *You are in a very precarious position*, he advised Will. *If you choose to remain in San Diego, it's imperative that you behave with the utmost discretion.*

And so he continued to live in the shadows. *Better hold off on a board for now*, he concluded. *Maybe later.*

It was at just that moment he was joined on the sea wall by a Hispanic male who looked to be in his early 40s. Will felt an instinctive jolt of alarm. This section of the boardwalk was deserted for hundreds of yards in either direction, and yet the man had chosen a position on the wall not more than 20 feet from Will's own.

In addition, the man's attire was wholly out of context. He wore a suit of light gray with a white dress shirt but no tie. While everyone on the boardwalk typically went barefoot or at most wore flip-flops, this man wore a pair of shiny black loafers with sharply pointed toes and black socks to match. He wore his sideburns long and accompanied by a chin beard but no other facial hair. His face was heavily scarred and pitted, as if he'd suffered severe acne during adolescence. *He doesn't* fit, Will thought. *Time to go. Quickly.*

As Will was preparing to make an inconspicuous exit, the man removed a pack of cigarettes from the breast pocket of his suit jacket, withdrew one and called over to Will, "*Amigo*, do you have a light?"

Will shook his head negatively in reply and arose from the wall, intending to walk in the opposite direction.

"Too bad," the man said in a voice intended to carry. He shook his head. "To smoke at day's end is a pleasure to be savored." He recited the words as if they were some sort of code.

Will ignored him and began to walk.

"*Senor* Rawlins," the man called after him. "Why be in such a hurry to leave? Come sit here beside me, and enjoy the last of this beautiful sunset."

Will slowed at the sound of his name spoken aloud by this stranger, but recovering rapidly he willed himself to remain composed. Turning, he addressed the man calmly. "I'm afraid you've confused me with someone else," he said.

The stranger smiled broadly and replied, "*No lo creo*. But," he paused, looking down at the ground, his face now solemn and brow wrinkled, "I must apologize. It is *Doctor* Rawlins, is it not?"

Will stared back at him without expression. "Mister or doctor," he said, "my name's not Rawlins. I'm afraid you're mistaken." He turned and began to walk away, more rapidly this time.

"It is you who are mistaken, Dr. Rawlins," the man called out after him, more loudly than before. "One cannot shed his identity as a snake sheds its skin. If you respect the welfare of the one who has given you refuge, you might do well to accept my humble invitation and come sit with me for a moment."

The man directed his gaze seaward and lowered his voice. "*Por favor,*" he implored. "*Un momentito solamente.* See now how quickly the sunset fades. How transient is its glory. Not unlike the life God grants us."

Both by nature and as a result of his medical training, Will was almost preternaturally observant. He'd sensed the man's presence at once, and reflexively he'd registered alarm. Already from their brief interaction Will knew the man was not an agent of the American government nor of California's; if he was officially busted, by now he'd have been cuffed, informed of his rights and on his way to a holding cell downtown. Was this man an official agent of Mexico, intent on spiriting him back to Sonora to face his legal music or, as was so typical amongst such agents, intent on extortion to spare Will that fate? Whoever he was, whomever he was working for, the man was not Mexican himself. Although the stranger was clearly Hispanic, the scant Spanish he'd spoken had been marked by a soft slurring that was distinctively South American in character.

Briefly scanning his face, Will saw he resembled the Puerto Ricans he'd known in college: acne-scarred youths who dressed in black, implored him to attend their parties and then drank too much rum while attempting to cut each other with the knives they kept concealed in their boots. *Colombian?* he wondered. *No. Argentine.* The slurring of his Spanish was diagnostic.

From his words "the one who has given you refuge", he assumed the man was speaking of Sally, and the surge of panic he'd felt nearly caused him to stagger. Was the man an envoy for Arivada, the Mexican *narcotraficker* whose wrath Will had incurred but escaped? Arivada could have no conceivable use for Will now. Revenge would be his only motive, and Sally could be a factor.

He remained standing twenty feet from where the other sat. Although the stranger's jacket was likely concealing a shoulder holster and pistol, Will would have taken his chances, bolted and run if he'd had a car parked nearby. But there was no car. Even so, he was inclined to test the man's resolve - and aim - by pursuing the cut and run option; he knew this area of the beach community well, and it contained a labyrinth of back streets and pedestrian alleys which would assist in foiling any pursuit.

As if reading his mind the man spoke again. "I again would suggest that you accept my invitation. I've no doubt your lovely friend in *la casita* on the hill can surely spare you for just a few minutes."

Observing Will's discomfiture, the man adopted a look of wounded innocence. "Do you question my sincerity?" he asked with mock sadness. "Then let us call the young lady and seek her approval." With one motion he reached into the breast pocket that had contained the cigarettes and extracted a sleek cell phone. "Let me see," he pondered, casting his eyes skyward. "*El numero es*, I think, 443. . . ."

"That's enough," Will broke in curtly. "Put the phone away." He closed his eyes briefly, in resignation. "What it is you want?" he asked.

The man smiled back at him companionably. "My friend!" he cried. "Already I have told you what I want. *Claro.* I wish only that you sit beside me for a moment to share what remains of this grand sunset."

In fact, the sunset had ended. And as the Santa Anna's influence diminished, the bleak, wet grayness of the marine layer was moving inexorably landward once again.

Will sat down on the sea wall to the man's right and faced the beach; he calculated this to be his most advantageous position should the man, by the odds right-handed, suddenly reach for the revolver presumably residing in a holster under his left armpit. The man offered Will a cigarette, and he shook his head in response. "What exactly is it you want?" he asked asgain, "What is it you want from me?"

The Hispanic stranger sighed heavily as if pained by the younger's man brusqueness, and now his previous attitude of disingenuous good will turned abruptly harsh.

"*Want* from you?" he repeated. "There's nothing you can do for me, *hombre*. Nada." He paused and took a long drag on his cigarette, exhaling twin plumes of smoke slowly thru his mouth and nose. "At issue here," he said, "are not *my* wants or needs. I come to you simply as a messenger." He reached again under his coat and this time brought out an envelope which he handed to Will.

"What's this?" Will asked sharply.

The man turned to face him and shrugged his shoulders. His expression was unreadable. "Although one hopes to acquire some measure of agility in passing through this life," he said, "there seems always to be something new that must be experienced and learned . . . as well as that which, although familiar, requires it to be learned once again." He stared at Will somberly as he spoke.

"Even the most trivial of one's actions ultimately provokes a reaction. It is said that nature will not tolerate an action left unanswered. Neither will certain men...or women. *En el final,* balance must be restored." He paused again to smoke.

"What is your point?" Will asked wearily. "Is this some type of threat? Is it Arivada you speak for?"

The man directed his gaze seaward. In the darkness that had gathered the waves were obscured, and only the foaming white collapse that followed their cresting was visible from the wall. Line after infinite line, marching ceaselessly onward.

It was growing cooler. The man used his right hand to tug at the sleeves of his jacket and shirt, briefly exposing the lower half of his forearm. Several inches above the crease of his wrist there was a tattoo. Small but expertly inscribed, it was a coiled rattlesnake, the head raised slightly as if preparing to strike. All of Arivada's men bore such a tattoo.

At last the Argentinia spoke. "This is no threat, my friend," he replied. "*No es necessario ahora.* As I told you before, I am simply a messenger sent to communicate these few words: *Mira a su pasado.* Look to your past.

Will stared at the man for a moment and then arose from the wall. He began to sprint in the direction of Mission Boulevard.

———

He'd run as quickly as he could back to Sally's home in Hillcrest, but much of the route was steeply uphill. Nearly an hour passed before he arrived at the front door, panting for breath and sweating profusely. The door was unlocked, and he feared what lay beyond the threshold.

Inside, however, the house was undisturbed. He could hear Sally in the kitchen, humming softly to herself. A cat lay curled up on the couch. The clock on the mantle read ten minutes past seven. Nothing seemed amiss.

He sat down beside the cat and, remembering, pulled the envelope from the waistband of his running shorts. "Dr. Will Rawlins" was inscribed on the outside; the words were printed and written in ink. Inside the envelope was a letter, a single page dense with sentences. The handwriting was neat and feminine. Within the folded letter was a photograph of a little boy dressed in a t-shirt and jeans and smiling at the camera. Putting the photograph aside, he began to read the letter:

Will,

I betrayed you, and I am so sorry. And so ashamed. I know that to ask for your assistance now is beyond all irony, but I am desperate and without recourse. There is little time for explanation, but I will tell you quickly what I can.

I was born on esta estancia and raised here by my father after my mother died giving birth to my youngest sister. My father, a gardener, worked for Manuel's father, El Diablo…may his soul burn in Hell.

I lived in the gatehouse with my father and my five siblings, all younger than me. As I grew older, I began to feel El Diablo's eyes upon me. When I was twelve, he tried to have his way with me. He was an old man by then, however, and I escaped him easily.

After he died I thought myself safe, but in the son resided the same evil as in the father. Manuelo wished to have me as a plaything. When he was twenty-six and I turned sixteen, he decreed that I should share his bed whenever it pleased him. As with his books, his guns and his great desk, I was simply another possession. When my father attempted to intercede, Manuelo had him beaten so badly that he could not arise from his bed for a full week.

Manuelo's interest in me quickly waned, but still he would not allow me to leave. La estancia had become my prison, the gatehouse my cell. Then his brother fell ill, and as el hermano's condition worsened, Manuelo grew distraught. Somehow learning of your presence nearby, he instructed me to engage with you. He told me he would kill my father and siblings if I failed to obey.

For whatever reason he has permitted me to live, but I fear for my child. My son. I know Manuelo will tolerate him no longer. He will have his men kill my Tomas, and he will revel in my grief.

My sins are beyond any atonement, and what happens to me now is of no consequence. But Tomas has hurt no one. He is an innocent boy who deserves to live. Please help him. Please hurry.

Elena

He put the letter on the end table beside him and picked up the photograph, inspecting it more closely this time. The little boy's skin was light and his hair almond brown, like Elena's. He left the photograph on the table with the letter and walked into the kitchen.

At his approach Sally turned from the pot of a red sauce she'd been stirring. "How was the run?" she asked pleasantly, but when she looked up and saw his expression, her smile vanished.

"What is it?" she asked. "Did someone recognize you?"

"Yes and no," he replied.

They sat together on the couch in the living room, the cat purring contentedly in Sally's lap, and he described his encounter with the pineapple-faced emissary at the seawall. When he'd finished, he handed her the letter and photograph. He watched her as she studied both carefully and at length.

Finished at last, she looked up. "What are you going to do?" she asked him.

"I'm not sure," he answered. "To begin with, I'm not sure Elena is alive. *If* she is, and *if* she wrote this letter, and even if what she wrote is true, the guy at the seawall clearly works for Arivada. Why would *he* deliver her message? Why would he betray his boss, a man who doesn't hesitate to murder? What's in it for him? It doesn't make sense." He paused, pondering.

"Either someone else wrote the letter - maybe Arivada - or she wrote it for him," he concluded. "Regardless, he wants to lure me back."

"But how can you be *sure*?" Sally asked, urgently "Maybe she's just a mom who wants to save her little boy." Her distress was obvious. "You can't just *assume*. We have to go get him."

Will shook his head. "You don't understand," he replied. "Your devoted 'mom' was responsible for my being kidnapped and almost killed. And 'getting him' is not just another trip to the Humane Society to pick up a stray dog."

She looked at him archly. Her compassion for helpless creatures was profound and irremediable. "We *have* to go get him," she repeated.

"Listen to me, Sally," he said. His tone now was urgent. "These cartel *nacotraficantes* are evil sociopaths. Unimaginably cruel. Murderers. There is no 'we' in this. I would never willingly allow you near them."

"Maybe it's my choice to make," she retorted. "Not yours."

"Negative," he said firmly. "Not going to happen."

"We'll see about that," she replied. And returned to her sauce in the kitchen.

———

He met again with the attorney Patrick had recommended, and at first the man was adamant in his opposition. Even after Will provided more background, he remained openly skeptical.

"Yes, he's a big fish," the lawyer conceded. "And yes, both the DEA and the FBI would be interested, *highly* interested, and more to the point, appreciative. But at best it would mean abandoning your old identity and starting over in a new location under some type of witness protection plan. And that's assuming your grab is successful and they stick to the bargain."

He paused. "Face it, Dr. Rawlins," he said grimly. "What you propose to undertake is difficult even for the pros, and you're definitely no pro. The odds of success are exceedingly slim. Anything *less* than success is likely to prove fatal."

Will grinned. "Too true," he replied. "And duly noted. Now let's see what kind of deal you can get for me. Ideally, I'd like a signed agreement by noon tomorrow."

The attorney sighed and picked up his phone. "You might want to skedaddle on out of here before I make this call," he said. "I'd hate to have to fight your extradition."

Will left and returned immediately home. He'd made his decision, and it was time to start preparing.

———

He packed only a few items: his papers and all the cash he had available; a change of clothes; binoculars, maps and rope; and the sturdy diving knife with its six inch blade that he'd sharpened to a fine edge.

The last would provide little advantage against men likely to be armed with automatic weapons, but he had nothing else. To have carried his old .38 with him as he walked across the border could have precipitated disaster, and he'd not attempted to obtain a replacement during his time in San Diego. As always, he would have to improvise.

Sally appeared at the bedroom's doorway. "I'm all packed and ready to go," she said brightly.

Will suppressed a grimace. Despite his protestations, she'd remained adamant in her determination to accompany him. He told her repeatedly that it was too dangerous. He told her that her presence would only complicate matters, that for him she would be a liability. "I can't afford to be distracted by having to worry about you, Sally," he said.

She dismissed his arguments. "I'm going with you, Will," she said. "Get used to it."

Now, grim-faced, Will settled himself behind the wheel of Sally's green Toyota to begin the long drive to Guerrero Negro and to Arivada. To the malevolent man who surely had beckoned him. And ultimately, he hoped, to freedom.

———

The three men had driven all day and reached San Diego in the late afternoon. There Hector spoke with one of their people who lived in the city and was charged with tracking the American. After Alejandro's meeting with Rawlins at Pacific Beach they turned south and drove to the marina on Shelter Island. Once they'd parked, Hector exited the black sedan and walked towards the boats. The other two men trailed behind, both burdened with large canvas sacks of some weight.

Their voyage northward along the coast was uneventful. The boat was a Grady-White, thirty-seven feet in length and refit with a 1,000 horsepower Volvo inboard that could push the cabin cruiser to over 50 knots on a flat sea. It was a saltwater fishing boat of considerable cost and luxury, a type endemic to the area. Except for a well-concealed storage area that lay beneath the cabin sole, the yacht was identical to a hundred others floating in their slips at Marina del Rey.

Hector stood beside the helm smoking a cigarette, staring out at the lights of San Pedro as they entered the large bay. Along the wharf were tethered a number of commercial ships, their cargo awaiting daylight and the attention of the huge cranes that would pluck their cargo. This blue-collar segment of the coast sat cheek-to-cheek with tony Palos Verdes just to the north.

They pulled into a slip near the end of a remote and unoc-cupied pier, and his two men hastened to secure the dock lines while the captain remained at the helm. Hector scowled. Dressed as they were and clearly unused to boats, the two men were notably conspicuous, but it was still quite dark, and no eyes marked their presence. The engine abruptly ceased its droning, and the hours began to drag by.

At precisely 2AM a group of six men suddenly appeared on the previously deserted pier, and an exchange took place. Hector's two men passed a number of parcels, each the size of a thick telephone book, to a tall *negro* from the other group, and he in turn passed them to another who placed the parcels in a wooden wheelbarrow of the type common to marinas. The exchange concluded, the parties separated, one departing the pier and the other re-boarding the boat.

Soon they were underway. As the Grady-White exited the harbor, the boat turned left. Southward back towards San Diego and then on to Baja Sur.

Chapter 4

REUNION

Afterwards Will could recall little of their nocturnal drive southward from Sally's house in Hillcrest. About two hours after sunrise he pulled into the dirt parking area of a small *tienda* some sixty kilometers north of Guerrero Negro. He'd driven all night, and he felt unwashed, hungry and exhausted. Sally lay curled up in the passenger seat, unmoving and deeply asleep

As he filled the Toyota's tank from the sole Pemex pump he willed his brain to arouse and devise some strategy. One obvious problem: aside from his knife, he had no weapon. While to enter Arivada's lair might be suicidal in any event, to do so unarmed would virtually ensure futility. He wished they'd taken the time for Sally to buy a handgun and rifle in San Diego. For either of them, *yanquis*, to obtain a firearm legally in Mexico would be impossible, and he hadn't the time to ferret out an illegal source.

As he stood pondering this dilemma, a potential solution presented itself. A battered old pick-up truck which appeared to lack any vestige of shocks rattled into the parking area and wheezed to a stop just beside the store's front entrance. Two equally ancient *campesinos* emerged from the cab, each wearing the ubiquitous straw cowboy hat, a flannel shirt and jeans which hung low on their shankless hips. From the passenger's right hand hung a brace of freshly shot quail, and after they entered the store Will could see suspended on a rack in the cab's back window the shotgun they'd used to bring down the birds.

He walked into the *tienda* to pay for his gas and marked the two *viejos* seated comfortably at a small table in the corner, sipping at mugs of coffee. He paid for his gas, asked the proprietor to prepare for him some *tacos de pollo para llevar* - to go - and then walked over to stand by the elderly hunters' table.

Their soft murmuring ceased abruptly at his approach, and one of the men raised his heavily creased face. *"En que le puedo server a usted?"* he asked, phrasing his question in the most formal manner. How could he be of assistance?

"Perdone que lo importune," Will replied. He hoped they would forgive his interrupting them. He had seen the fine quail they had shot. He himself was a *cazador* who had journeyed far to hunt the quail, grouse and dove for which this region was justly famous. He had arranged to meet his *tio* in Santo Tomas, but this uncle - who lived in Tecate - had become acutely ill and unable travel. To make matters worse, *el tio* had their shotguns. He was here, and the birds clearly were plentiful, but without a suitable weapon he would have no choice but to return home to El Cajon.

Both men listened carefully throughout. When Will finished, they looked down at the mugs of coffee they'd politely left untouched and said nothing.

He told them that he would like to buy their shotgun and any shells they might have. Their eyes widened slightly at this, and they remained silent. While in the hinterlands many *campesinos* used a rifle or shotgun to supplement the family larder, private ownership of guns was formally outlawed in Mexico.

Will removed two hundred dollars from his wallet and laid the money on the wooden table. The man who'd initially spoken to him lifted his cup, slowly drank what remained of his coffee and looked up.

The old *campesino* told Will it was possible that he had seen their red truck parked outside. He added that the day was already growing warm, and so it might be that he and his friend had left the truck's windows open. *Ventanas abiertas.* In deference to the rising heat, he and his *compadre* intended to remain as they were and perhaps enjoy *un refresco frio.* A cold soda. "*Quizas deberias ir a cazar ahora,*" he concluded. "*Puede que el dia estara mas caliente.*" It would be better if Will went hunting now, he advised. It might be too hot to do so later.

He casually folded the bills Will had placed on the table and slipped them into his shirt pocket. Then he turned away from Will, and both he and his companion gazed out the dusty window beside the table as if to contemplate at their leisure the aforementioned truck.

As Will walked by the counter, the proprietor handed him a grease-stained paper bag. Leaving the store, Will climbed back into Sally's car, started its engine and then quickly slipped back out, leaving the door widely ajar. He loped over to the pickup, reached through the open window on the driver's side and lifted the shotgun from its rack. On the seat was a leather pouch which by its heft presumably contained a few shells.

After extricating the shotgun and pouch from the *campesino*'s truck, he walked leisurely back to his car with the gun held tightly against his left side. Placing both carefully under the seat, he settled himself behind the wheel and slowly exited the parking area to regain the main highway. Sally appeared to remain soundly asleep. Glancing in the rear-view mirror he could see the proprietor standing in the doorway of his *tienda*, watching Will depart. He hoped the store had no phone.

After he'd driven about twenty kilometers he pulled off the main road and drove another two kilometers on a spur that led westward towards the sea. He stopped the car but left the engine on. Looking ahead through the windshield and behind him in the rear-view mirror, he was confident he could spot any approaching vehicle well in advance of its arrival. Reaching under the seat, he lifted the shotgun, placed it in his lap and with a sinking heart began to examine it more closely.

The weapon would not have been out of place in the hands of one of Villa's foot soldiers during the bloody campaigns of the early 1900's. Extensive use over the years had contrived to remove from its single barrel and firing mechanism any trace of engraving it once may have born, and its stock was obviously not the original. From what appeared to be a chunk of *palo fierro* - ironwood - the owner had shaped a triangular wedge and secured it to the gun itself with tightly wound strands of wire. An old, sweat-stained leather strap was fastened to the barrel and stock so as to allow one to carry the weapon slung over a shoulder.

Sighing, Will set the shotgun aside and opened the leather pouch. To his dismay it held only four shells, all presumably filled with birdshot. Good for bringing down quail on the wing, he thought, but less likely to drop a man.

After testing the mechanism a few times, Will loaded one of the four precious shells in the chamber, clicked on the safety and stepped out of the car. Opening the trunk, he found a place beneath the spare tire where the carpeting had become unattached. He slid the shotgun under the carpeting and replaced the spare tire.

Famished, he wolfed down two of the tacos from the paper sack and left the other two for Sally to eat when she awoke. Back behind the wheel once again, he circled about, drove back to the main highway and turned right. Still heading south.

———

To his relief, Will had no difficulty finding the unpaved road that departed the highway just north of Guerrero Negro and led to Arivada's *hacienda*. After some minutes he drove through the sandy wash where he'd shot and wounded two of Arivada's thugs in the process of what proved to be only a temporary escape. Sally was awake by then, but he made no comment to her of the events which had occurred in the arroyo almost three years prior.

Several kilometers further on he pulled off the road at a level spot, drove slowly through the scrubby desert for another five hundred meters and then parked the Toyota where a jumble of rocks and brush would render it invisible from the road. Retrieving the shotgun from the trunk, he marked the car's location, placed the keys under a distinctive rock and with Sally beside him began to walk westward towards the *hacienda*.

Soon enough they reached the edge of a small bluff that provided good cover and an unobscured view of *la casa grande* and its surrounding grounds. Even with the binoculars, he could see no activity below. Several vehicles were parked in the lot at the rear of the great house, but outside there was no one visible.

Peering more closely, he could see the grounds appeared untended and ill-kempt. The lawn, once lush and green, now blended seamlessly with the drab brown terrain surrounding the *hacienda*, and much of the shrubbery abutting the great house either had died or become so overgrown as to obscure many of the windows they had once simply shaded. Except for the vehicles, Will would have thought the *hacienda* long-deserted.

Will told Sally they should wait until dark before descending to the house, and the wait proved to be long and uncomfortable. Despite lying quietly in what shade they could find, their thirst grew to become almost intolerable. Anxiety muted hunger, but both sorely regretted the absence of water.

With sunset the air began to cool, but their desire for water grew ever more insistent. Finally Will decided it was time to move. He shouldered his ancient weapon and with Sally close behind began to pick his way carefully down the bluff's steep face. He thought to himself that whatever else might befall them in the house below, at least they might quench their tremendous thirst.

He drew closer to the *hacienda*, and he could see now that the unkempt nature of the grounds was duplicated by the dilapidated condition of the great house itself. All about there lay fragments of roof tiles presumably dislodged by the wind or simply time's passage. The façade of the building was deeply cracked and fissured, and here and there on the ground immediately below its walls lay great shards of stucco which had yielded to gravity. Where the plaster had fallen were exposed patches of the underlying block wall, and in the darkness the building's exterior resembled nothing so much as an old fortress battered by cannon fire.

Taken altogether, the *hacienda*'s aspect bespoke neglect and decay. Regardless, the memory of the violence produced within these walls was still fresh in Will's mind, and despite the air of abandonment he moved no less stealthily as he made his way to the rear of the great house.

He could see light streaming out through the kitchen windows, but so filthy was the glass that even at short distance he could perceive nothing of the interior. Indicating to Sally that she should stay back in the shadows beyond the light's reach, he ascended the three steps that led to the rear door and found it to be locked. Pausing to unlimber the old shotgun and to cock its well-worn trigger, he raised one foot, kicked the door open and stepped into the kitchen with his weapon at ready.

Once inside he immediately could see three adults and a child seated at a small table. They turned their faces towards him, their expressions calm, as if they'd been expecting him and were unperturbed by his noisy intrusion. Examining in turn those seated before him, Will saw it was Arivada, an older Mexican man simply dressed and, much altered but unmistakably alive, Elena. In her lap the young woman held an almond-haired little boy of toddler age.

Despite the reconstructive surgery she'd undergone, Elena's facial disfigurement was significant. On the side of the bullet's entrance wound a sizable skin graft contrasted sharply with the surrounding skin to which it had been sutured, and on the opposite side she appeared to have sustained a complete facial nerve injury. The eye was sutured shut, and the right side of her mouth hung slackly.

While Arivada displayed no such disfigurement, Will was struck by the change in the man's physical appearance. He appeared to have aged twenty years in the last three. His previously jet-black hair was streaked with gray, and it badly needed a trim. Previously lean, he was now cadaverous. His face was hollow-cheeked, his skin had an unhealthy yellow hue and he'd clearly not shaved in days. Most striking, however, was his bearing. Where before he'd exuded a dangerous intensity even in repose, he now appeared listless. Even seated, his posture was stooped. Stooped like that of a defeated and much older man.

Will wondered what events could have conspired to produce such profound change. Arivada's physical decline seemed to mirror both that of his previously majestic *estancia* and the disfigurement of the once-lovely Elena.

His old nemesis raised his face slightly to speak, and Will noted that the man's eyes were perhaps not so clouded by apathy as he'd initially perceived them to be. "Ah, Dr. Rawlins," the Mexican said calmly. "So it is that you come to us once again, here in the autumn of our discontent." He smiled faintly.

"Get up," Will commanded, leveling the shotgun at the other man's chest.

Arivada continued to sit, his smile broadening.

"Get up!" Will repeated, raising his voice. "Get up, or I'll blow your fucking head off."

The Mexican's smile faded, but he remained both seated and composed. "That would be unwise, Dr. Rawlins," he replied. "If you remove me from the scene, how will you ever find *su novia?*"

Will was not so distracted by the man's reference to Sally that he failed to notice Elena's eyes flit towards the door at his rear. Wheeling about and not bothering to aim, Will pulled the trigger on two burly Hispanic men standing in the doorway, each clad in the familiar black garb of Arivada's *pistoleros* and holding revolvers.

Despite the deafening explosion produced by the shotgun, both men remained standing. The shorter of the two was hunched over and clutching his chest, but the other, unharmed, was drawing a bead on Will's upper torso with his pistol.

From the table a male voice spoke sharply. "*Alto!*" It was Arivada, and in response the gunman lowered his weapon.

Now Arivada was standing. "Lower your weapon," he advised Will. Glancing away, in rapid Spanish he instructed the gunman to see to his companion and the others to remain seated at the kitchen table. Turning back to Will, he said, in English, "Please follow me."

They walked down the great hall to the man's library, and as they entered and sat across the desk from one another Will was visited by the unwelcome recollection that nothing arising from their prior discussions in this room had turned out well for him. The Mexican's black eyes were cold, and he was staring at Will like a serpent regarding its prey. *Curious*, Will thought. With the brief burst of violence in the kitchen the Mexican appeared suddenly a changed man. *El Santo* - the Dark One - apparently had returned.

The man wasted no time on preamble. "Dr. Rawlins," he said, "my colleagues and I deal in a product which, like fine diamonds, is small in physical volume but quite large in value." He opened the top drawer of his desk, and remembering the pistol the man had kept there, Will suppressed a flinch.

Instead of a pistol, however, Arivada withdrew a large plastic bag containing a faintly brownish powder. *Heroin*, Will guessed. *Maybe coke.*

Arivada slid the bag across the desktop. "*Su novia* was taken soon after you illegally entered my home, and she is now en route to a location far from here." He paused, now gazing at Will intently. "*Estas un intruso, no*? A trespasser." He nodded to indicate the package lying on the desk between them. "As penance for your trespass and to regain *su novia*, I would ask you to perform one simple errand. Deliver this product to the men who will be receiving her," he said. "Exchange this product for her."

Will stared stonily back across the desk at the Mexican. "Where is she?" he demanded. "What have you done with her?"

"She is quite safe," the Mexican replied. "And unharmed… for now. To ensure that she remains so will require that you perform for me *este favor muy poco*. This very small favor."

"What favor?" Will asked.

Arivada lightly tapped the bag that lay between them on the desktop. "As I said, simply take the package to the men who soon will be in possession of *su novia*," he said. "Exchange this product for her."

"I'm not your fucking mule," Will declared. "You and your 'product' can go to hell."

Arivada's expression was that of a parent amused by an unruly but ultimately hapless child. "These men, Dr. Rawlins, are devoid of what you might call *sympathy*," he said mildly. "Should they fail to receive what it is they await, they will not hesitate to focus their disappointment upon *tu amante*. And when they have tired of her, they will kill her. *Verdad.*"

"If this is heroin," Will replied, gesturing to the package, "it doesn't seem like enough to justify such drama." Surreptitiously he slipped a shell from his pocket and into the chamber of the shotgun resting on his lap.

"This particular product is *muy pura,*" the other man advised him. "And thus very valuable. Besides, what you will take to them is but a sample. Symbolic, in its way."

"What about Elena and the boy?" Will asked. "What will happen to them?"

"Dr. Rawlins," Arivada replied in a chiding tone. "Do you truly believe that you might descend upon my house as some manner of savior?" His tone was almost kindly.

This bastard has planned the whole thing, Will realized. *He lured us down here, apparently has kidnapped Sally and now has the leverage to manipulate me as he wishes.* He was thoroughly ensnared, and he could think of nothing to be done but comply. "Tell me what it is you want me to do," Will said tonelessly.

Arivada leaned forward over the desk, and his gaze was intense. "*Otra vez,* bring them the package," he said. "That is all *I* want. That is all *they* want."

"If I give them what they want, what's to stop them from killing us anyway?" Will asked.

"These men care for nothing but the product and the wealth it conveys," the Mexican replied smoothly. "Once it is in their possession, you and your woman will be to them irrelevant. Literally not worth the effort of killing."

He's lying, Will thought. But aloud he said, "Where is Sally? Where do I find her?"

"Thirty kilometers north of Ensenada there is a small town, La Mision," Arivada began. "There is an inn there. An inn and a restaurant. *La Fonda. En la calle libre.*"

Will knew it. *La Fonda* sat high on a bluff that overlooked a wide sandy beach. When the weather was fine, the restaurant's outdoor terrace was a pleasant place to drink margaritas and enjoy *langosta al Puerto Nuevo*, and there was fairly decent surfing off the beach. On summer weekends the modest resort was infested with *Los Angelenos* who drank too much and regarded their brief Mexican sojourn as license for coarse behavior, but during the week and especially in the off-season there wasn't a more charming establishment of its kind on the entire coast of northern Baja.

"I know the place," Will told him.

The Mexican continued without acknowledging Will's words. "Just to the south of *La Fonda* is an inconspicuous gravel road that exits *la calle libre* to the west and curves sharply before descending to the beach. At its end is a simple tower built of rock and mortar, standing alone." He paused and looked directly into Will's eyes. "This is where the transfer of product takes place," he said. "If you wish to retrieve *su novia, la casa roca* is where you will find her."

To his surprise, Will was also familiar with the house and its precise location. He'd seen it a number of times while walking or jogging on that stretch of beach, and he'd been intrigued by the structure's odd location, distinct architecture and apparent lack of function. The building's dun colored exterior blended perfectly with the surrounding sand and the scrubby bluff immediately behind it, and the cylindrical tower of rock lacked even the tiniest window through which its occupants could enjoy the magnificent view. The tower's only opening was the portal at its base, and barring entry was a stout wooden door reinforced with horizontal bands of rusty iron and secured with a large steel padlock.

Will had assumed it was some type of storage facility, albeit one poorly placed for that purpose. Tight though the building appeared to be, its lower portion undoubtedly would be flooded at intervals by winter's high tides and storms. The interior would be dank, poorly lit and dungeon-like. It was difficult to think of Sally imprisoned there alone with the men of whom Arivada spoke.

"Why are you doing this, Arivada?" Will asked the Mexican.

The other man smiled. "Why, to make a profit, of course," he replied. "Such is the nature of commerce."

"No," Will persisted. "Why me? Why Sally? Why go to the trouble of including us in your 'commerce'?"

Arivada's smile faded. He leaned forward, clasping his hands and resting his elbows on the desktop. "Trouble?" he repeated. He spoke as if puzzled. "But my dear Dr. Rawlins, I can assure you that your involvement poses no trouble for me." His black eyes glittered. "What trouble you have caused me lies in the past," he said gravely. "And that trouble was indeed considerable."

There was a long silence, and then abruptly his tone grew light, and his smile returned. "But how fortunate it is that you should have this opportunity to redress the imbalance which has existed between us."

Of course it's a set-up, Will thought. *How not? Whatever else may be at stake here, I'm not meant to come out of this alive.*

"Then I want to leave now," Will told the other man. "I want your best car and some food, and I'll need a decent weapon." The Mexican smiled and nodded slightly, again as one bemused by the belligerent demands of a willful child. "*Now, goddamit!*" Will shouted, and in one quick motion he swung the stolen shotgun to his shoulder and pulled its trigger.

There was a deafening explosion, and the spines of several large books located just beyond the Mexican's left ear exploded. Paper shards from the shattered volumes rose and fell slowly to the ground like confetti.

The bastard didn't even flinch; if anything, his smile grew broader. "That was unnecessary, Dr. Rawlins," he admonished. "And not worthy of your considerable intellect. Not only have you wasted one round of what I suspect is a very limited supply of ammunition, but even worse I can see that your shotgun possesses but a single barrel. If I wished, I could extract my own weapon from this desk's top drawer and easily take your life before you could reload." He shook his head with mock sadness.

"Regardless," he continued, "there is no time for such theatrics. Raul already has packed you food and beverage sufficient to see you comfortably to La Mision, and you are welcome to my fastest and most reliable vehicle. As for firearms, even now this house contains many weapons, and to exhibit them all would consume far too much of your precious time. Allow me to make a selection."

He motioned Will to remain sitting and left the room. When he returned, he carried a carbine that looked to be of the same type Will had taken from the *federales* that fateful night in San Carlos, along with a shiny automatic pistol that he assumed to be a Glock or its equivalent. The carbine was equipped with a night vision scope and laser sight. He placed the guns on the desktop between them. "I believe these will serve you more adequately than your antiquated shotgun," the Mexican observed.

Will wordlessly gathered up the weapons, accepted from the man two sacks containing loaded clips for each and turned to make his way to the kitchen and the rear exit from the house.

"Dr. Rawlins!" Arivada called. He tossed Will a set of keys. "The Expedition," he said. "The big black one."

———

Chapter 5

EL SANTO

*B*y *sea or by land?* he wondered.

The *yanqui* had left, and now Manuelo Arivada gazed westward into the darkness beyond the window.

Much had changed since he assumed control of the family business following his father's prolonged and ultimately fatal illness. What he'd inherited was a relatively simple operation, modestly profitable by current standards, and for some years he'd continued what his father had begun.

It had been a deceptively simple but effective business model. At times the producers in Sinaloa had found themselves burdened with a surplus of *marihuana*. Typically this occurred when the pressure exerted by the *yanquis* compelled the Mexican authorities to arrange a token intervention and temporarily close down a supply route. At such times his father would purchase the surplus at a bargain price.

To move the *marihuana* northward to its market he'd devised a method of transportation and distribution different from the land and air routes employed by the Sinaloans. This involved smuggling the bales of *marihuana* by boat from Ensenada to Los Angeles, Long Beach or San Pedro, alternating randomly between the three American ports to reduce the odds of detection. At dockside the cargo was sold directly to *los negros* who controlled so much of the trade in that area.

Manuelo had merely adapted his father's method to accomodate a less bulky and far more lucrative product. It had proven relatively simple for him to establish a connection to the Haitians. During law school he'd befriended a fellow student from Colombia who'd gone to work for one of his country's cartels after graduation. Enrique was based in Miami, and when there was reason for Manuelo to visit that city he'd spend an evening with his friend. The glamorous nightlife offered up by the clubs of South Beach contrasted pleasantly with the rustic solitude of coastal Baja.

On one such evening Enrique had introduced him to an impeccably dressed and soft-spoken Haitian who was rumored to be involved in the pan-American heroin trade. The Mexican cartels had faced a major problem in attempting to break into that flourishing trade: they were as yet unable to produce large volumes in their homeland, and transportation from its source in South America was inefficient, expensive and often unsuccessful. The Sinaloan's had continued to focus on *marihuana* instead.

This changed with the ascent of *El Chapo* ("Shorty") Guzman. An uneducated but ambitious thug, Guzman rose from obscure origins to develop dependable routes for the large volume transport of cocaine and heroin through Central America and western Mexico to markets in Chicago and the larger cities of both American coasts. In the process he managed to build what eventually became for a time Mexico's largest and wealthiest crime syndicate. No governmental representative, from the lowliest *federal* to, some said, *el presidente* himself, could oppose *El Chapo* and his gunmen. In Sinaloa and Jalisco, the only rule of law was Guzman's.

Such monopolization of the heroin trade was financially disadvantageous to the other parties involved, and so the Haitian now facing Arivada across glasses of champagne in the trendy South Beach club was keen to develop an alternative route and market for the products originating in Colombia. Ideally these new alternatives would be unknown to both the interdicting authorities and *El Chapo*. With care and patience the Haitian quietly had assembled all but one of the required components, and now what he needed to complete the circuit was a means of moving his products quietly northward from Mexico to eager new consumers in southern California.

Despite the formidable menace projected by the two large black men who stood still, silent and expressionless behind his chair, the Haitian was quite charming. When he learned of the Arivada's experience with the exportation of Sinoloan agricultural goods, he suggested they meet at his home the following day to discuss how their interests might coincide. From that meeting in Miami Beach had sprung a flourishing heroin pipeline through Baja.

At an airstrip on a remote section of the Baja coast Arivada's *traqueteros* received the Colombian product from Haitian middlemen. The product was driven north to Ensenada and then transported by boat to be off-loaded at one of the ports in greater Los Angeles. After returning to the point of departure in Ensenada, the crew drove to a secluded beach dwelling in La Mision, a tiny hamlet nearby, to give the middlemen their share of the cash received from *los negros*. All transactions were made hand-to-hand and on a cash basis, with no electronic footprint.

Arivada had made a great deal of money from this trade, but despite his efforts to keep the operation and himself obscure, *hombres malos* from the east, men of insatiable greed, unparalleled brutality and irresistible power, now intended to displace him. *Zetas*, they were called, members of the Mexican military's special forces recruited to serve as bodyguards for the leadership of the eastern cartel whose capital was Veracruz. Now they numbered ten thousand or more, and with their propensity for acts of stupefying violence and their seeming invincibility, they'd absorbed the cartel which had employed them and were bent on extending their dominion.

The *Zetas'* westward migration was as inevitable as that which the *yanquis* had undertaken in the north more than a hundred and fifty years prior. First they seized control of the border cities – Matamoros, Reynosa, Nuevo Loredo, Juarez, Nogales - and then they turned their attention southwestward.

By that time the Sinaloans had discovered methamphetamine and were abandoning their *marihuana* fields in favor of this cheaply produced and more profitable export. *El Chapo* and the other *jefes* who controlled the meth trade in Jalisco and Sinaloa were hardly novices at defending themselves against competitors, but these *Zetas*, these *diablos* from the east, could impose a level of ferocity that was unprecedented.

They fire-bombed buildings with abandon, and those they perceived as opponents they brazenly murdered, decapitating their corpses and depositing piles of the severed heads in highly public locations. Assisting their takeover was the fact that many of the foot soldiers who'd served the Sinaloan bosses had become hopelessly addicted to their new product.

Like a cloud of hungry locusts the *Zetas* descended upon Michoacan, obliterating all resistance, and within a matter of months the neighboring state of Jalisco was similarly consumed. In testimony to the cartel's absolute dominance of the region and the lawlessness within its borders, the area was now called *la Tierra Caliente*. The "Hot Land".

Sinaloa, Guzman's redoubt, was next in line, and those few of his bosses who survived the first weeks of slaughter rapidly fled. The others, not so cautious, wound up with their heads impaled on sticks before the charred remnants of a Culiacan police station. For weeks the heads remained in place, a public monument none dared to disturb or dispute. As for *El Chapo*, the deposed monarch wisely took luxurious refuge in his Parisian apartment.

With the western coast of the mainland now securely in their grip, Arivada knew these evil men eventually would turn their attention to him. Anticipating this, he was unsurprised when he learned that his best man, Hector, had been turned and was now secretly in their employ. What made the man so effective was the keen animal intelligence that accompanied his sociopathic nature. Hector knew all too well which way blew the winds of change. Already these *Zetas* were planning his employer's elimination, and Hector intended to stand with the victors.

With the methamphetamine trade so lucrative, the *Zetas* had been content to concentrate their efforts on assuming control of the Sinaloan operation and to leave Arivada's eradication for some later date. But then their primary transport point, *el Rancho Villa Real* in Guadalajara, was raided by the military. Many barrels of methamphetamine were confiscated, and, worse, this lucrative pipeline to the U.S. was irretrievably lost. The *Zeta* bosses were anxious to establish a new and more oblique route as quickly as possible, and if they could add heroin to their product line, then so much the better.

It was pointless to resist. While only Arivada knew the details of his operation in their entirety, Hector was privy to enough information to direct his new masters to the route they now required. From Arivada himself the *Zetas* would seek to extract whatever additional information they desired, and Manuelo had no illusions regarding the fate he would suffer once that particular transaction was complete.

As for the Haitians, they knew no loyalty. To them, one Mexican was as another, and his death would have no relevance as long as they retained a buyer for their product. What forces of his own he could muster would be eliminated or, as with Hector, simply purchased.

He smiled involuntarily. He liked the plan he'd devised. Not for him was the option of meekly surrendering the field, but he was equally disinclined to suffer the fate endured by those of *El Chapo's* bosses who'd chosen to resist. For him there was a middle road, and by traveling that road he intended to retain his wealth, have his revenge and emerge unscathed.

It was very simple, really. He'd slowly allowed his business, his home and his own physical presence to decline in a manner that suggested weakening and imminent collapse. To all appearances, *El Santo's* time was passing, and to Hector in particular he confided that he wished only to complete one last transaction and then depart.

Manuelo told his traitorous chief lieutenant that unexpectedly there had arrived a large amount of product which needed to be moved quickly. He told Hector that if he left at once with two men of his choosing, he could off-load this product in San Pedro and return in time to rendezvous with the Haitians at the stone tower to pay them their share of the proceeds. This time Hector could keep half of what remained: well over half a million in *yanqui* dollars. A parting gift for his loyal service, Arivada had said, smiling.

First Hector would complete one small errand in San Diego. Then he would supervise the delivery in San Pedro and meet the Haitians in La Mision. Accomplish *estas cosas*, and he would be rewarded most handsomely.

Hector's greed was such that he'd decided at once to undertake the now-familiar trip to Los Angeles and the tower one last time for the man he'd betrayed, with the exception that in this instance he'd simply keep for himself *el jefe's* share of the profit made from the exchange in San Pedro. Hector would not be so foolish as to bypass the tower and so deny the Haitians *their* share. He knew well how poorly those men tolerated any such subterfuge.

Unbeknownst to Hector, the heroin Arivada sent north to San Pedro with his lieutenant was heavily cut. Because this had no precedent, the buyers in Los Angeles had paid dockside as was customary, and they'd not discovered their purchase was tainted until Hector and his crew were well away. By now, however, the duped buyers undoubtedly had alerted the Haitians, and matters would not go well for Hector and his companions when all met in La Mision.

It was regrettable that he was not to share in the profit from the sale of the bogus product delivered to San Pedro, but that amount was but a fraction of the total value of the uncut heroin now residing beneath the floor of his gatehouse.

As for Rawlins, it would have been simple enough to have the dishonorable physician eliminated in San Diego, but Manuelo was unwelcome in *los estados unidos,* and to do so would deprive him of observing at first-hand the man's suffering and death. He'd been confident the American doctor would come to him. From an informant who worked in San Diego's legal community he knew the fugitive neurosurgeon was contriving to barter him - Arivada - for some measure of amnesty. The apprehension of *El Santo* inevitably must involve the Mexican authorities, and Arivada smiled at the thought of how unlikely it was those authorities would receive Rawlins' scheme with any enthusiasm, let alone recompense. Not for nothing these men feared *el jefe* and his organization, and many he had *en el bosillo.*

Confident that Elena's plea for help would motivate the American, he'd instructed the Argentine, Alejandro, to gain her trust and then convey her letter. Rawlins already had proven himself susceptible to the plight of attractive young women in distress, and the message from his past love would strike that weakness like a well-aimed arrow. *El raton* would come intending to rescue, and instead, after an appropriate interval devoted to torture, he would beg for death's release at Arivada's feet.

But now Arivada had changed his mind. He'd assumed the liaison between Rawlins and *la gringa* in San Diego to be a relationship of convenience only and decided that kidnapping her would not suffice to bring the man to him. This clearly was not so, and that Rawlins inexplicably had chosen to bring his *gringa* on a journey of such peril served only to sweeten the dish. Instead of simply killing Rawlins at the *hacienda,* he had presented the American with an inescapable obligation to retrieve his woman. While he would sacrifice the pleasure of witnessing his adversary's death, it was nonetheless gratifying to further manipulate the prideful *yanqui* and to contemplate Rawlins being forced to watch his beloved *gringa* suffer at the hands of the Haitians as a prelude to his own extinction.

His smile broadened when he considered the prospect of all parties intersecting sequentially in La Misíon: first Hector and his entourage with the Haitians; then the *gringa*; and, finally, the treacherous American *medico*. That the *torcidor*, Hector, and the American must be eliminated was necessary. *Un adjusticarando.* A balancing of accounts. Each had betrayed him, and each therefore must die. The Mexican retainers he'd sent to accompany Hector were similarly expendable. He cared little what happened to the American's new *puta*, for she was simply bait. That the Haitians would emerge from *la casa de roca* angry and eager to retrieve their heroin was inevitable, but he planned to be far from this place long before they arrived. Only Elena and the boy would be left to greet them.

To carry out his plan would require him to abandon the *estancia,* but this caused him small regret. Such had been the course of events since the American first was brought to him that he wished to be forever rid of his home and its unfortunate associations. In two days he would begin his drive northeast to Chihuahua and stay for a time with his uncle's family at their isolated *ranchero* in the heart of *la barranca del cobre*. The people of the region were Tarahumara. *Indios.* His mother's people. The Tarahumara's hostility towards the intrusion of uninvited strangers was longstanding and invariable. He would be safe there.

After a few months he would journey south to Mexico City, where under a pseudonym he owned a secure home in the central district. His mistress had furnished the house lavishly, and it was as secure as a fortress. From that home, through intermediaries, he could manage the sale of the heroin, and with the profit forthcoming they would live well and in perpetual anonymity.

Yes, he thought still gazing out the window towards the ocean and beyond. *Let them come if they wish. Whether by sea or by land, it is of no consequence.*

He lit one of the thin black cigars he'd long favored, and his thoughts strayed to the American. He frowned as he considered the irrevocable losses the man's chaotic behavior had wrought. His younger brother now two years in the grave. Elena disfigured beyond redemption. And the boy. Arivada grimaced reflexively. As with the rest, the boy required elimination.

Waiting is the hard thing, he thought. He'd set all parts in motion, and there was nothing else to be done. While he was confident of the end result, it now was left to the unwitting players to achieve that result.

He turned and began to walk out of the magnificent library, pausing to select a single item from the shelves that lined the walls. He was leaving behind him a small fortune in books, paintings, fine furniture and the like, but he carried away only the shotgun. The old weapon that had belonged to his mother's grandfather, a *Yaqui*, who chose to die fighting on his feet rather than on his knees as a slave in the mines of Diaz.

Satisfied, he strode down the hall towards the steps that led to his bedroom.

Chapter 6

SALLY

Sally was reclining on the large bed and wondering when she would see Will.

To her chagrin, two men - presumably agents of this Arivada - had captured her easily as she'd crouched in the shadows, straining to make sense of what was taking place within the house. Despite her struggling, they had effortlessly pinned her arms and dragged her into the *hacienda* and eventually to a large bedroom deep within the interior of the house. While the room was comfortable and well-appointed, its subterranean lack of windows and locked door gave it a cell-like aspect. She'd been there for over an hour. Her initial terror subsided, and she had grown more bored than afraid.

She'd been thinking of Will, and as always when she thought of him her feelings were complicated. Over the years Sally had endured a series of failed relationships with men unsuitable for one reason or another, and she worried that now with Will she was making her greatest mistake. Sally was a generous woman, but time and experience had taught her to be cautious with her heart, and the low expectations she typically maintained had served to spare her much distress when her relationships had turned sour. With Will that was no longer possible. She loved him, and that was that.

Was he able to commit, she'd wondered, or simply unwilling? Had the time spent alone as a fugitive, always wary, inoculated him against intimacy? She'd tried to be patient, placed no demands and avoided all talk of a future together, but it had become ever more difficult to sustain her insouciant façade. Beneath Will's warm, congenial exterior she sensed an absence, even a certain *coldness*. That was the best she could describe it to herself. Whatever the precise source of his emotional reserve, Sally feared that it bode poorly for their long-term prospects.

As was her tendency, Sally consciously chose to dismiss her ruminations and arose from the bed to wash up in the beautifully tiled bathroom. Glancing at a clock on the wall, she saw it was almost eight.

Three Mexican men suddenly appeared at the door, and before she could make even the slightest resistance they were upon her, pinning her arms behind her, cuffing her wrists and roughly thrusting some type of cloth within her mouth so as to silence her. Trying desperately to keep her wits about her, trying not to choke or faint, Sally felt herself spun about to face one of her attackers.

He was a muscular Hispanic man dressed in a manner that seemed to her straight out of central casting for a film that involved organized crime: shiny black jacket over a black turtle neck sweater, black dress pants and expensive-appearing, highly polished black loafers of a European cut. The man had withdrawn an enormous revolver from a holster beneath his jacket and pressed its barrel against the skin overlying her left carotid artery.

"Quiet," he'd advised her. "Be now so very quiet. If no, you will die." He had a thick Spanish accent. So fetid was his breath that she'd almost gagged.

Shifting her eyes a bit, Sally looked at the two other men standing beside her, each grasping an arm. Both were identical to Bad Breath in their attire. Unbidden had come to her the thought: *I may not survive this one.*

Bad Breath directed the others to release her, and Sally immediately made a dash for the door. Moving swiftly for a man of his size, Bad Breath blocked her exit, grabbed her upper arm with his enormous left hand that easily encircled her limb and with his pistol directed her to sit on the bed.

Bad Breath left her with the other two men, and the next ten minutes passed in silence. Then he returned and spoke to the others in rapid-fire Spanish she found difficult to follow. The two men abruptly seized her, forced her to her feet and half-dragged her out of the room, down the hall and up two sort flights of stairs to an exterior door. Bad Breath leading them, they'd exited the *hacienda* and unceremoniously dumped her in the open trunk of a large black sedan, slamming the lid after her. She heard the engine turn over, and immediately they were on their way.

———

After about an hour they'd stopped on an empty two-lane road and transferred her from the trunk to the back seat of the car. Although she disliked being trussed up, her only real discomfort resulted from their unbending refusal to stop and allow her to urinate.

After another few hours the car turned off the main coastal highway, slowed to a crawl and fitfully descended a steep, narrow track to a beach. Dragged from the car and placed on her feet, Sally saw before her in the darkness a cylinder of rock, its sightless façade ominous in the wet, gray fog pushed shoreward by the cooling sea of early winter. In her relief at being freed of her bonds and allowed to squat in the sand she'd barely noticed the three men who emerged from the tower to greet her abductors.

Then the strange dark men had come, erupting into the rock tower shortly after midnight. Their lilting speech was at odds with their hard, expressionless faces.

———

The leader of the Mexican crew, Hector, had been absent when the dark men arrived. He was seated at *La Fonda's* bar, preoccupied in morosely drinking one margarita after another in a futile attempt to shake the sense of foreboding that dogged him.

Never before had these Haitians failed to keep rigorously to their schedule, and they were three days overdue. When Diego and the others brought *la gringa* to the tower, they also brought a message from *el jefe*: the dark men had been delayed; after they arrived all should wait for another who would be coming from the *hacienda* with additional product.

These changes in their long-established pattern and the *gringa's* appearance had created a discordance, and with each hour that passed there grew ever greater in him the suspicion that something had gone very wrong.

He'd left them behind in the tower, the *gringa* and the two men who'd accompanied him to San Pedro. The woman and instructions delivered, the other three had departed immediately to return to Guerrero Negro. Hector was sorry to see them go. Who knew what was coming? The two back at the tower were untested in any real gunplay, and their reliability was therefore suspect. He could take comfort only in the tequila and the gym bag full of cash that he kept with him always.

———

Within the tower there was only a single, high-ceilinged room. Circular in shape with a concrete floor, the room's diameter was about twenty feet. The only illumination was supplied by a battery-powered lamp, and so tightly sealed was the tower that none of that light penetrated to the murky darkness outside.

Sally's fear and hunger had combined to eliminate any hope of sleep. She consequently was awake to hear the padlock succumb to a heavily delivered blow, and suddenly the door was flung open and the room filled with a blinding light.

The dark men were three in number, and only the tallest had spoken to them directly. "Lie you face down on de flo'," he commanded in heavily accented English. When the two men failed to obey, rubbing their eyes and looking bewildered as they remained sitting on their blankets, the other two intruders stepped rapidly forward. Each bore a rifle at his chest, and using the barrels of their weapons as clubs, they struck the two men's heads sharply and in unison, sending them sprawling to lie prone on the hard floor.

For the next hour the dark men spoke sparingly amongst themselves and brooked no movement or speech from their captives. The man with the acne-scarred face briefly whispered something to the tallest of them as he bent over him, listening, and when he'd finished, the one who had struck him previously strolled over and clubbed him as before. Although directed at

453

another, this act of reflexive brutality so unnerved Sally that she struggled to avoid emptying her bladder involuntarily.

Shortly thereafter the big Mexican returned. Not so inebriated as to overlook the damage inflicted on the padlock, he paused before opening the door to retrieve his *pistola* from its shoulder holster. As he did so, however, the door flew open, and he was cut down where he stood by a brief burst of fire from an automatic weapon.

His slayer, the tall dark man, walked over to where he lay, pressed the muzzle of his rifle against the fallen man's temple and administered a final *coup d'grace*. In a rhythmic language that Sally couldn't identify he called back over his shoulder to his two companions, and together the men dragged the large corpse into the already crowded room. The tall man followed, Hector's gym bag gripped in his huge hand.

————

Many hours had passed since the shooting, her initial shock had subsided and now Sally felt herself numb beyond despair. She and her two fellow captives were not allowed outside, and the stench within the room was overpowering. They'd been given a bottle containing a liter of water and for nourishment a single plastic bag containing stale flour tortillas. All the while there lay against the wall Hector's corpse, one of the gaily colored tourist blankets covering his face and upper body.

Sally registered her lack of fear and worried that it might signal resignation. Or, worse, surrender. True, the dark men ignored her, but she felt their persistent indifference no less unnerving than the violence that had gone before. They rarely spoke, even to one another. They seemed to be waiting. *But for what?* she wondered.

Chapter 7

THE STONE TOWER

As he drove north Will began to feel increasingly unwell, assailed by waves of nausea, intestinal cramping and diarrhea. Anxious to reach his destination he found the last to be especially vexing, as it required urgently executed and frequent stops by the side of the road. The symptoms were classic for food poisoning, and the timing of the onset suggested as culprit the chicken tacos he'd bought yesterday at the *tienda* along with the shotgun.

Just south of Ensenada he raced through Manandero, and in doing so he unknowingly passed the *orfanaterio* where Maria, once the object of his passion, had spent her youth. Ironically, it was that same young woman whose manipulations ultimately had served to precipitate the events now unfolding.

Nearly doubled over by another bout of intense intestinal cramping, Will worried that his increasing incapacitation would remove completely whatever slim chance he had of rescuing Sally. He pulled off onto the shoulder and parked quickly behind one of the ubiquitous mounds of debris that lay along the highway. Finishing quickly, he cleaned himself as best as he could, and when he arose, so low did his blood pressure drop from the accumulated volume depletion that he nearly fainted. Desperately he considered what he could do to alleviate his symptoms.

He'd left the engine running and was about to pull back onto the highway when he recalled the heroin. All morphine derivatives were potent inhibitors of gastric motility, so the trick would lie in taking just enough of the drug to suppress the cramps and diarrhea without promoting a drug-induced euphoria that might prove even more disabling.

He removed the parcel from its hiding place under the front seat, untied the twine and carefully unfolded the heavy paper. Revealed inside were five large transparent bags with zip locks, and within each bag was a fine white powder tinged brown and densely packed. He unzipped one bag slightly, moistened his index finger and stuck it through the opening to retrieve a small sample.

The taste was quite bitter. He'd no experience with heroin in any form, but he knew that it frequently was diluted with talc or quinine. This powder's bitterness suggested the latter. Will assumed purity of product to be a relative term in any commercial transaction involving heroin, and he assumed that what lay in his lap had been profoundly cut. He wondered briefly whether it contained any viable "product" whatsoever. For the sake of his cramps, he hoped so.

He snorted a small amount, rewrapped the package and almost immediately felt the heroin's impact. So profound was its effect that he nearly swooned, and it was an effort even to maintain the level of alertness required to start the engine and regain the highway. *Powerful stuff*, he thought. He hoped fervently that he'd recover sufficiently by the time he reached his destination.

As he resumed driving northward he forced down a few more gulps of water from the plastic bottle in his daypack. The dehydration he'd experienced from his repeated bouts of vomiting and diarrhea had left him weak and dizzy. He was determined not to stop again until he reached La Mision.

———

In November dusk came early, and in the gathering darkness Will missed the obscure turn-off that wound down to the beach. He pulled into the parking lot at *La Fonda* to double back, and as he did so it seemed to him exceedingly strange to hear the happy shouts and drunken laughter arising from within. He recalled a time six years prior, when he'd come to this place to relax after a demanding period at work. In the course of those three idyllic days he'd come to know the owner, Anatole, a vigorous, bald man who was fiftyish and of Turkish descent.

Despite the man's energetic intensity, the service provided at *La Fonda* was offhand. Decidedly casual. To make a reservation one sorted through the clutter on the owner's desk to find a simple spiral notebook. On each page was listed a date and a number corresponding to each of the rooms. Assuming the notebook could be located, one simply flipped through the pages to the desired date and wrote a name on the line next to the room's number. With regularity a usurper would erase or mark out a name and replace it with his own, and when confronted by the unhappy would-be guest who thus had lost his "reservation", Anatole typically exhibited little sympathy. It was a catch-as-catch-can proposition.

The service provided at the humble resort's restaurant was much in the same vein. Hours might pass before food was placed on the table, and despite a menu limited to lobster, *cabrilla* and *carne tampiquena* as entrees with refried beans and *chile con queso* as the sole side dishes, orders were confused or the various dishes arrived at irregular intervals.

It didn't really matter. To sit outside at one of the talavera tile-bedecked tables beneath a palm-thatched *palapa* that rustled with the on-shore breeze, to sip margaritas or *cervezas frias,* and to watch the dolphins hang suspended as they surfed the translucent waves was an experience to be savored. During the winter months, when the Los Angeles crowd was absent and the pace slowed, it had not been unusual on a Sunday afternoon for Will to recognize more than half of those at the neighboring tables on the terrace: surfers and other fellow travelers whom he knew from San Diego and North County.

But those tranquil days had long since passed, and tonight he had business elsewhere. Driving a short distance south from *La Fonda*, he pulled off on the road's narrow shoulder just before the turnoff that led eventually to the stone tower. He checked his weapons and loads, just as he'd done twice before on the journey north. Of the guns Arivada had gifted him, the pistol appeared as if it might function, but the rifle was useless. The clips supplied by the Mexican did not fit the weapon's chamber, and Will suspected the mismatch was no mistake.

This did little to allay his conviction that he was walking into a trap. He still had the humble shotgun, but disinclined to burden himself too heavily he stashed it under the seat; its stopping power was limited in any event. He jammed the pistol between his waistband and sacrum. He hid the parcel of heroin beneath the spare tire.

He left the car on the shoulder and walked quietly down the steep, narrow access road to the beach. Once he reached the sand, he crept along the foot of the bluff where the shadows were darkest. Even with the moonless, overcast night he easily could make out the cylindrical rock structure about one hundred yards distant. Approaching the building from the rear, he listened closely but could hear no sounds from within. The tower was dark and silent.

He waited a full thirty minutes, but the only sounds were those produced by the small waves breaking onshore and the occasional passing of a vehicle on the *calle libre* high above. Flattening himself against the building's exterior, Will slowly inched his way towards the door that fronted the sea. As he stood by the door, straining to hear above the sound of the surf, he suddenly felt something hard, cold and metallic press against the mastoid bone behind his left ear. *Fuck,* he thought.

A deep male voice spoke to him softly in English, the accent heavy but not Spanish. "Put op you honds," the voice commanded.

He raised his arms, and the man spoke again. "Lie down," he said. "On you belly. Slow."

Will complied. The man found the pistol immediately and extracted it from his waistband. "Now you get up, you," he said, and he used the barrel of his weapon to prod Will towards the door. For one desperate second Will considered spinning about and attacking his captor. As if anticipating this, he heard the man speak. "Don' do it, you," he warned. "My finga on de trigguh."

Feeling the pressure of the weapon's muzzle against his back increase, Will was pushed against the heavy wooden door, his weight causing it to swing open. Once inside the circular room it took a moment for his eyes to adjust from the darkness outside to the light cast by a fluorescent camping lantern set against the far wall.

Blinking, he saw several bodies wrapped in blankets and reclining on the floor in various positions, and in the middle of the room stood two men with shaved heads and skin the color of black ash. Their expressions were cold and distinctly unfriendly. One of the men was very tall.

He continued to glance about, and then in the shadows to his right he saw Sally lying on the floor, her face pale and drawn, her eyes wide, her gaze unfocused. He made to move towards her, and the man at his rear immediately brought him to a standstill with a sharp nudge of the weapon's muzzle against his flank. "Sally," Will called to her. "It's Will, Sally. Are you all right?"

The taller of the two men who stood before him stepped forward and slapped him roughly across the left cheek with his open hand. "Shot de fock op," he told Will, his accent similar to that of the gunman but his English more distinct. His assailant turned to two men of Hispanic appearance who were lying on the floor. "Who dis be? He be a couryuh?" he demanded of them. "Dis be de mon who be havin' de smock?"

The men on the floor remained silent under his inquiry, one staring blankly down at the concrete and the other obviously agitated, now trembling. The latter began to stutter in barely intelligible Spanish. "*Por favor*", he pleaded. "*No se nada.*" He knew nothing, he said. Even in the poor lighting Will could see it was the Argentine from the sea wall. The messenger.

"Den what de fock we need you fo'?" the tall man responded, shrugging. Reaching for the holster he wore at his left shoulder, he withdrew an enormous handgun and fired three rounds into the supplicant's face at a range of six feet. The bullets' effects were predictably gruesome, and the deafening echo of the explosions within the dimly lit tower set Will's ears to bell-ringing deafness.

The killer turned to the remaining Hispanic. "Now whot *you* got to say?" he asked, leveling his pistol at the other's face.

In the midst of suppressing another surge of nausea, Will glanced over at the freshly slain man. Even in the poorly illuminated room he could see the tattoo on his right wrist.. Looking beyond him Will saw a fourth person on the floor. He was wedged against the far wall, a large figure lying motionless and partially covered by a blanket.

Despite the pistol pointing at his face, the last surviving Hispanic continued to stare resignedly at the floor between his outstretched legs. Suddenly the tall man was screaming. "You tock to me, mon! You tock to me *now*, or I keel you de som as you fren!" In his fury the black man's expression assumed an insane malevolence.

The man sitting on the floor looked up and shrugged. "*Tu eres un perro negro,*" he said calmly. "*Nada mas.*" A black dog. Nothing more.

In the next instant there was a burst of gunfire, and the man's face disappeared.

This place is becoming a real charnel house, Will thought. The motionless body under the blanket presumably was also a corpse, and the floor of the cylindrical room now sported crimson patches containing small fragments of skull, brain and other gore. He glanced over at Sally and saw she still wore the same expression of wide-eyed horror he'd observed when he'd first entered the room. God only knew what acts she'd been compelled to observe or experience prior to this present spate of violence.

Turning to his compatriots, the tall man now seemed composed. He spoke to them briefly in a language unrecognizable to Will, and they proceeded to heap the two inert bodies atop the corpse lying against the wall. Then, with the two men flanking him, the Tall Man faced Will and spoke to him directly. "Do you hawv it wit you?" he demanded.

"Have what?" Will responded. And as he spoke he suddenly realized the full nature of what Arivada intended for him. And for Sally.

The man looked down and shook his head as if bemused. Rubbing his neck, he raised his head again and locked eyes with Will. "Whot de fock wrong wit' you, mon?" he asked. "You nawt jus see what hoppen to dem?" he nodded briefly towards the bodies stacked against the wall. "You mebbe wont to lie dere wit' dem?"

Will was at a loss. What could he say or do that would have any chance of saving their lives? "These men work for Manuelo Arivada," he said, finally. "The man they call *El Santo*. I don't."

As if suddenly infuriated by these words, the Tall Man clenched his right fist and shook it directly in front of Will's nose. "I don' care *who* de fock fo' who you wuck," he shouted. "Why you t'ink I care 'bout dis '*Santo*' mon?" Placing his face directly against Will's and enunciating his words slowly, he asked once again, "Do...you...hawv...*eet*?"

When Will remained silent, the man broke away from the American and seemed to ponder what to do next. Finally he turned back and spoke. "Dis you woman?" he asked, indicating Sally.

Will saw little point in denial. "I know her," he answered simply.

"She you guhlfren, yes?" the Tall Man inquired, leering grotesquely.

When Will failed to answer, the man abruptly became agitated as before, his eyes bulging, the sclerae yellow-tinged and bloodshot. "Mebbe you like to watch while fuhst we fock she up good," he suggested. Then, walking to where Sally sat motionless on the floor and placing the long barrel of his pistol carefully against her head, he asked, "Oh mebbe you jus' won' dot I keel she now?"

Thinking fast, Will said, "I know what it is you want. You want the heroin."

The Tall Man slowly withdrew his pistol and walked over to stand once again with his face just inches from Will's own. "Yessss," he replied softly. "De heroin. Where is eet, den? Where is de res' of de smock?"

"Arivada," Will answered. "I have a few bags in my car, but Arivada has the rest. He set them up." He indicated the dead men heaped against the wall. "He set you up," he continued, "and he set me up. He set us *all* up. The rest of the product is still with him."

"Den why you come to dis place, you?" the Tall Man demanded. "Why you boddah to come?"

"I came here for her," Will replied, nodding towards Sally. "Like I said, Arivada set me up, too. He told me she was here. He sent me here so you would kill me."

The Haitian stared into Will's eyes for a full thirty seconds as if attempting to gauge the veracity of his words. Finally he broke away and stood leaning against a portion of wall as yet uncontaminated by blood or other body fluids, his arms folded before him.

"Prawduck," he said in a tone softly sarcastic. "Yes, it dis 'praw-duck' dot be makin' de prollum for evyone. Fo' you. Fo' we. Fo' dem," he specified, flicking his gaze at the stack of corpses. "You take us to you cah," he concluded. "And if dere we find dis 'prawduck', den mebbe we jus' let you an' you pretty fren go on you way. If not . . .". He shrugged.

"But it's only a few bags in my car," Will insisted. "I told you. Arivada has the rest."

The Haitian simply stared at him for another moment and then shrugged as before.

———

The Tall Man's accomplice quickly found the shotgun and parcel, and he immediately passed the latter to his superior. The Tall Man folded his long frame on to the SUV's passenger seat, impatiently ripped off the external wrapping and unzipped one of the plastic bags. Much as Will had done, he sampled the powder with a moistened forefinger and then snorted a small amount. He repeated the act multiple times. At last he closed took the bag.

Turning about, he lowered his face to within an inch of Will's and glared at the American with his bulging eyes. Will was feeling ill again - whether from food poisoning or apprehension - but still he managed to stare back at the apparition before him and to speak calmly. "I told you, I don't have the heroin," he said. "I told you, the Mexican set me up. He sent me here with just these few bags. He sent me here so you would kill me."

The Haitian withdrew his face but continued to glower. "He right in dot," the Tall Man replied sullenly.

Will improvised. "Kill me if you want," he said, "but then you'll never see your heroin again. You don't know where it is."

"Den wheh de smock be?" demanded the Haitian. "You tell me now, you, or I tro you ovah dis cleef."

Will's gaze was steady. "I've told you already," he replied. "Arivada has it."

"How you know dis, you?" the Tall Man asked dubiously. "Whot you know 'bout dis mon?"

"I know where he lives," Will answered. "Wait too long, and he'll be gone… and your heroin with him. I'll bet your friends back home wouldn't be too happy about that."

The tall black man glared at him without speaking, but Will could sense his words had struck home. Will had gained them a reprieve. However brief.

———

They returned to the fetid room where Sally had remained with the third Haitian, and the three dark men left Will with her while they went outside to confer.

"Sally," Will said, grasping her upper arm lightly and shaking it. "Look at me."

She flinched reflexively at his touch but turned her head to face him, her eyes still wide and pupils dilated. *She looks almost psychotic,* he thought. *Small wonder.* "I'm so sorry," he told her.

Tears gathered at the corners of her eyes, began to leak out and traced their way down her cheeks. "Will," she said hoarsely. "I'm so frightened."

"Sally," he told her firmly. "I will get us out of this. You will be safe again, I promise." Although she looked at him doubtfully, he was relieved she at least seemed to comprehend what he was saying. *God knows*, he thought, *she has good reason to be skeptical.*

He was cradling her in his lap and stroking her hair when the Haitians re-entered the room. For some reason the Tall Man hung back and allowed the shortest and blackest of the three to speak for them. His English was shaky, but the message conveyed was all too clear. "We t'ink you lie. But mebbe we cot dis you guhl, den mebbe you tell us whot you know. And whot you nawt be knowin', too."

Cut your girl, the man had said. *Think fast*, Will told himself.

The Haitian who'd spoken looked back at the Tall Man as if for confirmation, and the latter dipped his head, closing his eyes and resting his chin on his chest as if saddened by the knowledge of what was to follow. The other two moved to grab Sally, but she scuttled away, kicking at them vigorously as she scooted backwards, halted finally by the rough wall. She called to Will, her voice wild with fear. "Will!" she screamed. "What is it they want? For God's sake, give it to them! *Please*. Give it to them!"

He cursed his helplessness. The two men now had Sally in their grasp and were in the process of pinning her down in the center of the room, spread-eagled and supine on the filthy concrete floor. From somewhere the Tall Man had produced a machete, and once the other two suppressed Sally's struggling and had her positioned as he wanted, he made ready to strike her right arm. Seeing his intent, she began to scream, at the same time renewing her struggle against the strong hands that gripped her wrists and ankles.

Here was the opening Will sought. With the three men distracted by Sally's screams and her desperate efforts to wrench free, he drove his fist into the small of the Tall Man's back, lunging forward from his seated position so as to put his full weight behind the impact. The man shouted out as he crumpled to the floor, the machete skittering across the concrete. The other two immediately released Sally and reached for their weapons, one a pistol holstered at the shoulder and the other a rifle lying on the floor.

Recovering from the assault, the Tall Man was struggling to his hands and knees. Will lunged again, and in a rapid sequence of actions more reflexive than volitional struck the Haitian a wicked blow just beneath his right eye, took advantage of the man's incapacitation to extract his pistol from its holster and crouched to assume a defensive position. He braced his back against the wall, hooked his left arm around the tall Haitian's neck and with his right hand pressed the muzzle of the man's pistol against his curiously small and slightly pointed right ear. He briefly wondered whether the human shield he held before him would be sufficient to stop multiple rounds shot at high velocity and close range. It seemed doubtful.

Sally had scrambled to that portion of the cylindrical wall farthest from the two men who'd pinned her. Immediately to her left were the corpses, stacked like oversized logs of firewood. "Sally," he called to her. "Keep against the wall, and come over here with me."

Complying, she inched her way towards him, her back to the wall and eyes fixed on the two Haitians now crouched low at the room's center. Will could sense their confusion. The Tall Man – presumably their leader – was barely conscious following the blow to his head. Without guidance they were a rudderless ship.

Once she'd completed her transit, Will bade Sally to sit beside him and then addressed the two Haitians. "Put your guns down," he commanded. They hesitated, and Will spoke more sharply, "Put your fucking guns *down,* I said!"

The responses of the two men contrasted sharply and were immediately apparent in their differing expressions. The younger of the two was obviously unnerved, his eyes wide with fear and his pistol already hanging uselessly from his right hand, its muzzle pointing downward at the floor. The other man – the burliest and blackest of the three, the one who'd initially accosted him outside - showed no trace of fear. Instead he radiated a primitive, almost reptilian malevolence. He kept his rifle trained on Will via the Tall Man's chest.

"I t'ink eef we poot down dese guns, den you jus' keel us all t'ree," he said flatly. "I t'ink mebbe I shoot you guhlfren fus', den you." As if to demonstrate, he shifted the rifle's position momentarily, bringing it to bear upon Kate's head.

Will spoke quickly. "If you shoot me, your boss man here dies. And if he dies, you go back to *his* boss man and explain how he died and why you're coming home empty- handed. Without your boss. Without your heroin." For emphasis, he jammed the pistol's barrel yet further into the Tall Man's ear. A scarlet trickle of blood descended down the angle of his jaw from a laceration the hard metal tore in the fragile skin of the external canal. "I t'ink den you be de one dey shoot," he mocked the rifleman. "Or mebbe dey jus' chop off *you* arm."

Will could see the man was considering his words, wavering. His companion, however, already had made his decision. Without being asked, he slid his pistol to where Will was standing.

"Pick it up," Will told Sally. "Grip the handle with both hands." He nodded towards the Haitian still holding the rifle and spoke to her slowly but distinctly, taking care that the other armed man should comprehend what he said. "If that man does not put down his rifle or he shoots me, kill him. Pull the trigger and hold it down; the pistol will keep firing until you release the trigger or the clip is empty."

Glancing over, he could see Sally holding the pistol precisely as he'd instructed, without any trace of hesitation. *What a woman,* he thought.

Unfortunately, it was at that critical moment that the tall Haitian regained full consciousness. He abruptly shouted something to his companion with the rifle, and the language he used was unknown to Will. Presumably Haitian.

Immediately the man fired a brief but deafening burst from his weapon. The lava rock and mortar just adjacent to Sally's left cheek exploded, and the blast knocked her to the floor. Now she lay sprawled across the Tall Man's feet, while Will stood behind both. As she fell, the pistol she'd held flew from her hand and clattered against the floor to Will's right.

The tall Haitian spoke quickly, in English now and directing his words to Will. "You guhl is not huht so bad. But eff you doan lay down de gun, dot mon" – he nodded towards the rifleman – "shoot you and den you guhl."

"Listen, friend," Will replied. "If he shoots me, you die, too."

The Tall Man actually smiled. "You doan unnastan', you" he said. "Dis nawht de U Ess A, and dis no cowboy movie or sumtink lak dot. Eef my fren' der doan keel you, de uddahs bock home jus' keel heem. Yesss. Keel dot mon ovuh dere wit' de gon. Me. Boaf. Dis be nudding to dem. I hawv ohdaws, and he" – he nodded towards the other Haitian – "now he hawv hees ohdaws, too."

Orders, Will thought, hopelessly. *Fucking killers with orders.* They all held their positions for another few seconds: the corpses stiff and silent against the wall; Sally sitting up now, picking out the small fragments of rock and mortar imbedded in her cheek, a thin circle of blood smeared there like poorly applied rouge; the youngest Haitian reunited with his automatic pistol, standing now and brandishing his weapon aggressively as if to negate his earlier surrender; the burly black man still crouched with one knee on the concrete floor, his rifle held with both hands and its muzzle now aimed at Will's chest. And, finally, Will and the Tall Man, the former still clutching the latter from behind, each staring straight ahead and calculating what might be the thoughts and intentions of the other.

The Tall Man broke the silence. "Poot down de gon, mon," he said gently. "Beddah you poot dat gon down queeck."

Slowly Will lowered the pistol and laid it on the floor beside him. The Tall Man arose, picked up his weapon and, gripping it tightly with his right hand, used the barrel and chamber to strike Will a vicious blow across his left temple.

Knocked off balance, Will fell heavily on his left side. As if reawakened from prolonged slumber the nerves involved in the old injury to his left shoulder screamed out in a sudden, rousing chorus of excruciating pain. He felt a series of electric shocks jolt his left arm from armpit to fingertip. He fought to remain conscious, and when he opened his eyes, his vision in the left was periodically obscured by lightening-like flashes that persisted even when he closed the eye once again. *Detached retina,* he thought. *Great.*

He felt himself being dragged across the room, and when he looked up, there seemed to be fireworks exploding upon the tower's high ceiling; these, too, were arising from his damaged left eye. Eventually the strong hands released him, and he was sitting with his back once again propped against the rough interior wall. Sally was sitting beside him, and he turned to find her searching his face with obvious concern. Perceiving him to be conscious, she murmured, "I'm sorry. Oh, Will. I'm so sorry."

Will presumed she was referring to her having dropped the automatic pistol, and he tried to smile. "Let's not start that game," he said. "Without me, you'd be back in Hillcrest waiting for some handsome surgeon to pick you up for dinner."

Shaking her head, she was about to respond to this, but the tall Haitian cut their conversation short. "Shot you boaf op," he said. His voice was cold, and he loomed directly above them, his arms folded over his chest and a gunman at either side. Without diverting his eyes from Will's, he spoke a few quick words to the burly man who'd earlier been prepared to let him die rather than surrender his weapon. Some type of command, apparently, issued in their own language. The man promptly left the stone tower, shutting the heavy wooden door behind him.

Then with his unblinking eyes still fixed on Will, he spoke to the other gunman, the one with the automatic pistol. "Keel dem," he commanded. "Guhl fust, mon fust. Eet doan mawta." He turned to follow the man who'd just left.

"Wait!" Will called after him. The Tall Man kept moving, hand now on the door. The smallest Haitian was raising his pistol, leveling it at them where they sat and preparing to fire.

"Wait!" Will shouted, desperate now. "I know you what *you* need to know, goddamit. I know where it is. I know *precisely* where the heroin is. Kill me, and you'll never find it. Only we can take you there."

During the brief lull just a few minutes before, Will had used the seconds to concoct this proposal. If the quantity and value of the drug these men sought was important enough to him and his employers, the Tall Man might let them live. It was a gamble born of desperation, but somehow he felt he was correct in his choice of bait. Besides, at this point what else did they have?

The Tall Man dropped his hand from the door handle, turned and looked back at Will. "Whot you *really* know 'bout dis heroin, you?" he demanded, disgustedly.

Will improvised. He was fairly sure these men would not know about the *hacienda*. "I know their boss ripped you off," he replied, nodding towards the dead Mexicans. I know where you can find their boss. *And* I know where he has your heroin. I also know you've killed the only other people here who could have taken you to him."

The Tall Man snorted derisively. "Now why dot mon tell *you* wheh he poot dis smock? You nudding but a go-boy."

"I know where to find the Mexican," Will repeated slowly, deliberately. "I know he has the heroin. I know where he keeps it."

"I doan t'ink you know nudding," the other man sneered. "I t'ink you jus' be sayin' anyting so mebbe you doan die."

"Then kill me," Will told him, "and let your people back home decide whether you made the right decision."

The Tall Man scowled at this and turned away. Will could see he was turning over the various permutations in his mind. Finally he turned back and spoke to his short henchman as he gestured towards Sally. "Keel de guhl," he said. "Wedda dis go-boy sayin' be true or no, we doan need huh."

Will reacted quickly. "Kill her," he said, "and I won't tell you a fucking thing."

The Tall Man looked upon him balefully. "White mon," he said, "eef I won, I con make you tell me any 'fockin' t'ing'. In fack, I can make you tell me *everyt'ing*... everyt'ing you know... and mebbe some t'ings you tawt you fawgot." He exchanged glances with the shorter black man. "But we spen' too moch de time ahready in dis dahmn stinkin' place. Get you up wit' you guhlfrien', and we go to dis mon. Dis '*Santo*'." He spat, as if he found the word distasteful.

The moment passed, no one moved and then the tall Haitian spoke. "Poott down yo' gon," he told his man. And then to Will more quietly, he muttered, "I steel t'ink you lyin', mon. Eef be so, den boaf you die ... die slow...slow and not hoppy. De guhl fus while you watch. Den you. Dis I promise."

"I'm telling you the truth," Will lied.

The Tall Man glared at him for another long moment. "I t'ink you lyin'," he repeated. "An' I t'ink we be killin' de boaf uff you. But fuss we aw be takin' de ride ahn pay dis call on you fren."

"He's no friend of mine," Will assured the man.

———

They'd been driving south for over an hour, and their captors had yet to speak. He and Sally sat in the back, staring ahead at the Haitians' shaved heads, their furtive attempts to whisper to one another rapidly aborted when the Tall Man jerked his head about to glare at them with his bloodshot eyes bulging.

At least this will buy some time, Will thought. *But time for what?* Arivada had set him up. Whether they found what they sought or were unable to recover the stolen heroin, these cruel men would kill them both. He could parley his knowledge of the *hacienda's* location and other particulars to insure their survival for a few more hours, but then what? Sally, his only ally in the enterprise, obviously possessed no information of value to the Haitians, and Will had no illusions that the Tall Man had exaggerated in his assurance that their deaths would be as painful as they were inevitable.

Yet again, as so often had occurred with the misfortune he'd experienced in Mexico, he'd have to improvise as events unfolded. He resolved to use the remaining hours they'd spend in traveling to the *hacienda* to formulate a plan.

Chapter 8

LA DANZA DEL MUERTE

Manuel Arivada stood at the window in his library, clasping his hands behind him while he looked out into the twilight.

Del mar o la tierra? he asked himself yet again. And then shrugged. Why should it matter what route his enemies chose? When they arrived, he'd be gone.

That they would come for him was likely. He knew well how these Haitians chose to operate, and it was a near certainty that the *yanqui,* Rawlins, would have told them of the *hacienda*'s location before he died. Or they would obtain that information by another means. They were relentless, and only after they recovered the heroin and permanently eliminated the man who had betrayed them would they cease their pursuit. Sooner or later, they would come. Here. To the *hacienda.*

He gazed at the moon rising over the hills to the west and smiled at the sight. Was this meant as a signal, indicating that his foes would be arriving by water? Reflexively he shrugged again. Their route was irrelevant.

His thoughts turned to Elena and the boy. *How strangely life deals with us,* he mused. He had intended to share his life with a family. With his brother, a devoted wife and sons of his own blood. How ironic was the reality: his brother dead, and in his house only Elena, disfigured and useless. And the boy. The infernal boy. A constant reminder of his home's defilement.

What was broken was not to be mended. Well he knew this. But to take revenge could be a satisfaction nonetheless.

He turned from the window. It was time to sleep. Were they coming, it would be prudent to leave at first light.

———

They made an odd group, Will thought, the five of them crowded together in the Haitians' mid-sized Mexican rental. The shortest man, the one who had surrendered so easily back at the rock house, had been exiled to the back seat and now sat between Will and Sally. The Tall Man rode shotgun while the third did all the driving.

The Haitians spoke little and stopped only once, at a shabby bus station in San Quintin, to empty their bladders and fill their bellies with pre-made cheese sandwiches and bags of fried pork rinds sold by a diffident old Mexican who also served as the station's ticket agent. Not once during the transaction did *el viejo* look up at the Haitians or the two white *yanquis* who accompanied them.

The station's bathroom was filthy, its single toilet broken and filled to the brim with human waste and discarded paper of various types. The dark men simply relieved themselves against an outside wall, but they indicated that Will and Sally should make do with *el bano*. And although they allowed them a sandwich and a bottle of sweet orange soda, they forbade any conversation between the two in the car or during their brief stop at the terminal.

He looked over at Sally. She appeared to be sleeping, her head resting against the car's side window. The three Haitians remained awake, staring ahead silently at the highway before them. Despite his exhaustion, he was unable to sleep but too stupefied to think clearly. They would reach the *hacienda* within another two hours, and he still lacked even the shred of a plan that might save them.

His nausea and intestinal cramping persisted, and from this, sleep deprivation and the dehydration he felt thoroughly ill and unfit. *This never happens in the movies*, he thought. Manly heroes of the screen apparently were immune to fatigue and the humiliating ravages of food poisoning.

In his mind he tried to assemble what he knew to be true and what was likely to be so. It appeared that his Mexican nemesis, Arivada, had conspired to divert a shipment of heroin, and the Haitians intended to retrieve their product and, presumably, take their revenge upon the man who'd betrayed them. That these men had permitted Sally and Will to survive clearly signaled their conviction that the Mexican retained access to the missing heroin. Will also assumed that they had no idea as to the location of the *hacienda*.

The last seemed strange to him. True, Arivada's bastion was hidden away in a particularly remote and sparsely populated area of Baja's Pacific coast, but these Haitians had found their way to the obscure rock tower south of tiny La Mision. To locate the sprawling *estancia* of the Mexican drug lord would hardly seem to pose any greater challenge.

Of one more thing Will was certain. Arivada had meant for him to die in the rock tower. He wondered why the Mexican had not simply killed him outright when he'd burst into the *hacienda's* kitchen. Was the man seeking a more intricate revenge? Did this account for Sally's involvement, with her serving to balance Elena's disfigurement? Did the man hope to use Will to try to conceal his theft of the heroin?

Impossible to know, he decided. But of one thing he was sure: Arivada was expecting the Haitians, but he would not be expecting Will to have remained alive to accompany them. With Will's guidance they would be arriving at the *hacienda* much earlier than Arivada was likely to have calculated, and it was this flaw in the Mexican's plan that Will was counting on for potential salvation.

———

The sun was rising as they approached the turn-off to the unpaved road that led to Arivada's home. "Slow down," Will told the driver. "We're getting close."

The Tall Man jabbered something to the driver, presumably speaking in Haitian. The man seemed to understand little English, and Will filed that small observation away for future use. The Tall Man twisted around in his seat and glared meaningfully at Will. "You fock wit' us now, you and de guhl be sorry fo' it. Doan be tryin' to set no trop."

Will stared back at him, unblinking. "I'm not setting any trap," he replied. They locked eyes for a moment longer, and then the Tall Man turned back to face the road.

As they bumped along the hard, rocky surface Will spoke again to the Tall Man. "This road dips down to cross some dry washes. The sand there can be deep and soft, and it's easy for a car like this to become stuck."

The Tall Man simply shrugged and responded without turning to face him. "We be stock, den we jus' poosh de caw out," he said, obviously unimpressed by his prisoner's warning.

Will settled back and said no more. *Have it your way then, fucker*, he thought.

Although they made it through the first wash without difficulty, halfway through the second the car became hopelessly stuck, buried to its axles in the soft sand. The smallest man was now in the driver's seat, gunning the engine and spinning the car's wheels ineffectually while the other two Haitians pushed and sweated.

Will and Sally sat together on a flat rock and made the most of the first opportunity they'd had to converse privately since her abduction. He asked her how she felt, and her stoic response ("I'm fine") immediately aroused in him more intense feelings of sympathy and shame than would have any amount of tearful distress or accusation.

"I love you, Sally," he told her.

Her response was neutral, almost dismissive. "Oh, Will" she said. "Right now you're in Sir Galahad mode, and I'm your damsel in distress. Let's concentrate on getting out of this mess alive, and then we can worry about romance."

Taking note of the deflating effect these words exerted, she smiled at him encouragingly. "Now don't pout, Sir Galahad," she teased. "Right now this particular damsel needs a gallant rescue and a hot bath a lot more than declarations of love. Put your testosterone where it's needed, and come up with a plan."

Will grinned in response. *She is really something*, he thought. *And she's right. The only problem is, I can't come up with a plan. For the life of me. Literally.* His smile faltered, and he looked away.

"Don't worry," Sally told him, rubbing his shoulders as if to sooth him. "You're a smart fella. *Something* will come to you."

Silently he watched the men continue to struggle with the car.

———

Finally, at mid-day and the sun directly above them, the Tall Man gave up. "How long it take to wock to dis place?" he demanded of Will.

"Less than an hour if we stick to the road," he replied. "Longer if we go overland." To illustrate, he pointed at the rough, uneven terrain to the south, a sea of rocky hills dotted here and there with stunted trees, scrubby bushes and an infinity of ubiquitous prickly pear. "But I'd suggest the longer way."

The Tall Man looked where he pointed and then turned back to him. "Why de fock we wan' to walk tru dat sheet lan'?" he snapped at Will angrily. He'd been in an increasingly foul temper since the car had bogged down.

"When I left Arivada's *hacienda*," Will said, "he had with him only his houseman and a crippled young woman. But now the place could be crawling with his thugs."

"He *thugs!*" the tall Haitian sneered. He called over something to his comrades in Haitian, and they laughed in response. "Dose 'thugs' you call dem eeder be daid now o fah away. Dese Mexicans, dey not so tough. Wid me and me frens' obah hee, dey cry lack de bay-bay. Ooo, dey sing lack de buhds." He put his long arm around the shoulder of the pocket-sized Haitian, and the man grinned up at him in response.

"Dot ugly mon wid de face lak de pineopple," he continued, "he t'ink cause he sing mebbe he be invahted to de pahty. Now

I t'ink he know bedda." Will supposed the Haitian leader was referring to the acne-scarred Argentine who was now one of the corpses stacked against the wall of the stone tower.

Will shrugged. "Then you know more than I do," he said. "But if it were me, I'd rather walk the extra distance than risk meeting a truckload of armed men coming at me down this road." He gestured towards the steep hillsides that bordered the narrow defile where they stood.

The Tall Man scowled in response but glanced about him to take in the surrounding topography. Were they to be caught in such a place, an approaching vehicle could simply run them down, and its occupants could pick off any survivors as they attempted to scramble up the confining walls.

"Fock dis," he said quietly to no one in particular. He called to his two comrades, and together they conferred for a moment by the car. The two minions then began to gather up from the car's trunk those articles they intended to bring with them, and the Tall Man spoke again to Will.

"You and you guhl, you get op now," he said. "And no mo' you tock wid de udder. We goin' obah dat sheet lan' now. De fahsta de bedda."

Looking over the man's shoulder, Will could see the other two Haitians walking towards them, each bearing an assortment of lethal-appearing firearms and dun-colored camo backpacks bulging with what he presumed to be ammunition. He smiled to himself. This trek would be difficult enough for a man unencumbered. So burdened, these two men would suffer.

The sun was beginning to drop slowly behind the coastal hills by the time they reached the *hacienda*. Will had led them on approximately the same overland route he'd taken with Sally in her car. *Was that only two days ago?* he thought. *It seems like months.*

As before, the *hacienda* appeared deserted and its grounds unkempt. In response to the Tall Man's demand, Will used a twig to sketch in the *caliche* a crude diagram of the *hacienda's* grounds and interior, emphasizing the various exterior and interior doors as best he could remember them.

When he'd finished, the Tall Man called over the shortest Haitian, showed him the map Will had scratched out and spoke to him at length in their native tongue. The man's visage grew increasingly grim, and when his chief was done, he shouldered a backpack and an automatic weapon and set off down the steep ridge to the sprawling *estancia* below.

They'd been waiting for hours, and night had come. Finally they heard someone scrambling up the hillside, the short Haitian returning from his reconnaissance. The three dark men huddled together and conferred. When they'd finished, the Tall Man gestured briefly to Will and Sally, indicating they should follow, and the entire group began the descent.

As he approached the main house Will could see that the front door stood ajar, and drawing yet closer he could make out in the dim light what appeared to be a body sprawled across the stoop and partially obstructing the threshold. It was Arivada's houseman, Raul, the man who'd sat beside Elena in the kitchen three nights prior. Or, at least, what was left of him. He appeared to have taken a round in the face at short range, and amidst the lacerated tissue and fractured facial bones his features were unrecognizable. Will could identify him only by his thin frame and the same clothing he'd worn in the kitchen: black trousers and a dark blue shirt with sleeves rolled up neatly to the elbows.

They stepped across the body, the middle-sized Haitian leading, the Tall Man following with Sally and Will and the short Haitian bringing up the rear. They walked down the hallway now so familiar to Will and entered the library where he'd experienced some of the most disquieting moments of his life.

The room was well lit, and Will could see Arivada in his accustomed position behind the great desk. This time, however, he sat restrained by the same type of strap Will once had used to secure his surfboards to a vehicle's roof rack. Even so, the Mexican seemed composed, and aside from a brief glance as Will entered with Sally, his eyes gave away nothing.

In the corner sat Elena, unrestrained; presumably the Haitian had considered her incapable of flight or any resistance. Seeing this, however, the Tall One spoke to the shortest man harshly, and in a moment she was bound as tightly as her *patron* behind the desk.

Arivada broke a lengthening silence. "Dr. Rawlins," he declared, "I see you were successful in retrieving *su novia*."

Shifting his gaze to Sally, Arivada addressed her in turn, his affect that of a gracious *don de una casa grande* receiving an honored guest. "Please forgive me if I am presumptuous," he told her. "We've not met nor been formally introduced, but given the circumstances it seemed to me a certainty that you are the young woman whom Dr. Rawlins was seeking when he came here to my home to request my assistance." He smiled at her pleasantly.

"Dot enuf!" shouted the tall Haitian. "You shot op, now, you. You be tellin' me where eez de smock, o you be de dead mon."

Arivada was able to shift slightly despite his restraints, and when he faced the man to reply his eyes were flat, cold and serpentine. "And if I give you what you want, you will kill me anyway," he said quietly. "Of what advantage is that?"

The Tall Man set his hands on the desk and leaned forward, bringing his face as close to Arivada's as he could. His eyes bulged. "Lissen you to me," he growled. "You days as de beeg mon be ovah. Yesss. You tell me now wheh is de smock, o I keel you woman and dese two muddafockers heah." He pointed with his long, bony index finger to indicate Will and Sally.

Arivada smiled at the man's words, but his eyes remained cold. "Whether or not you kill the two *yanquis* is your concern," he said calmly. "Not mine. And as for Elena over there in the corner, I fear that through his actions the good Dr. Rawlins already has deprived her of what one typically considers *una vida*. She is simply a shell, a husk *solamente*. Your threat to eliminate a husk is, I would venture, rather an empty one."

During these words the Haitian had not altered his position. Now he arose, drew back his right arm and struck the Mexican a hard blow to the face with his right fist. Arivada's chair toppled to the floor with him attached to it, and the other two dark men hastened over to set him up upright once again. The Mexican was bleeding heavily from a lacerated lip, but he remained fully conscious.

The tall Haitian screamed down at him, his neck veins bulging in synchrony with his bloodshot eyes. "I shoot you now, you muddafocker!" Accompanying his words, he pulled from his belt a wicked-looking automatic pistol and shoved its barrel hard against Arivada's left temple.

Even with all this, the Mexican maintained his composure. "Kill me now, *bastardo*," he said, blood dripping profusely from his torn lip, "and you will lose *un producto* worth millions of dollars. Do so, and your employers will make a tablecloth of your stinking black skin."

Will glanced over to where Elena still sat and saw the young woman was staring at him intently. Now that she had his attention, she began silently to mouth over and over a single word. He couldn't be certain, but he thought it might be *"amiga"*. *'Friend'? Now what the fuck does that mean?* he wondered.

The tall Haitian backed off. Although he still gripped his pistol, it hung at his side while he stood silent, pondering the Mexican's words. "We doan need you, mon," he said at last. "De white boy obah dere say he know weh ees de smock."

Arivada's left eye was now swollen shut, his face was beginning to bruise, and his mouth was a mess. Despite this, he managed a smile. "I fear Dr. Rawlins has misled you," he told the black man.

The Haitian was immediately outraged. Pivoting about to confront Will, he shouted, "Get de fock ovah heah!" Will complied, walking over to stand next to the battered Mexican.

Again the tall Haitian leaned forward on the desk, facing them with his pistol at the ready. "Now who gonna tell me de t'ing I wanna know?" he demanded. "Weh be de smock?"

Will was fumbling in his mind for some reply when Arivada spoke. "As I said before," he said, "to simply give you what you seek would only ensure my death." He paused as if to consider the circumstances. "And yet," he continued, "perhaps some gesture is required to preserve good faith."

He inclined his head to indicate the desktop. "If you'll pull out this drawer before me," he told the Tall Man, "you will find a generous sample of *un producto*."

Beckoning the middle-sized Haitian, the Tall Man waved the barrel of his revolver at the drawer. The man opened it and handed the Tall Man a small plastic bag that contained a beige-colored powder. Opening the bag, the tall Haitian dipped his little finger within to withdraw a sample, first sniffing it and then licking what off what residue remained.

He looked up at the Mexican. "Wheh de res'?" he asked quietly.

"Ah," replied Arivada. "Here we find ourselves yet again. A 'Mexican stand-off' is, I believe, how *los yanquis* describe it. *Verdad*. For you to receive the remainder of the valuable product that you hold in your hand, I will require some assurance of my safety."

The tall Haitian straightened up and blew out an exasperated sigh. "Enuf," he said wearily. "How we do dis?"

"First, untie me," Arivada replied. "Once unbound, I will give you a substantially larger sample of the product. You will find it to be as pure as that which you now hold. Tomorrow I will take you to the remainder, and in turn you will allow the woman and me to depart unharmed."

"How I know you cahn do dis?" the dark man demanded.

"Don't worry, my friend," the Mexican responded. "I can do it, and I will. And you must trust me on this. Otherwise your employers will sustain a great financial loss."

"An' dem?" the Haitian asked, indicating the two Americans.

"As I told you earlier," said the Mexican, "They are your concern. Not mine. Now untie me."

The Haitian paused, clearly uncertain. "Wheh de somple be you say?" he demanded.

Arivada stared back at the dark man, and his eyes once again were cold. "First untie me," he answered. "Then untie the woman. And then I will tell you."

The Tall One gave a nod that was almost imperceptible, and his two accomplices rapidly stepped forward and freed Arivada from the straps.

Even with his face in tatters, the red marks on his wrists where the restraining straps had chafed and the *hacienda's* sad state of disrepair, as he sat before them Manuelo Arivada was again *el jefe*, lord of all he surveyed.

He spoke dismissively to the Haitians, as if their significance had dissipated. "The sample is within the chest by the chair to which you've bound the woman."

The two Haitians scurried to the chest and after a moment nodded to their leader. The heroin apparently was there.

"In the morning I will take you to my office in the city," Arivada told the Tall Man, "where resides the far greater portion of the product. To ensure my cooperation, one of your men shall remain here with Elena."

He paused, his black eyes glittering as he focused intently on the Haitian. When he resumed, his tone and bearing bespoke command. "Once at my office, you will call your man and instruct him to release Elena," he said.

"After I know she is safe," he continued, "I will give you what you seek, and you will return to your island. When you have departed and my own safety is assured, you will have both the money and your heroin, and *los negros* in America will be none the wiser. It is I they will blame for their loss, and I would rather sacrifice my gains and risk their revenge than incur the persistent enmity of your employers. With both money and product in hand, the men who employ you should be well pleased."

He rubbed his chin thoughtfully, as if pondering which entrée to select from a menu. "Or," he suggested, "you can simply kill us all now." He shrugged.

"I leave you to your deliberations," he concluded. "We will be in the kitchen, awaiting your decision." Then, turning away, he linked Elena's arm with his and escorted her from the room.

—

Chapter 9

EL CAZADOR FORTUNADO

Manuelo Arivada was a man seldom unprepared for such adversity as came his way, but in this instance he'd severely miscalculated. He'd allowed himself to believe the Haitians would impulsively murder his three men and the American physician, Rawlins, the only people who could lead them to his *hacienda*. Even if the Haitians managed to unravel the convoluted knot he'd tied and contrived to find this place, he'd intended to depart long before before the revengeful dark ones arrived. When he heard the footsteps in the hall and the murmur of foreign voices, however, he knew at once how badly he'd erred and how serious could be the consequences.

The dark men had separated him from the others and left him here to pass what remained of the night. Although a prisoner in his own bedroom, Arivada found reason to feel amused. *It is only fitting,* he thought, *that the two former lovers, Elena and Rawlins, should be reunited here in the place where it all began. To be yoked together in death.*

For he was confident the Haitian left behind would be ordered to slaughter them all. Their leader, the Tall One, was as paranoid as he was violent, and he would not allow anyone with knowledge of this transaction to survive. Elena, her bastard son, the obnoxious *yanqui* and his new *puta,* he would see them all as potential threats. Without doubt, the Tall One would command the man left behind to eliminate these witnesses. Once in the city and with the heroin in his possession, the Tall Man would, of course, kill him as well.

As was his longstanding habit, however, Arivada had taken the precaution of conceiving a contingency plan. To mislead them all and Hector in particular, he'd allowed those involved with his work to believe that his strength and will had declined consequent to his brother's death.

Unknown to anyone directly affiliated with his organization, Arivada had imported a trio of experienced gunmen from a sympathetic business associate in Mexico City whose loyalty was insured by his desire to share in the profits generated from the sale of the diverted heroin. Arivada instructed the three *sicarios* that if they received no call from him on the anticipated day of his departure from *la estancia* they should assume the Haitians had arrived prematurely. They would prepare an ambush. Even now they were waiting in the so-called office Arivada had secured in Guerrero Negro. The Tall Man and his sideman would be slain by these gunmen.

Elena and the boy would be eliminated by the Haitian remaining behind at the *hacienda.* The *yanquis* would die as well, probably at the hands of that Haitian or certainly when he, Manuelo, returned from Guerrero Negro to retrieve the heroin he'd hidden in the gatehouse. Abandoning his original escape route, he then would drive directly to Mexico City.

The new plan lacked the elegance of the original *trampa,* but this alternative was not without its satisfactory elements. Hopefully before their departure in the morning he might

490

witness at first hand the execution of Rawlins, the man he held responsible for the death of his brother. And he was confident that he could elude any pursuit launched by his vengeful associates.

The house in *La Ciudad* would be sold at huge profit by an anonymous third party. With the Haitians having arrived on the scene prematurely and their elimination now a necessity, it would be dangerous for him to tarry too long in Mexico; their employers would be bent on revenge as well as retrieval of what they'd lost. Blanca, his long-term mistress, had spent two years and many thousands of his pesos to renovate the grand old house. She would be annoyed by the need to abandon her project, but the money she'd receive would assuage her disappointment.

Fortunately, over the years Manuelo had acquired several fine homes in places far from Mexico - in Madrid, Paris and Dubrovnik - and in any of these he and Blanca would be comfortable and safe.

Besides, he thought, he'd grown weary of his homeland and the forces with which he contended. Even before the *Zetas* had arrived, the avaricious *jefes* of the traditional cartels in Sinaloa had found methamphetamine to be a more efficient and profitable product to manufacture and distribute than the marihuana of days past or the cocaine and heroin of more recent years. He'd no respect for these men. They sold their infernal powder to anyone, including those within the communities where they lived, and as a consequence Sinaloa had become a societal wasteland populated by addicts with rotting teeth.

The newcomers, these *Zetas*, were worse, and he knew he was wise to fear them. These men were unimaginably violent and devoid of honor. To resist them was more than pointless;

it was impossible. And as bad as they were, even worse forces eventually would arise to succeed them.

He thought of Elena, presumably down the hall and closeted with her bastard son, *como siempre.* That he had allowed her to remain at the *hacienda* following her recovery and the birth of the boy was a matter of simple inertia. Like the books in his library, she was part of his home, no more nor less. As with departing Mexico, he found it pleasing to contemplate her elimination from his life.

Manuelo lay upon his great bed with his arms crossed behind his head and one leg casually draped over the other. His appearance was that of a man unconcerned and at his ease. He looked at his watch: 2:15 am. They would be coming for him at sunrise, and it would be best to get some rest. Satisfied, he closed his eyes and was immediately asleep.

———

Almost as an afterthought the Haitians had locked Will and Sally in a bedroom downstairs, and within a minute of toweling off from her shower and climbing into bed, Sally had fallen fell deeply asleep. She obviously was exhausted from her experiences over the last three days, and after the concrete floor at the gruesome stone tower the bed they lay in must have felt quite wonderful. *Unfortunately,* he thought, *for all its comforts our bedroom is still a cell.*

He could achieve no more than a fitful slumber, and when in the pre-dawn hours their door quietly opened, he was immediately awake. Silently cursing his lack of a weapon, he strained to see more clearly the form moving slowly towards the bed. It was Elena, and the surprise he felt only intensified when she reached out to caress his cheek - only once, and very softly - with her right hand.

Placing the same hand gently on his lips to indicate he should remain quiet, she sat beside him on the bed and began to speak earnestly but in a whisper that was barely audible.

"There is much I would say to you," she told him, "but there is no time. Unbeknownst to the dark men and even to Manuelo himself, I have a key that opens every lock in this house. With this key you can escape. You and your woman." She glanced over her shoulder at Sally sleeping peacefully. "She appears to be a good person," Elena said softly. "She will love you, Will. Just as I once did."

"If you loved me so much," Will asked, "then why didn't you keep me from returning after I'd escaped? Why didn't you just let me go? Was it simply to save your own skin?"

"*Si*," Elena replied simply. To save myself... and thus to save our child."

Will was stunned. "What?" he demanded.

She nodded in response. "Yes, by then I knew I was pregnant. Had you not returned, he would not have hesitated to kill me and the baby I was carrying. Tomas. I served only as an inducement for you to operate upon his brother."

"Why did Arivada allow you both to live after I escaped again and his brother died?" Will asked.

Even in the darkness he could see her face cloud with doubt. "I don't know," she answered, "but he has been intent upon gaining revenge. Perhaps my son and I were meant to play some role in that revenge."

"But his plan has failed," she continued. "That the dark men arrived here when they did was a surprise to him, a surprise most unwelcome. You must leave quickly, before the dark men come for you."

"Why are you so concerned about saving us?" he asked her.

She looked at him solemnly, and for an instant he could recognize in her good eye something of the woman he'd once known in Guererro Negro. "Manuelo is evil," she replied. "You have done no wrong, and there is no reason why you or your woman should suffer by his actions."

She hesitated before going on. "And there is also my son," she told him. "*Our* son." Tears began to course down the irregular contours of her face. "Tomas is a good little boy, very sweet and funny. He is all that is left to me now, and I beg you to help me ensure that he comes to no harm. I want you take him with you"

The tears continued, but so rigid was her damaged face that it remained expressionless, as if indifferent to her emotions. The effect was eerie.

"We need to take Arivada, too," Will told her. Briefly he explained his plan.

"Why aren't *you* coming with us?" he asked at last. "You know you won't be safe if you stay."

She looked back at him steadily, and there were both sadness and resignation in her voice when she replied. "No," she said. "There is something here left for me to do."

She squeezed Will's hand tightly with her own. "You must go now," she said firmly. "On the floor below us is a door that leads outside. The dark men will not be watching for you there. One whom I trust, *un hombre* who worked with my father, waits outside. I will ask him to seize Manuelo and take him to your car. *Vamanos ahora. Con la prisa.*"

She arose from the bed and walked to the doorway to speak with her father's *compadre*.

Hastily he aroused Sally, told her to dress and watched as she resolutely pulled on the same grimy sweatshirt and jeans she'd been wearing when she left home two days prior. Shaking his head, he marveled again at her resilience. As she finished, she looked at him expectantly. "We're getting out of here," he told her. "With Arivada. For now the rest is unimportant."

They waited in the bedroom for another ten minutes and then at her signal began to follow Elena down the hall. As Will trailed behind her something about her nightgown, her movements and the shadows cast by the dim flashlight she carried recalled to him Lady Macbeth. Midway down the hall a short flight of tiled steps led to the floor below, and gesturing silently with her hand Elena bade them descend.

They did so and then entered another long hallway identical to the one above. At intervals on each wall were doors that presumably led also to bedrooms, but when Elena stopped at one, unlocked it and opened the door it gave way instead to an alcove and yet another door. Beside the door stood a Mexican male of about fifty and the young boy Will had seen with Elena when he'd burst into the kitchen. The man told him that Arivada could be found in the car's trunk, gagged and securely bound.

Elena knelt beside the boy and whispered quietly into his ear. When he nodded in response, she arose and unlocked the final door. It swung open, and beyond it was visible only the darkness of the desert night.

Elena turned to face Will and Sally. "Go now," she said urgently. "And take my precious boy. I beg you, keep him safe."

When Will started to speak, she held up a hand to silence him and shook her head. Kneeling down once again, she held her son tightly for a moment and then released him. Arising, she walked back to the main hallway and closed the door behind her. They could hear its lock engage.

Will looked down at Tomas, and despite the boy's fear and bewilderment he managed to respond with a faint but hopeful smile. Gathering him up in his arms so as to speed their escape, Will turned to face Sally. "Well," he said, "let's go."

With Elena and her co-conspirator watching after them, they hurried out into the night.

———

The Haitian's name was Toussaint, and his enthusiasm for this job had dimmed considerably even before the Mexican *bruja* appeared suddenly before him. In her flowing white gown she emerged from the darkness like one of the wraiths his grandmother had described in the bedtime stories she'd told him when he was a young boy.

The butchery in the tower of stone had not moved him - despite his youth, he'd seen as bad or worse many times before - but the uneven course of subsequent events had been disturbing. Their chief was hardly what one would call a friend, but Toussaint had respected his cunning and ferocity. To observe how rapidly in the tower he'd transformed from predator to prey had been sobering, and the spectacle of the Tall One standing helplessly in the grasp of the *yanqui* had remained in the forefront of his thoughts.

Other than his name, Guilloteau, itself undoubtedly a pseudonym, he'd known little of the Tall Man prior to this job. The behavior he'd observed thus far had more than confirmed what he'd come to know regarding the Haitian's soulless capacity for violence, but the rising body count had produced no satisfactory conclusion. He was beginning to fear that the man's inherently evil nature had derailed his judgment.

And now there stood before him this apparition, this ghostly figure in white, this woman with a body the stuff of dreams but a face born of nightmare. "Wot you won'?" he asked her, struggling to keep the fear from his voice.

In response she silently drew from the folds of her gown a package the size of a shoebox, extended her arm and placed it in his lap. "I can take you to the rest," she whispered. "It is here on these grounds...not in the town." Without another word she turned from him, and in seconds the darkness had swallowed her up.

Toussaint looked down at the package. After a moment he carefully untied the twine which bound it and unfolded the outer layer of butcher paper. Lying within were eight small bags of thick plastic zipped tightly at the end and packed densely with the fine beige powder. He opened one bag, dipped his moistened finger into its contents and tasted the residue with the tip of his tongue.

Although no expert in the analysis of product, Toussaint knew at once it was heroin of unusual purity. If he was correct, he held in his lap a small fortune. Unfortunately, he thought, the path from here to there - from possession of the drug to the riches it promised - was not one easily navigated. Toussaint was an uneducated young man but no fool; he knew well how certain choices could provoke dire consequences.

And so he neatly rewrapped the package, arose from the chair where he'd been dozing and set off in search of Guilloteau.

Chapter 10

AFTERMATH

El Santo, the fabled cartel boss said to control much of southern Baja, was apprehended in San Diego by agents of the Drug Enforcement Agency who coincidentally happened to drive by the man as he stood at a corner on Friar's Road near Old Town. His claim of having been kidnapped by an American fugitive and transported illegally across the border in the trunk of a car was declared to lack foundation or relevance. His requests for deportation to Mexico or release on bail were denied. Multiple requests from the Mexican authorities for extradition were consistently refused. Following indictments on a wide range of charges, he remains incarcerated while awaiting trial.

———

The surf in Paia Bay matched the gentle weather that day. The beach break was serving up one to two foot waves that developed slowly, waves perfect for the little boy whose father shouted words of praise and encouragement according to his son's small successes. Their wet brown skin shone in the light, the son a shade darker than his father. They both were laughing,

The woman watched them from the lanai of their small house on the bluff above the beach, and she was thinking that she'd never seen anything more beautiful than the pair of them. Soon she would descend the path to join them, but she was very pregnant, and for a moment it was pleasant simply to sit and enjoy the breeze off the ocean.

Hawaii suits us, she thought. *Thank goodness he managed to pull it off.* Initially they'd been offered a forlorn refuge in some barren corner of western Oklahoma, but when Will insisted on this small island town which so easily absorbed newcomers, the Bureau relented. They needed his testimony.

The phone began to ring, and when she answered, it was the after-hours operator at the Maui Lanihi Clinic. "Kate," said the woman. "I apologize for bothering you on a Sunday, but it's that Mahelona girl again. She just won't take her medicine, and her mom just called to say she had another seizure."

"No big deal, Alani," she replied. "I'll let Brian know. He can meet her at the clinic in about thirty minutes."

After the older woman had hung up, she paused for a moment to admire the sun's reflection on the water. Far below her she could see Tomas playing in the shorebreak while Will sat nearby in the sand.

Mindful of the baby she was carrying, Sally began walking carefully down the trail to the beach and her husband.

———

The best of our stories have always been quests, and the most satisfying quests are those that grant us a clearer sense of who we are. An understanding and acceptance of what motivates our actions in the personal histories we create. And a chance to begin again.

CPSIA information can be obtained
at www.ICGtesting.com
Printed in the USA
BVHW071240150419
545535BV00008B/270/P